LOVE AND FRE[illegible]
AND OTHER YOUTHFUL WRITINGS

JANE AUSTEN was born on 16 December 1775 at Steventon, near Basingstoke, the seventh child of the rector of the parish. She lived with her family at Steventon until they moved to Bath when her father retired in 1801. After his death in 1805, she moved around with her mother and sister; in 1809 they settled in Chawton, near Alton, Hampshire. Here she remained, except for a few visits to London, until May 1817, when she moved to Winchester to be near her doctor. She died in Winchester on 18 July 1817.

In her youth Jane Austen wrote stories, including burlesques of popular romances, followed by a short epistolary novel, *Lady Susan*. Her works published in her lifetime include *Sense and Sensibility* (1811), *Pride and Prejudice* (1813), *Mansfield Park* (1814) and *Emma* (1816). Two other novels, *Northanger Abbey* and *Persuasion*, were published posthumously in 1818, with a biographical notice by her brother, Henry Austen, the first formal announcement of her authorship. *Persuasion* was written in a race against failing health in 1815–16. She also left two further compositions: an unfinished novel, *The Watsons*; and *Sanditon*, a fragmentary draft of a new novel she was working on at the time of her death.

CHRISTINE ALEXANDER is Emeritus Scientia Professor of English at the University of New South Wales, Fellow of the Australian Academy of the Humanities, and director and general editor of the Juvenilia Press. She has published extensively on the Brontës and literary juvenilia, including *The Early Writings of Charlotte Brontë* (1983), *The Art of the Brontës* (1995), *The Oxford Companion to the Brontës* (2003), a number of critical editions; and *The Brontës: Tales of Glass Town, Angria, and Gondal: Selected Early Writings* (2010). She has also co-edited the first book on literary juvenilia, *The Child Writer from Austen to Woolf* (2005), and published on gothic literature, Jane Austen, critical editing, and literature and landscape gardening. She was married to the late biographer and academic Emeritus Professor Peter F. Alexander.

PENGUIN CLASSICS

LOVE AND FRIENDSHIP AND OTHER JUVENILE WRITINGS

JANE AUSTEN was born on 16 December 1775 at Steventon, near Basingstoke, the seventh child of the rector of the parish. She lived with her family at Steventon until they moved to Bath when her father retired in 1801. After his death in 1805, she moved around with her mother and sister; in 1809 they settled in Chawton, near Alton, Hampshire. Here she remained, except for a few visits to London, until May 1817, when she moved to Winchester to be near her doctor. She died in Winchester on 18 July 1817.

In her youth Jane Austen wrote stories, including burlesques of popular romances, followed by a more mature story, *Lady Susan*. Her works published in her lifetime include *Sense and Sensibility* (1811), *Pride and Prejudice* (1813), *Mansfield Park* (1814) and *Emma* (1815). Two other novels, *Northanger Abbey* and *Persuasion*, were published posthumously in 1818 with a biographical notice by her brother Henry Austen, the first formal announcement of her authorship. *Persuasion* was written in a race against failing health in 1815–16. She also left two earlier compositions, an unfinished novel, *The Watsons*, and *Sanditon*, a fragmentary draft of a new novel she was working on at the time of her death.

CHRISTINE ALEXANDER is Scientia Professor of English at the University of New South Wales, Fellow of the Australian Academy of the Humanities, and director and general editor of the Juvenilia Press, and has published extensively on the Brontës and literary juvenilia, including *The Early Writings of Charlotte Brontë* (1983), *The Art of the Brontës* (1995), *The Oxford Companion to the Brontës* (2003), a number of critical editions, and *The Brontës: Tales of Glass Town, Angria, and Gondal: Selected Early Writings* (2010). She has also co-edited the first book on literary juvenilia, *The Child Writer from Austen to Woolf* (2005), and published on colonial literature, Jane Austen, critical editing, and literature and landscape. She was married to the late biographer [illegible] Professor Peter F. Alexander.

JANE AUSTEN

Love and Freindship and Other Youthful Writings

Edited and with an Introduction and Notes by
CHRISTINE ALEXANDER

PENGUIN BOOKS

PENGUIN CLASSICS

UK | USA | Canada | Ireland | Australia
India | New Zealand | South Africa

Penguin Books is part of the Penguin Random House group of companies
whose addresses can be found at global.penguinrandomhouse.com.

First published in Penguin Classics 2014
This edition published in penguin Classics 2015

015

Jane Austen's original spelling of her title 'Love and Freindship' has
been retained in this edition.

Set in 10.25/12.25 pt Adobe Sabon
Typeset by Jouve (UK), Milton Keynes
Printed and bound in Great Britain by Clays Ltd, Elcograf S.p.A.

ISBN: 978-0-141-39511-1

www.greenpenguin.co.uk

Contents

LOVE AND FREINDSHIP AND OTHER YOUTHFUL WRITINGS

Volume the First

Introduction

Jane Austen's brilliantly sophisticated teenage writings constitute her beginnings as a writer. We see in the works in this volume the sheer fun of her early sketches and their ridicule of human foibles, her parody of the absurdities of romance and sentimental fiction, her decision-making over choice of word and incident, her changing attitude towards character and style, and especially her early fascination with wordplay and hidden meanings that reveal her sprightly imagination. G. K. Chesterton called the young Austen 'naturally exuberant' and placed her writing in the comic tradition of Rabelais and Dickens: she possessed 'the inspiration of Gargantua and of Pickwick; it was the gigantic inspiration of laughter'.[1] Virginia Woolf, too, focused on the laughter in Austen's early writing, calling it 'Spirited, easy, full of fun verging with freedom upon sheer nonsense'; but she also detected seriousness behind the 'clever nonsense', a seriousness that clearly emerges in the last of the pieces in this volume and that reaffirms Woolf's conclusion that 'at fifteen she had few illusions about other people and none about herself'.[2] This young writer was a consummate observer and imitator, whose quick wit and mastery of style and manner enabled her to experiment in the techniques of fiction while producing at the same time works that are not only morally and aesthetically acute but also worthy of a talented entertainer.

Composed between 1787 and *c.*1794, these early writings all survive in fair-copy manuscript – unlike Jane Austen's six famous novels *Sense and Sensibility* (1811), *Pride and Prejudice* (1813), *Mansfield Park* (1814), *Emma* (1816), *Persuasion* and *Northanger Abbey* (both published posthumously 1818).[3]

Some of her juvenilia are unfinished, some deliberately so as part of a joke, but all bear witness to a young author in the making. Both their content and form suggest Austen's concerns at the time, in particular her fascination with various genres and their conventions, ranging from dramas, short tales, sketches, imaginary letters and novels of various forms to popular history, and her growing concern about the education of women. Partly in imitation, partly in parody, the young Austen gathered her early works (with the exception of *Lady Susan*) into three notebooks, labelling them with the grandiose titles 'Volume the First', 'Volume the Second' and 'Volume the Third'. Here we have a writer constructing herself as author, dedicating many of her productions to family and friends, and ensuring their preservation in bound vellum volumes that have stood the test of time. Together with *Lady Susan*, they allow us to chart Austen's development towards her celebrated novels – later works that critics now agree stand at the end of a rather different 'bright & sparkling'[4] early writing career.

FAMILY AND EARLY LIFE

Jane Austen was born on 16 December 1775, five years after William Wordsworth and four years after Sir Walter Scott, who later would so much admire the realistic and psychological artistry of her novels. Unlike such male authors, however, she seldom travelled far from home. She spent her early years in a rural rectory in Steventon, in the southern English county of Hampshire, where her father the Revd George Austen was the Anglican rector. Together with her older sister Cassandra and cousin Jane Cooper, Jane Austen spent a few months in 1783 at a small boarding-school in Oxford that then moved to Southampton – a disastrous experiment from which the girls caught 'putrid fever' (a form of typhoid) and were rapidly brought home. Then, in 1785–6, she spent a year and a half with Cassandra at The Abbey School in Reading where, like Harriet Smith in *Emma*, 'girls might be sent to be out of the way and scramble themselves into a little education, without any danger of coming back prodigies'.[5] Formal education was not seen as important for girls who, unlike the Austen boys, were not destined for professional life.

Jane Austen was the seventh child in a family of eight. She had six brothers who were tutored at home by their father, together with several wealthy boarders whom he prepared for university. James, the eldest child, went on to Oxford University and then followed his father into the Church, inheriting the Steventon living when his father retired to Bath in 1801 with his wife and two unmarried daughters, Cassandra and Jane. Edward was adopted by childless wealthy relatives, Mr Thomas Knight II and his wife, sometime in 1783, and later changed his name to Knight (1812), after inheriting in 1797 the estates of Godmersham Park in Kent, together with Chawton Manor and the Steventon living in Hampshire. He thus had the means to provide Jane, her mother and sister with a home in Chawton Cottage from 1809 until Jane's death on 18 July 1817. Her favourite brother Henry, after a time at Oxford University and in the militia, became a banker in London, where Jane visited him a number of times, until he was bankrupted in March 1816 by the post-war economic slump and subsequently entered the Church. Francis and Charles, the youngest sons, enrolled at the Royal Naval Academy as cadets about the age of eleven or twelve and rose through the ranks at sea during the Revolutionary and Napoleonic Wars with France; from the early hardships as midshipmen – acknowledged in dedications in the juvenilia – they both eventually attained the rank of admiral. The remaining son was George Austen, the second eldest, who appears to have been mentally handicapped and was sent to live first with a local village family in early 1773, and later, in 1791, to live with his mentally infirm uncle, Thomas Leigh, in the care of another family near Basingstoke, until his death in 1838.[6] Although George was not neglected he was seldom mentioned, not even later by family members whose works help to form the basis of our knowledge of Jane Austen: the 'Biographical Notice' (1817) by her brother Henry Austen and *A Memoir of Jane Austen* (1870) by her nephew James Edward Austen-Leigh. These accounts are inevitably coloured by a sense of fond remembrance of their now famous late relative and by pride in the status she adds to the family name. They are guarded, carefully framed to protect family interests and to bury embarrassments – including the often risqué performances of an exuberant young girl whose romantic imagination and ironic laughter burst forth in the juvenilia.

The close family circle was enlarged by a web of more distant relatives and friends, who might visit and be visited. Jane's aunt Mrs Hancock and her glamorous daughter Eliza, Madame la Comtesse de Feuillide, visited Steventon for the Christmas of 1787 and in subsequent years, bringing stories of India where Eliza had been raised and of revolutionary France where her husband was guillotined in Paris in 1794. With her parents and sister, Jane visited relatives in Kent via London in the summer of 1788, when she was twelve, and may have had her portrait painted.[7] In July 1791, the sisters appear to have accompanied their parents and brother Charles to Portsmouth when Charles entered the Royal Naval Academy there. They at least made a visit to the Hampshire coast in the second half of this year, since a letter dated 14 November 1791 from their cousin Eliza de Feuillide to another Austen cousin, Philadelphia Walter in Kent, refers to this and agrees that 'some Son of Neptune may have obtained [Cassandra's] Approbation as She probably experienced much homage from these very gallant Gentlemen during her Aquatic excursions. I hear her Sister and herself are two of the prettiest Girls in England.'[8] Mrs Austen, formerly Cassandra Leigh, was the daughter of a former Fellow of Oxford's All Souls College and had links with the aristocratic, rich and influential Leighs of Stoneleigh Abbey, whom the Austens visited at least three times between 1794 and 1806 while at Adlestrop rectory, the home of Revd Thomas Leigh, Mrs Austen's cousin.[9] Mr Austen's rich relatives the Knights of Godmersham acted as his patrons, helping him to acquire the living of Steventon and to rent a nearby farm to supplement his clerical income. An uncle, Francis Austen, helped him secure a second living at the nearby village of Deane. Such connections gave the young Jane Austen a glimpse of wealth and elegance, but also an awareness of her own social precariousness and vulnerable welfare.

Without land of their own, her family lived on the edge of gentry, always aware of the importance of a good education, good sense and industry. The juvenilia demonstrate Austen's early concern for money, her awareness of the nuances of class, and the gaping distance between the professional possibilities for young men and the restricted options for genteel women to gain an income. Jane and Cassandra, three years older than herself, had only £20 a year each from their father to spend on themselves,[10] a far cry from the £10,000 a year of Mr Darcy in *Pride and Prejudice* or the even greater income of her brother Edward once he inherited his estates from his adopted father, Thomas Knight II.[11] The sisters were expected to marry or, if they remained single, to teach or become lady companions like Jane Fairfax in *Emma*, or to be useful as child-minders and nurses for relatives. In later years the Austen sisters took turns to visit Edward at Godmersham to assist with his children, while the other stayed home to care for their mother. It is little wonder that an intelligent young woman with a bent for literature might harbour literary ambition in the hope of gaining some intellectual and financial freedom if not literary fame.

THE EARLY MANUSCRIPTS

By the age of eleven, Jane Austen was consciously constructing herself as 'author'. She made fair copies of twenty-seven early stories and dramatic sketches including a parody history of England, possibly after some selection,[12] transcribing them in a clear, legible hand into three manuscript notebooks. They amount to some 74,000 words. The composition dates of the various pieces range from the year 1787 (Austen turned twelve in December of that year) until June 1793 (when she was seventeen). As a rule of thumb, the age of twenty is usually used as the limit for juvenilia, but this is a moot point depending on one's definition of the word 'juvenilia'.[13] Generally classified as 'early writings or works written in one's youth', juvenilia are not simply immature or apprentice writings. As with the Brontës' famous juvenilia, or those of Lady Mary Wortley Montagu,

Lewis Carroll, John Ruskin or Katherine Mansfield, for example, Austen's early writings are not only apprentice works but of value in their own right as entertainment and as literary and historical documents – records of a youthful writer's response to her times, to mores and manners and to aesthetic values.

Lady Susan, often referred to as 'juvenilia', is not strictly speaking in this category since the fair copy was made sometime after the completion of her notebook volumes (the date 1805 appears on two watermarks on the manuscript). It is generally agreed, however, that the novel was originally composed about 1794 when she was eighteen, following the last of her juvenilia in the manuscript notebooks.[14] In style and content it is linked with the robust commentary and literary techniques of the juvenilia; yet, like much of the later juvenilia, it contains significant precedents that point to the mature author.[15] The manuscript itself, located in the Pierpont Morgan Library in New York, has been transcribed by Austen from a draft on to seventy-nine quarto leaves (19 × 15.5 cm), in her neat, expansive longhand. A note surviving with the manuscript – 'For Lady Knatchbull', almost certainly in Cassandra Austen's hand – indicates that Cassandra gave it to Jane Austen's favourite niece Fanny Knight (who became Lady Knatchbull in 1820). Austen never entitled the manuscript, but she clearly delineated the epistolary form of this early novel in her exact layout of letters, with their headings, announcement of correspondents, recipients and place of writing, and the conventional signatures at the end. In 1871, Lady Knatchbull allowed James Edward Austen-Leigh to publish *Lady Susan* in the appendix to his second edition of *A Memoir of Jane Austen*, where it received its title for the first time – a title that clearly denotes the central character but tends to obscure the more serious moral tone the young author was trying to inject into her writing.[16] This was the first (rather inaccurate) publication of any early Austen manuscripts, yet this alone indicates that it was viewed, at least by her family, as a more serious performance than others of her early writings.[17]

The three manuscript volumes of juvenilia also survive intact, the first in the Bodleian Library in Oxford and the other two in the British Library in London. The contents of the three volumes are not chronological. *Volume the First*, for example, contains not only the earliest pieces from 1787 to 1790 but also two of the last pieces. As Brian Southam surmises, after beginning chronologically 'it looks as if Jane Austen entered fresh material into whichever of the three notebooks was most conveniently to hand'.[18] There are a number of dates inscribed by Austen in each of the volumes; these, together with external evidence, allow scholars to date the individual pieces. The dating of the various items, some of which is conjectural, is discussed in the explanatory notes.

Volume the First is in a quarto-size notebook, bound in quarter calf and marbled boards. It is an elegant volume but has suffered wear and tear, chiefly in Jane Austen's lifetime when it circulated among members of the family. Apart from the last two items ('The Three Sisters' and 'Detached Pieces') that were written later, the handwriting is large and immature compared to that in the other two volumes. There are 180 pages numbered by Austen herself,[19] and following the final item she wrote: 'End of the first volume June 3^{d} 1793'. The front cover carries the title 'Volume the First' in her large early hand, and the inside cover has an inscription by Cassandra, who inherited Jane's manuscripts: 'For my Brother Charles'. Cassandra has also written a note on a scrap of paper that is pasted below: 'For my Brother Charles. I think I recollect that a few of the trifles in this Vol. were written expressly for his amusement. C. E. A.'

Volume the Second is a better-quality notebook in white vellum, given to Jane by her father. She has proudly written the Latin tag '*Ex dono mei Patris*' at the top of the contents page, and it is fair to assume – as Margaret Doody suggests – that her father was so impressed by his daughter's earlier works in *Volume the First* that 'he supplied the finer notebook as an encouragement to further productions'.[20] Again she has titled the cover in ink, 'Volume the Second', and inside the front cover a pencil inscription by Cassandra reads 'For my Brother Frank, C. E. A.' Two of the items are dated by Austen: 'Love and Freindship' (13 June 1790) and 'The History of England' (26 November 1791); and her brother Henry has added a comic reply to her dedication of 'Lesley Castle', pretending to order his bank to pay her one hundred guineas for the work. 'The History of England' is illustrated with thirteen pen and watercolour medallion portraits by Cassandra, designed to support and enhance the satire of her sister's prose portraits of kings and queens – a revealing collaborative project discussed below. *Volume the Second* is the longest of the notebooks, with 264 pages. Austen apparently numbered all the pages sometime after six leaves (twelve pages), scattered throughout in groups of one or two leaves, were removed from the notebook and before she wrote her contents page, so there is no knowing what was excised. However, Brian Southam has noted that one of the stubs left from a cut page 'shows the beginning of words', so demonstrating that the missing leaf 'was certainly completely written on both sides'.[21] This suggests that Austen may not have been simply copying early drafts but was also improving or composing into the notebook. Clearly she was keen to preserve the fair-copy look of her volume and removed any pages spoiled by deletions or false starts. One exception that further suggests Austen began composing directly into her notebooks is a short cancelled paragraph at the end of *Volume the First*, written after *Volume the Third* and titled: 'A fragment – written to inculcate the practise of Virtue', a tongue-in-cheek piece originally intended to accompany the three 'Detached Pieces' (1793) written by Austen for her new infant niece (see Textual Notes).

Volume the Third is another vellum-covered notebook, titled on the front by Austen and inscribed on the contents page 'Jane Austen – May 6th 1792', although the first of the two items, 'Evelyn', was probably written earlier.[22] The second, 'Catharine, or the Bower', is dated August 1792. Both pieces were left unfinished by Austen, who intended to complete at least 'Evelyn' since she left blank pages for a continuation before she began writing 'Catharine'; and both pieces have continuations by her nephew James Edward, son of the eldest brother James, who frequently visited his aunt and her family at Chawton in 1815 and 1816. On the first page of the notebook Cassandra has written 'for James Edward Austen' (in a different hand, someone has inserted 'Leigh' after 'Austen', presumably after James Edward added the name of his wealthy Leigh relatives to his own in 1837). The Revd George Austen may well have provided this third notebook as another gift to his writing daughter; inside the front cover he penned the following: 'Effusions of Fancy by a very Young Lady Consisting of Tales in a Style entirely new'. Unlike many fathers of the period who would have insisted their daughters confine their interests to needlework, he took an interest in Austen's writing, was clearly aware of much of its content and keen to encourage her authorship. The word 'Effusions' did not carry the negative aspersions it does today and 'Fancy' was not then the poor relation of 'imagination': 'effusions of fancy', a phrase Austen herself repeated in *Northanger Abbey* (I, v) to describe the novel, indicates Mr Austen's appreciation of his daughter's early frank and eager expression of her imagination. Although there are only 140 pages, mostly paginated by Austen, and only two unfinished items, the notebook shows interesting textual features that also indicate careful craftsmanship.

Even as a teenager, Austen was aware of her audience. Why, for example, did she change the name of her heroine 'Kitty' to the more formal 'Catharine' in her novel of the same name? Or delete the suggestive criticism Catharine receives from her aunt ('Her intimacies with Young men are abominable')? Or why did she delete the colloquial word 'cockalorum' ('little cock, bantam; self-important little man', *OED*) and attribute the more moralistic 'vanity' to Lady Jane Grey in 'The History of England'? Changes like these in her later juvenilia suggest a growing sense of public performance and its associated emphasis on moral decorum (see also Note on the Text). Further revisions in 'Evelyn' and 'Catharine', of new material indicating a later date, suggest that Austen returned to her juvenilia between 1809 and 1811, possibly during the rediscovery of her notebooks after unpacking her belongings at her new Chawton home in July 1809.[23] The emendations (such as inserted references to the 'Regency' period) show she was updating her stories, perhaps to enhance their appeal to nephews and nieces or using the notebooks as working copy for later writing. There is also evidence that during the draft composition of her first three novels she returned to her juvenilia as a kind of source book for the recycling of characters and ideas. The irresponsible and vacuous Camilla Stanley in 'Catharine', for example, suggests an early version of Isabella Thorpe in *Northanger Abbey*, and the haughty snobbery of Lady Greville towards Maria in 'A Collection of Letters' prefigures Lady Catherine De Bourgh's calculated arrogance towards Charlotte Collins in *Pride and Prejudice*. Even as late as 23 August 1814 Austen was still recalling incidents in her juvenilia, when she referred to some eccentric travel that 'put me in mind of my own Coach between Edinburgh & Sterling',[24] a reference to the bizarre coach travel that forms the denouement of 'Love and Freindship'.

FAMILY COLLABORATION AND HIDDEN MEANINGS

The Austen family, together with close friends, played a considerable role in the conception of the juvenilia. They provided inspiration for stories and characters, often becoming the butt of the youthful author's jokes; they modelled literary and dramatic enterprise, encouraged her critical stance in reading and, when necessary, were an encouraging audience. Their fostering of Austen's early creativity is seen especially in the dedications that are written to suit individual members. Although many of them were written after the actual composition of a tale, squeezed between title and text as in the cases of 'Jack and Alice' and 'The adventures of Mr Harley', or inserted in the blank page Austen had left at the beginning of each new piece, they represent her creative response to the people and events around her. Her play 'The Visit', for example, is dedicated to her brother James, an acknowledgement of his own dramatic talents in writing prologues and organizing family theatricals. 'The Mystery', inspired by Revd George Austen's favourite play *The Critic* (1779) by Richard Brinsley Sheridan, is dedicated accordingly to her father,[25] and he is also mentioned on the title page of her history. 'The beautifull Cassandra', whose heroine falls in love with an elegant bonnet, is dedicated to her beloved sister who shared Austen's love of bonnets and their trimmings. To Cassandra, Austen also dedicated her more ambitious works 'The History of England' and 'Catharine, or the Bower', works replete with hidden meanings and private concerns shared only by the sisters, as the following discussion suggests. All her early writings, apart from 'Edgar and Emma', are dedicated either to family members, including her cousins Jane Cooper and Eliza de Feuillide, or to her friend Martha Lloyd. The dedication to Martha, like most of the dedications, is a carefully worded joke: 'As a small testimony of the gratitude I feel for your late generosity to me in finishing my muslin Cloak, I beg leave to offer you this little production of your sincere Freind' ('Frederic and Elfrida'). The grandiose style of the usual dedication of the period is undercut here by the domestic chore of 'finishing [a] muslin Cloak'; as kind as the act might have been, functional needlework is not usually the subject of literary dedications. Juliet McMaster has demonstrated that these dedications are in themselves accomplished works, fragments that represent carefully crafted letters for public consumption.[26]

Austen's brother Henry reported that her writings 'were never heard to so much advantage as from her own mouth; for she partook largely in all the best gifts of the comic muse'.[27] Although this comment probably refers to her novels, it is possible that some of the juvenilia – at least those of *Volume the First* – may have been read aloud by Austen to the family circle and select friends.[28] She was known to be an excellent mimic, a talent she inherited from her mother who from an early age had delighted family audiences with her charades and 'Smart pieces' of comic verse.[29] Jane Austen's dramatic talents were early nurtured by family entertainments shared with neighbouring friends. One memorable occasion for a twelve-year-old Austen was the visit to Steventon rectory at Christmas 1787 of her 'very pleasure loving' cousin Eliza de Feuillide, whose interests stimulated the revival of a small amateur dramatic company organized by James and Henry. Neighbours and visitors like Eliza were recruited for the performance and Mr Austen's barn was fitted up 'quite like a theatre, & all the young folks [were] to take their part'.[30] The younger Austens staged Susanna Centlivre's *The Wonder! A Woman Keeps a Secret* (1714), characterized by William Hazlitt as 'a happy medium between grossness and refinement', with the dialogue rich 'in *double entendre*'.[31] Eliza's performance as 'the flirtatious leading lady', Donna Violante, opposite James and Henry Austen (the latter she eventually married) is thought to have provided material for the similar theatrical situation in *Mansfield Park*.[32] Also in this novel Austen observed: 'A love of the theatre is so general, an itch for acting so strong among young people' – a comment Penny Gay suggests must surely be based on autobiographical experience. Gay also demonstrates that the plays performed at Steventon during Austen's childhood 'present a conspectus of late eighteenth-century fashionable comic theatre'.[33] Much of the material of the juvenilia, especially the early burlesques but also the energetic and attractively wicked *Lady Susan*, echoes this comic theatre and the high spirits and repartee practised by the talented community of young readers, writers and actors at Steventon rectory.

Lady Susan is Austen's only literary excursion into the world of the aristocracy and it has much to do with her newly widowed but dazzling cousin Eliza de Feuillide, who as the wife of an officer in the *Dragons de Reine* had frequented the court of Marie-Antoinette at Versailles. Eliza had had ample opportunity to observe the intrigues of courtiers, including her own aristocratic husband and his mistress. With her quick wit and acting ability, she was a ready participant in the flirtation and subterfuge practised at the time, a likely model for the amoral attitude of a Lady Susan. Eliza brought a taste of the beau monde to the Austen rectory, even characterizing herself as the 'greatest rake imaginable'.[34] She was a welcome and lively visitor there during her widowhood and is said to have fascinated her young cousin Jane, even perhaps introducing her to Laclos's scandalous novel, *Les Liaisons Dangereuses* (1782). Stories of adultery and parental cruelty, Lady Susan's particular attributes, could also of course be found closer to home. Not much would have escaped the ears of a daughter of the rectory.

She would have heard from her friends Martha and Mary Lloyd, who for some time rented the nearby Deane rectory from Mr Austen and later became part of the Austen family, tales of their wicked grandmother, a Mrs Craven, who, like Lady Susan, imprisoned her daughters until they absconded and married.[35] She was 'a most courteous and fascinating woman in society' but with 'a stern tyrannical temper' in private and determined to acquire a wealthy second husband.[36] Austen would have known, too, of the desperate plight of her Aunt Philadelphia (Eliza's mother) whose best chance of a home was to travel to India to find a husband among the numerous Englishmen employed by the East India Company. Her story reappears in the fate of the eldest Miss Wynne in 'Catharine', who is 'obliged to accept the offer of one of her cousins to equip her for the East Indies, and tho' infinitely against her inclinations had been necessitated to embrace the only possibility that was offered to her, of a Maintenance'. Gossip among a lively circle of friends and relations contributed much to the young writer's surprisingly sophisticated knowledge of human nature and helped to fuel her imaginative response to her reading.

A richly educated family life was vital for a young woman whose two brief experiences of school had done little for her mind and who otherwise had to fend for herself. Despite the value placed on education by the Austens, formal tuition was reserved for the boys. Nevertheless, both father and brothers clearly guided the young Jane's learning; and like all youthful writers she was keen to imitate, to join their more adult pursuits and to receive their approbation. The witty minimalist plays she wrote – 'The Visit', 'The Mystery', 'The first Act of a Comedy' – would have been welcomed and performed at one of the more intimate family entertainments. Her father's five-hundred-volume library meant that, like her brothers, she could read voraciously a healthy mix of works: from Shakespeare to Pope, Fielding, Richardson, Sterne, Johnson, Sheridan, Cowper and Frances Burney (to name her favourites that are most frequently alluded to in the juvenilia) on the one hand, to the popular sentimental literature she later disingenuously described in *Sanditon* as 'The mere Trash of the common Circulating

Library'.[37] The Austen parents were remarkable for their enlightened view towards their children's reading, a view unencumbered either by contemporary gendered prejudice against women taxing their weaker female minds with history and philosophy (although Austen did not share her brothers' classical tuition) or the moralistic evangelical prejudice against the evils of novels for young women that Mrs Percival voices in 'Catharine'. Like Edward in 'Love and Freindship' and Henry Tilney in *Northanger Abbey*, her brothers enjoyed not only popular drama but also novels, generally considered female fare at the time, never missing an opportunity to mock the sentimentalism in both genres. A letter from Austen to her sister in 1798 records that even her father took delight in a newly published Gothic novel, *The Midnight Bell*, a work she later mentions in *Northanger Abbey*. Literature was a shared activity in the Austen household; it was fun and enlightening. It is little wonder it became embedded in the writing of an eager young author.

James and Henry Austen's magazine *The Loiterer*, written and published in Oxford about the same time as the writing of the juvenilia, has been seen as an index to Austen's early literary and social interests.[38] Certainly it has the same exuberance and mix of contents as her early writing and would have had a major influence on the development of her critical gifts. The articles that appeared weekly between January 1789 and March 1790, written almost entirely by the brothers themselves, satirize university life and parody popular fiction. Significantly, they also track the same critical stance as her juvenilia – in A. Walton Litz's words, 'from simple burlesque and parody towards a more complex merging of narrative structure with ironic methods', a tendency which foreshadows Jane Austen's own development after 'Love and Freindship'.[39] There are a number of parallels between articles in the magazine and the juvenilia that indicate her close reading of *The Loiterer*, and she may even have contributed the letter from 'Sophia Sentiment' (see Appendix B), published in the number for 28 March 1789. Her two brothers were also probably the chief recipients of Austen's early prose, of the many drafts she wrote that did not find their way into her three fair-copy manuscript notebooks.

If James and Henry were the young writer's mentors, her closest collaborator was her sister Cassandra. We know from the surviving letters that Cassandra was privy to all Austen's secrets: they shared a room throughout their lives and both faced the precarious future of the unmarried woman. Privacy was at a premium in the Austen home, especially with Mr Austen's three or four live-in male pupils, but by 1791 the brothers were no longer living at home and the sisters were allocated an upstairs sitting-room or 'dressing room', as they called it, adjoining their bedroom: 'This room belonged exclusively to the two sisters. Here they followed their favourite pursuits – Cassandra had her drawing materials, and Jane her desk and her piano'.[40] Here Austen wrote the bulk of her juvenilia and the first drafts of *Pride and Prejudice*, *Sense and Sensibility* and *Northanger Abbey*. Cassandra, who may have received drawing lessons from the famous water-colourist John Claude Nattes,[41] was a talented amateur whose ability to take an accurate likeness was valued by family members in those days before photography. R. W. Chapman, who in 1933 published the first scholarly edition of juvenilia, was surprised to find that some family members 'made it plain that Cassandra and her drawing were not less interesting in their eyes than Jane and her writing'.[42] It is to Cassandra that we owe the famous images of Austen: the pen and water-colour image of the later novelist (*c.*1810), and the water-colour sketch (1804) of a tantalizing rear-view of Austen sitting outdoors in her blue bonnet and gown, both now in the National Portrait Gallery, London. Less known is an early image of her sister that Cassandra secreted among her miniature caricature portraits for 'The History of England', a complex collaboration between the two sisters that plays with the possibilities of text and image. Here Jane Austen is portrayed as Mary, Queen of Scots, her favourite Stuart monarch, a heroine of romance but also calculatingly ambitious and tragically beheaded by her cousin Elizabeth I of England. Cassandra's image of Jane both parodies and confirms her sister's fierce partiality for the Stuarts demonstrated in her text. Brigid Brophy suggests that Austen's self-identification with Mary may derive from the pro-Stuart historian John

Whitaker (cited in Austen's text), who characterizes Mary, Queen of Scots as 'young, beautiful and accomplished', with an ambition to 'appear as a woman of intellect, and to be considered as a woman of taste'.[43] Both sisters sought intellectual validation in their creative talents. The format of Cassandra's signature on her miniature portrait, with its professional Latin abbreviation '*pinx*' (for '*pinxit*', meaning 'painted it') shows that she too was not only laughing at her own pretensions to professionalism but was also endorsing herself as a talented artist like her sister, with a strong desire for her work to be taken seriously.

'The History of England' demonstrates the close creative bond between the two sisters. Jane Austen dated her text 26 November 1791, a few weeks before her sixteenth birthday, and transcribed it into *Volume the Second* some time during May to November 1792. Cassandra contributed thirteen miniature images of monarchs, completing them by early 1793.[44] They are cleverly conceived and delicately executed, and in some cases may be copies of original sketches presented to the sitters. They are printed in this edition as they appear in the manuscript. They join in Austen's parody of Oliver Goldsmith's 1771 *The History of England*,[45] imitating the woodcut medallion images of his abridged edition but disrupting their historical pose by clothing the monarchs in brightly coloured modern dress and then enhancing the joke by using portraits of family members and friends to represent individual monarchs. This equation between Cassandra's portraits and Austen family likenesses has only recently been recognized – in the Juvenilia Press edition of *The History of England & Cassandra's Portraits* (2009) – and further confirms the link between family and imaginative creativity in the juvenilia.

Of Cassandra's thirteen portraits of monarchs, seven (possibly eight) – through a comparison of existing miniatures and other family representations, and supported by biographical evidence[46] – can be tentatively identified as Austen family members and friends. Textual references link the portraits to particular family members (see individual Notes at the end of this edition). The most obvious is the clue that the images correspond, wherever possible, to family members and friends of the same name. The brothers James, Edward and Henry, for example, are depicted as James I, Edward VI, and Henry V respectively and their friend Mary Lloyd is Mary Tudor. Jane Austen as the youthful and pretty Mary, Queen of Scots is particularly red-cheeked, a trademark feature Austen herself joked about in many of her heroines. She is dressed in 1790s formal costume, ready to impress at a ball – an image perhaps not inconsistent with the contemporary comment that 'she was *then* the prettiest, silliest, most affected, husband-hunting butterfly'.[47] In contrast, as Austen's text demands, Cassandra's portrayal of Mary's rival Elizabeth I is depicted as an 'over-dressed, over-rouged harridan', to use Brian Southam's words.[48] Critics have been quick to comment on the 'slanderously unflattering portrait of Elizabeth which features a greatly exaggerated version of the witch's proverbial pointy nose and chin',[49] a nose and chin that appear to be an exaggerated version of Mrs Austen's renowned aristocratic Leigh features of which she was especially proud.[50] Were the teenage sisters making a private joke at their mother's expense? The placement of the portraits is also suggestive. Unlike the other single portraits accompanying the text of each monarch, Cassandra has deliberately displayed Elizabeth and Mary confronting each another. As Jan Fergus puts it: these two queens 'confront one another as maiden and crone'.[51]Annette Upfal, who was the first to identify the witty concealment of family likeness in the portraits, convincingly argues that the semiotics of this representation suggest that the juxtaposed historical rivals Elizabeth (Mrs Austen) and Mary (Jane) might portray a family confrontation at the time between a strict mother and her independent-minded teenage daughter.[52] Certainly the phrases Austen uses for Elizabeth as 'the destroyer of all comfort, the deceitful Betrayer of trust reposed in her' are odd in a historical context and may be a reference to tension in Steventon rectory.

Although not every image in 'The History of England' can be identified or, in some cases, authenticated, the expert findings together with supporting biographical evidence show that Cassandra included not only portraits of her mother, sister and three of her brothers but also of her cousin Edward Cooper, her friend Mary Lloyd and possibly her future fiancé, Tom Fowle, who was to die tragically of yellow fever in the West Indies in 1797.[53] Just as there is no image of the unfortunate Edward V, who apparently 'lived so little a while that no body had time to draw his picture', there is no image of the midshipman brother Francis, perhaps because he had been away at sea for several years or perhaps simply because England has had no King Francis.[54] Austen however includes an elaborate compliment to Francis in her chapter on Elizabeth, where she compares him to Sir Francis Drake:

> It was about this time that Sir Francis Drake the first English Navigator who sailed round the World, lived, to be the ornament of his Country and his profession. Yet great as he was, and justly celebrated as a Sailor, I cannot help foreseeing that he will be equalled in this or the next Century by one who tho' now but young, already promises to answer all the ardent and sanguine expectations of his Relations and Freinds, amongst whom I may class the amiable Lady to whom this work is dedicated, and my no less amiable Self.

As in her dedications, Austen flatters her siblings with the same tongue-in-cheek ambiguity she applies to the historical monarchs themselves, and, as the final comment indicates, she is also quick to undercut her own outrageously intrusive narrative pose. The playful compliment to her seventeen-year-old sailor brother is both wishful thinking and comic extravagance. For her favourite brother Henry, both she and Cassandra flattered his ambitions by depicting him as the great military leader Henry V, whose victory at Agincourt is referred to in the text, and by dressing him as an officer of the Royal Regiment of Artillery, using an officer's image from a popular satiric print by H. W. Bunbury as her model.[55] Cassandra used another contemporary caricature by Bunbury[56] as the model for her pompous cousin the Revd Edward Cooper as Edward IV, playing with the original in the same way as Jane was burlesquing historical precedent in her text. In Cassandra's portrait, Cousin

Edward's dress as an evangelical clergyman parodies the orthodox image of Edward IV in Goldsmith's original text, and the gross posture of Bunbury's caricature taints both the cousin she dislikes and the monarch. Cassandra's technique is as witty and accomplished as her sister's risky *double entendre*. We surely encounter here a lively artistic mind capable of engaging and encouraging the daring creativity of her younger sister. This is a far cry from the characterization of the later Cassandra handed down by her nephew in his *Memoir* as 'colder and calmer', 'always prudent and well-judging, but with less outward demonstration of feeling and less sunniness of temper than Jane possessed'.[57] Cassandra was clearly a kindred spirit to her sister, who on 1 September 1796 wrote admiringly:

> The letter which I have this moment received from you [Cassandra] has diverted me beyond moderation. I could die of laughter at it, as they used to say at school. You are indeed the finest comic writer of the present age.[58]

Austen's 'The History of England', then, with its visual and verbal reference, is in some sense a covert representation of the Austen family scene. It laughs both at and with family and friends, and demonstrates the way juvenilia, like autobiography, can be an empowering act that enables the young writer to 'circumvent social prohibitions', to 'think forbidden thoughts' and to express them in a literary (and in this case historical) code with impunity.[59] Park Honan comments on the significance of the sisters' room of their own and its impact on Austen's early writing: the 'daily freedom behind a shut door' to say or do whatever she liked.[60] Austen's forthright stories in the juvenilia, with their sexual innuendos and jokes on deformity and drunkenness, would repeatedly violate the rules of contemporary conduct books on feminine behaviour in polite society and the topics that a girl was permitted to discuss. The joke on James I's homosexuality in 'The History of England', for example, is daringly risqué for a young girl of this period, and Cassandra's grotesque portrait of Mrs Austen as Elizabeth would have been equally offensive to later family members, if not to Austen's immediate family. It is unlikely that this particular manuscript would have been circulated widely among family and friends. Reginald Farrer suggests 'it is significant that only upstairs, behind her shut door, did [Austen] read her own work aloud, for the benefit of her chosen circle in the younger generation'.[61] He is surely not speaking of *Volume the First*, but this may well have been the case with Austen's 'History' and with other juvenilia in *Volume the Second* and *Volume the Third*. They are all dedicated to members of this 'chosen circle' of supportive young people that would have included her brothers James and Henry, Cassandra, the cousins Eliza de Feuillide and Jane Cooper, Mr Austen's pupil Richard Buller and probably Tom Fowle, all of whom were either staying at or in the vicinity of Steventon rectory in late 1792 when the bulk of the juvenilia had been completed.

'TALES IN A STYLE ENTIRELY NEW'

A much grander portrait of the young Jane Austen by the artist Ozias Humphrey has more recently returned to the spotlight and, although some scholars are still uneasy about the authenticity of its subject, it is helpful in suggesting the un-childlike disposition of the young writer we encounter in the juvenilia. Margaret Anne Doody characterizes this portrait as that of 'a young girl of the new revolutionary decade of the 1790s. She takes care of no one and nothing . . . but walks freely towards life, with open eyes and curious amused gaze.'[62] This same gaze is encountered in the juvenilia. Whether she turns her probing ironic eye on her family and friends or engages with the wider context of her life, her written response is almost always parodic – 'rattling burlesque' is how G. K. Chesterton first characterized it and since then many critics have pointed to elements of the burlesque in the juvenilia. Perhaps this is what George Austen had in mind when he described his daughter's early writing as 'Tales in a Style entirely new'.[63] Burlesque, 'an incongruous imitation',[64] may be written in sheer fun, but it is usually seen as a form of satire with some serious mocking intent. Austen's juvenilia are witty and entertaining – 'light-hearted', 'exuberant', 'hilarious', 'raucous' are adjectives applied to it – but it would be wrong to assume that because they are youthful writings they are not intentionally serious, even subversive. A remarkable feature of the juvenilia is its ability to subvert limitations imposed on young women, especially in the field of education. The form of burlesque Austen uses to achieve this is parody, which deflates the serious original by applying the imitation to a comically inappropriate subject. Practice in parody honed her critical skills and assisted the development of the witty ironic voice for which she is famous. In *Jane Austen: Irony as Defence and Discovery* (1952), Marvin Mudrick demonstrated the way her use of irony for contrasting what is with what should be is intimately related to her contemporary literature.

Austen was an avid reader of the romantic, sentimental and Gothic novels that flooded the popular market in the second half of the eighteenth century. Simply by using 'Love', 'Friendship' or 'Castle' in her titles, she conjures up expectations of the sentimental or Gothic ready to be subverted by her wicked sense of humour. Horace Walpole's *The Castle of Otranto* (1765) is usually considered the first novel to associate castles with Gothic motifs: remote and foreign settings, gloom and decay, dark secrets associated with a villainous tyrant and persecuted heroine, crime and the supernatural; but Austen would also have in mind more recent novels like Ann Radcliffe's first novel *The Castles of Athlin and Dunbayne: A Highland Story* (1789) and Charlotte Smith's *Emmeline, the Orphan of the Castle* (1788), a novel she alludes to in 'Catharine'. 'Lesley Castle', however, debunks any such conventions found in these novels. The castle may be 'Mouldering' and set 'on a bold projecting Rock' in the Highlands of Scotland, but it is merely two miles from a populous town and commands delightful views over its environs. Its characters are equally cosmopolitan, unintentionally disclosing their jealousy, greed and egotism in a series of comic letters that reveal Austen's familiarity with the epistolary novels of her favourite novelist Samuel Richardson, whose *Sir Charles Grandison* she is said to have known 'almost by heart'.[65] The letter novel was another genre she practised and satirized with great gusto in early pieces like 'The Three Sisters', 'A Collection of Letters' and 'Love and Freindship', and then perfected in *Lady Susan*. The popular literary form of the memoir, too, is parodied in 'Memoirs of Mr Clifford', whose hero records a journey in which he does nothing of interest.

But it is the sentimental novel that is the chief butt of her early satire. Characterized by Mudrick as the 'lachrymose novel, compounded of sentiment, morality, manners, instruction, sensibility, and adventure',[66] it focused on the heroine's 'sensibility', a feeling response that is seen as virtuous. By the 1790s a 'cult of sensibility' had developed, fuelled largely by imitations of two popular continental novels: Goethe's *The Sorrows of Young Werther* (1774) and Jean-Jacques Rousseau's *Julie, ou La Nouvelle Héloïse* (1761), both of which Austen satirizes in her juvenilia. Rousseau's message that we should abandon social mores and listen to our natural instincts for guidance motivates most of the heroines of the juvenilia. In 'Henry and Eliza' the characters follow their instincts in gleeful fashion, indulging their natural cravings for violence and self-gratification: the Harcourts 'cudgel' their workers, Eliza steals money from her benefactors, the 'Dutchess' locks her up and the babies eat two of her fingers. Her 'inhuman' benefactor, Sir George Harcourt, named for Rousseau's English patron, dispenses Rousseauean rewards for virtue and industry to his haymakers in the manner of Julie in *La Nouvelle Héloïse*. In Goethe's novel, the virtuous young hero Werther (whose 'blue sattin Waistcoat' is emulated by Austen's hero in 'Love and Freindship') is so distressed on hearing that Charlotte, the girl he loves, is betrothed to his friend that he gives way to his uncontrolled feelings and commits suicide – a novelistic event that led to hundreds of copycat suicides all over Europe at the time. In her earliest surviving story, 'Frederic and Elfrida', the eleven-year-old Austen responds by creating her own heroine Charlotte, who is so virtuous and obliging that she cannot refuse anyone anything. Consequently she agrees to marry both the men who propose to her and then finds a sentimental solution to her ensuing problem: rather than hurt the feelings of either of the men by a rejection, she commits suicide. Austen further exploits the irony of the situation in a direct challenge to the reader: if we read the pathetic lines on Charlotte's epitaph 'without a shower of tears, which if they should fail of exciting in you, Reader, your mind must be unworthy to peruse them'. Her challenge suggests we are unsympathetic if we do not respond appropriately and herein rests the absurdity of expecting a uniform tearful response to a sentimental scene. This way affectation and hypocrisy lie, the prime target of Austen's satire.

'Jack and Alice' takes issue with the model of the popular sentimental hero. Like the hero of *Sir Charles Grandison*, Charles Adams is a model of the Enlightenment man, a paragon of virtue and reason (his very name suggests his original perfection). Austen sends him to a masquerade where he shines resplendent in a mask that represents the sun: 'The Beams that darted from his Eyes were like those of that glorious Luminary tho' infinitely superior. So strong were they that no one dared venture within half a mile of them; he had therefore the best part of the Room to himself'. Such perfection, Austen suggests, is unapproachable and the hero is best left in the company of his own egotism. Not so Mr Gower, the hero of 'Evelyn', who is surrounded by the extravagant hospitality of a family who cannot lavish enough sentimental benevolence on their self-absorbed guest. His egotism, like that of Charlotte Lutterell in 'Lesley Castle', manifests itself in a boundless sense of entitlement. His appetite for both the food and possessions of these 'virtuous' strangers is insatiable, and they relinquish chattels, house and daughter to him in an absurd exaggeration of sentimental values.

'Love and Freindship' (1790) from *Volume the Second* has been called 'the most amusing and incisive of all eighteenth-century attacks upon sentimental fiction'.[67] The earliest juvenilia, 'Frederic and Elfrida', 'Jack and Alice' and other contributions to *Volume the First* (apart from 'The Three Sisters' [1791] and 'Detached Pieces' [1793], written later), are in many ways exercises for this extraordinary assault on the genre. They all exhibit a knowing awareness of the false values and absurd conventions of sentimental fiction, not least women's assumed fragility of body and mind. The anonymous epistolary novel *Laura and Augustus* (1784), with its suggestive names of the central players in 'Love and Freindship', was probably the main focus of Austen's mockery;[68] but sentimental excess in general is everywhere displayed: friendships are formed 'instantaneously', heroines swoon 'Alternately on a Sofa' when they are not pro-active in stealing and moral corruption, long-lost relations are discovered in rapid succession, and lovers determine 'not to transgress the rules of Propriety by owning their attachment, either to the object beloved, or to any one else'. The sentimental convention of recounting inward secrets or one's life adventures as a sign of true intimacy and committed feeling is ridiculed mercilessly throughout the story, until the end when Laura's insistence on again hearing everyone's separate adventures enables Austen to wind up all the threads of her story neatly. When Sir Edward wonders where his son picked up his absurd habits and language, his answer betrays a nice self-reflexive irony: '"Where, Edward, in the name of wonder" (said he) "did you pick up this unmeaning Gibberish? You have been studying Novels I suspect."' Austen is acknowledging here her own voracious appetite for popular novels and laughing at herself for indulging in writing 'gibberish' about them. She is displaying what Jan Fergus refers to as her 'double vision':[69] the ability to laugh at her own prejudices while still maintaining them. Her practice is that of Henry Tilney, the hero of *Northanger Abbey*, who delights in parodying the Gothic novels he so thoroughly enjoys reading.

Her double vision is more complex and less secure in *Lady Susan*, a brilliantly cynical study of a voracious and witty heroine that introduces a seriousness of tone and intent that is new in Austen's early writing and that heralds the moral tenor of her later (and longer) novels. The character Lady Susan shows none of the naivety of the narrator Laura in 'Love and Freindship', who endorses the crazy fainting fits and outrageous sensibility that engage our laughter but not our judgement. In contrast, Lady Susan positively exults in her own sophistication and duplicity, so we are forced to consider the morality of her disingenuous and malicious behaviour. However, she also 'possesses an uncommon union of Symmetry, Brilliancy and Grace' and, like the polished Mary Crawford in *Mansfield Park*, she is an entertaining and intelligent woman. She may flaunt the wit and energy that align Austen's earlier heroines with Restoration comedy and the plays of Sheridan; she may display the blatant hypocrisy and coquetry of Fielding's artful Shamela;[70] and she may be a skilful practitioner of language, a quality the young novelist herself much admires in her heroine, but this is not enough to condemn her. Austen's voice even appears to be endorsing her heroine's eloquent revelations: 'If I am vain of anything, it is of my eloquence. Consideration and Esteem as surely follow command of Language, as Admiration waits on Beauty.' But Lady Susan's cruelty to her daughter injects a black humour that is central to the plot and that obliges the audience to make a moral judgement. She is bent on disposing of Frederica with the same cold-hearted materialism as Sir George Fitzgibbon and 'Every body' in 'Catharine' who assist in shipping off one of the Wynne sisters to Bengal to find a husband. Through the worthy Mrs Vernon, who rescues Frederica, we encounter (perhaps for the first time if we discount the sensible Lady Dorothea in 'Love and Freindship', who is not permitted to speak for herself) an antagonistic voice whose morality is not mocked. Lady Susan is eventually foiled. But she remains disarmingly attractive to her rival Mrs Vernon, to the reader and to her creator. In the contrast between Lady Susan and Mrs Vernon – and the concomitant gap between Town and Country, and London and Churchill – we see the young Austen struggling to find a balance between the morality that was to inform her later novels and the subversive charm of her earlier heroines.

IN DEFENCE OF THE NOVEL AND FEMALE EDUCATION

The juvenilia can be read as astute exercises in intertextuality: their formal structure mimics and mocks conventional publication practice, their events play with paradigms in the popular novel, and the speeches echo contemporary texts. Even in 'Frederic and Elfrida', the very earliest of her writings, Austen demonstrates her skill in juggling tropes, figures and vocabulary from contemporary literature. She plays with the clichéd phrases in Gothic and romantic fiction ('tremblingly alive', 'weltering in their blood', 'the horrid Spectacle') and pastoral poetry ('purling Stream', 'Valley of Tempé'); adapts phrases and figures from the poetry of Alexander Pope ('Patches, Powder, Pomatum and Paint', 'seven days . . . expired, together with the lovely Charlotte'); and demonstrates the fun she has with nomenclature by choosing to use traditional names for rustic lovers in pastoral poetry (Damon, Corydon), pseudo-biblical names (Jezalinda), the names of a famous sentimental hero and heroine (Frederic, Charlotte), and the requisite uncommon name for a sentimental heroine (the Old-English 'Elfrida'). Even the disarming laughter at deformity (to many later readers embarrassing and crude) imitates a strain of early eighteenth-century ironic humour found in writers like Fielding and Smollett. Austen's correspondence and earliest juvenilia reflect this broad and bawdy humour. In 'Frederic and Elfrida', the heroine and her companions visit Mrs Fitzroy and her two daughters, and are struck by 'the engaging Exterior and beautifull outside' of Jezalinda and 'the Wit and Charms' resplendent in the conversation of Rebecca:

> 'Lovely and too charming Fair one, notwithstanding your forbidding Squint, your greazy tresses and your swelling Back, which are more frightfull than imagination can paint or pen describe, I cannot refrain from expressing my raptures, at the engaging Qualities of your Mind, which so amply atone for the Horror, with which your first appearance must ever inspire the unwary visitor.'

The characters' comment on Rebecca's repulsive appearance suggests the popular caricatures of Gillray, Rowlandson or Cruickshank, with their grotesque distortions of humanity; and the ironic emphasis on 'first appearance', so important to young women keen to attract a husband, and on the qualities of Rebecca's mind, mock the conventional focus on women's physical attributes rather than their mental abilities. Even the salutation 'Lovely and too charming Fair one' mocks the extravagant form of address found in romantic novels. The Notes to this edition document Austen's fertile subversion of a variety of literary devices and of what she refers to as 'novel slang'.[71]

Yet, for all the absurdities they reveal in contemporary fiction, her early burlesques do not necessarily suggest disapproval of the novel as a form. As Juliet McMaster reminds us, parody need not imply contempt.[72] Although its reputation was at an especially low level in the 1780s and 1790s, Austen famously defended the novel. Whereas contemporary women novelists like Maria Edgeworth, Amelia Opie, Elizabeth Inchbald and even Frances Burney were uneasy about their relationship with the genre, Austen was unapologetic in her support of what she saw as an undervalued species of fiction. At the end of chapter 5 of *Northanger Abbey*, she writes:

> [T]here seems almost a general wish of decrying the capacity and undervaluing the labour of the novelist, and of slighting the performances which have only genius, wit, and taste to recommend them . . . in which the greatest powers of the mind are displayed, in which the most thorough knowledge of human nature, the happiest delineation of its varieties, the liveliest effusion of wit and humour are conveyed to the world in the best chosen language.

Despite the light irony in the voice, this must surely be the most famous tribute addressed to any literary form. It is a vision not necessarily *of* but *for* the novel, subtly arguing for its educative value. The juvenilia suggest that Austen realized early on that the novel was something of a facilitator, generating and disseminating 'knowledge of human nature' to a ready audience. Although we learn nothing in her early works by example – the educative value of the sentimental novel is burlesqued – we learn indirectly, by understanding the ridicule and irony, to appreciate the 'truth' of this young writer's ideas. Thus the writer of juvenilia can be seen to be entering the education debate by indirect means, like any good ironist who dissembles not to deceive but to enlighten.

The education of young women was a major topic of discussion in Austen's youth. Because of its widespread popularity and because it appealed chiefly to women, religious and moral educationalists considered the novel harmful to young female readers who were ill-equipped to judge its overwhelming appeal to the senses. Enlightenment attributes of rationality and individualism were male prerogatives of the Charles Adamses of this world, seen as irrelevant to women who were to be educated as wives and mothers rather than thinkers. 'The Three Sisters' and 'Evelyn' in particular reveal Austen's concerns about the way this focus on marriage defines a woman's life. Writers of the fashionable conduct books, such as Dr John Gregory, the Revd James Fordyce, Mrs Chapone and Hannah More – all alluded to in Austen's writing – agreed on the importance of limiting the scope of the intellectual interests of young women. If women must read, said Dr Gregory, they might read the scriptures.[73] Although such writers were vehemently opposed to novels, however, ironically they promoted them by reinforcing society's expectations that women should be virtuous, delicate vessels (Hannah More spoke of 'porcelain clay') appealing to men. As we've seen, the popular novels idealized this fragile heroine who fainted when she was terrified or swooned when her virtue was assaulted. Janet Todd argues that this lack of robustness (so contrary to Austen's juvenilia heroines!) embodied not only purity but also an underlying seductive quality.[74] Both the female body and mind were portrayed as inherently weaker, and therefore more appealing to the opposite sex, than those of men.

Liberal thinkers like Austen's family, however, encouraged a rational (though unstructured) education for their daughters that would lead to a strong mind and sensible decision-making. When, in *Pride and Prejudice*, Elizabeth Bennet rejects Mr Collins's offer of marriage she is caught in the dilemma of the intelligent woman of the time: he believes she is feigning delicacy and bashfulness, 'the usual practice of elegant females',[75] and Elizabeth must reply: 'Do not consider me now as an elegant female intending to plague you, but as a rational creature speaking the truth directly from her heart.' The statement could be seen as Austen's creed as a writer, one that the author conceived almost as soon as she put pen to paper. For at the heart of all her early writing Austen is both advocating and demonstrating through her skill in parody the importance of a rational education for young women that will allow them to read critically and respond intelligently to their role in society.

We see something of Austen's endorsement of 'interpretative reading'[76] in 'Catharine, or the Bower', her first experiment in third-person narrative, the form she eventually used for her later novels. Catharine, or Kitty as she is affectionately called, always has a book on hand ready to amuse or console her when she is irritated. She is deeply disappointed when she finds that Camilla, who professes to be equally fond of books, has got little further than the covers of Charlotte Smith's *Emmeline* and *Ethelinde* and can say nothing sensible about them. Not to be able to appreciate novels intelligently or to read with critical awareness is a severe fault. The dangers of confusing novels with life is plainly spelled out in *Sense and Sensibility* and *Northanger Abbey*, but here in the juvenilia Austen is already clear about the importance of developing a critical response in reading. Camilla's superficial response is an index to her character, as both Kitty and the reader soon discover.

Hannah More's novel *Coelebs in Search of a Wife* (1809), substituted for an earlier novel in the text of 'Catharine', provides a further clue to Austen's early intention to critique the unrealistic attitudes to men and women she found in the novel – an ambitious (and serious) project for a young writer. Both More and her novel were a calculated choice. More was an evangelical religious writer and conservative propagandist who saw her mission as an educator of young women. She was keen to douse the bush fires of incipient feminism and secular republicanism, thus endearing herself to the influential middle-class as a preceptress to their daughters. Her novel presents an impossibly good man in search of an equally improbable good wife. The hero's examination of the flaws in a series of young women reinforces the dangers of rejection for those who usurp masculine prerogatives. His choice finally alights on a self-effacing girl not unlike the Sophie of Rousseau's *Emile* (1762), a novelistic model Austen was familiar with. She would have known, too, of More's 1799 *Strictures on Female Education* that confirmed the backlash against the campaign for women's rights and education by Catharine Macaulay and Mary Wollstonecraft. Thus, in 'Catharine', Mrs Percival's conservative taste and the advice she administers to her niece are not as ridiculous as they may seem to a modern-day audience or, indeed, as Austen parodically represents them. She is something of a touchstone for the contemporary moral code advocated by the conduct-book writers. Austen uses her as a foil to the spontaneous, fun-loving Catharine, who questions the gendered boundaries of her education (her name carries shades of Catharine Macaulay, who had just died the previous year and whose *Letters on Education*, 1790, advocated an enlightened education for women).

Catharine's natural responses are not those of the demure heroines of Rousseau and his followers. Like Austen herself, and like any intelligent young girl, she is learning to negotiate entrenched mores and seeking a meaningful role in society. But the novel 'Catharine' is unfinished. Critics have suggested that the challenge of working out Catharine's natural rebellion in the plot structure of her novel may have proved too great for the adolescent writer aware of social pressures and of her ambition to publish. Doody makes a strong case for Austen's calculated change of tack about this time from 'the rich and energetic comedy of the heartless world' to the tamer, more morally acceptable style that would appeal to a more conservative audience: 'In order to get published, she had to retrick her beams, redefine herself as a "serious" novelist.'[77]

'Catharine', with its more sober tone and less engaged, omniscient narration, may have been the first gesture towards this new approach to publication, but its unfinished state suggests that its heroine was still too rebellious to please publishers. Austen abandoned 'Catharine' for *Lady Susan*, a subject with greater ethical scope, that allows us to gain insight into the first steps from her short, sophisticated parodies to her more moral, novel-length fiction. Her ambition to be a published writer is reiterated throughout her juvenilia in the many signatures 'The Author'. In the last of her dedications to her sister she expresses, in preposterously exaggerated terms as always, the power she longs for: that her books should have 'obtained a place in every library in the Kingdom, and run through threescore Editions', and that

> the following Novel . . . I humbly flatter myself, possesses Merit beyond any already published, or any that will ever in future appear, except such as may proceed from the pen of Your Most Grateful Humble Serv[t]
>
> The Author

During her youth, Jane Austen received encouragement for her writings; her family was proud of her early 'Effusions of Fancy'. After her death, however, they were reluctant to release the juvenilia for publication, arguing that 'it would be as unfair to expose this preliminary process to the world, as it would be to display all that goes on behind the curtain of the theatre before it is drawn up'.[78] Her nephew James Edward Austen-Leigh spoke disparagingly of the juvenilia in his *Memoir* as 'transitory amusements', 'of a slight and flimsy texture'.[79] Even in 1933, R. W. Chapman patronizingly stated: 'it will always be disputed whether such effusions as these ought to be published; and it may be that we have enough already of Jane Austen's early scraps'.[80] Even as late as 1978, critics still allotted her 'first creative period' to the composition of *Pride and Prejudice*, alluding to the juvenilia and *Lady Susan* as 'trifling enough, consisting mainly of squibs and skits on the light literature of the day'.[81] The tide has now turned and readers and scholars cannot get enough of her early writings. They are clearly recognized as accomplished works in their own right. Like all juvenilia, they document the author's early delight in the process of creation and her gradual progression towards the artistic and moral maturity of her first published novels. But they also reveal the seriousness of an intelligent young writer behind the bravado and 'clever nonsense'. Jane Austen is a singular example of the many adolescents who take the pen into their own hands to entertain themselves and family, to interpret and critique their reading and experiences of life, and to express hidden desires and ambitions.

NOTES

1. Preface to *Love & Freindship and Other Early Works, Now first printed from the original MS by Jane Austen* (London: Chatto & Windus, 1922), pp. xiv–xv.
2. See Virginia Woolf, 'Jane Austen', in *The Common Reader* (London: Hogarth Press, 1925), pp. 168–72.
3. The sole exception is two cancelled chapters of *Persuasion*, but, as Kathryn Sutherland points out, they 'represent an alternative ending to the one that made it into print' (*Jane Austen's Fiction Manuscripts Digital Edition*, 'Introduction to the Edition'; *Jane Austen's Textual Lives: From Aeschylus to Bollywood* [Oxford: Oxford University Press, 2005], p. 148). Apart from this, the only other surviving fiction manuscripts by JA are the short play 'Sir Charles Grandison' (*c.*?1793–1800), the unfinished drafts of *The Watsons* (1803–4) and *Sanditon* (1817); and a fair copy of *Plan of a Novel* (*c.*1815). Most critics now date the first act of JA's 'Sir Charles Grandison' to the early 1790s (following Brian Southam, ed., *Jane Austen's 'Sir Charles Grandison'* [Oxford: Clarendon Press, 1980]), although other critics like Deirdre Le Faye date the whole play to *c.*1800–5 (Deirdre Le Faye, *Jane Austen: A Family Record*, 2nd edition [Cambridge: Cambridge University Press, 2004] [hereafter referred to as *FR*], p. 150).
4. JA's own words: *Jane Austen's Letters*, ed. Deirdre Le Faye, 3rd edition (Oxford: Oxford University Press, 1995) (hereafter referred to as *Letters*), p. 203.
5. *Emma*, I, iii.
6. *FR*, pp. 22 and 71.
7. Owned by the Rice family, direct descendants of the Kent branch of the Austens, the authenticity of the 'Rice Portrait' executed by Ozias Humphrey RA in 1788 remains unresolved. Many scholars, including Claudia Johnson, believe there is 'strong evidence in family testimony and provenance' that the portrait depicts JA in her early teens (Claudia Johnson, *Jane Austen's Cults and Cultures* [Chicago: University of Chicago Press, 2012], p. 47).

8. *FR*, p. 72.
9. *FR*, p. 155, and pp. xxi, xxiii, xxv.
10. In 1794 (just after JA wrote the last of the juvenilia) the Austens' benefactor Thomas Knight II died and left £50 each to Jane and Cassandra (*FR*, p. 87); and in February 1797, on the death of her fiancé Tom Fowle, Cassandra inherited his savings of £1,000 which might have provided an income of £35 pound a year from investments (*FR*, p. 101).
11. When Edward inherited the estates of Thomas Knight II in 1797, he 'eventually enjoyed an income greater than Mr Darcy's, nearly £15,000 a year' (Janet Todd, ed., *Jane Austen in Context* [Cambridge: Cambridge University Press, 2005], p. 5). For an approximate amount in today's terms, multiply this number by fifty.
12. James Edward Austen-Leigh, *A Memoir of Jane Austen* (1871), in *A Memoir of Jane Austen and Other Family Recollections*, ed. Kathryn Sutherland (Oxford: Oxford University Press, 2002), p. 217.
13. For a discussion of juvenilia and their wide-ranging value, see Christine Alexander and Juliet McMaster, eds, *The Child Writer from Austen to Woolf* (Cambridge: Cambridge University Press, 2005).
14. See Christine Alexander and David Owen, '*Lady Susan*: A Re-evaluation of Jane Austen's Epistolary Novel', in *Persuasions: The Jane Austen Journal* 27 (2005), p. 57.
15. See David Owen, *Rethinking Jane Austen's Lady Susan: The Case for Her 'failed' Epistolary Novella* (Lewiston, NY: Edwin Mellen Press, 2010) for a revisionary view of the importance of *Lady Susan* among Austen's works.
16. For a discussion of this issue, see the Introduction to the Juvenilia Press edition of *Lady Susan*, ed. Christine Alexander and David Owen (Sydney: Juvenilia Press, 2005), pp. ix–xii.
17. The text of *Lady Susan*, which appeared together with 'The Mystery' from *Volume the First*, was printed from an inaccurate copy because the original was currently missing. It is curious that neither Austen-Leigh nor other family members at the time appear to have been troubled by the subversive qualities of *Lady Susan*, an attitude that was resoundingly corrected in the early twentieth century by W. and R. A. Austen-Leigh in *Jane Austen: Her Life and Letters. A Family Record* [1913] (New York, 1965), p. 81.
18. Brian Southam, 'Juvenilia', in *The Jane Austen Handbook*, ed. J. David Grey (London: Athlone Press, 1986), p. 245.

19. The initial pages with contents are unnumbered. Page 167 is misnumbered 177, and page 175 is unnumbered.
20. Introduction to *Catharine and Other Writings*, ed. Margaret Anne Doody and Douglas Murray (Oxford: Oxford University Press, 1993), p. xvi.
21. *Volume the Second*, ed. B. C. Southam (Oxford: Clarendon Press, 1963), p. 210.
22. Le Faye suggests that 'Evelyn' was originally written immediately after 'The History of England' (*FR*, p. 74).
23. *Catharine*, ed. Doody and Murray, p. xix.
24. *Letters*, p. 270.
25. Paula Byrne, *Jane Austen and the Theatre* (London: Hambledon and London, 2002), p. 21.
26. Juliet McMaster, 'Your sincere Freind, The Author', *Persuasions On-Line* 27.1 (Winter 2006).
27. Henry Austen, 'Biographical Notice of the Author', in Austen-Leigh, *Memoir*, ed. Sutherland, p. 140.
28. A suggestion first made by Brian Southam (*Volume the Second*, p. xi). It is less probable, however, that the items in *Volume the Second* and *Volume the Third* were 'performed' to a general family audience in the same way as the earliest, more comic juvenilia.
29. In 1745 the Master of Balliol praised his six-year-old niece (JA's mother) for her impromptu charades and 'Smart pieces promising a great Genius'; and years later, Mrs Austen's granddaughter Anna Lefroy spoke of 'a quick-witted woman' who wrote 'simple playful common sense in rhyme' (*FR*, p. 10).
30. *Ibid.*, p. 61.
31. Quoted in Penny Gay, *Jane Austen and the Theatre* (Cambridge: Cambridge University Press, 2002), p. 4; see pp. 1–6 for a discussion of Austen's early theatrical experience.
32. George Holbert Tucker was the first to suggest this speculation in his discussion of the family tradition of theatricals (*Jane Austen the Woman: Some Biographical Insights* [London: Robert Hale, 1994], pp. 88–92).
33. Gay, *Jane Austen and the Theatre*, pp. 3 and 4ff.
34. George Holbert Tucker, *A Goodly Heritage: A History of Jane Austen's Family* (Manchester: Carcanet New Press, 1983), p. 47.
35. Louis Kronenberger describes 'the terrible Mrs C., who, all tenderness to her children in public, in private beat and starved and locked them up' (*The Polished Surface* [New York: Alfred A. Knopf, 1969], p. 135).
36. *FR*, p. 69.

37. *Sanditon*, ch. viii.
38. A. Walton Litz in particular emphasizes the significance of *The Loiterer* in 'Jane Austen: The Juvenilia', in *Jane Austen's Beginnings: The Juvenilia and Lady Susan*, ed. J. David Grey (Ann Arbor, Michigan and London: UMI Research Press, 1989), p. 4.
39. *Ibid.*, p. 5.
40. Constance Hill, *Jane Austen: Her Homes & Her Friends* (John Lane, The Bodley Head, 1923), p. 84.
41. Irene Collins, *Jane Austen: The Parson's Daughter* (London: The Hambledon Press, 1998), p. 35.
42. R. W. Chapman, *Jane Austen: Facts and Problems* (Oxford: Clarendon Press, 1948), p. 17. Park Honan also notes that Cassandra's 'amateur drawing was said to be good' (*Jane Austen*, p. 290).
43. Brigid Brophy, 'Jane Austen and the Stuarts', in *Critical Essays on Jane Austen*, ed. B. C. Southam (London: Routledge, 1968), p. 30.
44. A detailed discussion of the dating can be found in Annette Upfal's Introduction to *Jane Austen's 'The History of England' & Cassandra's Portraits*, ed. Annette Upfal and Christine Alexander (Sydney: Juvenilia Press, 2009), pp. xxvii–xxx.
45. The family copy of Goldsmith's *History* contains over a hundred marginal comments by JA, written about 1791 and reflecting her distaste for the text: see relevant Notes to her 'History of England' at the end of this edition.
46. *History & Cassandra's Portraits*, ed. Upfal and Alexander, pp. xix–xxxvii.
47. Remark made by Mary Russell Mitford (1787–1855), quoted in Austen-Leigh, *Memoir*, ed. Sutherland, p. 133.
48. *Volume the Second*, ed. Southam, p. 214.
49. Clara Tuite, *Romantic Austen: Sexual Politics and the Literary Canon* (Cambridge: Cambridge University Press, 2002), p. 46.
50. *FR*, p. 10.
51. *The History of England*, ed. Jan Fergus (Edmonton: Juvenilia Press, 1995), p. viii.
52. See Introduction to *History & Cassandra's Portraits*, ed. Upfal and Alexander. Catherine Hubback (daughter of Francis Austen) states that Mrs Austen was 'strict with her children' (John H. and Edith C. Hubback, *Jane Austen's Sailor Brothers* [1906] [Folcroft, PA: Folcroft Library Editions, 1976], p. 9).
53. See *History & Cassandra's Portraits*, ed. Upfal and Alexander, Introduction and pp. 59–68 for a comparison of illustrations with sketches of the originals and for authentication by experts in the fields of odontology and geometrics.

54. Francis Austen was at sea from 23 December 1788 until Winter 1793 (*FR*, pp. xx–xxi). Thirteen-year-old Charles, away at Naval College, is also excluded from the illustrations, although it is possible his portrait may exist in one of the still unidentified images.
55. *The Relief* by H. W. Bunbury, 1781; first noted in *History & Cassandra's Portraits*, ed. Upfal and Alexander, p. xxix.
56. *Recruits* by H. W. Bunbury (1780); first noted by Mary Millard: see *The History of England*, ed. Fergus, pp. iv–v.
57. Austen-Leigh, *Memoir*, ed. Sutherland, p. 19.
58. *Letters*, p. 5.
59. Christine Alexander, 'Autobiography and Juvenilia', in *The Child Writer*, p. 162.
60. Honan, *Jane Austen*, p. 37.
61. Reginald Farrer, 'Farrer on Jane Austen', in *Jane Austen: The Critical Heritage, Volume* 2, ed. B. C. Southam (London: Routledge, 1987), p. 247.
62. Margaret Anne Doody, 'Jane Austen, that disconcerting "child"', in *The Child Writer*, p. 101. Doody uses 'The Rice Portrait' (that appears on p. 102) to argue that JA's juvenilia are 'disconcertingly sophisticated' and distinct from the later novels, the works of 'another Austen, a comic writer of harder tone and more fearless satire' (p. 103) that had to be veiled in order to be published. For the Rice portrait, see note 7 above.
63. Brian Southam points out that Mr Austen's inscription inside the front cover of *Volume the Third* is particularly appropriate for 'Evelyn', which is in 'a Style entirely new', but not for 'Catharine', the other story in this volume (*Jane Austen's Literary Manuscripts: A Study of the Novelist's Development through the Surviving Papers* [Oxford: Oxford University Press, 1964], p. 36), suggesting that he might have read 'Evelyn' but not 'Catharine'.
64. M. H. Abrams and Geoffrey Galt Harpham, *A Glossary of Literary Terms*, 10th edition (Boston, MA: Wadsworth, 2012), p. 37.
65. David Cecil, *A Portrait of Jane Austen* (London: Penguin, 1980), p. 47.
66. Marvin Mudrick, *Jane Austen: Irony as Defence and Discovery* (Princeton, NJ: Princeton University Press, 1952), p. 5.
67. Southam, *Literary Manuscripts*, p. 3.
68. Mudrick, *JA*: *Irony as Defence and Discovery*, p. 5. See also Juliet McMaster, 'From *Laura and Augustus* to *Love and Freindship*', *Thalia: Studies in Literary Humor* 16: 1–2 (1996), pp. 16–26.

69. *The History of England*, ed. Fergus, p. vii.
70. The heroine of *Shamela* (1741), Fielding's spoof on Richardson's novel *Pamela* (see *Lady Susan*, ed. Alexander and Owen, p. xiv).
71. In a letter to her niece Anna Austen critiquing her writing, 28 September 1814 (*Letters*, p. 277).
72. Juliet McMaster, 'Young Jane Austen: Author', in *A Companion to Jane Austen*, ed. Claudia L. Johnson and Clara Tuite (Chichester: Wiley-Blackwell, 2009), p. 83.
73. Frank W. Bradbrook, *Jane Austen and Her Predecessors* (Cambridge: Cambridge University Press, (1966; 2010), p. 24.
74. Janet Todd, *Sensibility: An Introduction* (New York: Methuen, 1986), p. 80.
75. *Pride and Prejudice*, I, xix.
76. Mary Gaither Marshall, who argues that the young Austen was skilled in a family tradition of 'interpretative reading': 'Jane Austen's Manuscripts of the Juvenilia and *Lady Susan: A History and Description*', in *Jane Austen's Beginnings*, ed. Grey, p. 108.
77. Doody, 'Jane Austen, that disconcerting "child"', p. 118.
78. Austen-Leigh, *Memoir*, ed. Sutherland, p. 43.
79. *Ibid.*, p. 40; he included a tiny sample of Jane Austen's juvenilia ('The Mystery').
80. *Volume the First*, ed. R. W. Chapman (Oxford: Clarendon Press, 1933), p. ix. Over fifty years later, Chapman's misgivings were echoed by Joan Austen-Leigh, great-granddaughter of James Edward Austen-Leigh, who declared that her ancestor was right to suppress Austen's 'earliest scraps', many of which 'would never have seen the light of day if they had been by another hand' ('The Juvenilia: A Family "Veiw"', in *Jane Austen's Beginnings*, ed. Grey, p. 177).
81. Cecil, *A Portrait of Jane Austen*, p. 59.

69. The History of England [illegible], preface, p. vii.
70. The [illegible] (1773) [illegible] Richardson [illegible] p. xxvi.
71. Jane Austen to her niece Anna Austen [illegible] 9 September 1814 (Letters, p. 275).
72. Juliet McMaster, 'Young Jane Austen: Author', in A Companion to Jane Austen, ed. Claudia L. Johnson and Clara Tuite (Chichester: Wiley-Blackwell, 2009), p. 85.
73. Frank W. Bradbrook, Jane Austen and Her Predecessors (Cambridge: Cambridge University Press, 1966), p. 24.
74. [illegible] (New York: Methuen, 1986), p. 61.
75. Frederic and Elfrida, p. [illegible].
76. [illegible] who agrees that the young Austen was skilled in a family tradition of [illegible]; James Austen-Leigh, Memoir [illegible] (Oxford [illegible]), p. [illegible].
77. [illegible] discovering 'child' [illegible].
78. Austen-Leigh, Memoir, ed. Sutherland, p. [illegible].
79. Ibid., p. [illegible] [illegible] 'The Mystery'.
80. Volume the First, ed. R. W. Chapman (Oxford: Clarendon Press, 1933), p. [illegible]. Over fifty years later, Chapman's [illegible] echoed by [illegible] great-granddaughter of James Edward Austen-Leigh, who declared [illegible] would [illegible] if they had been [illegible]. (The [illegible]: A Family Record [illegible].)
81. Cecil, A Portrait of Jane Austen, p. [illegible].

Note on the Text

This is the first occasion on which Jane Austen's *Lady Susan* has been published together with her three early volumes of juvenilia. *Lady Susan*, like the juvenilia, is significant in Austen studies as one of her few early surviving manuscripts; yet it is almost always published with the later fragmentary 'The Watsons' and with 'Sanditon', the last of her extant manuscripts, presumably because these pieces are all relatively short. Publishing *Lady Susan* chronologically, however, following the three manuscript volumes of juvenilia, allows us to assess the significant position of this early novel in Austen's development as a writer.

The present edition is based on the three manuscript volumes of juvenilia, located in the Bodleian Library (*Volume the First*: MS.Don.e.7) and in the British Library (*Volume the Second*: Add.59874 and *Volume the Third*: Add.65381), and on the manuscript of *Lady Susan*, located in the Pierpont Morgan Library. A further brief manuscript poem is included in Appendix A since it was not part of Austen's notebooks; the letter in *The Loiterer* from 'Sophia Sentiment', attributed to Austen, is included in Appendix B; and, although the first act of Austen's play 'Sir Charles Grandison' was probably written in the 1790s, the remainder of the play belongs to a later period of her work and is not included in this volume.

All texts have been newly transcribed from the manuscripts. There are few problems of transcription since all three volumes of juvenilia and *Lady Susan* are basically fair copies, written in a large clear hand and requiring only minimal editorial emendation, as noted below. Occasionally it is difficult to distinguish the difference between an upper- and lower-case letter, or whether or not an indentation signifies a new paragraph; in such cases, an editorial judgement has been made based on the context and Austen's usual practice.

THE MANUSCRIPTS

The script of *Volume the First* (apart from its last two items that were transcribed much later) is less mature than that of the other two volumes of juvenilia, but there are very few major authorial revisions in any of the volumes or *Lady Susan*. The manuscript errors are chiefly of the kind we make when we are copying: words misspelled, words repeated or omitted, letters or words transposed. Most of these minor mistakes Austen neatly corrected. Occasionally her revisions refine the comedy or tone down her enthusiasm and bravura; some of these more significant changes of mind are commented on in the Notes and all are recorded in the Textual Notes at the back of this edition, so that readers can gain an insight into the process of Austen's composition. Those who wish to examine all authorial revisions should consult Peter Sabor's detailed textual footnotes in his scholarly edition *Juvenilia* (Cambridge: Cambridge University Press, 2006) or a copy of the actual manuscripts themselves that has recently been made available online, expertly presented by Kathryn Sutherland as *Jane Austen's Fiction Manuscripts Digital Edition*.

Austen's juvenilia are writings of a private character to which criteria of standardized correctness were not applied. While the printed form of the language had largely been standardized by the late eighteenth century, spelling in those forms of writing not intended for publication was not expected to adhere to such regulation, as Barbara Strang explains in *A History of English* (London: Methuen, 1970, p. 107). Thus spellings that are clearly anomalous to standard modern written British English (including the notorious 'ei' example that appears in the title 'Love and Freindship' and throughout the three volumes of juvenilia, with the exception of two instances in 'Detached Pieces' and three instances in 'Scraps') have been preserved in this edition as alternative forms. This example and other spelling anomalies should no longer be seen – somewhat condescendingly – as indications of immaturity. Furthermore, these variant early spellings, including the use of the suffix 'full' in words like 'beautifull', 'wonderfull' and 'faithfull', congregate in the earliest items of juvenilia before Austen's spelling became more consistent and conventional, and thus they assist scholars in dating the various items (see Brian Southam, 'The Manuscript of Jane Austen's Volume the First', in *The Library*, vol. XVII, No. 3 [Sept 1962], p. 236).

THE PRESENT EDITION

The aim of this edition is to present an easily readable text while remaining as close as possible to the content and form of what Austen wrote. Thus the layout of the titles and dedications is represented as in the manuscripts, apart from two occasions in *Volume the First* where Austen's irregular use of ruled lines in headings has been made consistent. Words and phrases that Austen underlined for emphasis are retained; and her spellings (such as 'sat-off', 'inshort' and the anomalous 'ei' and '-full' forms mentioned above) are preserved. Minor editorial emendations have been made only where the original is misleading (such as variations in the spelling of names). The very few editorial insertions are included in square brackets.

Jane Austen's punctuation has been preserved wherever possible, except when it appears eccentric to a modern audience and has no bearing on the meaning of her text. For example, she includes many interjections within the quoted text, as can be seen in the following sentences from 'Jack and Alice': 'My dear Kitty she said. Good night t'ye', where we would now use inverted commas to separate the dramatic aside 'she said' from the actual words spoken. *Lady Susan*, too, follows this practice and has been emended accordingly. Occasionally, as in 'Love and Freindship', Austen signals her asides with brackets, which have been preserved in this edition. Speech marks are often incomplete in the manuscripts and, in *Volume the First*, Austen uses double inverted commas at the beginning and end of each manuscript line of speech; these have been regularized to conform to a modern rendering of direct speech. In Austen's youthful dramas, too, her irregular use of a colon followed by a bracket to separate a character from speech has been emended to the use of a colon alone.

Other minor emendations include punctuation in headings and the indentation of initial paragraphs in chapters, both of which have been made consistent; the removal of Austen's use of the colon before a superscript letter in contractions such as 'Capt:^{n}' and in place of a hyphen to indicate a word broken at the end of a line; the occasional insertion of a comma for clarity, or of an inverted comma in cases of possession and in contractions such as 'don't', and the correction of 'its/it's' to conform with modern usage (although anomalous possessive forms were acceptable at the time Austen was writing). Austen's occasional use of the long 's' has been regularized to a modern 's'; and her ampersand (&) and '&c' have been regularized to 'and' and 'etc' accordingly. However, her use of shorthand for common superscript tags used in letters (such as 'Y^{r} affec^{te}' for 'Your affectionate' and 'in Comp^{ts}' for 'with Compliments') has been preserved throughout.

This edition preserves all Austen's manuscript dashes, including the many apparently unnecessary dashes that seem to carry no grammatical significance: they often appear as line fillers or are used before or after a full stop to separate sentences. Yet, on close inspection, they can be seen to signal a variety of meaning: a pause, a moment of introspection or indecision on the part of the writer; an innuendo or hint of further significance to the reader; a dramatic conclusion to a sentence; or a change in thought that may equate to a new paragraph. The subtlety of such punctuation that provides a trace of the composition process demands to be preserved, especially in the case of a young writer where her creative development is on display.

Every effort has been made to preserve not only the content but also the shape and 'flavour' of these manuscripts. The layout of mock dedications, title pages and the exuberant use of accidentals (even the variant spellings) express a sense of progression from the playful nature of the early juvenile pieces to the more serious concerns of 'Catharine' and *Lady Susan* at the end of this volume. In keeping with this policy, Cassandra's portraits that are vital to the meaning of the collaborative 'History of England', produced by the two sisters, are included in their original positions in the text. The continuations of her two stories in *Volume the Third* made by her nephew James Edward Austen-Leigh have also been included (with clear indication to the reader), since they are an integral part of the manuscript volume and at least two of them may have been authorized by Austen herself (see notes to the continuations).

Further Reading

EDITIONS

Austen, Jane, *Catharine and Other Writings*, ed. Margaret Anne Doody and Douglas Murray (Oxford: Oxford University Press, 1993). The first annotated edition of Austen's juvenilia and later prayers and poems, with an excellent introduction by Doody.

— *Jane Austen's 'Sir Charles Grandison'*, ed. Brian Southam (Oxford: Clarendon Press, 1980). A short play written about 1800–5, although most critics believe that the first act was written much earlier, when JA was playing with '*Grandison* jokes' in her juvenilia.

— *Jane Austen's 'The History of England' & Cassandra's Portraits*, ed. Annette Upfal and Christine Alexander (Sydney: Juvenilia Press, 2009). The emphasis of this edition is on the collaboration between the Austen sisters, and the identification and meaning of the portraits in relation to the text.

— *Juvenilia*, ed. Peter Sabor, The Cambridge Edition of the Works of Jane Austen (Cambridge: Cambridge University Press, 2006). A scholarly, comprehensive and detailed source for all manuscript queries.

— *Lady Susan*, ed. Christine Alexander and David Owen (Sydney: Juvenilia Press, 2005). The first fully annotated edition of *Lady Susan*, with appendix on historical punctuation and spelling.

— *Later Manuscripts*, ed. Janet Todd and Linda Bree, The Cambridge Edition of the Works of Jane Austen (Cambridge:

Cambridge University Press, 2008). Despite the misleading title, *Lady Susan* appears in this edition.

— *Minor Works*, vol. 6 of *The Works of Jane Austen*, ed. R. W. Chapman (Oxford: Clarendon Press, 1954; revised by B. C. Southam, London: Oxford University Press, 1975). For many years, Chapman's editions of Austen's juvenilia were the only ones available, subsequently updated by Southam. An important work in the history of Austen scholarship.

Austen-Leigh, James Edward, *A Memoir of Jane Austen, to which is added Lady Susan and fragments of two other unfinished tales by Miss Austen*, 2nd edition (London: Richard Bentley, 1871). The first publication of *Lady Susan*.

See also other Juvenilia Press editions of Jane Austen's individual works: *A Collection of Letters* (1998, repr. 2006), *Catharine, or The Bower* (1996, repr. 2005), *Evelyn* (1999, repr. 2011), *Frederic & Elfrida* (2002), *Jack and Alice* (2001), *Jane Austen's Men* (2007), *Lesley Castle* (1998, repr. 2006), *Love and Freindship* (1995, repr. 2008), *The Three Sisters* (2004), and *Three Mini-Dramas* (2006).

TEXTUAL STUDIES

Gilson, David J., and J. David Grey, 'Jane Austen's Juvenilia and *Lady Susan*: An Annotated Bibliography', in *Jane Austen's Beginnings: The Juvenilia and Lady Susan*, ed. J. David Grey (Ann Arbor, Michigan, and London: University of Michigan Research Press, 1989), pp. 243–62. An important work that did much to inspire and direct future scholarly work on the juvenilia; still a valuable resource.

Marshall, Mary Gaither, 'Jane Austen's Manuscripts of the Juvenilia and *Lady Susan*: A History and Description', in *Jane Austen's Beginnings*, pp. 107–21.

Southam, B. C., *Jane Austen's Literary Manuscripts: A Study of the Novelist's Development through the Surviving Papers* (1964), revised edition (London: Althone Press, 2001). Chapters 1 and 2 deal exclusively with the juvenilia, and chapter 3 with *Lady Susan*. A seminal work in the field.

Sutherland, Kathryn, *Jane Austen's Textual Lives: From Aeschylus to Bollywood* (Oxford: Oxford University Press, 2005). A fascinating history of textual transmission, with insights into the way the 'myth' of Jane Austen affected the reception of the juvenilia.

Sutherland, Kathryn, ed., *Jane Austen's Fiction Manuscripts Digital Edition* (http://www.janeausten.ac.uk/index.html). The manuscripts are readily available here online.

BIOGRAPHY

Austen, Jane, *Jane Austen's Letters*, ed. Deirdre LeFaye, 3rd edition (Oxford: Oxford University Press, 1995). An important primary resource.

Austen-Leigh, James Edward, *A Memoir of Jane Austen*, 2nd edition (1871), in *A Memoir of Jane Austen and Other Family Recollections*, ed. Kathryn Sutherland (Oxford: Oxford University Press, 2002). A new revised edition that includes Henry Austen's two biographical essays, Caroline Austen's *My Aunt Jane Austen: A Memoir* (1867) and Anna Lefroy's 'Recollections of Aunt Jane' (1864).

Byrne, Paula, *The Real Jane Austen: A Life in Small Things* (London: Harper Press, 2013). A revisionary biography, featuring a 'far tougher' Jane Austen. Chapter 3 features the juvenilia.

Le Faye, Deirdre, *Jane Austen: A Family Record*, 2nd edition (Cambridge: Cambridge University Press, 2004). An indispensable resource on Austen family matters and her early life.

Spence, Jon, *Becoming Jane Austen: A Life* (London and New York: Hambledon and London, 2003). Focuses heavily on Austen's early relationships with her cousin Eliza and Tom Lefroy.

Tomalin, Claire, *Jane Austen: A Life* [1997], revised edition (London: Penguin, 2000). A balanced, sensitive biography that asks some of the big questions.

CRITICISM

Alexander, Christine and Juliet McMaster, eds, *The Child Writer from Austen to Woolf* (Cambridge: Cambridge University Press, 2005). Contains essays by Margaret Anne Doody, 'Jane Austen, that disconcerting "child"', and Rachel M. Brownstein, 'Endless imitation: Austen's and Byron's juvenilia'. Other numerous references to Austen and literary juvenilia.

Byrne, Paula, *Jane Austen and the Theatre* (London: Hambledon and London, 2002).

Copeland, Edward and Juliet McMaster, eds, *The Cambridge Companion to Jane Austen*, 2nd edition (Cambridge: Cambridge University Press, 2011). Chapter 5, 'The early short fiction' by Margaret Anne Doody, discusses the juvenilia.

Gay, Penny, *Jane Austen and the Theatre* (Cambridge: Cambridge University Press, 2002). Chapter 1 discusses Austen's early experience of the theatre.

Harris, Jocelyn, *Jane Austen's Art of Memory* (Cambridge: Cambridge University Press, 1989). Examines the reading and imaginative life of Austen. The Appendices address allusions to Sir Charles Grandison in the juvenilia.

Johnson, Claudia L., *Jane Austen: Women, Politics and the Novel* (Chicago: University of Chicago Press, 1988). Places Austen's work in political, cultural and literary history.

Kent, Christopher, 'Learning History with, and from, Jane Austen', in *Jane Austen's Beginnings: The Juvenilia and Lady Susan*, ed. J. David Grey (Ann Arbor, Michigan, and London: UMI Research Press, 1989), pp. 59–72. Important for Austen's 'The History of England'.

Litz, A. Walton, 'Jane Austen: The Juvenilia', in *Jane Austen's Beginnings*, ed. Grey, pp. 1–6.

McMaster, Juliet, 'The Juvenilia: Energy Versus Sympathy', in *A Companion to Jane Austen Studies*, ed. Laura Cooner

Lambdin and Robert Thomas Lambdin (Westport, CT, and London: Greenwood Press, 2000), 173–90.

— 'Young Jane Austen: Author', in *A Companion to Jane Austen*, ed. Claudia L. Johnson and Clara Tuite (Chichester: Wiley-Blackwell, 2009), pp. 81–90.

— 'Your sincere Freind, The Author', *Persuasions On-Line* 27.1 (Winter 2006).

Owen, David, *Rethinking Jane Austen's Lady Susan: The Case for Her 'failed' Epistolary Novella* (Lewiston, NY: Edwin Mellen Press, 2010).

Todd, Janet, ed., *Jane Austen in Context*, The Cambridge Edition of the Works of Jane Austen (Cambridge: Cambridge University Press, 2005). A comprehensive resource on the life and times of Austen.

Tuite, Clara, *Romantic Austen: Sexual Politics and the Literary Canon* (Cambridge: Cambridge University Press, 2002). Chapter 1 addresses the historical context of the juvenilia.

Lambdin and Robert Thomas Lambdin (Westport, CT, and London: Greenwood Press, 2000), 287–310.

— 'Young Jane Austen: Author', in *A Companion to Jane Austen*, ed. Claudia L. Johnson and Clara Tuite (Chichester: Wiley-Blackwell, 2009), pp. 82–91.

— '"Your sincere Friend, the Author": Forewords to Lady Susan', *Persuasions On-Line* 23.1 (Winter 2002).

Owen, David, *Refashioning Jane Austen's Lady Susan: The Case for Her 'Ideal' Epistolary Novella* (Lewiston, NY: Edwin Mellen Press, 2010).

Sabor, Peter, ed., *Jane Austen's Juvenilia*, The Cambridge Edition of the Works of Jane Austen (Cambridge: Cambridge University Press, 2006). A comprehensive resource on the life and times of Austen.

Tuite, Clara, *Romantic Austen: Sexual Politics and the Literary Canon* (Cambridge: Cambridge University Press, 2002). Chapter 1 addresses the historical context of the juvenilia.

Chronology

1775 16 December: Jane Austen born at Steventon, Hampshire, seventh child of the Revd George Austen, Rector of Steventon and Deane, and Cassandra Austen, née Leigh. Her elder siblings are James, George, Edward, Henry, Cassandra and Francis; Charles is born one year later.

1779 3 July: JA's eldest brother James matriculates at St John's College, Oxford, aged fourteen.

1782 December: First amateur theatrical production at Steventon, of Dr Thomas Franklin's tragedy *Matilda* (1775). Numerous family productions in subsequent years include such comedies as Richard Brinsley Sheridan's *The Rivals* (1775), Susanna Centlivre's *The Wonder* (1714) and John Fletcher's *The Chances* (*c.*1617); Henry Fielding's burlesque *Tom Thumb* (1731); and two farces, Isaac Bickerstaffe's *The Sultan* (1775) and Revd James Townley's *High Life Below Stairs* (1759).

1783 JA's brother Edward is adopted by Mr and Mrs Thomas Knight II of Godmersham in Kent.

March: JA, Cassandra and cousin Jane Cooper go to Mrs Cawley's boarding school in Oxford.

Summer: Mrs Cawley moves to Southampton and the girls contract typhoid fever in early September; Aunt Jane Cooper, after nursing her daughter, dies of typhoid in Bath (25 October).

1785 August: JA and Cassandra go to the Abbey House School, Reading.

1786 Edward on Grand Tour of Europe (1786–90).

15 April: JA's brother Francis enters Royal Naval Academy at Portsmouth.

November: JA's brother James goes to the Continent.

December: JA and Cassandra leave the Abbey House School and return to Steventon. Between now and 1793, JA writes her three volumes of juvenilia.

1787 JA begins work on *Volume the First* (final pieces dated 1793).

1788 1 July: JA's brother Henry matriculates at St John's College, Oxford.

Summer: JA and Cassandra taken to Kent and London by their parents.

23 December: Francis sails to East Indies with the Royal Navy aboard the *Perseverance* (returns 1793).

1790 13 June: JA completes 'Love and Freindship' (*Volume the Second*).

1791 20 July: JA's youngest brother Charles enters the Royal Naval Academy, Portsmouth.

26 November: JA completes 'The History of England' (*Volume the Second*).

27 December: Edward marries Elizabeth Bridges in Kent, and goes to live at Rowling.

1792 January: Date of JA's earliest extant verses.

27 March: James marries Anne Mathew; they live at Deane parsonage.

Spring: JA writes 'Lesley Castle' (*Volume the Second*).

6 May: JA dates contents page of *Volume the Third*.

August: JA's dedication to 'Catharine, or the Bower' dated.

1793 8 April: Henry becomes a lieutenant in the Oxfordshire Militia.

3 June: JA completes and dates *Volume the Third*.

1794 *Lady Susan* probably written in this period.

Summer: JA and Cassandra visit the Leighs at Adlestrop, and later Edward and Elizabeth at Rowling.

1795 Cassandra becomes engaged to Revd Tom Fowle.

JA probably writes 'Elinor and Marianne' (later *Sense and Sensibility*).

December: Tom Lefroy visits Ashe Rectory: JA and Tom have a flirtation over the Christmas holidays.

1796 October: JA begins 'First Impressions' (later *Pride and Prejudice*).

1797 17 January: James marries Mary Lloyd (his first wife died in 1795).

February: Tom Fowle, Cassandra's fiancé, dies of fever at San Domingo and is buried at sea.

August: JA completes 'First Impressions'; Mr Austen offers it to Thomas Cadell for publication but it is rejected.

1 November: Edward takes possession of Godmersham estate in Kent.

November: JA begins to revise 'Elinor and Marianne' into *Sense and Sensibility*. JA and Cassandra visit Bath with their mother.

31 December: Henry marries cousin, the widowed Eliza de Feuillide, in London.

1798 August: JA and Cassandra visit Godmersham with their parents (JA returns in October). JA works on 'Susan' (later *Northanger Abbey*); probably finishes the following summer.

1799 17 May: JA and Mrs Austen, with Edward and Elizabeth, visit Bath until end of June.

1800 December: Revd George Austen retires and decides to settle in Bath.

1801 May: JA, Cassandra and their parents leave Steventon for Bath; they then go on a West Country holiday until September, when they visit Steventon before returning to Bath on 5 October.

1802 September–October: JA and Cassandra pay visits to James at Steventon and Edward at Godmersham.

2 December: JA and Cassandra visit Steventon; while there, JA accepts a proposal from Harris Bigg-Wither, but withdraws her consent the following day.

1803 Spring: 'Susan' sold to Crosby & Son of London for £10.

September: JA, Cassandra and their parents visit Ramsgate in Kent and Godmersham, returning to Bath 24 October.

November: The Austens visit Lyme Regis.

1804 JA probably begins *The Watsons*, leaving it unfinished.

Summer: The Austens visit Lyme Regis, returning to Bath on 25 October.

1805 21 January: Revd George Austen dies in Bath.

June: Mrs Austen and her daughters visit Godmersham.

Summer: Martha Lloyd decides to live with Mrs Austen and her daughters.

1806 2 July: JA, Cassandra and Mrs Austen leave Bath; they visit Clifton (near Bristol) and Adlestrop.

24 July: JA's brother Francis marries Mary Gibson.

5–14 August: JA, Cassandra and Mrs Austen visit relations at Stoneleigh Abbey.

October: JA settles in Southampton with Cassandra and Mrs Austen.

1807 19 May: Charles marries Fanny Palmer, in Bermuda.

1809 7 July: JA, Cassandra and Mrs Austen, with Martha Lloyd, move into Chawton Cottage, Hampshire, owned by Edward.

1811 February: JA begins *Mansfield Park.*

March–May: JA stays with Henry in London and corrects proofs of *Sense and Sensibility*.

30 October: *Sense and Sensibility* published by Egerton.

?Winter: JA begins to revise 'First Impressions' into *Pride and Prejudice*.

1812 9–25 June: JA visits Steventon with Mrs Austen.

14 October: Mrs Thomas Knight II dies, and Edward officially takes Knight as his surname.

1813 28 January: *Pride and Prejudice* published.

22 April: JA goes to London to attend cousin Eliza, who dies on 24 April.

1 May: JA returns to Chawton; spending two weeks in London with Henry from 19 May.

?July: JA finishes *Mansfield Park*.

September: JA visits Godmersham for the last time, returning to Chawton on 13 November.

1814 21 January: JA begins writing *Emma* (finished 29 March 1815).

1 March: JA visits Henry in London; and again in August and November.

9 May: *Mansfield Park* published by Egerton.

1815 2–16 January: JA and Cassandra stay at Steventon.

8 August: JA begins *Persuasion* (finished 6 August 1816).

August: JA goes to London, probably to secure publication of *Emma*, and returns early September.

4 October: JA visits Henry in London; he falls ill and she doesn't return to Chawton until 16 December.

13 November: JA visits Charlton House, and is invited to dedicate a future novel to the Prince Regent.

1816 *Emma* published by John Murray, dedicated to the Prince Regent (title page 1816, but actually printed the previous December). JA writes 'Plan of a Novel'.

Spring: JA begins to feel unwell. Henry buys back MS of 'Susan' (*Northanger Abbey*) so JA can revise and resubmit for publication; Henry's bank fails and he leaves London on 15 March.

22 May: JA and Cassandra visit Steventon; returning to Chawton 15 June.

December: Henry ordained, becomes curate of Chawton.

1817 January: From 27 January to 18 March JA works on *Sanditon*, leaving it unfinished.

27 April: JA makes her Will.

24 May: Cassandra takes JA to Winchester for medical attention; they lodge at No. 8, College Street.

18 July: JA dies; buried in Winchester Cathedral.

December: *Northanger Abbey* and *Persuasion* published together by John Murray (title page dated 1818), with Henry Austen's 'Biographical Notice'.

LOVE AND FREINDSHIP AND OTHER YOUTHFUL WRITINGS

Volume the First

Frederic & Elfrida

a novel.

Chapter the First.

The Uncle of Elfrida was the Father of Frederic; in other words, they were first cousins by the Father's side.

Being both born in one day & both brought up at one school, it was not wonderfull that they should look on each other with something more than bare politeness. They loved with mutual sincerity but were both determined not to transgress the rules of Propriety by owning their attachment, either to the object beloved, or to any one else.

Manuscript page 1 of 'Frederic and Elfrida', in Jane Austen's notebook *Volume the First*. (By permission of The Bodleian Libraries, University of Oxford.)

VOLUME THE FIRST

Contents

To Miss Lloyd[1]

My dear Martha

As a small testimony of the gratitude I feel for your late generosity to me in finishing my muslin Cloak,[2] I beg leave to offer you this little production of your sincere Freind[3]

The Author

Frederic and Elfrida
a novel

Chapter the First

The Uncle of Elfrida was the Father of Frederic;[4] in other words, they were first cousins by the Father's side.

Being both born in one day and both brought up at one school,[5] it was not wonderfull that they should look on each other with something more than bare politeness. They loved with mutual sincerity but were both determined not to transgress the rules of Propriety[6] by owning their attachment, either to the object beloved, or to any one else.

They were exceedingly handsome and so much alike, that it was not every one who knew them apart.[7] Nay even their most intimate freinds had nothing to distinguish them by, but the shape of the face, the colour of the Eye, the length of the Nose and the difference of the complexion.

Elfrida had an intimate freind to whom, being on a visit to an Aunt, she wrote the following Letter:

To Miss Drummond

Dear Charlotte

I should be obliged to you, if you would buy me, during your stay with Mrs Williamson, a new and fashionable Bonnet, to suit the complexion of your

E. Falknor.

Charlotte, whose character was a willingness to oblige every one, when she returned into the Country, brought her Freind the wished-for Bonnet, and so ended this little adventure, much to the satisfaction of all parties.

On her return to Crankhumdunberry[8] (of which sweet village her father was Rector) Charlotte was received with the greatest Joy by Frederic and Elfrida, who, after pressing her alternately to their Bosoms, proposed to her to take a walk in a Grove of Poplars which led from the Parsonage to a verdant Lawn enamelled with a variety of variegated flowers[9] and watered by a purling Stream, brought from the Valley of Tempé[10] by a passage under ground.

In this Grove they had scarcely remained above 9 hours, when they were suddenly agreably surprized by hearing a most delightfull voice warble the following stanza.

Song.

That Damon[11] was in love with me
I once thought and beleiv'd
But now that he is not I see,
I fear I was deceiv'd.

No sooner were the lines finished than they beheld by a turning in the Grove 2 elegant young women leaning on each other's arm, who immediately on perceiving them, took a different path and disappeared from their sight.

Chapter the Second

As Elfrida and her companions, had seen enough of them to know that they were neither the 2 Miss Greens, nor M[rs] Jackson and her Daughter, they could not help expressing their surprise at their appearance; till at length recollecting, that a new family had lately taken a House not far from the Grove, they hastened home, determined to lose no time in forming an acquaintance with 2 such amiable and worthy Girls, of which family they rightly imagined them to be a part.

Agreable to such a determination, they went that very evening[12] to pay their respects to Mrs Fitzroy and her two Daughters. On being shewn into an elegant dressing room, ornamented with festoons of artificial flowers,[13] they were struck with the engaging Exterior and beautifull outside of Jezalinda the eldest of the young Ladies; but e'er they had been many minutes seated, the Wit and Charms which shone resplendant in the conversation of the amiable Rebecca, enchanted them so much that they all with one accord jumped up and exclaimed.

'Lovely and too charming Fair one,[14] notwithstanding your forbidding Squint, your greazy tresses and your swelling Back, which are more frightfull than imagination can paint or pen describe, I cannot refrain from expressing my raptures, at the engaging Qualities of your Mind,[15] which so amply atone for the Horror, with which your first appearance must ever inspire the unwary visitor.

'Your sentiments so nobly expressed on the different excellencies of Indian and English Muslins, and the judicious preference[16] you give the former, have excited in me an admiration of which I can alone give an adequate idea, by assuring you it is nearly equal to what I feel for myself.'

Then making a profound Curtesy[17] to the amiable and abashed Rebecca, they left the room and hurried home.

From this period, the intimacy between the Families of Fitzroy, Drummond, and Falknor, daily increased till at length it grew to such a pitch, that they did not scruple to kick one another out of the window on the slightest provocation.

During this happy state of Harmony, the eldest Miss Fitzroy ran off with the Coachman[18] and the amiable Rebecca was asked in marriage by Captain Roger of Buckinghamshire.

Mrs Fitzroy did not approve of the match on account of the tender years of the young couple, Rebecca being but 36 and Captain Roger little more than 63. To remedy this objection, it was agreed that they should wait a little while till they were a good deal older.

Chapter the Third

In the mean time the parents of Frederic proposed to those of Elfrida,[19] an union between them, which being accepted with pleasure, the wedding cloathes were brought and nothing remained to be settled but the naming of the Day.

As to the lovely Charlotte, being importuned with eagerness to pay another visit to her Aunt, she determined to accept the invitation and in consequence of it walked to Mrs Fitzroys to take leave of the amiable Rebecca, whom she found surrounded by Patches, Powder, Pomatum and Paint[20] with which she was vainly endeavouring to remedy the natural plainness of her face.

'I am come my amiable Rebecca, to take my leave of you for the fortnight I am destined to spend with my Aunt. Beleive me this separation is painfull to me, but it is as necessary as the labour which now engages you.'

'Why to tell you the truth my Love,' replied Rebecca, 'I have lately taken it into my head to think (perhaps with little reason) that my complexion is by no means equal to the rest of my face and have therefore taken, as you see, to white and red paint which I would scorn to use on any other occasion as I hate art.'

Charlotte, who perfectly understood the meaning of her freind's speech, was too goodtempered and obliging to refuse her, what she knew she wished,— a compliment; and they parted the best freinds in the world.

With a heavy heart and streaming Eyes did she ascend the lovely vehicle*[21] which bore her from her freinds and home; but greived as she was, she little thought in what a strange and different manner she should return to it.

On her entrance into the city of London which was the place of Mrs Williamson's abode, the postilion,[22] whose stupidity was amazing, declared and declared even without the least shame

* a post chaise [JA's note]

or Compunction, that having never been informed he was totally ignorant of what part of the Town, he was to drive to.

Charlotte, whose nature we have before intimated, was an earnest desire to oblige every one, with the greatest Condescension and Good humour informed him that he was to drive to Portland Place,[23] which he accordingly did and Charlotte soon found herself in the arms of a fond Aunt.

Scarcely were they seated as usual, in the most affectionate manner in one chair, than the Door suddenly opened and an aged gentleman with a sallow face and old pink Coat,[24] partly by intention and partly thro' weakness was at the feet of the lovely Charlotte, declaring his attachment to her and beseeching her pity in the most moving manner.

Not being able to resolve to make any one miserable, she consented to become his wife; where upon the Gentleman left the room and all was quiet.

Their quiet however continued but a short time, for on a second opening of the door a young and Handsome Gentleman with a new blue coat,[25] entered and intreated from the lovely Charlotte, permission to pay to her, his addresses.

There was a something in the appearance of the second Stranger, that influenced Charlotte in his favour, to the full as much as the appearance of the first: she could not account for it,[26] but so it was.

Having therefore agreable to that and the natural turn of her mind to make every one happy, promised to become his Wife the next morning, he took his leave and the two Ladies sat down to Supper on a young Leveret, a brace of Partridges, a leash of Pheasants[27] and a Dozen of Pigeons.

Chapter the Fourth

It was not till the next morning that Charlotte recollected the double engagement she had entered into; but when she did, the reflection of her past folly, operated so strongly on her mind, that she resolved to be guilty of a greater, and to that end threw herself into a deep stream which ran thro' her Aunt's pleasure Grounds in Portland Place.[28]

She floated to Crankhumdunberry where she was picked up and buried; the following epitaph, composed by Frederic, Elfrida and Rebecca, was placed on her tomb.

Epitaph

Here lies our freind who having promis-ed
That unto two she would be marri-ed
Threw her sweet Body and her lovely face
Into the Stream that runs thro' Portland Place

These sweet lines, as pathetic as beautifull were never read by any one who passed that way, without a shower of tears, which if they should fail of exciting in you, Reader, your mind must be unworthy to peruse them.[29]

Having performed the last sad office to their departed freind, Frederic and Elfrida together with Captain Roger and Rebecca returned to M[rs] Fitzroy's at whose feet they threw themselves with one accord and addressed her in the following Manner.

'Madam

'When the sweet Captain Roger first addressed the amiable Rebecca, you alone objected to their union on account of the tender years of the Parties. That plea can be no more, seven days being now expired, together with the lovely Charlotte, since the Captain first spoke to you on the subject.

'Consent then Madam to their union and as a reward, this smelling Bottle[30] which I enclose in my right hand, shall be yours and yours forever; I never will claim it again. But if you refuse to join their hands in 3 days time, this dagger[31] which I enclose in my left shall be steeped in your hearts blood.

'Speak then Madam and decide their fate and yours.'

Such gentle and sweet persuasion could not fail of having the desired effect. The answer they received, was this.

'My dear young freinds

'The arguments you have used are too just and too eloquent to be withstood; Rebecca in 3 days time, you shall be united to the Captain.'

This speech, than which nothing could be more satisfactory, was received with Joy by all; and peace being once more restored on all sides, Captain Roger intreated Rebecca to favour them with a Song, in compliance with which request having first assured them that she had a terrible cold, she sung as follows.

Song

When Corydon went to the fair
He bought a red ribbon for Bess,
With which she encircled her hair
And made herself look very fess.[32]

Chapter the Fifth

At the end of 3 days Captain Roger and Rebecca were united and immediately after the Ceremony set off in the Stage Waggon[33] for the Captain's seat in Buckinghamshire.[34]

The parents of Elfrida, alltho' they earnestly wished to see her married to Frederic before they died, yet knowing the delicate frame of her mind could ill bear the least excertion and rightly judging that naming her wedding day would be too great a one, forebore to press her on the subject.

Weeks and Fortnights flew away without gaining the least ground; the Cloathes grew out of fashion and at length Capt.

Roger and his Lady arrived to pay a visit to their Mother and introduce to her their beautifull Daughter of eighteen.

Elfrida, who had found her former acquaintance were growing too old and too ugly to be any longer agreable, was rejoiced to hear of the arrival of so pretty a girl as Eleanor with whom she determined to form the strictest freindship.

But the Happiness she had expected from an acquaintance with Eleanor, she soon found was not to be received, for she had not only the mortification of finding herself treated by her as little less than an old woman, but had actually the horror of perceiving a growing passion in the Bosom of Frederic for the Daughter of the amiable Rebecca.

The instant she had the first idea of such an attachment, she flew to Frederic and in a manner truly heroick, spluttered out to him her intention of being married the next Day.

To one in his predicament who possessed less personal Courage than Frederic was master of, such a speech would have been Death; but he not being the least terrified boldly replied,

'Damme Elfrida—you may be married tomorrow but I won't.'

This answer distressed her too much for her delicate Constitution. She accordingly fainted and was in such a hurry to have a succession of fainting fits, that she had scarcely patience enough to recover from one before she fell into another.

Tho', in any threatening Danger to his Life or Liberty, Frederic was as bold as brass yet in other respects his heart was as soft as cotton and immediately on hearing of the dangerous way Elfrida was in,[35] he flew to her and finding her better than he had been taught to expect, was united to her Forever—.

Finis

Jack and Alice

a novel

Is respectfully inscribed to Francis William Austen Esqr Midshipman on board his Majesty's Ship the Perseverance[1]

by his obedient humble
Servant The Author

Chapter the First

Mr Johnson[2] was once upon a time about 53; in a twelvemonth afterwards he was 54, which so much delighted him that he was determined to celebrate his next Birth day by giving a Masquerade[3] to his Children and Freinds. Accordingly on the Day he attained his 55th year tickets[4] were dispatched to all his Neighbours to that purpose. His acquaintance indeed in that part of the World were not very numerous as they consisted only of Lady Williams, M^r and Mrs Jones, Charles Adams and the 3 Miss Simpsons, who composed the neighbourhood of Pammydiddle[5] and formed the Masquerade.

Before I proceed to give an account of the Evening, it will be proper to describe to my reader, the persons and Characters of the party introduced to his acquaintance.

M^r and Mrs Jones were both rather tall and very passionate, but were in other respects, good tempered, wellbehaved People. Charles Adams[6] was an amiable, accomplished and bewitching young Man; of so dazzling a Beauty that none but Eagles could look him in the Face.[7]

Miss Simpson was pleasing in her person, in her Manners and in her Disposition; an unbounded ambition was her only fault. Her second sister Sukey[8] was Envious, Spitefull and Malicious. Her person was short, fat and disagreable. Cecilia (the youngest) was perfectly handsome but too affected to be pleasing.

In Lady Williams every virtue met. She was a widow with a handsome Jointure[9] and the remains of a very handsome face. Tho' Benevolent and Candid, she was Generous and sincere; Tho' Pious and Good, she was Religious and amiable, and Tho' Elegant and Agreable, she was Polished and Entertaining.[10]

The Johnsons were a family of Love,[11] and though a little addicted to the Bottle and the Dice, had many good Qualities.

Such was the party assembled in the elegant Drawing Room[12] of Johnson Court, amongst which the pleasing figure of a Sultana was the most remarkable of the female Masks.[13] Of the Males a Mask representing the Sun,[14] was the most universally admired. The Beams that darted from his Eyes were like those of that glorious Luminary tho' infinitely superior. So strong were they that no one dared venture within half a mile of them; he had therefore the best part of the Room to himself, its size not amounting to more than 3 quarters of a mile in length and half a one in breadth. The Gentleman at last finding the feirceness of his beams to be very inconvenient to the concourse by obliging them to croud together in one corner of the room, half shut his eyes by which means, the Company discovered him to be Charles Adams in his plain green Coat, without any mask at all.

When their astonishment was a little subsided their attention was attracted by 2 Dominos[15] who advanced in a horrible Passion; they were both very tall, but seemed in other respects to have many good qualities. 'These,' said the witty Charles, 'these are M^r^ and Mrs Jones,' and so indeed they were.

No one could imagine who was the Sultana! Till at length on her addressing a beautifull Flora[16] who was reclining in a studied attitude on a couch, with 'Oh Cecilia, I wish I was really what I pretend to be', she was discovered by the never failing genius of Charles Adams, to be the elegant but ambitious Caroline Simpson, and the person to whom she addressed herself, he rightly imagined to be her lovely but affected sister Cecilia.

The Company now advanced to a Gaming Table where sat 3 Dominos (each with a bottle in their hand) deeply engaged; but a female in the character of Virtue fled with hasty footsteps from the shocking scene, whilst a little fat woman representing Envy, sate alternately on the foreheads of the 3 Gamesters. Charles Adams was still as bright as ever; he soon discovered the party at play to be the 3 Johnsons, Envy to be Sukey Simpson and Virtue to be Lady Williams.

The Masks were then all removed and the Company retired to another room, to partake of an elegant and well managed Entertainment,[17] after which the Bottle being pretty briskly pushed about by the 3 Johnsons, the whole party not excepting even Virtue were carried home, Dead Drunk.

Chapter the Second

For three months did the Masquerade afford ample subject for conversation to the inhabitants of Pammydiddle; but no character at it was so fully expatiated on as Charles Adams. The singularity of his appearance, the beams which darted from his eyes, the brightness of his Wit, and the whole <u>tout ensemble</u>[18] of his person had subdued the hearts of so many of the young Ladies, that of the six present at the Masquerade but five had returned uncaptivated. Alice Johnson was the unhappy sixth whose heart had not been able to withstand the power of his Charms. But as it may appear strange to my Readers, that so much worth and Excellence as he possessed should have conquered only hers, it will be necessary to inform them that the Miss Simpsons were defended from his Power by Ambition, Envy, and Selfadmiration.

Every wish of Caroline was centered in a titled Husband; whilst in Sukey such superior excellence could only raise her Envy not her Love, and Cecilia was too tenderly attached to herself to be pleased with any one besides. As for Lady Williams and Mrs Jones, the former of them was too sensible, to fall in love with one so much her Junior[19] and the latter, tho' very tall and very passionate was too fond of her Husband to think of such a thing.

Yet in spite of every endeavour on the part of Miss Johnson to discover any attachment to her in him; the cold and indifferent heart of Charles Adams still to all appearance, preserved its native freedom; polite to all but partial to none, he still remained the lovely, the lively, but insensible Charles Adams.

One evening, Alice finding herself somewhat heated by wine (no very uncommon case) determined to seek a releif for her disordered Head and Love-sick Heart in the Conversation of the intelligent Lady Williams.

She found her Ladyship at home as was in general the Case, for she was not fond of going out, and like the great Sir Charles Grandison scorned to deny herself when at Home,[20] as she looked on that fashionable method of shutting out disagreable Visitors, as little less than downright Bigamy.

In spite of the wine she had been drinking, poor Alice was uncommonly out of spirits;[21] she could think of nothing but Charles Adams, she could talk of nothing but him, and in short spoke so openly that Lady Williams soon discovered the unreturned affection she bore him, which excited her Pity and Compassion so strongly that she addressed her in the following Manner.

'I perceive but too plainly my dear Miss Johnson, that your Heart has not been able to withstand the fascinating Charms of this Young Man and I pity you sincerely. Is it a first Love?'

'It is.'

'I am still more greived to hear <u>that</u>; I am myself a sad example of the Miseries, in general attendant on a first Love and I am determined for the future to avoid the like Misfortune. I wish it may not be too late for you to do the same; if it is not endeavour my dear Girl to secure yourself from so great a Danger. A second attachment[22] is seldom attended with any serious consequences; against <u>that</u> therefore I have nothing to say. Preserve yourself from a first Love and you need not fear a second.'

'You mentioned Madam something of your having yourself

been a sufferer by the misfortune you are so good as to wish me to avoid. Will you favour me with your Life and Adventures?'[23]

'Willingly my Love.'

Chapter the Third

'My Father was a gentleman of considerable Fortune in Berkshire; myself and a few more his only Children. I was but six years old when I had the misfortune of losing my Mother and being at that time young and Tender, my father instead of sending me to School, procured an able handed Governess to superintend my Education at Home. My Brothers were placed at Schools suitable to their Ages and my Sisters being all younger than myself, remained still under the Care of their Nurse.

'Miss Dickins was an excellent Governess. She instructed me in the Paths of Virtue; under her tuition I daily became more amiable, and might perhaps by this time have nearly attained perfection, had not my worthy Preceptoress been torn from my arms, e'er I had attained my seventeenth year. I never shall forget her last words. "My dear Kitty" she said. "Good night t'ye." I never saw her afterwards,' continued Lady Williams wiping her eyes, 'She eloped with the Butler the same night.

'I was invited the following year by a distant relation of my Father's to spend the Winter with her in town.[24] Mrs Watkins was a Lady of Fashion, Family and fortune; she was in general esteemed a pretty Woman, but I never thought her very handsome, for my part. She had too high a forehead, Her eyes were too small and she had too much colour.'

'How can <u>that</u> be?' interrupted Miss Johnson reddening with anger; 'Do you think that any one can have too much colour?'

'Indeed I do, and I'll tell you why I do my dear Alice; when a person has too great a degree of red in their Complexion, it gives their face in my opinion, too red a look.'

'But can a face my Lady have too red a look?'

'Certainly my dear Miss Johnson and I'll [tell] you why.

When a face has too red a look it does not appear to so much advantage as it would were it paler.'

'Pray Ma'am proceed in your story.'

'Well, as I said before, I was invited by this Lady to spend some weeks with her in town. Many Gentlemen thought her Handsome but in my opinion, Her forehead was too high, her eyes too small and she had too much colour.'

'In that Madam as I said before your Ladyship must have been mistaken. Mrs Watkins could not have too much colour since no one can have too much.'

'Excuse me my Love if I do not agree with you in that particular. Let me explain myself clearly; my idea of the case is this. When a Woman has too great a proportion of red in her Cheeks, she must have too much colour.'[25]

'But Madam I deny that it is possible for any one to have too great a proportion of red in their Cheeks.'

'What my Love not if they have too much colour?'

Miss Johnson was now out of all patience, the more so perhaps as Lady Williams still remained so inflexibly cool. It must be remembered however that her Ladyship had in one respect by far the advantage of Alice; I mean in not being drunk, for heated with wine and raised by Passion, she could have little command of her Temper.

The Dispute at length grew so hot on the part of Alice that 'From Words she almost came to Blows'[26] When Mr Johnson luckily entered and with some difficulty forced her away from Lady Williams, Mrs Watkins and her red cheeks.

Chapter the Fourth

My Readers may perhaps imagine that after such a fracas, no intimacy could longer subsist between the Johnsons and Lady Williams, but in that they are mistaken for her Ladyship was too sensible to be angry at a conduct which she could not help perceiving to be the natural consequence of inebriety and Alice had too sincere a respect for Lady Williams and too great a relish for her Claret,[27] not to make every concession in her power.

A few days after their reconciliation Lady Williams called on Miss Johnson to propose a walk in a Citron Grove[28] which led from her Ladyship's pigstye to Charles Adams's Horsepond.[29] Alice was too sensible of Lady Williams's kindness in proposing such a walk and too much pleased with the prospect of seeing at the end of it, a Horsepond of Charles's, not to accept it with visible delight. They had not proceeded far before she was roused from the reflection of the happiness she was going to enjoy, by Lady Williams's thus addressing her.

'I have as yet forborn my dear Alice to continue the narrative of my Life from an unwillingness of recalling to your Memory a scene which (since it reflects on you rather disgrace than credit) had better be forgot than remembered.'

Alice had already begun to colour up and was beginning to speak, when her Ladyship perceiving her displeasure, continued thus.

'I am afraid my dear Girl that I have offended you by what I have just said; I assure you I do not mean to distress you by a retrospection of what cannot now be helped; considering all things I do not think you so much to blame as many People do; for when a person is in Liquor, there is no answering for what they may do.'

'Madam, this is not to be borne; I insist—'

'My dear Girl don't vex yourself about the matter; I assure you I have entirely forgiven every thing respecting it; indeed I was not angry at the time, because as I saw all along, you were nearly dead drunk. I knew you could not help saying the strange things you did. But I see I distress you; so I will change the subject and desire it may never again be mentioned; remember it is all forgot—I will now pursue my story; but I must insist upon not giving you any description of Mrs Watkins; it would only be reviving old stories and as you never saw her, it can be nothing to you, if her forehead <u>was</u> too high, her eyes <u>were</u> too small, or if she <u>had</u> too much colour.'

'Again! Lady Williams: this is too much—'

So provoked was poor Alice at this renewal of the old story, that I know not what might have been the consequence of it, had not their attention been engaged by another object. A lovely young Woman lying apparently in great pain beneath a Citron-tree, was an object too interesting not to attract their notice. Forgetting their own dispute they both with simpathizing Tenderness advanced towards her and accosted her in these terms.

'You seem fair Nymph[30] to be labouring under some misfortune which we shall be happy to releive if you will inform us what it is. Will you favour us with your Life and adventures?'[31]

'Willingly Ladies, if you will be so kind as to be seated.' They took their places and she thus began.

Chapter the Fifth

'I am a native of North Wales[32] and my Father is one of the most capital Taylors in it. Having a numerous family, he was easily prevailed on by a sister of my Mother's who is a widow in good circumstances and keeps an alehouse in the next Village to ours, to let her take me and breed me up at her own expence.[33] Accordingly I have lived with her for the last 8 years of my Life, during which time she provided me with some of the first rate Masters, who taught me all the accomplishments requisite for one of my sex and rank. Under their instructions I learned Dancing, Music, Drawing and various Languages,[34] by which means I became more accomplished than any other Taylor's Daughter in Wales. Never was there a happier Creature than I was, till within the last half year—but I should have told you before that the principal Estate in our Neighbourhood belongs to Charles Adams, the owner of the brick House, you see yonder.'

'Charles Adams!' exclaimed the astonished Alice; 'are you acquainted with Charles Adams?'

'To my sorrow madam I am. He came about half a year ago to receive the rents of the Estate[35] I have just mentioned. At that time I first saw him; as you seem ma'am acquainted with him, I need not describe to you how charming he is. I could not resist his attractions;—'

'Ah! who can,' said Alice with a deep sigh.

'My Aunt being in terms of the greatest intimacy with his cook, determined, at my request, to try whether she could discover, by means of her freind if there were any chance of his returning my affection. For this purpose she went one evening to drink tea with Mrs Susan,[36] who in the course of Conversation mentioned the goodness of her Place[37] and the Goodness of her Master; upon which my Aunt began pumping her with so much dexterity that in a short time Susan owned, that she did not think her Master would ever marry, "for (said she) he has often and often declared to me that his wife, whoever she might be, must possess, Youth, Beauty, Birth, Wit, Merit, and Money.[38] I have many a time (she continued) endeavoured to reason him out of his resolution[39] and to convince him of the improbability of his ever meeting with such a Lady; but my arguments have had no effect and he continues as firm in his determination as ever." You may imagine Ladies my distress on hearing this; for I was fearfull that tho' possessed of Youth, Beauty, Wit and Merit, and tho' the probable Heiress of my Aunts House and business, he might think me deficient in Rank, and in being so, unworthy of his hand.

'However I was determined to make a bold push and therefore wrote him a very kind letter, offering him with great tenderness my hand and heart.[40] To this I received an angry and peremptory refusal, but thinking it might be rather the effect of his modesty than any thing else, I pressed him again on the subject.[41] But he never answered any more of my Letters and very soon afterwards left the Country. As soon as I heard of his departure I wrote to him here, informing him that I should shortly do myself the honour of waiting on him at Pammydiddle, to which I received no answer; therefore choosing to take, Silence for Consent, I left Wales, unknown to my Aunt, and arrived here after a tedious Journey this Morning. On enquiring for his House I was directed thro' this Wood, to the one you there see. With a heart elated by the expected happiness of beholding him I entered it and had proceeded thus far in my progress thro' it, when I found myself suddenly seized by the leg and on examining the cause of it, found that I was caught in one of the steel traps[42] so common in gentlemen's grounds.'

'Ah,' cried Lady Williams, 'how fortunate we are to meet with you; since we might otherwise perhaps have shared the like misfortune—'

'It is indeed happy for you Ladies, that I should have been a short time before you. I screamed as you may easily imagine till the woods resounded again and till one of the inhuman Wretch's servants came to my assistance and released me from my dreadfull prison, but not before one of my legs was entirely broken.'

Chapter the Sixth

At this melancholy recital the fair eyes of Lady Williams, were suffused in tears and Alice could not help exclaiming,

'Oh! cruel Charles to wound the hearts and legs[43] of all the fair.'

Lady Williams now interposed and observed that the young Lady's leg ought to be set without farther delay. After examining the fracture therefore, she immediately began and performed the operation with great skill which was the more wonderfull on account of her having never performed such a one before. Lucy, then arose from the ground and finding that she could walk with the greatest ease, accompanied them to Lady Williams's House at her Ladyship's particular request.

The perfect form, the beautifull face, and elegant manners of Lucy so won on the affections of Alice that when they parted, which was not till after Supper, she assured her that except her Father, Brother, Uncles, Aunts, Cousins and other relations, Lady Williams, Charles Adams and a few dozen more of particular freinds, she loved her better than almost any other person in the world.

Such a flattering assurance of her regard would justly have given much pleasure to the object of it, had she not plainly perceived that the amiable Alice had partaken too freely of Lady Williams's claret.

Her Ladyship (whose discernment was great) read in the intelligent countenance of Lucy her thoughts on the subject and as soon as Miss Johnson had taken her leave, thus addressed her.

'When you are more intimately acquainted with my Alice you will not be surprised, Lucy, to see the dear Creature drink a little too much; for such things happen every day. She has many rare and charming qualities, but Sobriety is not one of them. The whole Family are indeed a sad drunken set. I am sorry to say too that I never knew three such thorough Gamesters as they are, more particularly Alice. But she is a charming girl. I fancy not one of the sweetest tempers in the world; to be sure I have seen her in such passions! However she is a sweet young Woman. I am sure you'll like her. I scarcely know any one so amiable.—Oh! that you could but have seen her the other Evening! How she raved! and on such a trifle too! She is indeed a most pleasing Girl! I shall always love her!'

'She appears by your ladyship's account to have many good qualities', replied Lucy. 'Oh! a thousand,' answered Lady Williams; 'tho' I am very partial to her, and perhaps am blinded by my affection, to her real defects.'[44]

Chapter the Seventh

The next morning brought the three Miss Simpsons to wait on Lady Williams, who received them with the utmost politeness and introduced to their acquaintance Lucy, with whom the eldest was so much pleased that at parting she declared her sole <u>ambition</u> was to have her accompany them the next morning to Bath,[45] whither they were going for some weeks.

'Lucy,' said Lady Williams, 'is quite at her own disposal and if she chooses to accept so kind an invitation, I hope she will not hesitate, from any motives of delicacy on my account. I know not indeed how I shall ever be able to part with her. She never was at Bath and I should think that it would be a most agreable Jaunt to her. Speak my Love,' continued she, turning to Lucy, 'what say you to accompanying these Ladies? I shall be miserable without you—t'will be a most pleasant tour to you—I hope you'll go; if you do I am sure t'will be the Death of me—pray be persuaded'—

Lucy begged leave to decline the honour of accompanying them, with many expressions of gratitude for the extream politeness of Miss Simpson in inviting her.

Miss Simpson appeared much disappointed by her refusal. Lady Williams insisted on her going—declared that she would never forgive her if she did not, and that she should never survive it if she did, and inshort used such persuasive arguments that it was at length resolved she was to go. The Miss Simpsons called for her at ten o'clock the next morning and Lady Williams had soon the satisfaction of receiving from her young freind, the pleasing intelligence of their safe arrival in Bath.

It may now be proper to return to the Hero of this Novel, the brother of Alice, of whom I beleive I have scarcely ever had occasion to speak; which may perhaps be partly oweing to his unfortunate propensity to Liquor, which so compleatly deprived him of the use of those faculties Nature had endowed him with, that he never did anything worth mentioning. His Death happened a short time after Lucy's departure and was the natural Consequence of this pernicious practice. By his decease, his sister became the sole inheritress of a very large fortune, which as it gave her fresh Hopes of rendering herself acceptable as a wife to Charles Adams could not fail of being most pleasing to her—and as the effect was Joyfull the Cause could scarcely be lamented.

Finding the violence of her attachment to him daily augment, she at length disclosed it to her Father and desired him to propose a union between them to Charles. Her father consented and set out one morning to open the affair to the young Man. Mr Johnson being a man of few words his part was soon performed and the answer he received was as follows—

'Sir, I may perhaps be expected to appear pleased at and gratefull for the offer you have made me: but let me tell you that I consider it as an affront. I look upon myself to be Sir a perfect Beauty—where would you see a finer figure or a more charming face. Then, sir I imagine my Manners and Address to be of the most polished kind; there is a certain elegance a peculiar sweetness in them that I never saw equalled and cannot describe—. Partiality aside, I am certainly more accomplished in every Language, every Science, every Art and every thing than any other person in Europe. My temper is even, my virtues innumerable, my self unparalelled.[46] Since such Sir is my character, what do you mean by wishing me to marry your Daughter? Let me give you a short sketch of yourself and of her. I look upon you Sir to be a very good sort of Man in the main; a drunken old Dog to be sure, but that's nothing to me. Your daughter sir, is neither sufficiently beautifull, sufficiently amiable, sufficiently witty, nor sufficiently rich for me—. I expect nothing more in my wife than my wife will find in me—Perfection. These sir, are my sentiments and I honour myself for having such. One freind I have and glory in having but one—.[47] She is at present preparing my Dinner, but if you choose to see her, she shall come and she will inform you that these have ever been my sentiments.'

Mr Johnson was satisfied; and expressing himself to be much obliged to Mr Adams for the characters he had favoured him with of himself and his Daughter, took his leave.

The unfortunate Alice on receiving from her father the sad account of the ill success his visit had been attended with, could scarcely support the disappointment—She flew to her Bottle and it was soon forgot.

Chapter the Eighth

While these affairs were transacting at Pammydiddle, Lucy was conquering every Heart at Bath. A fortnight's residence there had nearly effaced from her remembrance the captivating form of Charles—The recollection of what her Heart had formerly suffered by his charms and her Leg by his trap, enabled her to forget him with tolerable Ease, which was what she determined to do; and for that purpose dedicated five minutes in every day to the employment of driving him from her remembrance.

Her second Letter to Lady Williams contained the pleasing intelligence of her having accomplished her undertaking to her entire satisfaction; she mentioned in it also an offer of marriage she had received from the Duke of —— an elderly Man of noble fortune whose ill health was the chief inducement of his Journey to Bath. 'I am distressed (she continued) to know whether I mean to accept him or not. There are a thousand advantages to be derived from a marriage with the Duke, for besides those more inferior ones of Rank and Fortune it will procure me a home, which of all other things is what I most desire.[48] Your Ladyship's kind wish of my always remaining with you, is noble and generous but I cannot think of becoming so great a burden on one I so much love and esteem. That One should receive obligations only from those we despise, is a sentiment instilled into my mind by my worthy Aunt, in my early years, and cannot in my opinion be too strictly adhered to. The excellent woman of whom I now speak, is I hear too much incensed by my imprudent departure from Wales, to receive me again—. I most earnestly wish to leave the Ladies I am now with. Miss Simpson is indeed (setting aside ambition) very amiable, but her 2[d] Sister the envious and malvolent Sukey is too disagreable to live with.—I have reason to think that the admiration I have met with in the circles of the great at this Place, has raised her Hatred and Envy; for often has she threatened, and sometimes endeavoured to cut my throat.—Your Ladyship will therefore allow that I am not wrong in wishing to leave Bath, and in wishing to have a home to receive me, when I do. I shall expect with impatience your advice concerning the Duke and am your most obliged

etc etc—Lucy.'

Lady Williams sent her, her opinion on the subject in the following Manner.

'Why do you hesitate my dearest Lucy, a moment with respect to the Duke? I have enquired into his Character and find him to be an unprincipaled, illiterate Man. Never shall my Lucy be united to such a one! He has a princely fortune, which is every day encreasing. How nobly will you spend it!, what credit will you give him in the eyes of all! How much will he be respected on his Wife's account! But why my dearest Lucy, why will you not at once decide this affair by returning to me and never leaving me again? Altho' I admire your noble sentiments with respect to obligations, yet, let me beg that they may not prevent your making me happy. It will to be sure be a great expence to me, to have you always with me—I shall not be able to support it—but what is that in comparison with the happiness I shall enjoy in your society?—'twill ruin me I know—you will not therefore surely, withstand these arguments, or refuse to return to yours most affectionately—etc etc.

C. Williams'

Chapter the Ninth

What might have been the effect of her Ladyship's advice, had it ever been received by Lucy, is uncertain, as it reached Bath a few Hours after she had breathed her last. She fell a sacrifice to the Envy and Malice of Sukey who jealous of her superior charms took her by poison from an admiring World at the age of seventeen.[49]

Thus fell the amiable and lovely Lucy whose Life had been marked by no crime, and stained by no blemish but her imprudent departure from her Aunts, and whose death was sincerely lamented by every one who knew her. Among the most afflicted of her freinds were Lady Williams, Miss Johnson and the Duke; the 2 last of whom had a most sincere regard for her, more particularly Alice, who had spent a whole evening in her company and had never thought of her since. His Grace's affliction may likewise be easily accounted for, since he lost one for whom he had experienced during the last ten days, a tender affection and sincere regard. He mourned her loss with unshaken constancy for the next fortnight at the end of which time, he gratified the ambition of Caroline Simpson by raising her to the rank of a Dutchess. Thus was she at length rendered compleatly happy in the gratification of her favourite passion. Her sister the perfidious Sukey, was likewise shortly after exalted in a manner she truly deserved, and by her actions appeared to have always desired. Her barbarous Murder was discovered and in spite of every interceding freind she was speedily raised to the Gallows—.[50] The beautifull but affected Cecilia was too sensible of her own superior charms, not to imagine that if Caroline could engage a Duke, she might without censure aspire to the affections of some Prince—and knowing that those of her native Country were cheifly engaged,[51] she left England and I have since heard is at present the favourite Sultana of the great Mogul—.[52]

In the mean time the inhabitants of Pammydiddle were in a state of the greatest astonishment and Wonder, a report being circulated of the intended marriage of Charles Adams. The Lady's name was still a secret. M^{r} and Mrs Jones imagined it to be, Miss Johnson; but *she* knew better; all *her* fears were centered in his Cook, when to the astonishment of every one, he was publicly united to Lady Williams—

Finis

Edgar and Emma

a tale[1]

Chapter the First

'I cannot imagine,' said Sir Godfrey to his Lady, 'why we continue in such deplorable Lodgings as these, in a paltry Market-town, while we have 3 good Houses of our own situated in some of the finest parts of England, and perfectly ready to receive us!'

'I'm sure Sir Godfrey,' replied Lady Marlow, 'it has been much against my inclination that we have staid here so long; or why we should ever have come at all indeed, has been to me a wonder, as none of our Houses have been in the least want of repair.'

'Nay my dear,' answered Sir Godfrey, 'you are the last person who ought to be displeased with what was always meant as a compliment to you; for you cannot but be sensible of the very great inconvenience your Daughters and I have been put to during the 2 years we have remained crowded in these Lodgings in order to give you pleasure.'

'My dear,' replied Lady Marlow, 'How can you stand and tell such lies, when you very well know that it was merely to oblige the Girls and you, that I left a most commodious House situated in a most delightfull Country and surrounded by a most agreable Neighbourhood, to live 2 years cramped up in Lodgings three pair of stairs high,[2] in a smokey and unwholesome town, which has given me a continual fever and almost thrown me into a Consumption.'

As, after a few more speeches on both sides they could not

determine which was the most to blame, they prudently laid aside the debate, and having packed up their Cloathes and paid their rent, they set out the next morning with their 2 Daughters for their seat in Sussex.

Sir Godfrey and Lady Marlow were indeed very sensible people and tho' (as in this instance) like many other sensible People, they sometimes did a foolish thing, yet in general their actions were guided by Prudence and regulated by discretion.

After a Journey of two Days and a half they arrived at Marlhurst in good health and high spirits; so overjoyed were they all to inhabit again a place, they had left with mutual regret for two years, that they ordered the bells to be rung and distributed ninepence among the Ringers.[3]

Chapter the Second

The news of their arrival being quickly spread throughout the Country, brought them in a few Days visits of congratulation from every family in it.

Amongst the rest came the inhabitants of Willmot Lodge a beautifull Villa[4] not far from Marlhurst. Mr Willmot[5] was the representative of a very ancient Family and possessed besides his paternal Estate, a considerable share in a Lead mine[6] and a ticket in the Lottery.[7] His Lady was an agreable Woman. Their Children were too numerous to be particularly described; it is sufficient to say that in general they were virtuously inclined and not given to any wicked ways. Their family being too large to accompany them in every visit, they took nine with them alternately. When their Coach stopped at Sir Godfrey's door, the Miss Marlow's Hearts throbbed in the eager expectation of once more beholding a family so dear to them. Emma the youngest (who was more particularly interested in their arrival, being attached to their eldest Son) continued at her Dressing-room window in anxious Hopes of seeing young Edgar descend from the Carriage.[8]

Mr and Mrs Willmot with their three eldest Daughters first appeared—Emma began to tremble—.[9] Robert, Richard, Ralph, and Rodolphus followed—Emma turned pale—. Their two youngest Girls were lifted from the Coach—Emma sunk breathless on a Sopha.[10] A footman came to announce to her the arrival of Company; her heart was too full to contain its afflictions. A confidante[11] was necessary—In Thomas she hoped to experience a faithfull one—for one she must have and Thomas was the only one at Hand. To him she unbosomed herself without restraint[12] and after owning her passion for young Willmot, requested his advice in what manner she should conduct herself in the melancholy Disappointment under which she laboured.

Thomas, who would gladly have been excused from listening to her complaint, begged leave to decline giving any advice concerning it, which much against her will, she was obliged to comply with.

Having dispatched him therefore with many injunctions of secrecy, she descended with a heavy heart into the Parlour, where she found the good Party seated in a social Manner[13] round a blazing fire.

Chapter the Third

Emma had continued in the Parlour some time before she could summon up sufficient courage to ask Mrs Willmot after the rest of her family; and when she did, it was in so low, so faltering a voice that no one knew she spoke. Dejected by the ill success of her first attempt she made no other, till on Mrs Willmot's desiring one of the little Girls to ring the bell for their Carriage, she stepped across the room and seizing the string said in a resolute manner.

'Mrs Willmot, you do not stir from this House till you let me know how all the rest of your family do, particularly your eldest son.'

They were all greatly surprised by such an unexpected address and the more so, on account of the manner in which it was spoken; but Emma, who would not be again disappointed, requesting an answer, Mrs Willmot made the following eloquent oration.

'Our children are all extremely well but at present most of them from home. Amy is with my sister Clayton. Sam at Eton. David with his Uncle John. Jem and Will at Winchester. Kitty at Queen's Square. Ned with his Grandmother. Hetty and Patty in a Convent at Brussells. Edgar at college,[14] Peter at Nurse,[15] and all the rest (except the nine here) at home.'

It was with difficulty that Emma could refrain from tears on hearing of the absence of Edgar; she remained however tolerably composed till the Willmots were gone when having no check to the overflowings of her greif, she gave free vent to them, and retiring to her own room, continued in tears the remainder of her Life.

Finis

Henry and Eliza[1]
a novel

Is humbly dedicated to Miss Cooper[2] by her obedient
Humble Servant
The Author

As Sir George and Lady Harcourt were superintending the Labours of their Haymakers, rewarding the industry of some by smiles of approbation,[3] and punishing the idleness of others, by a cudgel,[4] they perceived lying closely concealed beneath the thick foliage of a Haycock,[5] a beautifull little Girl not more than 3 months old.[6]

Touched with the enchanting Graces of her face and delighted with the infantine tho' sprightly answers she returned to their many questions, they resolved to take her home and, having no Children of their own, to educate her with care and cost.

Being good People themselves, their first and principal care was to incite in her a Love of Virtue and a Hatred of Vice, in which they so well succeeded (Eliza having a natural turn that way herself) that when she grew up, she was the delight of all who knew her.

Beloved by Lady Harcourt, adored by Sir George and admired by all the World, she lived in a continued course of uninterrupted Happiness, till she had attained her eighteenth year, when happening one day to be detected in stealing a banknote of 50£, she was turned out of doors by her inhuman Benefactors.[7] Such a transition to one who did not possess so noble and exalted a mind as Eliza, would have been Death, but she, happy in the conscious knowledge of her own Excellence, amused herself, as she sate beneath a tree with making and singing the following Lines.

Song.

Though misfortunes my footsteps may ever attend
I hope I shall never have need of a Freind
as an innocent Heart I will ever preserve
and will never from Virtue's dear boundaries swerve.

Having amused herself some hours, with this song and her own pleasing reflections, she arose and took the road to M.[8] a small market town of which place her most intimate freind kept the red Lion.[9]

To this freind she immediately went, to whom having recounted her late misfortune, she communicated her wish of getting into some family in the capacity of Humble Companion.[10]

Mrs Wilson, who was the most amiable creature on earth, was no sooner acquainted with her Desire, than she sate down in the Bar[11] and wrote the following Letter to the Dutchess of F, the woman whom of all others, she most Esteemed.

'To the Dutchess of F.'

Receive into your Family, at my request a young woman of unexceptionable Character, who is so good as to choose your Society in preference to going to Service.[12] Hasten, and take her from the arms of your

Sarah Wilson.

The Dutchess, whose freindship for Mrs Wilson would have carried her any lengths, was overjoyed at such an opportunity of obliging her and accordingly sate out immediately on the receipt of her letter for the red Lion, which she reached the same Evening.[13] The Dutchess of F. was about 45 and a half; Her passions were strong, her freindships firm and her Enmities, unconquerable. She was a widow and had only one Daughter who was on the point of marriage with a young Man of considerable fortune.

The Dutchess no sooner beheld our Heroine than throwing her arms around her neck, she declared herself so much pleased with her, that she was resolved they never more should part. Eliza was delighted with such a protestation of freindship, and after taking a most affecting leave of her dear Mrs Wilson, accompanied her grace the next morning to her seat in Surry.[14]

With every expression of regard did the Dutchess introduce her to Lady Harriet, who was so much pleased with her appearance that she besought her, to consider her as her Sister, which Eliza with the greatest Condescension promised to do.

Mr Cecil, the Lover of Lady Harriet, being often with the family was often with Eliza. A mutual Love took place and Cecil having declared his first, prevailed on Eliza to consent to a private union,[15] which was easy to be effected, as the Dutchess's chaplain[16] being very much in love with Eliza himself, would they were certain do anything to oblige her.

The Dutchess and Lady Harriet being engaged one evening to an assembly,[17] they took the opportunity of their absence and were united by the enamoured Chaplain.

When the Ladies returned, their amazement was great at finding instead of Eliza the following Note.

'Madam

We are married and gone.

Henry and Eliza Cecil.'

Her Grace as soon as she had read the letter, which sufficiently explained the whole affair, flew into the most violent passion and after having spent an agreable half hour, in calling them by all the shocking Names her rage could suggest to her, sent out after them 300 armed Men, with orders not to return without their Bodies, dead or alive; intending that if they should be brought to her in the latter condition to have them put to Death in some torturelike manner,[18] after a few years Confinement.

In the mean time Cecil and Eliza continued their flight to the Continent, which they judged to be more secure than their native Land, from the dreadfull effects of the Dutchess's vengeance, which they had so much reason to apprehend.

In France they remained 3 years, during which time they became the parents of two Boys, and at the end of it Eliza became a widow without any thing to support either her or her Children. They had lived since their Marriage at the rate of 12,000£ a year,[19] of which Mr Cecil's estate being rather less than the twentieth part, they had been able to save but a trifle, having lived to the utmost extent of their Income.

Eliza, being perfectly conscious of the derangement in their affairs, immediately on her Husband's death set sail for England, in a man of War of 55 Guns, which they had built[20] in their more prosperous Days. But no sooner had she stepped on Shore at Dover,[21] with a Child in each hand, than she was seized by the officers of the Dutchess, and conducted by them to a snug little Newgate[22] of their Lady's which she had erected for the reception of her own private Prisoners.

No sooner had Eliza entered her Dungeon than the first thought which occurred to her, was how to get out of it again.

She went to the Door; but it was locked. She looked at the Window; but it was barred with iron; disappointed in both her expectations, she dispaired of effecting her Escape, when she fortunately perceived in a Corner of her Cell, a small saw and Ladder of ropes. With the saw she instantly went to work and in a few weeks had displaced every Bar but one to which she fastened the Ladder.

A difficulty then occurred which for some time, she knew not how to obviate. Her Children were too small to get down the Ladder by themselves, nor would it be possible for her to take them in her arms, when <u>she</u> did. At last she determined to fling down all her Cloathes, of which she had a large Quantity, and then having given them strict Charge not to hurt themselves, threw her Children after them. She herself with ease discended by the Ladder, at the bottom of which she had the pleasure of finding Her little boys in perfect Health and fast asleep.

Her wardrobe she now saw a fatal necessity of selling, both for the preservation of her Children and herself. With tears in her eyes, she parted with these last reliques of her former Glory, and with the money she got for them, bought others more usefull, some playthings for her Boys and a gold Watch for herself.[23]

But scarcely was she provided with the above-mentioned necessaries, than she began to find herself rather hungry, and had reason to think, by their biting off two of her fingers, that her Children were much in the same situation.

To remedy these unavoidable misfortunes, she determined to return to her old freinds, Sir George and Lady Harcourt, whose generosity she had so often experienced and hoped to experience as often again.

She had about 40 miles to travel before she could reach their hospitable Mansion, of which having walked 30 without stopping, she found herself at the Entrance of a Town, where often in happier times, she had accompanied Sir George and Lady Harcourt to regale themselves with a cold collation at one of the Inns.[24]

The reflections that her adventures since the last time she had partaken of these happy Junketings,[25] afforded her, occupied her mind, for some time, as she sate on the steps at the door of a Gentleman's house. As soon as these reflections were ended, she arose and determined to take her station at the very inn, she remembered with so much delight, from the Company of which, as they went in and out, she hoped to receive some Charitable Gratuity.[26]

She had but just taken her post at the Innyard before a Carriage drove out of it, and on turning the Corner at which she was stationed, stopped to give the Postilion an opportunity of admiring the beauty of the prospect.[27] Eliza then advanced to the carriage and was going to request their Charity, when on fixing her Eyes on the Lady, within it, she exclaimed,

'Lady Harcourt!'

To which the lady replied,

'Eliza!'

'Yes Madam it is the wretched Eliza herself.'

Sir George, who was also in the Carriage, but too much amazed to speek, was proceeding to demand an explanation from Eliza of the Situation she was then in, when Lady Harcourt in transports of Joy, exclaimed.

'Sir George, Sir George, she is not only Eliza our adopted Daughter, but our real Child.'[28]

'Our real Child! What Lady Harcourt, do you mean? You know you never even was with child. Explain yourself, I beseech you.'

'You must remember Sir George that when you sailed for America, you left me breeding.'

'I do, I do, go on dear Polly.'

'Four months after you were gone, I was delivered of this Girl, but dreading your just resentment at her not proving the Boy you wished, I took her to a Haycock and laid her down. A few weeks afterwards, you returned, and fortunately for me, made no enquiries on the subject. Satisfied within myself of the wellfare of my Child,[29] I soon forgot I had one, insomuch that when, we shortly after found her in the very Haycock, I had placed her, I had no more idea of her being my own, than you had, and nothing I will venture to say would have recalled the circumstance to my remembrance, but my thus accidentally hearing her voice, which now strikes me as being the very counterpart of my own Child's.'

'The rational and convincing Account you have given of the whole affair,' said Sir George, 'leaves no doubt of her being our Daughter and as such I freely forgive the robbery she was guilty of.'

A mutual Reconciliation then took place, and Eliza, ascending the Carriage with her two Children returned to that home from which she had been absent nearly four years.

No sooner was she reinstated in her accustomed power at Harcourt Hall, than she raised an Army, with which she entirely demolished the Dutchess's Newgate, snug as it was, and by that act, gained the Blessings of thousands, and the Applause of her own Heart.

Finis

The adventures of Mr Harley[1]

a short, but interesting Tale, is with all imaginable Respect inscribed to Mr Francis William Austen Midshipman[2] on board his Majesty's Ship the Perseverance by his Obedient Servant

The Author.

Mr Harley was one of many Children. Destined by his father for the Church and by his Mother for the Sea,[3] desirous of pleasing both, he prevailed on Sir John[4] to obtain for him a Chaplaincy on board a Man of War. He accordingly, cut his Hair and sailed.

In half a year he returned and sat-off[5] in the Stage Coach for Hogsworth Green, the seat of Emma.[6] His fellow travellers were, A man without a Hat, Another with two,[7] An old maid and a young Wife.

This last appeared about 17 with fine dark Eyes[8] and an elegant Shape; inshort Mr Harley soon found out, that she was his Emma and recollected he had married her[9] a few weeks before he left England.

Finis

Sir William Mountague[1]

an unfinished performance

is humbly dedicated to Charles John Austen Esqre,[2] by his most obedient humble Servant

The Author.

Sir William Mountague was the son of Sir Henry Mountague, who was the son of Sir John Mountague, a descendant of Sir Christopher Mountague, who was the nephew of Sir Edward Mountague, whose ancestor was Sir James Mountague a near relation of Sir Robert Mountague, who inherited the Title and Estate from Sir Frederic Mountague.[3]

Sir William was about 17 when his Father died, and left him a handsome fortune, an ancient House and a Park well stocked with Deer.[4] Sir William had not been long in the possession of his Estate before he fell in Love with the 3 Miss Cliftons of Kilhoobery Park.[5] These young Ladies were all equally young, equally handsome, equally rich and equally amiable—Sir William was equally in Love with them all, and knowing not which to prefer, he left the Country and took Lodgings in a small Village near Dover.

In this retreat, to which he had retired in the hope of finding a shelter from the Pangs of Love, he became enamoured of a young Widow of Quality, who came for change of air to the same Village, after the death of a Husband, whom she had always tenderly loved and now sincerely lamented.

Lady Percival was young, accomplished and lovely. Sir William adored her and she consented to become his Wife. Vehemently pressed by Sir William to name the Day in which he might conduct her to the Altar, she at length fixed on the following Monday, which was the first of September.[6] Sir William was a Shot[7] and could not support the idea of losing such a Day, even for such a Cause.[8] He begged her to delay the Wedding a short time. Lady Percival was enraged and returned to London the next Morning.

Sir William was sorry to lose her, but as he knew that he should have been much more greived by the Loss of the 1st of September, his Sorrow was not without a mixture of Happiness, and his Affliction was considerably lessened by his Joy.

After staying at the Village a few weeks longer, he left it and went to a freind's House in Surry.[9] Mr Brudenell was a sensible Man, and had a beautifull Neice with whom Sir William soon fell in love. But Miss Arundel was cruel; she preferred a Mr Stanhope:[10] Sir William shot Mr Stanhope; the lady had then no reason to refuse him; she accepted him, and they were to be married on the 27th of October. But on the 25th Sir William received a visit from Emma Stanhope the sister of the unfortunate Victim of his rage. She begged some recompence, some atonement for the cruel Murder of her Brother. Sir William bade her name her price. She fixed on 14s.[11] Sir William offered her himself and Fortune. They went to London the next day and were there privately married.[12] For a fortnight Sir William was compleatly happy, but chancing one day to see a charming young Woman entering a Chariot[13] in Brook Street,[14] he became again most violently in love. On enquiring the name of this fair Unknown, he found that she was the Sister of his old freind Lady Percival, at which he was much rejoiced, as he hoped to have, by his acquaintance with her Ladyship, free access to Miss Wentworth . . . . .[15]

Finis

To Charles John Austen Esqre

Sir,

Your generous patronage[1] of the unfinished tale, I have already taken the Liberty of dedicating to you, encourages me to dedicate to you a second, as unfinished as the first.

I am Sir with every expression
of regard for you and yr noble
Family, your most obed^{t}
etc etc. . . .
The Author

Memoirs[2] of M[r] Clifford

an unfinished tale

M[r] Clifford lived at Bath; and having never seen London, set off one monday morning determined to feast his eyes with a sight of that great Metropolis. He travelled in his Coach and Four, for he was a very rich young Man and kept a great many Carriages of which I do not recollect half. I can only remember that he had a Coach, a Chariot, a Chaise, a Landeau, a Landeaulet, a Phaeton, a Gig, a Whisky, an italian Chair, a Buggy, a Curricle and a wheelbarrow.[3] He had likewise an amazing fine stud of Horses. To my knowledge he had six Greys, 4 Bays, eight Blacks and a poney.[4]

In his Coach and 4 Bays M[r] Clifford sate forward about 5 o'clock on Monday Morning the 1st of May for London. He always travelled remarkably expeditiously and contrived therefore to get to Devizes[5] from Bath, which is no less than nineteen miles, the first Day. To be sure he did not get in till eleven at night and pretty tight work it was as you may imagine.

However when he was once got to Devizes he was determined to comfort himself with a good hot Supper and therefore ordered a whole Egg to be boiled for him and his Servants. The next morning he pursued his Journey and in the course of 3 days hard labour reached Overton,[6] where he was seized with a dangerous fever the Consequence of too violent Excercise.

Five months did our Hero remain in this celebrated City under the care of its no less celebrated Physician,[7] who at length compleatly cured him of his troublesome Desease.

As M[r] Clifford still continued very weak, his first Day's Journey carried him only to Dean Gate,[8] where he remained a few Days and found himself much benefited by the change of Air.

In easy Stages he proceeded to Basingstoke.[9] One day Carrying him to Clarkengreen, the next to Worting,[10] the 3d to the bottom of Basingstoke Hill, and the fourth, to Mr Robins's. . . .[11]

Finis

The beautifull Cassandra

a novel in twelve Chapters dedicated by permission to Miss Austen.[1]

Dedication.

Madam

You are a Phoenix.[2] Your taste is refined, your Sentiments are noble, and your Virtues innumerable. Your Person is lovely, your Figure, elegant, and your Form, magestic. Your Manners are polished, your Conversation is rational and your appearance singular. If therefore the following Tale will afford one moment's amusement to you, every wish will be gratified of

your most obedient
humble Servant
The Author

The beautifull Cassandra

a novel, in twelve Chapters

Chapter the First

Cassandra was the Daughter and the only Daughter of a celebrated Millener in Bond Street.[3] Her father was of noble Birth, being the near relation of the Dutchess of ——'s Butler.

Chapter the 2d

When Cassandra had attained her 16th year, she was lovely and amiable and chancing to fall in love with an elegant Bonnet,[4] her Mother had just compleated bespoke by the Countess of —— she placed it on her gentle Head and walked from her Mother's shop to make her Fortune.

Chapter the 3d

The first person she met, was the Viscount of —— a young Man, no less celebrated for his Accomplishments and Virtues, than for his Elegance and Beauty. She curtseyed and walked on.

Chapter the 4th

She then proceeded to a Pastry-cooks where she devoured six ices,[5] refused to pay for them, knocked down the Pastry Cook and walked away.

Chapter the 5th

She next ascended a Hackney Coach[6] and ordered it to Hampstead,[7] where she was no sooner arrived than she ordered the Coachman to turn round and drive her back again.

Chapter the 6th

Being returned to the same spot of the same Street she had sate out from, the Coachman demanded his Pay.

Chapter the 7th

She searched her pockets over again and again; but every search was unsuccessfull. No money could she find. The man grew peremptory. She placed her bonnet on his head and ran away.

Chapter the 8th

Thro' many a street she then proceeded and met in none the least Adventure till on turning a Corner of Bloomsbury Square,[8] she met Maria.

Chapter the 9th

Cassandra started and Maria seemed surprised; they trembled, blushed, turned pale and passed each other in a mutual silence.

Chapter the 10th

Cassandra was next accosted by her freind the Widow, who squeezing out her little Head thro' her less window, asked her how she did? Cassandra curtseyed and went on.

Chapter the 11th

A quarter of a mile brought her to her paternal roof in Bond Street from which she had now been absent nearly 7 hours.

Chapter the 12th

She entered it and was pressed to her Mother's bosom by that worthy woman. Cassandra smiled and whispered to herself 'This is a day well spent.'

Finis

Amelia Webster

an interesting and well written Tale

is dedicated by Permission
to
Mrs Austen[1]
by
Her humble Servant
The Author.

Letter the first

To Miss Webster

My dear Amelia

You will rejoice to hear of the return of my amiable Brother from abroad.[2] He arrived on thursday, and never did I see a finer form, save that of your sincere freind

Matilda[3] Hervey

Letter the 2d

To H. Beverley[4] Esqre

Dear Beverley

I arrived here last thursday and met with a hearty reception from my Father, Mother and Sisters. The latter are both fine Girls—particularly Maud,[5] who I think would suit you as a Wife well enough. What say you to this? She will have two thousand Pounds[6] and as much more as you can get. If you don't marry her you will mortally offend

George Hervey

Letter the 3d

To Miss Hervey

Dear Maud

Beleive me I'm happy to hear of your Brother's arrival. I have a thousand things to tell you, but my paper will only permit me to add[7] that I am yr affect Freind

Amelia Webster

Letter the 4th

To Miss S. Hervey

Dear Sally[8]

I have found a very convenient old hollow oak[9] to put our Letters in; for you know we have long maintained a private Correspondence.[10] It is about a mile from my House and seven from yours. You may perhaps imagine that I might have made choice of a tree which would have divided the Distance more equally—I was sensible of this at the time, but as I considered that the walk would be of benefit to you in your weak and uncertain state of Health, I preferred it to one nearer your House, and am yr faithfull

Benjamin Bar

Letter the 5th

To Miss Hervey

Dear Maud

I write now to inform you that I did not stop at your house in my way to Bath last Monday.—I have many things to inform you of besides; but my Paper reminds me of concluding;[11] and beleive me yrs ever etc.

Amelia Webster

Letter the 6th

To Miss Webster

Madam Saturday

An humble Admirer now addresses you—I saw you lovely Fair one as you passed on Monday last, before our House in your way to Bath. I saw you thro' a telescope,[12] and was so struck by your Charms that from that time to this I have not tasted human food.

George Hervey

Letter the 7th

To Jack

As I was this morning at Breakfast the Newspaper was brought me, and in the list of Marriages I read the following.

'George Hervey Esqre to Miss Amelia Webster'
'Henry Beverley Esqre to Miss Hervey'
and
'Benjamin Bar Esqre to Miss Sarah Hervey'.

yours, Tom[13]

Finis

The Visit

a comedy in 2 acts

Dedication
To the Revd James Austen.[1]

Sir,

The following Drama, which I humbly recommend to your Protection and Patronage, tho' inferior to those celebrated Comedies called 'The school for Jealousy' and 'The travelled Man',[2] will I hope afford some amusement to so respectable a Curate[3] as yourself; which was the end in veiw when it was first composed[4] by your Humble Servant the Author.

Dramatis Personae

Sir Arthur Hampton	Lady Hampton
Lord Fitzgerald	Miss Fitzgerald
Stanly	Sophy Hampton
Willoughby, Sir Arthur's nephew	Cloe[5] Willoughby

The scenes are laid in
Lord Fitzgerald's House.

Act the First

Scene the first, a Parlour—
enter Lord Fitzgerald and Stanly

Stanly: Cousin your servant.

Fitzgerald: Stanly, good morning to you. I hope you slept well last night.

Stanly: Remarkably well, I thank you.

Fitzgerald: I am afraid you found your Bed too short.[6] It was bought in my Grandmother's time, who was herself a very short woman and made a point of suiting all her Beds to her own length, as she never wished to have any company in the House, on account of an unfortunate impediment in her speech, which she was sensible of being very disagreable to her inmates.

Stanly: Make no more excuses dear Fitzgerald.

Fitzgerald: I will not distress you by too much civility—I only beg you will consider yourself as much at home as in your Father's house. Remember, 'The more free, the more Wellcome.'[7]

(exit Fitzgerald)

Stanly: Amiable Youth!
'Your virtues could he imitate
How happy would be Stanly's fate!'

(exit Stanly)

Scene the 2[d]
Stanly and Miss Fitzgerald, discovered.[8]

Stanly: What Company is it you expect to dine with you to Day, Cousin?

Miss F: Sir Arthur and Lady Hampton; their Daughter, Nephew and Neice.

Stanly: Miss Hampton and her Cousin are both Handsome, are they not?

Miss F: Miss Willoughby is extreamly so. Miss Hampton is a fine Girl, but not equal to her.

Stanly: Is not your Brother attached to the Latter?

Miss F: He admires her I know, but I beleive nothing more. Indeed I have heard him say that she was the most beautifull, pleasing, and amiable Girl in the world, and that of all others he should prefer her for his Wife. But it never went any farther I'm certain.

Stanly: And yet my Cousin never says a thing he does not mean.

Miss F: Never. From his Cradle he has always been a strict adherent to Truth.

(Exeunt Severally)[9]

End of the First Act.

Act the Second

Scene the first. The Drawing Room.
Chairs set round in a row.[10] Lord Fitzgerald, Miss Fitzgerald and Stanly seated.
Enter a Servant.

Servant: Sir Arthur and Lady Hampton. Miss Hampton, M^r^ and Miss Willoughby.

(exit Servant)

Enter the Company.

Miss F: I hope I have the pleasure of seeing your Ladyship well. Sir Arthur, your servant. Y^rs^ Mr Willoughby.
Dear Sophy, Dear Cloe,—

(They pay their Compliments alternately.)

Miss F: Pray be seated.

(They sit)

Bless me! there ought to be 8 Chairs and there are but 6. However, if your Ladyship will but take Sir Arthur in your Lap, and Sophy my Brother in hers, I beleive we shall do pretty well.

Lady H: Oh! with pleasure . . .

Sophy: I beg his Lordship would be seated.

Miss F: I am really shocked at crouding you in such a manner, but my Grandmother (who bought all the furniture of this room) as she had never a very large Party, did not think it necessary to buy more Chairs than were sufficient for her own family and two of her particular freinds.

Sophy: I beg you will make no apologies. Your Brother is very light.

Stanly, aside) What a cherub is Cloe!

Cloe, aside) What a seraph is Stanly!

Enter a Servant.

Servant: Dinner is on table.

They all rise.

Miss F: Lady Hampton, Miss Hampton, Miss Willoughby.

Stanly hands[11] Cloe, Lord Fitzgerald, Sophy, Willoughby, Miss Fitzgerald, and Sir Arthur, Lady Hampton.

(Exeunt.)

Scene the 2[d]

The Dining Parlour.

Miss Fitzgerald at top. Lord Fitzgerald at bottom. Company ranged on each side.[12]

Servants waiting.

Cloe: I shall trouble M[r] Stanly for a Little of the fried Cowheel and Onion.[13]

Stanly: Oh Madam, there is a secret pleasure in helping so amiable a Lady.

Lady H: I assure you my Lord, Sir Arthur never touches wine; but Sophy will toss off a bumper[14] I am sure to oblige your Lordship.

Lord F: Elder wine or Mead,[15] Miss Hampton?

Sophy: If it is equal to you Sir, I should prefer some warm ale with a toast and nutmeg.[16]

Lord F: Two glasses of warmed ale with a toast and nutmeg.

Miss F: I am afraid M[r] Willoughby you take no care of yourself. I fear you don't meet with any thing to your liking.

Willoughby: Oh! Madam, I can want for nothing while there are red herrings[17] on table.

Lord F: Sir Arthur taste that Tripe. I think you will not find it amiss.

Lady H: Sir Arthur never eats Tripe; 'tis too savoury for him you know my Lord.

Miss F: Take away the Liver and Crow[18] and bring in the suet pudding.[19]

(a short Pause.)

Miss F: Sir Arthur shan't I send you a bit of pudding?

Lady H: Sir Arthur never eats suet pudding Ma'am. It is too high a Dish for him.

Miss F: Will no one allow me the honour of helping them? Then John take away the Pudding, and bring the Wine.

(Servants take away the things and bring in the Bottles and Glasses.)

Lord F: I wish we had any Desert to offer you. But my Grandmother in her Lifetime, destroyed the Hothouse in order to build a receptacle for the Turkies with its materials;[20] and we have never been able to raise another tolerable one.

Lady H: I beg you will make no apologies my Lord.

Willoughby: Come Girls, let us circulate the Bottle.[21]

Sophy: A very good motion, Cousin; and I will second it with all my Heart. Stanly, you don't drink.

Stanly: Madam, I am drinking draughts of Love from Cloe's eyes.

Sophy: That's poor nourishment truly. Come, drink to her better acquaintance.

(Miss Fitzgerald goes to a Closet and brings out a bottle)

Miss F: This, Ladies and Gentlemen is some of my dear Grandmother's own manufacture. She excelled in Goose-berry Wine.[22] Pray taste it Lady Hampton?

Lady H: How refreshing it is!

Miss F: I should think with your Ladyship's permission, that Sir Arthur might taste a little of it.

Lady H: Not for Worlds. Sir Arthur never drinks any thing so high.

Lord F: And now my amiable Sophia condescend to marry me.

(He takes her hand and leads her to the front)

Stanly: Oh! Cloe, could I but hope you would make me blessed—

Chloe: I will.

(They advance.)

Miss F: Since you Willoughby are the only one left, I cannot refuse your earnest solicitations—There is my Hand.—

Lady H: And may you all be Happy!

Finis

The Mystery[1]

an unfinished Comedy

Dedication
To the Rev[d] George Austen[2]

Sir,

I humbly solicit your Patronage to the following Comedy, which tho' an unfinished one, is I flatter myself as complete a Mystery as any of its kind.

I am Sir your most Hum[le]
Servant
The Author

The Mystery
a Comedy

Dramatis Personae

Men	Women
Colonel Elliott	Fanny[3] Elliott
Sir Edward Spangle[4]	M[rs] Humbug
Old Humbug[5]	and
Young Humbug	Daphne
and	
Corydon[6]	

Act the First

Scene the 1st

A Garden.

Enter Corydon.

Cory: But Hush! I am interrupted.

(Exit Corydon.)

Enter Old Humbug and his Son, talking.

Old Hum: It is for that reason I wish you to follow my advice. Are you convinced of its propriety?

Young Hum: I am, Sir, and will certainly act in the manner you have pointed out to me.

Old Hum: Then let us return to the House.

(Exeunt)

Scene the 2d

A Parlour in Humbug's house.

Mrs Humbug and Fanny, discovered at work.[7]

Mrs Hum: You understand me my Love?

Fanny: Perfectly ma'am. Pray continue your narration.

Mrs Hum: Alas! it is nearly concluded, for I have nothing more to say on the Subject.

Fanny: Ah! here's Daphne.

Enter Daphne.

Daphne: My dear Mrs Humbug, how d'ye do? Oh! Fanny, 'tis all over.

Fanny: It is indeed!

Mrs Hum: I'm very sorry to hear it.

Fanny: Then t'was to no purpose that I . . . .

Daphne: None upon Earth.

Mrs Hum: And what is to become of? . . . .

Daphne: Oh! that's all settled.

(whispers Mrs Humbug)

Fanny: And how is it determined?

Daphne: I'll tell you.

(whispers Fanny)

Mrs Hum: And is he to? . . .

Daphne: I'll tell you all I know of the matter.

(whispers Mrs Humbug and Fanny)

Fanny: Well! now I know everything about it, I'll go away.

Mrs Hum:
Daphne: } And so will I.

(Exeunt)

Scene the 3^d

The Curtain rises and discovers Sir Edward Spangle reclined in an elegant Attitude[8] on a Sofa, fast asleep. Enter Colonel Elliott.

Colonel: My Daughter is not here I see . . . there lies Sir Edward . . . Shall I tell him the secret? . . . No, he'll certainly blab it . . . But he is asleep and won't hear me . . . So I'll e'en venture.

(Goes up to Sir Edward, whispers him, and Exit)

End of the 1st Act.

Finis

To Edward Austen Esqre [1]
The following unfinished Novel
is respectfully inscribed
by
His obedient Hum^ble Servt
The Author

The Three Sisters

a novel

Letter 1st

Miss Stanhope to Mrs ——

My dear Fanny

I am the happiest creature in the World, for I have received an offer of marriage from Mr Watts. It is the first I have ever had and I hardly know how to value it enough. How I will triumph over the Duttons! I do not intend to accept it, at least I beleive not, but as I am not quite certain I gave him an equivocal answer and left him. And now my dear Fanny I want your Advice whether I should accept his offer or not, but that you may be able to judge of his merits and the situation of affairs I will give you an account of them. He is quite an old Man, about two and thirty, very plain so plain that I cannot bear to look at him. He is extremely disagreable and I hate him more than any body else in the world. He has a large fortune and will make great Settlements[2] on me, but then he is very healthy. In short I do not know what to do. If I refuse him he as good as told me that he should offer himself to Sophia and if she refused him to Georgiana, and I could not bear to have either of them married before me.[3] If I accept him I know I shall be miserable all the rest of my Life, for he is very ill tempered and peevish extremely jealous, and so stingy that there is no living in the house with him. He told me he should mention the affair to Mama, but I insisted upon it that he did not for very likely she would make me marry him whether I would or no; however probably he has before now, for he never does anything he is desired to do. I believe I shall have him. It will be such a triumph to be married before Sophy, Georgiana and the Duttons; And he promised to have a new Carriage on the occasion, but we almost quarrelled about the colour, for I insisted upon its being blue spotted with silver, and he declared it should be a plain Chocolate;[4] and to provoke me more said it should be just as low as his old one.[5] I won't have him I declare. He said he should come again tomorrow and take my final answer, so I believe I must get him while I can. I know the Duttons will envy me and I shall be able to chaprone[6] Sophy and Georgiana to all the Winter Balls.[7] But then what will be the use of that when very likely he won't let me go myself, for I know he hates dancing and what he hates himself he has no idea of any other person's liking; and besides he talks a great deal of Women's always Staying at home and such stuff. I beleive I shan't have him; I would refuse him at once if I were certain that neither of my Sisters would accept him, and that if they did not, he would not offer to the Duttons. I cannot run such a risk, so, if he will promise to have the Carriage ordered as I like, I will have him, if not he may ride in it by himself for me. I hope you like my determination; I can think of nothing better;

And am your ever affec^{te}

Mary Stanhope

From the Same to the Same

Dear Fanny

I had but just sealed my last letter to you when my Mother came up and told me she wanted to speak to me on a very particular subject.

'Ah! I know what you mean;' (said I) 'That old fool Mr Watts has told you all about it, tho' I bid him not. However you shan't force me to have him if I don't like it.'

'I am not going to force you, Child, but only want to know what your resolution is with regard to his Proposals, and to insist upon your making up your mind one way or t'other, that if <u>you</u> don't accept him <u>Sophy</u> may.'

'Indeed' (replied I hastily) 'Sophy need not trouble herself for I shall certainly marry him myself.'

'If that is your resolution' (said my Mother) 'why should you be afraid of my forcing your inclinations?'

'Why, because I have not settled whether I shall have him or not.'

'You are the strangest Girl in the World Mary. What you say one moment, you unsay the next. Do tell me once for all, whether you intend to marry Mr Watts or not?'

'Law[8] Mama, how can I tell you what I don't know myself?'

'Then I desire you will know, and quickly too, for Mr Watts says he won't be kept in suspense.'

'That depends upon me.'

'No it does not, for if you do not give him your final answer tomorrow when he drinks Tea[9] with us, he intends to pay his Addresses to Sophy.'

'Then I shall tell all the World that he behaved very ill to me.'

'What good will that do? Mr Watts has been too long abused by all the World to mind it now.'

'I wish I had a Father or a Brother because then they should fight him.'[10]

'They would be cunning if they did, for Mr Watts would run away first; and therefore you must and shall resolve either to accept or refuse him before tomorrow evening.'

'But why if I don't have him, must he offer to my Sisters?'

'Why! because he wishes to be allied to the Family and because they are as pretty as you are.'

'But will Sophy marry him, Mama, if he offers to her?'

'Most likely. Why should not she? If however she does not choose it, then Georgiana must, for I am determined not to let such an opportunity escape of settling one of my Daughters so advantageously. So, make the most of your time; I leave you to settle the Matter with yourself.' And then she went away. The only thing I can think of my dear Fanny is to ask Sophy and Georgiana whether they would have him were he to make proposals to them, and if they say they would not I am resolved to refuse him too, for I hate him more than you can imagine. As for the Duttons if he marries one of <u>them</u> I shall still have the triumph of having refused him first. So, adeiu my dear Freind—

Y^rs ever M. S.

Miss Georgiana Stanhope to Miss x x x[11]

My dear Anne Wednesday

Sophy and I have just been practising a little deceit on our eldest Sister, to which we are not perfectly reconciled, and yet the circumstances were such that if any thing will excuse it, they must. Our neighbour M[r] Watts has made proposals to Mary; Proposals which she knew not how to receive, for tho' she has a particular Dislike to him (in which she is not singular) yet she would willingly marry him sooner than risk his offering to Sophy or me which in case of a refusal from herself, he told her he should do, for you must know that the poor Girl considers our marrying before her as one of the greatest misfortunes that can possibly befall her, and to prevent it would willingly ensure herself everlasting Misery by a Marriage with M[r] Watts. An hour ago she came to us to sound our inclinations respecting the affair which were to determine hers. A little before she came my Mother had given us an account of it, telling us that she certainly would not let him go farther than our family for a Wife. 'And therefore' (said she) 'If Mary won't have him Sophy must, and if Sophy won't Georgiana shall.' Poor Georgiana!— We neither of us attempted to alter my Mother's resolution, which I am sorry to say is generally more strictly kept than rationally formed. As soon as she was gone however I broke silence to assure Sophy that if Mary should refuse M[r] Watts I should not expect her to sacrifice her happiness by becoming his Wife from a motive of Generosity to me, which I was afraid her Good nature and Sisterly affection might induce her to do.

'Let us flatter ourselves' (replied She) 'that Mary will not refuse him. Yet how can I hope that my Sister may accept a Man who cannot make her happy.'

'He cannot it is true but his Fortune, his Name, his House, his Carriage will and I have no doubt but that Mary will marry him; indeed why should she not? He is not more than two and thirty; a very proper age for a Man to marry at; He is rather plain to be sure, but then what is Beauty in a Man; if he has but a genteel figure and a sensible looking Face it is quite sufficient.'

'This is all very true, Georgiana, but M[r] Watts's figure is unfortunately extremely vulgar and his Countenance is very heavy.'

'And then as to his temper; it has been reckoned bad, but may not the World be deceived in their Judgement of it. There is an open Frankness in his Disposition which becomes a Man; They say he is stingy; We'll call that Prudence. They say he is suspicious. That proceeds from a warmth of Heart always excusable in Youth, and inshort I see no reason why he should not make a very good Husband, or why Mary should not be very happy with him.'

Sophy laughed; I continued,

'However whether Mary accepts him or not I am resolved. My determination is made. I never would marry M[r] Watts were Beggary the only alternative. So deficient in every respect! Hideous in his person and without one good Quality to make amends for it. His fortune to be sure is good. Yet not so very large! Three thousand a year.[12] What is three thousand a year? It is but six times as much as my Mother's income. It will not tempt me.'

'Yet it will be a noble fortune for Mary' said Sophy laughing again.

'For Mary! Yes indeed it will give me pleasure to see her in such affluence.'

Thus I ran on to the great Entertainment of my Sister till Mary came into the room to appearance in great agitation. She sate down. We made room for her at the fire. She seemed at a loss how to begin and at last said in some confusion.

'Pray, Sophy, have you any mind to be married?'

'To be married! None in the least. But why do you ask me? Are you acquainted with any one who means to make me proposals?'

'I—no, how should I? But mayn't I ask a common question?'

'Not a very common one, Mary, surely.' (said I). She paused and after some moments silence went on—

'How should you like to marry M[r] Watts, Sophy?'

I winked at Sophy and replied for her. 'Who is there but must rejoice to marry a man of three thousand a year?'

'Very true' (she replied) 'That's very true. So you would have him if he would offer, Georgiana And would you Sophy?'

Sophy did not like the idea of telling a lie and deceiving her Sister; she prevented the first and saved half her conscience by equivocation.

'I should certainly act just as Georgiana would do.'

'Well then,' said Mary with triumph in her Eyes, 'I have had an offer from Mr Watts.'

We were of course very much surprised; 'Oh! do not accept him,' said I, 'and then perhaps he may have me.'

In short my scheme took and Mary is resolved to do that to prevent our supposed happiness which she would not have done to ensure it in reality. Yet after all my Heart cannot acquit me and Sophy is even more scrupulous. Quiet our Minds my dear Anne[13] by writing and telling us you approve our conduct. Consider it well over. Mary will have real pleasure in being a married Woman, and able to chaprone us, which she certainly shall do, for I think myself bound to contribute as much as possible to her happiness in a State I have made her choose. They will probably have a new Carriage, which will be paradise to her, and if we can prevail on Mr W. to set up his Phaeton[14] she will be too happy. These things however would be no consolation to Sophy or me for domestic Misery. Remember all this and do not condemn us.

Friday

Last night Mr Watts by appointment drank tea with us. As soon as his Carriage stopped at the Door, Mary went to the Window.

'Would you beleive it, Sophy' (said she) 'the old Fool wants to have his new Chaise[15] just the colour of the old one, and hung as low too. But it shan't—I will carry my point. And if he won't let it be as high as the Duttons, and blue spotted with Silver, I won't have him. Yes I will too. Here he comes. I know he'll be rude; I know he'll be ill tempered and won't say one civil thing to me! nor behave at all like a Lover.' She then sate down and Mr Watts entered.

'Ladies your most obedient.' We paid our Compliments and he seated himself.

'Fine Weather, Ladies.' Then turning to Mary, 'Well Miss Stanhope, I hope you have *at last* settled the Matter in your own mind; and will be so good as to let me know whether you will *condescend* to marry me or not.'

'I think Sir' (said Mary) 'You might have asked in a genteeler way than that. I do not know whether I *shall* have you if you behave so odd.'

'Mary!' (said my Mother). 'Well Mama, if he will be so cross . . .'

'Hush, hush, Mary, you shall not be rude to Mr Watts.'

'Pray, Madam, do not lay any restraint on Miss Stanhope by obliging her to be civil. If she does not choose to accept my hand, I can offer it else where, for as I am by no means guided by a particular preference to you above your Sisters it is equally the same to me which I marry of the three.' Was there ever such a Wretch! Sophy reddened with anger and I felt *so* spiteful!

'Well then' (said Mary in a peevish Accent) 'I *will* have you if I *must*.'

'I should have thought, Miss Stanhope, that when such Settlements are offered as I have offered to you there can be no great violence done to the inclinations in accepting of them.'

Mary mumbled out something, which I who sate close to her could just distinguish to be 'What's the use of a great Jointure if Men live forever?' And then audibly 'Remember the pin money;[16] two hundred a year.'

'A hundred and seventy-five Madam.'

'Two hundred indeed Sir' said my Mother.

'And Remember I am to have a new Carriage hung as high as the Duttons', and blue spotted with silver; and I shall expect a new saddle horse,[17] a suit of fine lace, and an infinite number of the most valuable Jewels. Diamonds such as never were seen! and Pearls, Rubies, Emeralds, and Beads out of number.[18] You must set up your Phaeton which must be cream coloured with a wreath of silver flowers round it, You must buy 4 of the finest Bays in the Kingdom and you must drive me in it every day. This is not all; You must entirely new furnish your House after my Taste, You must hire two more Footmen to attend me, two Women to wait on me, must always let me do just as I please and make a very good husband.'

Here she stopped, I beleive rather out of breath.

'This is all very reasonable, Mr Watts, for my Daughter to expect.'

'And it is very reasonable, Mrs Stanhope, that your daughter should be disappointed.' He was going on but Mary interrupted him.

'You must build me an elegant Greenhouse[19] and stock it with plants. You must let me spend every Winter in Bath, every Spring in Town, Every Summer in taking some Tour, and every Autumn at a Watering Place,[20] and if we are at home the rest of the year' (Sophy and I laughed) 'You must do nothing but give Balls and Masquerades. You must build a room on purpose and a Theatre to act Plays in. The first Play we have shall be <u>Which is the Man</u>[21] and I will do Lady Bell Bloomer.'

'And pray Miss Stanhope' (said Mr Watts) 'What am I to expect from you in return for all this?'

'Expect? why you may expect to have me pleased.'

'It would be odd if I did not. Your expectations, Madam, are too high for me, and I must apply to Miss Sophy who perhaps may not have raised her's so much.'

'You are mistaken, Sir, in supposing so,' (said Sophy) 'for tho' they may not be exactly in the same Line, yet my expectations are to the full as high as my Sister's; for I expect my Husband to be good tempered and Chearful; to consult my Happiness in all his Actions, and to love me with Constancy and Sincerity.'

Mr Watts stared. 'These are very odd Ideas truly, young Lady. You had better discard them before you marry, or you will be obliged to do it afterwards.'

My Mother in the meantime was lecturing Mary who was sensible that she had gone too far, and when Mr Watts was just turning towards me in order I beleive to address me, she spoke to him in a voice half humble, half sulky.

'You are mistaken, Mr Watts, if you think I was in earnest when I said I expected so much. However I must have a new Chaise.'

'Yes Sir, you must allow that Mary has a right to expect that.'

'Mrs Stanhope, I *mean* and have always meant to have a new one on my Marriage. But it shall be the colour of my present one.'

'I think, Mr Watts, you should pay my Girl the compliment of consulting her Taste on such Matters.'

Mr Watts would not agree to this, and for some time insisted upon its being a Chocolate colour, while Mary was as eager for having it blue with silver Spots. At length however Sophy proposed that to please Mr W. it should be a dark brown and to please Mary it should be hung rather high and have a silver Border. This was at length agreed to, tho' reluctantly on both sides, as each had intended to carry their point entire. We then proceeded to other Matters, and it was settled that they should be married as soon as the Writings[22] could be completed. Mary was very eager for a Special Licence and Mr Watts talked of Banns. A common Licence[23] was at last agreed on. Mary is to have all the Family Jewels which are very inconsiderable I beleive and Mr W. promised to buy her a Saddle horse; but in return she is not to expect to go to Town or any other public place for these three Years. She is to have neither Greenhouse, Theatre or Phaeton; to be contented with one Maid without an additional Footman. It engrossed the whole Evening to settle these affairs: Mr W. supped with us and did not go till twelve. As soon as he was gone Mary exclaimed 'Thank Heaven! he's off at last; how I do hate him!' It was in vain that Mama represented to her the impropriety she was guilty of in disliking him who was to be her Husband, for she persisted in declaring her aversion to him and hoping she might never see him again. What a Wedding will this be!

Adeiu my dear Anne.

Yr faithfully Sincere
Georgiana Stanhope

From the Same to the Same

Dear Anne Saturday

Mary, eager to have every one know of her approaching Wedding and more particularly desirous of triumphing as she called it over the Duttons, desired us to walk with her this Morning to Stoneham. As we had nothing else to do we readily agreed, and had as pleasant a walk as we could have with Mary whose conversation entirely consisted in abusing the Man she is soon to marry and in longing for a blue Chaise spotted with Silver. When we reached the Duttons we found the two Girls in the dressing-room with a very handsome Young Man, who was of course introduced to us. He is the son of Sir Henry Brudenell of Leicestershire.[24] Mr Brudenell is the handsomest Man I ever saw in my Life; we are all three very much pleased with him. Mary, who from the moment of our reaching the Dressing-room had been swelling with the knowledge of her own importance and with the Desire of making it known, could not remain long silent on the Subject after we were seated, and soon addressing herself to Kitty said,

'Don't you think it will be necessary to have all the Jewels new set?'

'Necessary for what?'

'For What! Why for my appearance.'

'I beg your pardon but I really do not understand you. What Jewels do you speak of, and where is your appearance[25] to be made?'

'At the next Ball to be sure after I am married.'

You may imagine their Surprise. They were at first incredulous, but on our joining in the Story they at last beleived it. 'And who is it to' was of course the first Question. Mary pretended Bashfulness, and answered in Confusion her Eyes cast down 'to Mr Watts'. This also required Confirmation from us, for that anyone who had the Beauty and fortune (tho' small yet a provision) of Mary would willingly marry Mr Watts, could by them scarcely be credited. The subject being now fairly introduced and she found herself the object of every one's attention in company, she lost all her confusion and became perfectly unreserved and communicative.

'I wonder you should never have heard of it before for in general things of this Nature are very well known in the Neighbourhood.'

'I assure you,' said Jemima, 'I never had the least suspicion of such an affair. Has it been in agitation long?'

'Oh! Yes, ever since Wednesday.'

They all smiled particularly Mr Brudenell.

'You must know Mr Watts is very much in love with me, so that it is quite a match of Affection on his side.'

'Not on his only, I suppose' said Kitty.

'Oh! when there is so much Love on one side there is no occasion for it on the other. However I do not much dislike him tho' he is very plain to be sure.'

Mr Brudenell stared, the Miss Duttons laughed and Sophy and I were heartily ashamed of our Sister. She went on.

'We are to have a new Postchaise and very likely may set up our Phaeton.'

This we knew to be false but the poor Girl was pleased at the idea of persuading the company that such a thing was to be and I would not deprive her of so harmless an Enjoyment. She continued.

'Mr Watts is to present me with the family Jewels which I fancy are very considerable.'

I could not help whispering Sophy 'I fancy not'.

'These Jewels are what I suppose must be new set before they can be worn. I shall not wear them till the first Ball I go to after my Marriage. If Mrs Dutton should not go to it, I hope you will let me chaprone you; I shall certainly take Sophy and Georgiana.'

'You are very good' (said Kitty) 'and since you are inclined to undertake the Care of young Ladies, I should advise you to prevail on Mrs Edgecumbe to let you chaprone her six Daughters which with your two Sisters and ourselves will make your Entrée very respectable.'[26]

Kitty made us all smile except Mary who did not understand her Meaning and coolly said that she should not like to chaperone so many.

Sophy and I now endeavoured to change the conversation

but succeeded only for a few Minutes, for Mary took care to bring back their attention to her and her approaching Wedding.

I was sorry for my Sister's sake to see that M[r] Brudenell seemed to take pleasure in listening to her account of it, and even encouraged her by his Questions and Remarks, for it was evident that his only Aim was to laugh at her. I am afraid he found her very ridiculous. He kept his Countenance extremely well, yet it was easy to see that it was with difficulty he kept it. At length however he seemed fatigued and Disgusted with her ridiculous Conversation, as he turned from her to us, and spoke but little to her for about half an hour before we left Stoneham. As soon as we were out of the House we all joined in praising the Person and Manners of M[r] Brudenell.

We found M[r] Watts at home.

'So, Miss Stanhope' (said he) 'you see I am come a courting in a true Lover like Manner.'

'Well you need not have <u>told</u> me that. I knew why you came very well.'

Sophy and I then left the room, imagining of course that we must be in the way, if a Scene of Courtship were to begin. We were surprised at being followed almost immediately by Mary.

'And is your Courting so soon over?' said Sophy.

'Courting!' (replied Mary) 'we have been quarrelling. Watts is such a Fool! I hope I shall never see him again.'

'I am afraid you will,' (said I) 'as he dines here today. But what has been your dispute?'

'Why only because I told him that I had seen a Man much handsomer than he was this Morning, he flew into a great Passion and called me a Vixen,[27] so I only stayed to tell him I thought him a Blackguard[28] and came away.'

'Short and sweet,' (said Sophy) 'but pray, Mary, how will this be made up?'

'He ought to ask my pardon; but if he did, I would not forgive him.'

'His Submission then would not be very useful.'

When we were dressed[29] we returned to the Parlour where Mama and M[r] Watts were in close Conversation. It seems that he had been complaining to her of her Daughter's behaviour, and she had persuaded him to think no more of it. He therefore met Mary with all his accustomed Civility, and except one touch at the Phaeton and another at the Greenhouse, the Evening went off with a great Harmony and Cordiality. Watts is going to Town to hasten the preparations for the Wedding.

I am your affec[te] Freind G. S.

[Detached pieces]

To Miss Jane Anna Elizabeth Austen[1]

My Dear Neice

Though you are at this period not many degrees removed from Infancy, Yet trusting that you will in time be older, and that through the care of your excellent Parents, You will one day or another be able to read written hand, I dedicate to You the following Miscellanious Morsels, convinced that if you seriously attend to them, You will derive from them very important Instructions, with regard to your Conduct in Life.—If such my hopes should hereafter be realized, never shall I regret the Days and Nights that have been spent in composing these Treatises for your Benefit.[2] I am my dear Neice

Your very Affectionate
Aunt.
The Author

June 2[d]
1793—[3]

A beautiful description of the different effects of Sensibility[4] on different Minds

I am but just returned from Melissa's Bedside, and in my Life tho' it has been a pretty long one, and I have during the course of it been at many Bedsides, I never saw so affecting an object as she exhibits. She lies wrapped in a book muslin bedgown, a chambray gauze shift, and a french net nightcap.[5] Sir William is constantly at her bedside. The only repose he takes is on the Sopha in the Drawing room, where for five minutes every fortnight he remains in an imperfect Slumber, starting up every Moment and exclaiming 'Oh! Melissa, Ah! Melissa,' then sinking down again, raises his left arm and scratches his head. Poor Mrs Burnaby is beyond measure afflicted. She sighs every now and then, that is about once a week; while the melancholy Charles says every Moment 'Melissa, how are you?' The lovely Sisters are much to be pitied. Julia is ever lamenting the situation of her friend, while lying behind her pillow and supporting her head—Maria more mild in her greif talks of going to Town next week, and Anna is always recurring to the pleasures we once enjoyed when Melissa was well.—I am usually at the fire cooking some little delicacy for the unhappy invalid—Perhaps hashing up[6] the remains of an old Duck, toasting some cheese[7] or making a Curry[8] which are the favourite Dishes of our poor friend.—

In these situations we were this morning surprised by receiving a visit from Dr Dowkins; 'I am come to see Melissa,' said he. 'How is She?'

'Very weak indeed,' said the fainting Melissa—

'Very weak,' replied the punning Doctor, 'aye indeed it is more than a very <u>week</u> since you have taken to your bed—How is your appetite?'

'Bad, very bad,' said Julia.

'That <u>is</u> very bad'—replied he. 'Are her spirits good, Madam?'

'So poorly, Sir, that we are obliged to strengthen her with cordials[9] every Minute.'—

'Well then she receives <u>Spirits</u> from your being with her. Does she sleep?'

'Scarcely ever—.'

'And Ever Scarcely I suppose when she does. Poor thing! Does she think of dieing?'

'She has not strength to think at all.'

'Nay then she cannot think to have Strength.'—

The Generous Curate[10] a moral Tale,[11] setting forth the Advantages of being Generous and a Curate.

In a part little known of the County of Warwick, a very worthy Clergyman[12] lately resided. The income of his living[13] which amounted to about two hundred pound, and the interest of his Wife's fortune which was nothing at all, was entirely sufficient for the Wants and Wishes of a Family who neither wanted or wished for anything beyond what their income afforded them. Mr Williams had been in possession of his living above twenty Years, when this history commences, and his Marriage which had taken place soon after his presentation to it, had made him the father of six very fine Children. The eldest had been placed at the Royal Academy for Seamen at Portsmouth[14] when about thirteen years old, and from thence had been discharged on board of one of the Vessels of a small fleet destined for Newfoundland,[15] where his promising and amiable disposition had procured him many freinds among the Natives, and from whence he regularly sent home a large Newfoundland Dog[16] every Month to his family. The second, who was also a Son, had been adopted by a neighbouring Clergyman with the intention of educating him at his own expence, which would have been a very desirable Circumstance had the Gentleman's fortune been equal to his generosity, but as he had nothing to support himself and a very large family but a Curacy of fifty pound a year,[17] Young Williams knew nothing more at the age of 18 than what a twopenny Dame's School[18] in the village could teach him. His Character however was perfectly amiable though his genius[19] might be cramped, and he was addicted to no vice, or ever guilty of any fault beyond what his age and situation rendered perfectly excusable. He had indeed sometimes been detected in flinging Stones at a Duck or putting brickbats[20] into his Benefactor's bed; but these innocent efforts of wit were considered by that good Man rather as the effects of a lively imagination, than of anything bad in his Nature, and if any punishment were decreed for the offence it was in general no greater than that the Culprit should pick up the Stones or take the brickbats away.—

Finis

To Miss Austen,[1] the following Ode to Pity[2] is dedicated, from a thorough knowledge of her pitiful Nature, by her obed^t hum^le Servt

The Author

Ode to Pity

1

Ever musing I delight to tread
  The Paths of honour and the Myrtle[3] Grove
Whilst the pale Moon her beams doth shed
  On disappointed Love.
While Philomel[4] on airy hawthorn Bush
  Sings sweet and Melancholy, And the thrush
Converses with the Dove.

2

Gently brawling down the turnpike road,[5]
  Sweetly noisy falls the Silent Stream—
The Moon emerges from behind a Cloud
  And darts upon the Myrtle Grove her beam.
Ah! then what Lovely Scenes appear,
  The hut, the Cot, the Grot, and Chapel queer,[6]
And eke the Abbey too a mouldering heap,[7]
  Conceal'd by aged pines her head doth rear
And quite invisible doth take a peep.

End of the first volume

June 3^d 1793

Volume the Second

60

Lesley Castle

an unfinished Novel in Letters.

Letter The first is from

Miss Margaret Lesley to Miss Charlotte Lutterell

Lesley Castle Janry 3d 1792.

My Brother has just left us. "Matilda (said he at parting) you and Margaret will I am certain take all the care of my dear little one, that she might have received from an indulgent, an affectionate an amiable Mother." Tears rolled down his Cheeks as he spoke these words—the remembrance of her who had so wantonly disgraced the Maternal character and so openly violated the conjugal Duties, prevented his adding anything farther; he embraced his sweet Child and after saluting Matilda & Me hastily broke from us and seating himself in his Chaise, pursued the road to Aberdeen. Never was

Manuscript page 1 of 'Lesley Castle', in Jane Austen's notebook *Volume the Second*. (By permission of the British Library.)

VOLUME THE SECOND

Ex dono mei Patris[1]

Contents[2]

To Madame La Comtesse De Feuillide[1]
This Novel is inscribed
by
Her obliged Humble Servant
The Author

Love and Freindship

a novel
in a series of Letters[2]

'Deceived in Freindship and Betrayed in Love.'[3]

Letter the First

From Isabel to Laura[4]

How often, in answer to my repeated intreaties that you would give my Daughter a regular detail of the Misfortunes and Adventures of your Life, have you said 'No, my freind, never will I comply with your request till I may be no longer in Danger of again experiencing such dreadful ones.'

Surely that time is now at hand. You are this Day 55. If a woman may ever be said to be in safety from the determined Perseverance of disagreable Lovers and the cruel Persecutions of obstinate Fathers, surely it must be at such a time of Life.

Isabel

Letter 2[d]

Laura to Isabel

Altho' I cannot agree with you in supposing that I shall never again be exposed to Misfortunes as unmerited as those I have already experienced, yet to avoid the imputation of Obstinacy or ill-nature, I will gratify the curiosity of your Daughter; and may the fortitude with which I have suffered the many Afflictions of my past Life, prove to her a useful Lesson for the support of those which may befall her in her own.

Laura

Letter 3[d]

Laura to Marianne[5]

As the Daughter of my most intimate freind I think you entitled to that knowledge of my unhappy Story, which your Mother has so often solicited me to give you.

My Father was a native of Ireland and an inhabitant of Wales; my Mother was the natural[6] Daughter of a Scotch Peer by an italian Opera-girl[7]—I was born in Spain and received my Education at a Convent in France.

When I had reached my eighteenth Year I was recalled by my Parents to my paternal roof in Wales. Our mansion was situated in one of the most romantic[8] parts of the Vale of Uske.[9] Tho' my Charms are now considerably softened and somewhat impaired by the Misfortunes I have undergone, I was once beautiful. But lovely as I was the Graces of my Person were the least of my Perfections. Of every accomplishment accustomary to my sex, I was Mistress.—When in the Convent, my progress had always exceeded my instructions, my Acquirements had been wonderfull for my Age, and I had shortly surpassed my Masters.

In my Mind, every Virtue that could adorn it was centered; it was the Rendez-vous[10] of every good Quality and of every noble sentiment.

A sensibility too tremblingly alive[11] to every affliction of my Freinds, my Acquaintance and particularly to every affliction of my own, was my only fault, if a fault it could be called. Alas! how altered now! Tho' indeed my own misfortunes do not make less impression on me than they ever did, yet now I never feel for those of an other. My accomplishments too, begin to fade—I can neither sing so well nor Dance so gracefully as I once did—and I have entirely forgot the Minuet Dela Cour— [12]

Adeiu.
Laura

Letter 4th

Laura to Marianne

Our neighbourhood was small, for it consisted only of your Mother. She may probably have already told you that being left by her Parents in indigent Circumstances she had retired into Wales on eoconomical motives. There it was, our freindship first commenced—. Isabel was then one and twenty—Tho' pleasing both in her Person and Manners (between ourselves) she never possessed the hundredth part of my Beauty or Accomplishments. Isabel had seen the World. She had passed 2 Years at one of the first Boarding-schools in London;[13] had spent a fortnight in Bath and had supped one night in Southampton.[14]

'Beware my Laura' (she would often say) 'Beware of the insipid Vanities and idle Dissipations of the Metropolis of England; Beware of the unmeaning Luxuries of Bath and of the Stinking fish of Southampton.'

'Alas!' (exclaimed I) 'how am I to avoid those evils I shall never be exposed to? What probability is there of my ever tasting the Dissipations of London, the Luxuries of Bath or the stinking Fish of Southampton? I who am doomed to waste my Days of Youth and Beauty in an humble Cottage in the Vale of Uske.'

Ah! little did I then think I was ordained so soon to quit that humble Cottage for the Deceitfull Pleasures of the World.

adeiu
Laura

Letter 5th

Laura to Marianne

One Evening in December as my Father, my Mother and myself, were arranged in social converse round our Fireside, we were on a sudden, greatly astonished, by hearing a violent knocking on the outward Door of our rustic Cot.[15]

My Father started— 'What noise is that,' (said he.) 'It sounds like a loud rapping at the Door'—(replied my Mother.) 'It does indeed,' (cried I.) 'I am of your opinion;' (said my Father) 'it certainly does appear to proceed from some uncommon violence exerted against our unoffending Door.'

'Yes,' (exclaimed I) 'I cannot help thinking it must be somebody who knocks for Admittance.'

'That is another point' (replied he;) 'We must not pretend to determine on what motive the person may Knock—tho' that someone does rap at the Door, I am partly convinced.'[16]

Here, a 2d tremendous rap interrupted my Father in his speech and somewhat alarmed my Mother and me.

'Had we not better go and see who it is?' (said she), 'the Servants are out.' 'I think we had,' (replied I.) 'Certainly,' (added my Father) 'by all means.' 'Shall we go now?' (said my Mother.) 'The sooner the better,' (answered he.) 'Oh! let no time be lost,' (cried I.)

A third more violent Rap than ever again assaulted our ears. 'I am certain there is somebody knocking at the Door,' (said my Mother.) 'I think there must,' (replied my Father) 'I fancy the Servants are returned;' (said I) 'I think I hear Mary going to the Door.' 'I'm glad of it' (cried my Father) 'for I long to know who it is.'

I was right in my Conjecture; for Mary instantly entering the Room, informed us that a young Gentleman and his Servant were at the Door, who had lossed their way, were very cold and begged leave to warm themselves by our fire.

'Won't you admit them?' (said I) 'You have no objection, my Dear?' (said my Father.) 'None in the World,' (replied my Mother.)

Mary, without waiting for any further commands, immediately left the room and quickly returned introducing the most beauteous and amiable Youth, I had ever beheld. The servant, She kept to herself.

My natural Sensibility had already been greatly affected by the sufferings of the unfortunate Stranger and no sooner did I first behold him, than I felt that on him the happiness or Misery of my future Life must depend.—[17]

adeiu
Laura

Letter 6th

Laura to Marianne

The noble Youth informed us that his name was Lindsay—for particular reasons however I shall conceal it under that of Talbot.[18] He told us that he was the son of an English Baronet,[19] that his Mother had been many years no more and that he had a Sister of the middle size. 'My Father' (he continued) 'is a mean and mercenary wretch—it is only to such particular freinds as this Dear Party that I would thus betray his failings—.

Your Virtues my amiable Polydore'[20] (addressing himself to my father) 'yours Dear Claudia, and yours my Charming Laura, call on me to repose in you, my Confidence.' We bowed. 'My Father, seduced by the false glare of Fortune and the Deluding Pomp of Title, insisted on my giving my hand to Lady Dorothea. No never exclaimed I. Lady Dorothea is lovely and Engaging; I prefer no woman to her; but Know Sir, that I scorn to marry her in compliance with your Wishes. No! Never shall it be said that I obliged my Father.'[21]

We all admired the noble Manliness of his reply. He continued.

'Sir Edward was surprised; he had perhaps little expected to meet with so spirited an opposition to his will. "Where, Edward, in the name of wonder" (said he) "did you pick up this unmeaning Gibberish? You have been studying Novels I suspect."[22] I scorned to answer: it would have been beneath my Dignity. I mounted my Horse and followed by my faithful William set forwards for my Aunt's.'

'My Father's house is situated in Bedfordshire, my Aunt's in Middlesex,[23] and tho' I flatter myself with being a tolerable proficient in Geography, I know not how it happened, but I found myself entering this beautifull Vale which I find is in South Wales, when I had expected to have reached my Aunt's.

'After having wandered some time on the Banks of the Uske without knowing which way to go, I began to lament my cruel Destiny in the bitterest and most pathetic Manner. It was now perfectly Dark, not a single Star was there to direct my steps, and I know not what might have befallen me had I not at length discerned thro' the solemn Gloom that surrounded me a distant Light, which as I approached it, I discovered to be the chearfull Blaze of your fire. Impelled by the combination of Misfortunes under which I laboured, namely Fear, Cold and Hunger I hesitated not to ask admittance which at length I have gained; and now, my Adorable Laura' (continued he taking my Hand) 'when may I hope to receive that reward of all the painfull sufferings I have undergone during the course of my Attachment to you, to which I have ever aspired? Oh! when will you reward me with Yourself?'

'This instant, Dear and Amiable Edward,' (replied I). We were immediately united by my Father, who tho' he had never taken orders had been bred to the Church.[24]

adeiu
Laura

Letter 7th

Laura to Marianne

We remained but a few Days after our Marriage, in the Vale of Uske—. After taking my affecting Farewell of my Father, my Mother and my Isabel, I accompanied Edward to his Aunt's in Middlesex. Philippa received us both with every expression of affectionate Love. My arrival was indeed a most agreable surprize to her as she had not only been totally ignorant of my Marriage with her Nephew, but had never even had the slightest idea of there being such a person in the World.

Augusta, the sister of Edward was on a visit to her when we arrived. I found her exactly what her Brother had described her to be—of the middle size. She received me with equal surprize though not with equal Cordiality, as Philippa. There was a Disagreable Coldness and Forbidding Reserve in her reception of me which was equally Distressing and Unexpected. None of that interesting Sensibility or amiable Simpathy in her Manners and Address to me when we first met which should have Distinguished our introduction to each other—. Her Language was neither warm, nor affectionate, her expressions of regard were neither animated nor cordial; her arms were not opened to receive me to her Heart, tho' my own were extended to press her to mine.

A short Conversation between Augusta and her Brother, which I accidentally overheard encreased my Dislike to her, and convinced me that her Heart was no more formed for the soft ties of Love than for the endearing intercourse of Freindship.

'But do you think that my Father will ever be reconciled to this imprudent connection?' (said Augusta.)

'Augusta,' (replied the noble Youth) 'I thought you had a better opinion of me, than to imagine I would so abjectly degrade myself as to consider my Father's Concurrence in any of my Affairs, either of Consequence or concern to me—. Tell me Augusta tell me with sincerity; did you ever know me consult his inclinations or follow his Advice in the least trifling Particular since the age of fifteen?'

'Edward,' (replied she) 'you are surely too diffident in your own praise—. Since you were fifteen only!—My Dear Brother since you were five years old, I entirely acquit you of ever having willingly contributed to the Satisfaction of your Father. But still I am not without apprehensions of your being shortly obliged to degrade yourself in your own eyes by seeking a Support for your Wife in the Generosity of Sir Edward.'

'Never, never Augusta will I so demean myself,' (said Edward). 'Support! What Support will Laura want which she can receive from him?'

'Only those very insignificant ones of Victuals and Drink,' (answered she.)

'Victuals and Drink!' (replied my Husband in a most nobly contemptuous Manner) 'and dost thou then imagine that there is no other support for an exalted Mind (such as is my Laura's) than the mean and indelicate employment of Eating and Drinking?'

'None that I know of, so efficacious,' (returned Augusta).

'And did you then never feel the pleasing Pangs of Love, Augusta?' (replied my Edward). 'Does it appear impossible to your vile and corrupted Palate, to exist on Love? Can you not conceive the Luxury of living in every Distress that Poverty can inflict, with the object of your tenderest affection?'

'You are too ridiculous' (said Augusta) 'to argue with; perhaps however you may in time be convinced that . . . .'

Here I was prevented from hearing the remainder of her Speech, by the Appearance of a very Handsome young Woman, who was ushered into the Room at the Door of which I had been listening. On hearing her announced by the Name of

'Lady Dorothea', I instantly quitted my Post and followed her into the Parlour, for I well remembered that she was the Lady, proposed as a Wife for my Edward by the Cruel and Unrelenting Baronet.

Altho' Lady Dorothea's visit was nominally to Philippa and Augusta, yet I have some reason to imagine that (acquainted with the Marriage and arrival of Edward) to see me was a principal motive to it.

I soon perceived that tho' Lovely and Elegant in her Person and tho' Easy and Polite in her Address, she was of that inferior order of Beings with regard to Delicate Feeling, tender Sentiments, and refined Sensibility, of which Augusta was one.

She staid but half an hour and neither in the Course of her Visit, confided to me any of her Secret thoughts, nor requested me to confide in her, any of Mine. You will easily imagine therefore my Dear Marianne that I could not feel any ardent Affection or very sincere Attachment for Lady Dorothea.

Adeiu
Laura

Letter 8th

Laura to Marianne, in continuation

Lady Dorothea had not left us long before another visitor as unexpected a one as her Ladyship, was announced. It was Sir Edward, who informed by Augusta of her Brother's marriage, came doubtless to reproach him for having dared to unite himself to me without his Knowledge. But Edward foreseeing his Design, approached him with heroic fortitude as soon as he entered the Room, and addressed him in the following Manner.

'Sir Edward, I know the motive of your Journey here—You come with the base Design of reproaching me for having entered into an indissoluble engagement with my Laura without your Consent—But Sir, I glory in the Act—. It is my greatest boast that I have incurred the Displeasure of my Father!'

So saying, he took my hand and whilst Sir Edward, Philippa, and Augusta were doubtless reflecting with Admiration on his undaunted Bravery, led me from the Parlour to his Father's Carriage which yet remained at the Door and in which we were instantly conveyed from the pursuit of Sir Edward.

The Postilions had at first received orders only to take the London road; as soon as we had sufficiently reflected However, we ordered them to Drive to M——. the seat of Edward's most particular freind, which was but a few miles distant.

At M——. we arrived in a few hours; and on sending in our names were immediately admitted to Sophia,[25] the Wife of Edward's freind. After having been deprived during the course of 3 weeks of a real freind (for such I term your Mother) imagine my transports at beholding one, most truly worthy of the Name. Sophia was rather above the middle size; most elegantly formed. A soft Languor spread over her lovely features, but increased their Beauty—. It was the Charectarestic of her Mind—. She was all Sensibility and Feeling. We flew into each others arms and after having exchanged vows of mutual Freindship for the rest of our Lives, instantly unfolded to each other the most inward Secrets of our Hearts—. We were interrupted in this Delightfull Employment by the entrance of Augustus, (Edward's freind) who was just returned from a solitary ramble.

Never did I see such an affecting Scene as was the meeting of Edward and Augustus.

'My Life! my Soul!' (exclaimed the former). 'My Adorable Angel!'[26] (replied the latter) as they flew into each other's arms.—It was too pathetic[27] for the feelings of Sophia and myself—We fainted Alternately on a Sofa.[28]

Adeiu
Laura

Letter the 9th

From the Same to the Same

Towards the close of the Day we received the following Letter from Philippa.

'Sir Edward is greatly incensed by your abrupt departure; he has taken back Augusta with him to Bedfordshire. Much as I wish to enjoy again your charming Society, I cannot determine to snatch you from that, of such dear and deserving Freinds— When your Visit to them is terminated, I trust you will return to the arms of your

Philippa.'

We returned a suitable answer to this affectionate Note and after thanking her for her kind invitation assured her that we would certainly avail ourselves of it, whenever we might have no other place to go to. Tho' certainly nothing could to any reasonable Being, have appeared more satisfactory, than so gratefull a reply to her invitation, yet I know not how it was, but she was certainly capricious enough to be displeased with our behaviour and in a few weeks after, either to revenge our Conduct, or releive her own solitude, married a young and illiterate Fortune-hunter. This imprudent Step (tho' we were sensible that it would probably deprive us of that fortune which Philippa had ever taught us to expect) could not on our own accounts, excite from our exalted Minds a single sigh; yet fearfull lest it might prove a source of endless misery to the deluded Bride, our trembling Sensibility was greatly affected when we were first informed of the Event. The affectionate Entreaties of Augustus and Sophia that we would for ever consider their House as our Home, easily prevailed on us to determine never more to leave them—. In the Society of my Edward and this Amiable Pair, I passed the happiest moments of my Life; Our time was most delightfully spent, in mutual Protestations of Freindship, and in vows of unalterable Love, in which we were secure from being interrupted, by intruding and disagreable

Visitors, as Augustus and Sophia had on their first Entrance in the Neighbourhood, taken due care to inform the surrounding Families, that as their Happiness centered wholly in themselves, they wished for no other society. But alas! my Dear Marianne such Happiness as I then enjoyed was too perfect to be lasting. A most severe and unexpected Blow at once destroyed every Sensation of Pleasure. Convinced as you must be from what I have already told you concerning Augustus and Sophia, that there never were a happier Couple, I need not I imagine inform you that their union had been contrary to the inclinations of their Cruel and Mercenary Parents; who had vainly endeavoured with obstinate Perseverance to force them into a Marriage with those whom they had ever abhorred; but with an Heroic Fortitude worthy to be related and Admired, they had both, constantly refused to submit to such despotic Power.

After having so nobly disentangled themselves from the Shackles of Parental Authority, by a Clandestine Marriage,[29] they were determined never to forfeit the good opinion they had gained in the World, in so doing, by accepting any proposals of reconciliation that might be offered them by their Fathers—to this farther tryal of their noble independance however they never were exposed.

They had been married but a few months when our visit to them commenced during which time they had been amply supported by a considerable sum of Money which Augustus had gracefully purloined from his Unworthy father's Escritoire,[30] a few days before his union with Sophia.

By our arrival their Expences were considerably encreased tho' their means for supplying them were then nearly exhausted. But they, Exalted Creatures! scorned to reflect a moment on their pecuniary Distresses and would have blushed at the idea of paying their Debts.[31]—Alas! what was their Reward for such disinterested Behaviour! The beautifull Augustus was arrested and we were all undone. Such perfidious Treachery in the merciless perpetrators of the Deed will shock your gentle nature Dearest Marianne as much as it then affected the Delicate Sensibility of Edward, Sophia, your Laura, and of Augustus himself. To compleat such unparalelled Barbarity we were informed that an Execution in the House[32] would shortly take place. Ah! what could we do but what we did! We sighed and fainted on the Sofa.

Adeiu
Laura

Letter 10th

Laura in continuation

When we were somewhat recovered from the overpowering Effusions of our Grief, Edward desired that we would consider what was the most prudent step to be taken in our unhappy situation while he repaired to his imprisoned freind to lament over his misfortunes. We promised that we would, and he set forwards on his Journey to Town. During his Absence we faithfully complied with his Desire and after the most mature Deliberation, at length agreed that the best thing we could do was to leave the House; of which we every moment expected the Officers of Justice[33] to take possession. We waited therefore with the greatest impatience, for the return of Edward in order to impart to him the result of our Deliberations—. But no Edward appeared—. In vain did we count the tedious Moments of his Absence—in vain did we weep—in vain even did we sigh—no Edward returned—. This was too cruel, too unexpected a Blow to our Gentle Sensibility—. we could not support it—we could only faint—. At length collecting all the Resolution I was Mistress of, I arose and after packing up some necessary Apparel for Sophia and myself, I dragged her to a Carriage I had ordered and we instantly set out for London. As the Habitation of Augustus was within twelve miles of Town, it was not long e'er we arrived there, and no sooner had we entered Holbourn[34] than letting down one of the Front Glasses I enquired of every decent-looking Person that we passed 'If they had seen my Edward'?

But as we drove too rapidly to allow them to answer my repeated Enquiries, I gained little, or indeed, no information concerning him. 'Where am I to Drive?' said the Postilion.[35] 'To Newgate,[36] Gentle Youth,' (replied I), 'to see Augustus.' 'Oh! no, no,' (exclaimed Sophia), 'I cannot go to Newgate; I shall not be able to support the sight of my Augustus in so cruel a confinement—my feelings are sufficiently shocked by the recital, of his Distress, but to behold it will overpower my Sensibility.' As I perfectly agreed with her in the Justice of her Sentiments the Postilion was instantly directed to return into the Country. You may perhaps have been somewhat surprised my Dearest Marianne, that in the Distress I then endured, destitute of any Support, and unprovided with any Habitation, I should never once have remembered my Father and Mother or my paternal Cottage in the Vale of Uske. To account for this seeming forgetfullness I must inform you of a trifling Circumstance concerning them which I have as yet never mentioned—. The death of my Parents a few weeks after my Departure, is the circumstance I allude to. By their decease I became the lawfull Inheritress of their House and Fortune. But alas! the House had never been their own and their Fortune had only been an Annuity[37] on their own Lives.—Such is the Depravity of the World! To your Mother I should have returned with Pleasure, should have been happy to have introduced to her, my Charming Sophia and should have with Chearfullness have passed the remainder of my Life in their dear Society in the Vale of Uske, had not one obstacle to the execution of so agreable a Scheme, intervened; which was the Marriage and Removal of your Mother to a Distant part of Ireland.

Adeiu.
Laura

Letter 11th

Laura in continuation

'I have a Relation in Scotland' (said Sophia to me as we left London) 'who I am certain would not hesitate in receiving me.' 'Shall I order the Boy to drive there?' said I—but instantly recollecting myself, exclaimed 'Alas, I fear it will be too long a Journey for the Horses.' Unwilling however to act only from my own inadequate Knowledge of the Strength and Abilities of Horses, I consulted the Postilion, who was entirely of my Opinion concerning the Affair. We therefore determined to change Horses at the next Town and to travel Post[38] the remainder of the Journey—. When we arrived at the last Inn we were to stop at, which was but a few miles from the House of Sophia's Relation, unwilling to intrude our Society on him unexpected and unthought of, we wrote a very elegant and well-penned Note to him containing an Account of our Destitute and melancholy Situation, and of our intention to spend some months with him in Scotland. As soon as we had dispatched this Letter, we immediately prepared to follow it in person and were stepping into the Carriage for that Purpose when our Attention was attracted by the Entrance of a coroneted Coach[39] and 4 into the Inn-yard. A Gentleman considerably advanced in years, descended from it—. At his first Appearance my Sensibility was wonderfully affected and e'er I had gazed at him a 2d time, an instinctive Sympathy whispered to my Heart, that he was my Grandfather.

Convinced that I could not be mistaken in my conjecture I instantly sprang from the Carriage I had just entered, and following the Venerable Stranger into the Room he had been shewn to, I threw myself on my knees before him and besought him to acknowledge me as his Grand-Child.—He started, and after having attentively examined my features, raised me from the Ground and throwing his Grand-fatherly arms around my Neck, exclaimed, 'Acknowledge thee! Yes dear resemblance of my Laurina and my Laurina's Daughter, sweet image of my Claudia and my Claudia's Mother, I do acknowledge thee as the Daughter of the one and the Grandaughter of the other.' While he was thus tenderly embracing me, Sophia, astonished at my precipitate Departure, entered the Room in search of me—. No sooner had she caught the eye of the venerable Peer, than he exclaimed with every mark of Astonishment—'Another Grandaughter! Yes, yes, I see you are the Daughter of my Laurina's eldest Girl; Your resemblance to the beauteous Matilda[40] sufficiently proclaims it.' 'Oh!' replied Sophia, 'when I first beheld you the instinct of Nature whispered me that we were in some degree related—But whether Grandfathers, or Grandmothers, I could not pretend to determine.' He folded her in his arms, and whilst they were tenderly embracing, the Door of the Apartment opened and a most beautifull Young Man appeared. On perceiving him Lord St Clair started and retreating back a few paces, with uplifted Hands, said, 'Another Grand-Child! What an unexpected Happiness is this! to discover in the space of 3 minutes, as many of my Descendants! This, I am certain is Philander[41] the son of my Laurina's 3^d^ Girl, the amiable Bertha; there wants now but the presence of Gustavus to compleat the Union of my Laurina's Grand-Children.'

'And here he is;' (said a Gracefull Youth who that instant entered the room) 'here is the Gustavus you desire to see. I am the son of Agatha, your Laurina's 4th and Youngest Daughter.' 'I see you are indeed;' replied Lord St Clair—But tell me' (continued he looking fearfully towards the Door) 'tell me, have I any other Grand-Children in the House?'[42] 'None, my Lord.' 'Then I will provide for you all without farther delay—Here are 4 Banknotes of 50£ each—Take them and remember I have done the Duty of a Grandfather—.' He instantly left the Room and immediately afterwards the House.

Adeiu.
Laura

Letter the 12th

Laura in continuation

You may imagine how greatly we were surprized by the sudden departure of Lord St Clair—. 'Ignoble Grandsire!' exclaimed Sophia. 'Unworthy Grandfather!' said I, and instantly fainted in each other's arms. How long we remained in this situation I know not; but when we recovered we found ourselves alone, without either Gustavus, Philander or the Bank-notes. As we were deploring our unhappy fate, the Door of the Apartment opened and 'Macdonald' was announced. He was Sophia's cousin. The haste with which he came to our releif so soon after the receipt of our Note, spoke so greatly in his favour that I hesitated not to pronounce him at first sight, a tender and simpathetic Freind. Alas! he little deserved the name—for though he told us that he was much concerned at our Misfortunes, yet by his own account it appeared that the perusal of them, had neither drawn from him a single sigh, nor induced him to bestow one curse on our vindictive Stars—. He told Sophia that his Daughter depended on her returning with him to Macdonald-Hall, and that as his Cousin's freind he should be happy to see me there also. To Macdonald-Hall, therefore we went, and were received with great kindness by Janetta the daughter of Macdonald, and the Mistress of the Mansion. Janetta was then only fifteen; naturally well disposed, endowed with a susceptible Heart, and a simpathetic Disposition, she might, had these amiable Qualities been properly encouraged, have been an ornament to human Nature; but unfortunately her Father possessed not a soul sufficiently exalted to admire so promising a Disposition, and had endeavoured by every means in his power to prevent its encreasing with her Years. He had actually so far extinguished the natural noble Sensibility of her Heart, as to prevail on her to accept an offer from a young Man of his Recommendation. They were to be married in a few Months, and Graham, was in the House when we arrived. We soon saw through his Character—. He was just such a Man as one might have expected to be the choice of Macdonald. They said he was Sensible, well-informed, and Agreable; we did not pretend to Judge of such trifles, but as we were convinced he had no soul, that he had never read the Sorrows of Werter,[43] and that his Hair bore not the least resemblance to Auburn,[44] we were certain that Janetta could feel no affection for him, at least that she ought to feel none. The very circumstance of his being her father's choice too, was so much in his disfavour, that had he been deserving her, in every other respect yet that of itself ought to have been a sufficient reason in the Eyes of Janetta for rejecting him. These considerations we were determined to represent to her in their proper light and doubted not of meeting with the desired Success from one naturally so well disposed, whose errors in the affair had only arisen from a want of proper confidence in her own opinion, and a suitable contempt of her father's. We found her indeed all that our warmest wishes could have hoped for; we had no difficulty to convince her that it was impossible she could love Graham, or that it was her Duty to disobey her Father; the only thing at which she rather seemed to hesitate was our assertion that she must be attached to some other Person. For some time, she persevered in declaring that she knew no other young Man for whom she had the smallest Affection; but upon explaining the impossibility of such a thing she said that she beleived she did like Captain M'Kenzie better than any one she knew besides. This confession satisfied us and after having enumerated the good Qualities of M'Kenzie and assured her that she was violently in love with him, we desired to know whether he had ever in any wise declared his Affection to her.

'So far from having ever declared it, I have no reason to imagine that he has ever felt any for me,' said Janetta. 'That he certainly adores you' (replied Sophia) 'there can be no doubt—. The Attachment must be reciprocal—. Did he never gaze on you with Admiration—tenderly press your hand—drop an involantary tear—and leave the room abruptly?' 'Never' (replied She) 'that I remember—he has always left the room indeed when his visit has been ended, but has never gone away particularly abruptly or without making a bow.'

'Indeed my Love' (said I) 'you must be mistaken—: for it is absolutely impossible that he should ever have left you but with Confusion, Despair, and Precipitation—. Consider but for a moment Janetta, and you must be convinced how absurd it is to suppose that he could ever make a Bow, or behave like any other Person.' Having settled this Point to our satisfaction, the next we took into consideration was, to determine in what manner we should inform M'Kenzie of the favourable Opinion Janetta entertained of him—. We at length agreed to acquaint him with it by an anonymous Letter which Sophia drew up in the following Manner.

'Oh! happy Lover of the beautifull Janetta, oh! enviable Possessor of <u>her</u> Heart whose hand is destined to another, why do you thus delay a confession of your Attachment to the amiable Object of it? Oh! consider that a few weeks will at once put an end to every flattering Hope that you may now entertain, by uniting the unfortunate Victim of her father's Cruelty to the execrable and detested Graham.

'Alas! why do you thus so cruelly connive at the projected Misery of her and of yourself by delaying to communicate that scheme which has doubtless long possessed your imagination? A secret Union will at once secure the felicity of both.'

The amiable M'Kenzie, whose modesty as he afterwards assured us had been the only reason of his having so long concealed the violence of his affection for Janetta, on receiving this Billet flew on the wings of Love to Macdonald-Hall, and so powerfully pleaded his Attachment to her who inspired it, that after a few more private interveiws, Sophia and I experienced the Satisfaction of seeing them depart for Gretna-Green,[45] which they chose for the celebration of their Nuptials, in preference to any other place although it was at a considerable distance from Macdonald-Hall.

Adeiu—
Laura

Letter the 13th

Laura in Continuation

They had been gone nearly a couple of Hours, before either Macdonald or Graham had entertained any suspicion of the affair—. And they might not even then have suspected it, but for the following little Accident. Sophia happening one Day to open a private Drawer in Macdonald's Library with one of her own keys, discovered that it was the Place where he kept his Papers of consequence and amongst them some bank notes of considerable amount. This discovery she imparted to me; and having agreed together that it would be a proper treatment of so vile a Wretch as Macdonald to deprive him of Money, perhaps dishonestly gained, it was determined that the next time we should either of us happen to go that way, we would take one or more of the Bank notes from the drawer. This well-meant Plan we had often successfully put in Execution; but alas! on the very day of Janetta's Escape, as Sophia was majestically removing the 5th Bank-note from the Drawer to her own purse, she was suddenly most impertinently interrupted in her employment by the entrance of Macdonald himself, in a most abrupt and precipitate Manner. Sophia (who though naturally all winning sweetness could when occasions demanded it call forth the Dignity of her Sex) instantly put on a most forbiding look, and darting an angry frown on the undaunted Culprit, demanded in a haughty tone of voice 'Wherefore her retirement was thus insolently broken in on?' The unblushing Macdonald, without even endeavouring to exculpate himself from the crime he was charged with, meanly endeavoured to reproach Sophia with ignobly defrauding him of his Money . . . The dignity of Sophia was wounded; 'Wretch' (exclaimed she, hastily replacing the Bank-note in the Drawer) 'how darest thou to accuse me of an Act, of which the bare idea makes me blush?' The base wretch was still unconvinced and continued to upbraid the justly-offended Sophia in such opprobrious

Language, that at length he so greatly provoked the gentle sweetness of her Nature, as to induce her to revenge herself on him by informing him of Janetta's Elopement, and of the active Part we had both taken in the Affair. At this period of their Quarrel I entered the Library and was as you may imagine equally offended as Sophia at the ill-grounded Accusations of the malevolent and contemptible Macdonald. 'Base Miscreant!' (cried I) 'how canst thou thus undauntedly endeavour to sully the spotless reputation of such bright Excellence? Why dost thou not suspect my innocence as soon?'

'Be satisfied, Madam' (replied he) 'I do suspect it, and therefore must desire that you will both leave this House in less than half an hour.'

'We shall go willingly;' (answered Sophia) 'our hearts have long detested thee, and nothing but our freindship for thy Daughter could have induced us to remain so long beneath thy roof.'

'Your Freindship for my Daughter has indeed been most powerfully exerted by throwing her into the arms of an unprincipled Fortune-hunter,' (replied he).

'Yes,' (exclaimed I) 'amidst every misfortune, it will afford us some consolation to reflect that by this one act of Freindship to Janetta, we have amply discharged every obligation that we have received from her father.'

'It must indeed be a most gratefull reflection, to your exalted minds' (said he).

As soon as we had packed up our wardrobe and valuables, we left Macdonald Hall, and after having walked about a mile and a half we sate down by the side of a clear limpid stream to refresh our exhausted limbs. The place was suited to meditation—. A Grove of full-grown Elms sheltered us from the East—. A Bed of full-grown Nettles from the West—. Before us ran the murmuring brook and behind us ran the turn-pike road.[46] We were in a mood for contemplation and in a Disposition to enjoy so beautifull a spot. A mutual Silence which had for some time reigned between us, was at length broke by my exclaiming—'What a lovely Scene! Alas, why are not Edward and Augustus here to enjoy its Beauties with us?'

'Ah! my beloved Laura' (cried Sophia) 'for pity's sake forbear recalling to my remembrance the unhappy situation of my imprisoned Husband. Alas, what would I not give to learn the fate of my Augustus!—to know if he is still in Newgate, or if he is yet hung.—But never shall I be able so far to conquer my tender sensibility as to enquire after him. Oh! do not I beseech you ever let me again hear you repeat his beloved Name—. It affects me too deeply—. I cannot bear to hear him mentioned, it wounds my feelings.'

'Excuse me my Sophia for having thus unwillingly offended you—' replied I—and then changing the conversation, desired her to admire the Noble Grandeur of the Elms which Sheltered us from the Eastern Zephyr.[47] 'Alas! my Laura' (returned she) 'avoid so melancholy a subject, I intreat you.—Do not again wound my Sensibility by Observations on those elms—. They remind me of Augustus—. He was like them, tall, magestic—he possessed that noble grandeur which you admire in them.'

I was silent, fearfull lest I might any more unwillingly distress her by fixing on any other subject of conversation which might again remind her of Augustus.

'Why do you not speak my Laura?' (said she after a short pause) 'I cannot support this silence—you must not leave me to my own reflections; they ever recur to Augustus.'

'What a beautifull Sky!' (said I) 'How charmingly is the azure varied by those delicate streaks of white!'

'Oh! my Laura' (replied she hastily withdrawing her Eyes from a momentary glance at the sky) 'do not thus distress me by calling my Attention to an object which so cruelly reminds me of my Augustus's blue sattin Waistcoat[48] striped with white! In pity to your unhappy freind avoid a subject so distressing.' What could I do? The feelings of Sophia were at that time so exquisite, and the tenderness she felt for Augustus so poignant that I had not the power to start any other topic, justly fearing that it might in some unforseen manner again awaken all her sensibility by directing her thoughts to her Husband.—Yet to be silent would be cruel; She had intreated me to talk.

From this Dilemma I was most fortunately releived by an accident truly apropos;[49] it was the lucky overturning of a

Gentleman's Phaeton,[50] on the road which ran murmuring behind us. It was a most fortunate Accident as it diverted the Attention of Sophia from the melancholy reflections which she had been before indulging.

We instantly quitted our seats and ran to the rescue of those who but a few moments before had been in so elevated a situation as a fashionably high Phaeton, but who were now laid low and sprawling in the Dust—. 'What an ample subject for reflection on the uncertain Enjoyments of this World, would not that Phaeton and the Life of Cardinal Wolsey[51] afford a thinking Mind!' said I to Sophia as we were hastening to the field of Action.

She had not time to answer me, for every thought was now engaged by the horrid Spectacle before us. Two Gentlemen most elegantly attired but weltering in their blood was what first struck our Eyes—we approached—they were Edward and Augustus—Yes, dearest Marianne, they were our Husbands. Sophia shreiked and fainted on the Ground—I screamed and instantly ran mad—. We remained thus mutually deprived of our Senses some minutes, and on regaining them were deprived of them again—. For an Hour and a Quarter did we continue in this unfortunate Situation—Sophia fainting every moment and I running Mad as often—. At length a Groan from the hapless Edward (who alone retained any share of Life) restored us to ourselves—. Had we indeed before imagined that either of them lived, we should have been more sparing of our Greif—but as we had supposed when we first beheld them that they were no more, we knew that nothing could remain to be done but what we were about—. No sooner therefore did we hear my Edward's groan than postponing our Lamentations for the present, we hastily ran to the Dear Youth and kneeling on each side of him implored him not to die—. 'Laura' (said He fixing his now languid Eyes on me) 'I fear I have been overturned.'

I was overjoyed to find him yet sensible—.[52]

'Oh! tell me Edward' (said I) 'tell me I beseech you before you die, what has befallen you since that unhappy Day in which Augustus was arrested and we were separated—'

'I will' (said he) and instantly fetching a Deep sigh, Expired—.

Sophia immediately sunk again into a swoon—. My Greif was more audible, My Voice faltered, My Eyes assumed a vacant Stare, My face became as pale as Death, and my Senses were considerably impaired—.

'Talk not to me of Phaetons' (said I, raving in a frantic, incoherent manner)— 'Give me a violin—. I'll play to him and sooth him in his melancholy Hours—Beware ye gentle Nymphs of Cupid's Thunderbolts, avoid the piercing Shafts of Jupiter[53]—Look at that Grove of Firs—I see a Leg of Mutton—They told me Edward was not Dead; but they deceived me—they took him for a Cucumber[54]—' Thus I continued wildly exclaiming on my Edward's Death—. For two Hours did I rave thus madly and should not then have left off, as I was not in the least fatigued, had not Sophia who was just recovered from her swoon, intreated me to consider that Night was now approaching and that the Damps began to fall. 'And whither shall we go' (said I) 'to shelter us from either?' 'To that white Cottage.' (replied she pointing to a neat Building which rose up amidst the Grove of Elms and which I had not before observed—). I agreed and we instantly walked to it—we knocked at the door—it was opened by an old Woman; on being requested to afford us a Night's Lodging, she informed us that her House was but small, that she had only two Bed-rooms, but that However we should be wellcome to one of them. We were satisfied and followed the good Woman into the House where we were greatly cheered by the sight of a comfortable fire—. She was a Widow and had only one Daughter, who was then just Seventeen—One of the best of ages; but alas! she was very plain and her name was Bridget[55]. . . . Nothing therefore could be expected from her . . . she could not be supposed to possess either exalted Ideas, Delicate Feelings or refined Sensibilities—She was nothing more than a mere good-tempered, civil and obliging Young Woman; as such we could scarcely dislike her—she was only an Object of Contempt—.

Adeiu
Laura

Letter the 14th

Laura in continuation

Arm yourself, my amiable Young Freind, with all the philosophy you are Mistress of; summon up all the fortitude you possess, for Alas! in the perusal of the following Pages your sensibility will be most severely tried. Ah! what were the Misfortunes I had before experienced and which I have already related to you, to the one I am now going to inform you of. The Death of my Father, my Mother, and my Husband, though almost more than my gentle Nature could support, were trifles in comparison to the misfortune I am now proceeding to relate. The morning after our arrival at the Cottage, Sophia complained of a violent pain in her delicate limbs, accompanied with a disagreable Head-ake. She attributed it to a cold caught by her continued faintings in the open Air as the Dew was falling the Evening before. This I feared was but too probably the case; since how could it be otherwise accounted for that I should have escaped the same indisposition, but by supposing that the bodily Exertions I had undergone in my repeated fits of frenzy, had so effectually circulated and warmed my Blood as to make me proof against the chilling Damps of Night, whereas, Sophia lying totally inactive on the Ground must have been exposed to all their Severity. I was most seriously alarmed by her illness which trifling as it may appear to you, a certain instinctive Sensibility whispered me, would in the End be fatal to her.

Alas! my fears were but too fully justified; she grew gradually worse—and I daily became more alarmed for her.—At length she was obliged to confine herself solely to the Bed allotted us by our worthy Landlady—. Her disorder turned to a galloping Consumption[56] and in a few Days carried her off. Amidst all my Lamentations for her (and violent you may suppose they were) I yet received some consolation in the reflection of my having paid every Attention to her, that could be offered, in her illness. I had wept over her every Day—had bathed her sweet face with my tears and had pressed her fair Hands continually in mine—. 'My beloved Laura' (said she to me a few Hours before she died) 'take warning from my unhappy End and avoid the imprudent conduct which has occasioned it . . . Beware of fainting-fits . . . Though at the time they may be refreshing and Agreable yet beleive me they will in the end, too often repeated and at improper seasons, prove destructive to your Constitution . . . My fate will teach you this . . . I die a Martyr to my greif for the loss of Augustus . . . One fatal swoon has cost me my Life . . . Beware of swoons Dear Laura . . . . A frenzy fit is not one quarter so pernicious; it is an exercise to the Body and if not too violent, is I dare say conducive to Health in its consequences—Run mad as often as you chuse; but do not faint—'.

These were the last words she ever addressed to me . . . It was her dieing Advice to her afflicted Laura, who has ever most faithfully adhered to it.

After having attended my lamented freind to her Early Grave, I immediately (tho' late at night) left the detested Village in which she died, and near which had expired my Husband and Augustus. I had not walked many yards from it before I was overtaken by a Stage-Coach, in which I instantly took a place, determined to proceed in it to Edinburgh, where I hoped to find some kind some pitying Freind who would receive and comfort me in my Afflictions.

It was so dark when I entered the Coach that I could not distinguish the Number of my Fellow-travellers; I could only perceive that they were Many. Regardless however of any thing concerning them, I gave myself up to my own sad Reflections. A general Silence prevailed—A Silence, which was by nothing interrupted but by the loud and repeated Snores of one of the Party.

'What an illiterate villain must that Man be!' (thought I to myself). 'What a total Want of delicate refinement must he have, who can thus shock our senses by such a brutal Noise! He must I am certain be capable of every bad Action! There is no crime too black for such a Character!' Thus reasoned I within myself, and doubtless such were the reflections of my fellow travellers.

At length, returning Day enabled me to behold the unprincipled Scoundrel who had so violently disturbed my feelings. It was Sir Edward the father of my Deceased Husband. By his side, sate Augusta, and on the same seat with me were your Mother and Lady Dorothea. Imagine my Surprize at finding myself thus seated amongst my old Acquaintance. Great as was my astonishment, it was yet increased, when on looking out of Windows, I beheld the Husband of Philippa, with Philippa by his side, on the Coach-box, and when on looking behind, I beheld, Philander and Gustavus in the Basket.[57] 'Oh! Heavens,' (exclaimed I) 'is it possible that I should so unexpectedly be surrounded by my nearest Relations and Connections?' These words rouzed the rest of the Party, and every eye was directed to the corner in which I sat. 'Oh! my Isabel' (continued I throwing myself, across Lady Dorothea into her arms) 'receive once more to your Bosom the unfortunate Laura. Alas! when we last parted in the Vale of Usk, I was happy in being united to the best of Edwards; I had then a Father and a Mother, and had never known misfortunes—But now deprived of every freind but you—'

'What!' (interrupted Augusta) 'is my Brother dead then? Tell us, I intreat you, what is become of him?'

'Yes, cold and insensible Nymph,' (replied I) 'that luckless Swain your Brother, is no more, and you may now glory in being the Heiress of Sir Edward's fortune.'

Although I had always despised her from the Day I had overheard her conversation with my Edward, yet in civility complied with hers and Sir Edward's intreaties that I would inform them of the whole melancholy Affair. They were greatly shocked—Even the obdurate Heart of Sir Edward and the insensible one of Augusta, were touched with Sorrow, by the unhappy tale. At the request of your Mother I related to them every other misfortune which had befallen me since we parted. Of the imprisonment of Augustus and the absence of Edward—of our arrival in Scotland—of our unexpected Meeting with our Grandfather and our cousins—of our visit to Macdonald-Hall—of the singular Service we there performed towards Janetta—her Father's ingratitude for it . . . of his inhuman Behaviour, unaccountable suspicions, and barbarous treatent of us, in obliging us to leave the House . . . of our Lamentations on the loss of Edward and Augustus and finally of the melancholy Death of my beloved Companion.

Pity and Surprise were strongly depictured in your Mother's Countenance, during the whole of my narration, but I am sorry to say, that to the eternal reproach of her Sensibility, the latter infinitely predominated. Nay, faultless as my Conduct had certainly been during the whole Course of my late Misfortunes and Adventures, she pretended to find fault with my Behaviour in many of the situations in which I had been placed. As I was sensible myself, that I had always behaved in a manner which reflected Honour on my Feelings and Refinement, I paid little attention to what she said, and desired her to satisfy my Curiosity by informing me how she came there, instead of wounding my spotless reputation with unjustifiable Reproaches. As soon as she had complyed with my wishes in this particular and had given me an accurate detail of every thing that had fallen her since our separation (the particulars of which you are not already acquainted with, your Mother will give you) I applied to Augusta for the same information respecting herself, Sir Edward and Lady Dorothea.

She told me that having a considerable taste for the Beauties of Nature, her curiosity to behold the delightful scenes it exhibited in that part of the World had been so much raised by Gilpin's Tour to the Highlands,[58] that she had prevailed on her Father to undertake a Tour of Scotland and had persuaded Lady Dorothea to accompany them. That they had arrived at Edinburgh a few Days before and from thence had made daily Excursions into the Country around in the Stage Coach[59] they were then in, from one of which Excursions they were at that time returning. My next enquiries were concerning Philippa and her Husband, the latter of whom I learned having spent all her fortune, had recourse for subsistance to the talent in which, he had always most excelled, namely, Driving, and that having sold every thing which belonged to them except their Coach, had converted it into a Stage,[60] and in order to be removed from any of his former Acquaintance, had driven it to Edinburgh from whence he went to Sterling[61] every other Day; That Philippa still retaining her affection for her ungratefull Husband, had followed him to Scotland and generally accompanied him in his little Excursions to Sterling. 'It has only been to throw a little money into their Pockets' (continued Augusta) 'that my Father has always travelled in their Coach to veiw the beauties of the Country since our arrival in Scotland—for it would certainly have been much more agreable to us, to visit the Highlands in a Postchaise[62] than merely to travel from Edinburgh to Sterling and from Sterling to Edinburgh every other Day in a crouded and uncomfortable Stage.' I perfectly agreed with her in her sentiments on the Affair, and secretly blamed Sir Edward for thus sacrificing his Daughter's Pleasure for the sake of a ridiculous old Woman whose folly in marrying so young a Man ought to be punished. His Behaviour however was entirely of a peice with his general Character; for what could be expected from a Man who possessed not the smallest atom of Sensibility, who scarcely knew the meaning of Simpathy, and who actually snored—.

Adeiu
Laura

Letter the 15th

Laura in continuation

When we arrived at the town where we were to Breakfast, I was determined to speak with Philander and Gustavus, and to that purpose as soon as I left the Carriage, I went to the Basket and tenderly enquired after their Health, expressing my fears of the uneasiness of their Situation. At first they seemed rather confused at my Appearance, dreading no doubt that I might call them to account for the money which our Grandfather had left me and which they had unjustly deprived me of, but finding that I mentioned nothing of the Matter, they desired me to step into the Basket[63] as we might there converse with greater ease. Accordingly I entered and whilst the rest of the party were devouring Green tea and buttered toast, we feasted ourselves in a more refined and Sentimental[64] Manner by a confidential Conversation. I informed them of every thing which had befallen me during the course of my Life, and at my request they related to me every incident of theirs.

'We are the sons as you already know, of the two youngest Daughters which Lord St Clair had by Laurina, an italian Opera girl. Our mothers could neither of them exactly ascertain who were our Fathers; though it is generally beleived that Philander, is the son of one Philip Jones a Bricklayer and that my father was Gregory Staves a Staymaker[65] of Edinburgh. This is however of little consequence, for as our Mothers were certainly never married to either of them, it reflects no Dishonour on our Blood, which is of a most ancient and unpolluted kind. Bertha (the Mother of Philander) and Agatha (my own Mother) always lived together. They were neither of them very rich; their united fortunes had originally amounted to nine thousand Pounds, but as they had always lived upon the principal of it, when we were fifteen it was diminished to nine Hundred.[66] This nine Hundred, they always kept in a Drawer in one of the Tables which stood in our common sitting Parlour, for the Convenience of having it always at Hand. Whether it was from this circumstance, of its being easily taken, or from a wish of being independant, or from an excess of Sensibility (for which we were always remarkable) I cannot now determine, but certain it is that when we had reached our 15th Year, we took the Nine Hundred Pounds and ran away. Having obtained this prize we were determined to manage it with eoconomy and not to spend it either with folly or Extravagance. To this purpose we therefore divided it into nine parcels, one of which we devoted to Victuals, the 2^{d} to Drink, the 3^{d} to House-keeping, the 4th to Carriages, the 5th to Horses, the 6th to Servants, the 7th to Amusements, the 8th to Cloathes and the 9th to Silver Buckles.[67] Having thus arranged our Expences for two Months (for we expected to make the nine Hundred Pounds last as long) we hastened to London and had the good luck to spend it in 7 weeks and a Day which was 6 Days sooner than we had intended. As soon as we had thus happily disencumbered ourselves from the weight of so much Money, we began to think of returning to our Mothers, but accidentally hearing that they were both starved to Death, we gave over the design and determined to engage ourselves to some strolling Company of Players,[68] as we had always a turn for the Stage. Accordingly we offered our Services to one and were accepted; our Company was indeed rather small, as it consisted only of the Manager, his Wife and ourselves, but there were fewer to pay and the only inconvenience attending it was the Scarcity of Plays which for want of People to fill the Characters, we could perform—. We did not mind trifles however—. One of our most admired Performances was *Macbeth*, in which we were truly great. The Manager always played *Banquo* himself, his Wife my *Lady Macbeth*. I did the *Three Witches* and Philander acted *all the rest*. To say the truth this tragedy was not only the Best, but the only Play we ever performed; and after having acted it all over England, and Wales, we came to Scotland to exhibit it over the remainder of Great Britain. We happened to be quartered in that very Town, where you came and met your Grandfather—. We were in the Inn-yard when his Carriage entered and perceiving by the Arms to whom it belonged, and knowing that Lord St Clair was our Grandfather, we agreed to endeavour to get something from him by discovering the Relationship—. You know how well it succeeded—. Having obtained the two Hundred pounds, we instantly left the Town, leaving our Manager and his wife to act *Macbeth* by themselves, and took the road to Sterling, where we spent our little fortune with great *eclat*.[69] We are now returning to Edinburgh in order to get some preferment[70] in the Acting way; and such, my Dear Cousin, is our History.'

I thanked the amiable Youth for his entertaining Narration, and after expressing my Wishes for their Welfare and Happiness, left them in their little Habitation and returned to my other Freinds who impatiently expected me.

My Adventures are now drawing to a close my dearest Marianne; at least for the present.

When we arrived at Edinburgh Sir Edward told me that as the Widow of his Son, he desired I would accept from his Hands of four Hundred a year. I graciously promised that I would, but could not help observing that the unsimpathetic Baronet offered it more on account of my being the Widow of Edward than in being the refined and Amiable Laura.

I took up my Residence in a romantic Village in the Highlands of Scotland, where I have ever since continued, and where I can uninterrupted by unmeaning Visits, indulge in a melancholy Solitude, my unceasing Lamentations for the Death of my Father, my Mother, my Husband and my Freind.

Augusta has been for several Years united to Graham the Man of all others most suited to her; she became acquainted with him during her stay in Scotland.

Sir Edward in hopes of gaining an Heir to his Title and Estate, at the same time married Lady Dorothea—. His wishes have been answered.

Philander and Gustavus, after having raised their reputation by their Performances in the Theatrical Line at Edinburgh, removed to Covent Garden, where they still Exhibit under the assumed names of Lewis and Quick.[71]

Philippa has long paid the Debt of Nature,[72] Her Husband however still continues to drive the Stage-Coach from Edinburgh to Sterling:—

Adeiu my Dearest Marianne.

Laura

Finis

June 13th 1790

To Henry Thomas Austen Esqre—.[1]

Sir

I am now availing myself of the Liberty you have frequently honoured me with of dedicating one of my Novels to you. That it is unfinished, I greive; yet fear that from me, it will always remain so; that as far as it is carried, it Should be so trifling and so unworthy of you, is

another concern to your obliged humble

Servant

The Author

Messrs Demand and Co[2]—please to pay Jane Austen Spinster the sum of one hundred guineas on account of your Hum^{bl} Servant.

H T Austen

£105.0.0

Lesley Castle
an unfinished Novel in Letters

Letter The first is from

Miss Margaret Lesley to Miss Charlotte Lutterell

Lesley-Castle Jan^{ry} 3^{d}—1792

My Brother has just left us. 'Matilda'[3] (said he at parting) 'you and Margaret will I am certain take all the care of my dear little one, that she might have received from an indulgent, an affectionate an amiable Mother.' Tears rolled down his cheeks as he spoke these words—the remembrance of her, who had so wantonly disgraced the Maternal character and so openly violated the conjugal Duties, prevented his adding anything farther; he embraced his sweet Child and after saluting Matilda and Me hastily broke from us—and seating himself in his Chaise, pursued the road to Aberdeen.[4] Never was there a better young Man! Ah! how little did he deserve the misfortunes he has experienced in the Marriage State. So good a Husband to so bad a Wife! for you know my dear Charlotte that the Worthless Louisa left him, her Child and reputation a few weeks ago in company with Danvers and *dishonour.[5] Never was there a sweeter face, a finer form, or a less amiable Heart than Louisa owned! Her child already possesses the personal Charms of her unhappy Mother! May she inherit from her Father all his mental ones! Lesley is at present but five and twenty, and has already given himself up to Melancholy and

* Rakehelly Dishonor Esqre [JA's note]

Despair; what a difference between him and his Father! Sir George is 57 and still remains the Beau, the flighty stripling, the gay Lad and sprightly Youngster, that his Son was really about five years back, and that he has affected to appear ever since my remembrance. While our father is fluttering about the streets of London, gay, dissipated, and Thoughtless at the age of 57, Matilda and I continue secluded from Mankind in our old and Mouldering Castle, which is situated two miles from Perth[6] on a bold projecting Rock, and commands an extensive veiw of the Town and its delightful Environs. But tho' retired from almost all the World, (for we visit no one but the M'Leods, The M'Kenzies, the M'Phersons, the M'Cartneys, the M'donalds, The M'Kinnons, the M'lellans, the M'Kays, the Macbeths and the Macduffs)[7] we are neither dull nor unhappy; on the contrary there never were two more lively, more agreable or more witty Girls, than we are; not an hour in the Day hangs heavy on our hands. We read, we work, we walk, and when fatigued with these Employments releive our spirits, either by a lively song, a graceful Dance, or by some smart bon-mot, and witty repartée.[8] We are handsome my dear Charlotte, very handsome and the greatest of our Perfections is, that we are entirely insensible of them ourselves. But why do I thus dwell on myself? Let me rather repeat the praise of our dear little Neice the innocent Louisa, who is at present sweetly smiling in a gentle Nap, as she reposes on the Sofa. The dear Creature is just turned of two years old; as handsome as tho' 2 and 20, as sensible as tho' 2 and 30, and as prudent as tho' 2 and 40. To convince you of this, I must inform you that she has a very fine complexion and very pretty features, that she already knows the two first Letters in the Alphabet, and that she never tears her frocks—. If I have not now convinced you of her Beauty, Sense and Prudence, I have nothing more to urge in support of my assertion, and you will therefore have no way of deciding the Affair but by coming to Lesley-castle, and by a personal acquaintance with Louisa, determine for yourself. Ah! my dear Freind, how happy should I be to see you within these venerable Walls! It is now four years since my removal from School has separated me from you; that two such tender Hearts, so closely linked together by the ties of simpathy and Freindship, should be so widely removed from each other, is vastly moving. I live in Perthshire, You in Sussex.[9] We might meet in London, were my Father disposed to carry me there, and were your Mother to be there at the same time. We might meet at Bath, at Tunbridge,[10] or any where else indeed, could we but be at the same place together. We have only to hope that such a period may arrive. My Father does not return to us till Autumn; my Brother will leave Scotland in a few Days; he is impatient to travel. Mistaken Youth! He vainly flatters himself that change of Air will heal the Wounds of a broken Heart! You will join with me I am certain my dear Charlotte, in prayers for the recovery of the unhappy Lesley's peace of Mind, which must ever be essential to that of your sincere freind

M. Lesley

Letter the second

From Miss C. Lutterell to Miss M. Lesley in answer

Glenford Feb[ry] 12

I have a thousand excuses to beg for having so long delayed thanking you my dear Peggy[11] for your agreable Letter, which beleive me I should not have deferred doing, had not every moment of my time during the last five weeks been so fully employed in the necessary arrangements for my sister's Wedding, as to allow me no time to devote either to you or myself. And now what provokes me more than anything else is that the Match is broke off, and all my Labour thrown away. Imagine how great the Dissapointment must be to me, when you consider that after having laboured both by Night and by Day, in order to get the Wedding dinner ready by the time appointed, after having roasted Beef, Broiled Mutton, and Stewed Soup[12] enough to last the new-married Couple through the Honey-moon, I had the mortification of finding that I had been Roasting,

Broiling and Stewing both the Meat and Myself to no purpose. Indeed my dear Freind, I never remember suffering any vexation equal to what I experienced on last Monday when my Sister came running to me in the Store-room with her face as White as a Whipt syllabub,[13] and told me that Hervey had been thrown from his Horse, had fractured his Scull and was pronounced by his Surgeon to be in the most emminent Danger.

'Good God!' (said I) 'you don't say so? why what in the name of Heaven will become of all the Victuals! We shall never be able to eat it while it is good. However, we'll call in the Surgeon to help us—. I shall be able to manage the Sir-loin myself; my Mother will eat the Soup, and You and the Doctor must finish the rest.' Here I was interrupted, by seeing my poor Sister fall down to appearance Lifeless upon one of the Chests, where we keep our Table linen. I immediately called my Mother and the Maids, and at last we brought her to herself again; as soon as ever she was sensible, she expressed a determination of going instantly to Henry, and was so wildly bent on this Scheme, that we had the greatest Difficulty in the World to prevent her putting it in execution; at last however more by Force than Entreaty we prevailed on her to go into her room; we laid her upon the Bed, and she continued for some Hours in the most dreadful Convulsions. My Mother and I continued in the room with her, and when any intervals of tolerable Composure in Eloisa[14] would allow us, we joined in heartfelt lamentations on the dreadful Waste in our provisions which this Event must occasion, and in concerting some plan for getting rid of them. We agreed that the best thing we could do was to begin eating them immediately, and accordingly we ordered up the cold Ham and Fowls, and instantly began our Devouring Plan on them with great Alacrity. We would have persuaded Eloisa to have taken a Wing of a Chicken, but she would not be persuaded. She was however much quieter than she had been; the Convulsions she had before suffered having given way to an almost perfect Insensibility. We endeavoured to rouse her by every means in our power, but to no purpose. I talked to her of Henry.

'Dear Eloisa' (said I) 'there's no occasion for your crying so much about such a trifle' (for I was willing to make light of it in order to comfort her) 'I beg you would not mind it—. You see it does not vex me in the least; though perhaps I may suffer most from it after all; for I shall not only be obliged to eat up all the Victuals I have dressed[15] already, but must if Hervey should recover (which however is not very likely) dress as much for you again; or should he die (as I suppose he will) I shall still have to prepare a Dinner for you whenever you marry any one else. So you see that tho' perhaps for the present it may afflict you to think of Henry's sufferings, Yet I dare say he'll die soon, and then his pain will be over and you will be easy, whereas my Trouble will last much longer for work as hard as I may, I am certain that the pantry cannot be cleared in less than a fortnight.' Thus I did all in my power to console her, but without any effect, and at last as I saw that she did not seem to listen to me, I said no more, but leaving her with my Mother I took down the remains of The Ham and Chicken, and sent William to ask how Hervey did. He was not expected to live many Hours; he died the same day. We took all possible Care to break the Melancholy Event to Eloisa in the tenderest manner; yet in spite of every precaution, her Sufferings on hearing it were too violent for her reason, and she continued for many hours in a high Delirium. She is still extremely ill, and her Physicians are greatly afraid of her going into a Decline.[16] We are therefore preparing for Bristol,[17] where we mean to be in the course of the next Week. And now my dear Margaret let me talk a little of your affairs; and in the first place I must inform you that it is confidently reported, your Father is going to be married; I am very unwilling to beleive so unpleasing a report, and at the same time cannot wholly discredit it. I have written to my freind Susan Fitzgerald, for information concerning it, which as she is at present in Town, she will be very able to give me. I know not who is the Lady. I think your Brother is extremely right in the resolution he has taken of travelling, as it will perhaps contribute to obliterate from his remembrance, those disagreable Events, which have lately so much afflicted him—I am happy to find that tho' secluded from all the World, neither You nor Matilda are dull or unhappy—that you may never know what it is to be either is the Wish of your Sincerely Affectionate

C. L.

P.S. I have this instant received an answer from my freind Susan, which I enclose to you, and on which you will make your own reflections.

The enclosed Letter

My dear Charlotte

You could not have applied for information concerning the report of Sir George Lesley's Marriage, to any one better able to give it you than I am. Sir George is certainly married; I was myself present at the Ceremony, which you will not be surprised at when I subscribe myself your

Affectionate Susan Lesley

Letter the third

From Miss Margaret Lesley to Miss C. Lutterell

Lesley Castle February the 16th

I have made my own reflections on the letter you enclosed to me, my Dear Charlotte and I will now tell you what those reflections were. I reflected that if by this second Marriage Sir George should have a second family, our fortunes must be considerably diminushed—that if his Wife should be of an extravagant turn, she would encourage him to persevere that Gay and Dissipated way of Life to which little encouragement would be necessary, and which has I fear already proved but too detrimental to his health and fortune—that she would now become Mistress of those Jewels which once adorned our Mother,[18] and which Sir George had always promised us—that if they did not come into Perthshire I should not be able to gratify my curiosity of beholding my Mother-in-law, and that if they did, Matilda would no longer sit at the head of her Father's table—. These my dear Charlotte were the melancholy reflections which crouded into my imagination after perusing Susan's letter to you, and which instantly occurred to Matilda when she had perused it likewise. The same ideas, the same fears, immediately occupied her Mind, and I know not which reflection distressed her most, whether the probable Diminution of our Fortunes, or her own Consequence. We both wish very much to know whether Lady Lesley is handsome and what is your opinion of her; as you honour her with the appellation of your freind, we flatter ourselves that she must be amiable. My Brother is already in Paris. He intends to quit it in a few Days, and to begin his route to Italy. He writes in a most chearfull Manner, says that the air of France has greatly recovered both his Health and Spirits; that he has now entirely ceased to think of Louisa with any degree either of Pity or Affection, that he even feels himself obliged to her for her Elopement, as he thinks it very good fun to be single again. By this, you may perceive that he has entirely regained that chearful Gaiety, and sprightly Wit, for which he was once so remarkable. When he first became acquainted with Louisa which was little more than three Years ago, he was one of the most lively, the most agreable young Men of the age—. I beleive you never yet heard the particulars of his first acquaintance with her. It commenced at our cousin Colonel Drummond's; at whose house in Cumberland he spent the Christmas, in which he attained the age of two and twenty. Louisa Burton was the Daughter of a distant Relation of Mrs Drummond, who dieing a few Months before in extreme poverty, left his only Child then about eighteen to the protection of any of his Relations who would protect her. Mrs Drummond was the only one who found herself so disposed—Louisa was therefore removed from a miserable Cottage in Yorkshire to an elegant Mansion in Cumberland, and from every pecuniary Distress that Poverty could inflict, to every elegant Enjoyment that Money could purchase—. Louisa was naturally ill-tempered and Cunning; but she had been taught to disguise her real Disposition, under the appearance of insinuating Sweetness by a father who but too well knew, that to be married, would be the only chance she would have of not being starved, and who flattered himself that with such an extroidinary share of personal beauty, joined to a gentleness of Manners, and an engaging address, she might stand a good chance of pleasing some young Man who might afford to marry a Girl without a Shilling. Louisa perfectly entered into her father's schemes and was determined to forward them with all her care and attention. By dint of Perseverance and Application, she had at length so thoroughly disguised her natural disposition under the mask of Innocence and Softness, as to impose upon every one who had not by a long and constant intimacy with her discovered her real Character. Such was Louisa when the hapless Lesley first beheld her at Drummond-house. His heart which (to use your favourite comparison) was as delicate as sweet and as tender as a Whipt-syllabub, could not resist her attractions. In a very few Days, he was falling in love, shortly afterwards actually fell, and before he had known her a Month, he had married her. My Father was at first highly displeased at so hasty and imprudent a connection; but when he found that they did not mind it, he soon became perfectly reconciled to the match. The Estate near Aberdeen which my brother possesses by the bounty of his great Uncle independant of Sir George, was entirely sufficient to support him and my Sister in Elegance and Ease. For the first twelvemonth, no one could be happier than Lesley, and no one more amiable to appearance than Louisa, and so plausibly did she act and so cautiously behave that tho' Matilda and I often spent several weeks together with them, yet we neither of us had any suspicion of her real Disposition. After the birth of Louisa however, which one would have thought would have strengthened her regard for Lesley, the mask she had so long supported was by degrees thrown aside, and as probably she then thought herself secure in the affection of her Husband (which did indeed appear if possible augmented by the birth of his Child) She seemed to take no pains to prevent that affection from ever diminushing. Our visits therefore to Dunbeath,[19] were now less frequent and by far less agreable than they used to be. Our absence was however never either mentioned or lamented by Louisa who in the society of young Danvers with whom she became acquainted at Aberdeen (he was at one of the Universities there,) felt infinitely happier than in that of Matilda and your freind, tho' there certainly never were pleasanter Girls than we are. You know the sad end of all Lesley's connubial happiness; I will not repeat it—. Adeiu my dear Charlotte; although I have not yet mentioned any thing of the matter, I hope you will do me the justice to beleive that I think and feel, a great deal for your Sister's affliction. I do not doubt but that the healthy air of the Bristol-downs,[20] will intirely remove it, by erasing from her Mind the remembrance of Henry. I am my dear Charlotte y^rs ever

ML

Letter the fourth

From Miss C. Lutterell to Miss M. Lesley

Bristol February 27th

My dear Peggy

I have but just received your letter, which being directed to Sussex while I was at Bristol was obliged to be forwarded to me here, and from some unaccountable Delay, has but this instant reached me—. I return you many thanks for the account it contains of Lesley's acquaintance, Love and Marriage with Louisa, which has not the less entertained me for having often been repeated to me before.

I have the satisfaction of informing you that we have every reason to imagine our pantry is by this time nearly cleared, as we left particular orders with the Servants to eat as hard as they possibly could, and to call in a couple of Chairwomen[21] to assist them. We brought a cold Pigeon-pye, a cold turkey, a cold tongue, and half a dozen Jellies[22] with us, which we were lucky enough with the help of our Landlady, her husband, and their three children, to get rid of, in less than two days after our arrival. Poor Eloisa is still so very indifferent both in Health and Spirits, that I very much fear, the air of the Bristol-downs, healthy as it is, has not been able to drive poor Henry from her remembrance—.

You ask me whether your new Mother in law is handsome and amiable—I will now give you an exact description of her bodily and Mental charms. She is short, and extremely well-made; is naturally pale, but rouges a good deal;[23] has fine eyes, and fine teeth, as she will take care to let you know as soon as she sees you, and is altogether very pretty. She is remarkably good-tempered when she has her own way, and very lively when she is not out of humour. She is naturally extravagant and not very affected; she never reads anything but the letters she receives from me, and never writes anything but her answers to them. She plays, sings and Dances, but has no taste for either, and excells in none, tho' she says she is passionately fond of all. Perhaps you may flatter me so far as to be surprised that one of whom I speak with so little affection should be my particular freind; but to tell you the truth, our freindship arose rather from Caprice on her side, than Esteem on mine. We spent two or three days together with a Lady in Berkshire with whom we both happened to be connected—During our visit, the Weather being remarkably bad, and our party particularly stupid, she was so good as to conceive a violent partiality for me, which very soon settled in a downright Freindship, and ended in an established correspondence. She is probably by this time as tired of me, as I am of her; but as she is too polite and I am too civil to say so, our letters are still as frequent and affectionate as ever, and our Attachment as firm and sincere as when it first commenced.—As she has a great taste for the pleasures of London, and of Brighthelmstone,[24] she will I dare say find some difficulty in prevailing on herself even to satisfy the curiosity I dare say she feels of beholding you, at the expence of quitting those favourite haunts of Dissipation, for the melancholy tho' venerable gloom of the castle you inhabit. Perhaps however if she finds her health impaired by too much amusement, she may acquire fortitude sufficient to undertake a Journey to Scotland in the hope of its proving at least beneficial to her health, if not conducive to her happiness. Your fears I am sorry to say, concerning your father's extravagance, your own fortunes, your Mother's Jewels and your Sister's consequence, I should suppose are but too well founded. My freind herself has four thousand pounds,[25] and will probably spend nearly as much every year in Dress and Public places, if she can get it—she will certainly not endeavour to reclaim Sir George from the manner of living to which he has been so long accustomed, and there is therefore some reason to fear that you will be very well off, if you get any fortune at all. The Jewels I should imagine too will undoubtedly be hers, and there is too much reason to think that she will preside at her Husband's table in preference to his Daughter. But as so melancholy a subject must necessarily extremely distress you, I will no longer dwell on it—.

Eloisa's indisposition has brought us to Bristol at so unfashionable a season of the year, that we have actually seen but one genteel family since we came. M^r and Mrs Marlowe are very agreable people; the ill health of their little boy occasioned their arrival here; you may imagine that being the only family with whom we can converse, we are of course on a footing of intimacy with them; we see them indeed almost every day, and dined with them yesterday. We spent a very pleasant Day, and had a very good Dinner, tho' to be sure the Veal was terribly underdone, and the Curry[26] had no seasoning. I could not help wishing all dinner-time that I had been at the dressing it—. A brother of Mrs Marlowe, Mr Cleveland, is with them at present; he is a good-looking young Man and seems to have a good deal to say for himself. I tell Eloisa that she should set her cap at him,[27] but she does not at all seem to relish the proposal. I should like to see the girl married and Cleveland has a very good estate. Perhaps you may wonder that I do not consider myself as well as my Sister in my matrimonial Projects; but to tell you the truth I never wish to act a more principal part at a Wedding than the superintending and directing the Dinner, and therefore while I can get any of my acquaintance to marry for me, I shall never think of doing it myself, as I very much suspect that I should not have so much time for dressing my own Wedding-dinner, as for dressing that of my freinds. Y[rs] sincerely

CL

Letter the fifth

Miss Margaret Lesley to Miss Charlotte Lutterell

Lesley-Castle March 18th

On the same day that I received your last kind letter, Matilda received one from Sir George which was dated from Edinburgh, and informed us that he should do himself the pleasure of introducing Lady Lesley to us on the following evening. This as you may suppose considerably surprised us, particularly as your account of her Ladyship had given us reason to imagine there was little chance of her visiting Scotland at a time that London must be so gay. As it was our business however to be delighted at such a mark of condescension as a visit from Sir George and Lady Lesley, we prepared to return them an answer expressive of the happiness we enjoyed in expectation of such a Blessing, when luckily recollecting that as they were to reach the Castle the next Evening, it would be impossible for my father to receive it before he left Edinburgh, We contented ourselves with leaving them to suppose that we were as happy as we ought to be. At nine in the Evening on the following day, they came, accompanied by one of Lady Lesley's brothers. Her Ladyship perfectly answers the description you sent me of her, except that I do not think her so pretty as you seem to consider her. She has not a bad face, but there is something so extremely unmajestic in her little diminutive figure, as to render her in comparison with the elegant height of Matilda and Myself, an insignificant Dwarf. Her curiosity to see us (which must have been great to bring her more than four hundred miles) being now perfectly gratified, she already begins to mention their return to town, and has desired us to accompany her—. We cannot refuse her request since it is seconded by the commands of our Father, and thirded by the entreaties of Mr Fitzgerald who is certainly one of the most pleasing young Men, I ever beheld. It is not yet determined when we are to go, but when ever we do we shall certainly take our little Louisa with us. Adeiu my dear Charlotte; Matilda unites in best Wishes to You and Eloisa, with yours ever

ML

Letter the sixth

Lady Lesley to Miss Charlotte Lutterell

Lesley-Castle March 20th

We arrived here my sweet Freind about a fortnight ago, and I already heartily repent that I ever left our charming House in Portman-Square[28] for such a dismal old Weather-beaten Castle as this. You can form no idea sufficiently hideous, of its dungeon-like form. It is actually perched upon a Rock to appearance so totally inaccessible, that I expected to have been pulled up by a rope; and sincerely repented having gratified my curiosity to behold my Daughters at the expence of being obliged to enter their prison in so dangerous and ridiculous a Manner. But as soon as I once found myself safely arrived in the inside of this tremendous building, I comforted myself with the hope of having my spirits revived, by the sight of the two beautifull Girls, such as the Miss Lesleys had been represented to me, at Edinburgh. But here again, I met with nothing but Dissapointment and Surprise. Matilda and Margaret Lesley are two great, tall, out of the way, overgrown Girls, just of a proper size to inhabit a Castle almost as Large in comparison as themselves. I wish my dear Charlotte that you could but behold these Scotch Giants; I am sure they would frighten you out of your wits. They will do very well as foils to myself, so I have invited them to accompany me to London where I hope to be in the course of a fortnight. Besides these two fair Damsels, I found a little humoured Brat here who I beleive is some relation to them; they told me who she was, and gave me a long rigmerole Story of her father and Miss Somebody which I have entirely forgot. I hate Scandal and detest Children.—I have been plagued ever since I came here with tiresome visits from a parcel of Scotch wretches, with terrible hard-names; they were so civil, gave me so many invitations, and talked of coming again so soon, that I could not help affronting them. I suppose I shall not see them any more, and yet as a family party we are so stupid, that I do not know what to do with myself. These girls have no Music, but Scotch Airs, no Drawings but Scotch Mountains, and no Books but Scotch Poems—And I hate everything Scotch.[29] In general I can spend half the Day at my toilett[30] with a great deal of pleasure, but why should I dress here, since there is not a creature in the House whom I have any wish to please.—I have just had a conversation with my Brother in which he has greatly offended me, and which as I have nothing more entertaining to send you I will give you the particulars of. You must know that I have for these 4 or 5 Days past strongly suspected William of entertaining a partiality for my eldest Daughter. I own indeed that had I been inclined to fall in love with any woman, I should not have made choice of Matilda Lesley for the object of my passion; for there is nothing I hate so much as a tall Woman: but however there is no accounting for some men's taste and as William is himself nearly six feet high, it is not wonderful that he should be partial to that height. Now as I have a very great Affection for my Brother and should be extremely sorry to see him unhappy, which I suppose he means to be if he cannot marry Matilda, as moreover I know that his Circumstances will not allow him to marry any one with out a fortune, and that Matilda's is entirely dependant on her Father, who will neither have his own inclination, nor my permission to give her anything at present, I thought it would be doing a good-natured action by my Brother to let him know as much, in order that he might choose for himself, whether to conquer his passion, or Love and Despair. Accordingly finding myself this Morning alone with him in one of the horrid old rooms of this Castle, I opened the Cause to him in the following Manner.

'Well my dear William what do you think of these girls? for my part, I do not find them so plain as I expected: but perhaps you may think me partial to the Daughters of my Husband and perhaps you are right—They are indeed so very like Sir George that it is natural to think . . . .'

'My Dear Susan' (cried he in a tone of the greatest amazement), 'You do not really think they bear the least resemblance to their Father! He is so very plain!—but I beg your pardon—I had entirely forgotten to whom I was speaking—'

'Oh! pray don't mind me;' (replied I) 'every one knows Sir George is horribly ugly, and I assure you I always thought him a fright.'

'You surprise me extremely' (answered William) 'by what you say both with respect to Sir George and his Daughters. You cannot think your Husband so deficient in personal Charms as you speak of, nor can you surely see any resemblance between him and the Miss Lesleys who are in my opinion perfectly unlike him and perfectly Handsome.'

'If that is your opinion with regard to the Girls it certainly is no proof of their Father's beauty, for if they are perfectly unlike him and very handsome at the same time, it is natural to suppose that he is very plain.'

'By no means,' (said he) 'for what may be pretty in a Woman, may be very unpleasing in a Man.'

'But you yourself' (replied I) 'but a few Minutes ago allowed him to be very plain.'

'Men are no Judges of Beauty in their own Sex,' (said he).

'Neither Men nor Women can think Sir George tolerable.'

'Well, well,' (said he) 'we will not dispute about <u>his</u> Beauty, but your opinion of his <u>Daughters</u> is surely very singular, for if I understood you right, you said you did not find them so plain as you expected to do!'

'Why, do <u>you</u> find them plainer then?' (said I).

'I can scarcely beleive you to be serious' (returned he) 'when you speak of their persons in so extroidinary a Manner. Do not you think the Miss Lesleys are two very handsome Young Women?'

'Lord! No!' (cried I) 'I think them terribly plain!'

'Plain!' (replied He) 'My dear Susan, you cannot really think so! Why what single Feature in the face of either of them, can you possibly find fault with?'

'Oh! trust me for that;' (replied I). 'Come, I will begin with the eldest—with Matilda. Shall I, William?' (I looked as cunning as I could when I said it, in order to shame him.)

'They are so much alike' (said he) 'that I should suppose the faults of one, would be the faults of both.'

'Well, then, in the first place, they are both so horribly tall!'

'They are <u>taller</u> than you are indeed,' (said he with a saucy smile).

'Nay,' (said I); 'I know nothing of that.'

'Well, but' (he continued) 'tho' they may be above the common size, their figures are perfectly elegant; and as to their faces, their Eyes are beautifull—.'

'I never can think such tremendous, knock-me-down figures in the least degree elegant, and as for their eyes, they are so tall that I never could strain my neck enough to look at them.'

'Nay,' (replied he), 'I know not whether you may not be in the right in not attempting it, for perhaps they might dazzle you with their Lustre.'

'Oh! Certainly.' (said I, with the greatest Complacency, for I assure you my dearest Charlotte I was not in the least offended tho' by what followed, one would suppose that William was conscious of having given me just cause to be so, for coming up to me and taking my hand, he said) 'You must not look so grave Susan; you will make me fear I have offended you!'

'Offended me! Dear Brother, how came such a thought in your head!' (returned I) 'No, really! I assure you that I am not in the least surprised at your being so warm an advocate for the Beauty of these Girls—'

'Well, but' (interrupted William) 'remember that we have not yet concluded our dispute concerning them. What fault do you find with their complexion?'

'They are so horridly pale.'

'They always have a little colour, and after any exercise it is considerably heightened.'

'Yes, but if there should ever happen to be any rain in this part of the world, they will never be able to raise more than their common stock—except indeed they amuse themselves with running up and Down these horrid old Galleries and Antichambers—'[31]

'Well,' (replied my Brother in a tone of vexation, and glancing an impertinent Look at me) 'if they <u>have</u> but little colour, at least, it is all their own.'

This was too much my dear Charlotte, for I am certain that he had the impudence by that look, of pretending to suspect the reality of mine. But you I am sure will vindicate my character whenever you may hear it so cruelly aspersed, for you can witness how often I have protested against wearing Rouge, and how much I always told you I disliked it. And I assure you that my opinions are still the same.—Well, not bearing to be so suspected by my Brother, I left the room immediately, and have ever since been in my own Dressing-room writing to you. What a long Letter have I made of it! But you must not expect to receive such from me when I get to Town; for it is only at Lesley castle, that one has time to write even to a Charlotte Lutterell.—I was so much vexed by William's Glance, that I could not summon Patience enough, to stay and give him that Advice respecting his Attachment to Matilda which had first induced me from pure Love to him to begin the conversation; and I am now so thoroughly convinced by it, of his violent passion for her, that I am certain he would never hear reason on the Subject, and I shall therefore give myself no more trouble either about him or his favourite. Adeiu my dear Girl—

Y[rs] Affectionately Susan L

Letter the Seventh

From Miss C. Lutterell to Miss M. Lesley

Bristol the 27th of March

I have received Letters from You and your Mother-in-law within this week which have greatly entertained me, as I find by them that you are both downright jealous of each other's Beauty. It is very odd that two pretty Women tho' actually Mother and Daughter cannot be in the same House without falling out about their faces. Do be convinced that you are both perfectly handsome and say no more of the Matter. I suppose this Letter must be directed to Portman Square where probably (great as is your affection for Lesley Castle) you will not be sorry to find yourself. In spite of all that People may say about Green fields and the Country I was always of the opinion that London and its Amusements must be very agreable for a while, and should be very happy could my Mother's income allow her to jockey us into its Public-places,[32] during Winter. I always longed particularly to go to Vaux-hall,[33] to see whether the cold Beef there is cut so thin[34] as it is reported, for I have a sly suspicion that few people understand the art of cutting a slice of cold Beef so well as I do: nay it would be hard if I did not know something of the Matter, for it was a part of my Education that I took by far the most pains with. Mama always found me <u>her</u> best Scholar, tho' when Papa was alive Eloisa was <u>his</u>. Never to be sure were there two more different Dispositions in the World. We both loved Reading. <u>She</u> preferred Histories, and <u>I</u> Receipts.[35] She loved drawing Pictures, and I drawing Pullets.[36] No one could sing a better Song than She, and no one make a better Pye than I.—And so it has always continued since we have been no longer Children. The only difference is that all disputes on the superior excellence of our Employments <u>then</u> so frequent are now no more. We have for many years entered into an agreement always to admire each other's works; I never fail listening to <u>her</u> Music, and she is as constant in eating <u>my</u>

pies. Such at least was the case till Henry Hervey made his appearance in Sussex. Before the arrival of his Aunt in our neighbourhood where she established herself you know about a twelvemonth ago, his visits to her had been at stated times, and of equal and settled Duration; but on her removal to the Hall which is within a walk from our House, they became both more frequent and longer. This as you may suppose could not be pleasing to Mrs Diana who is a professed Enemy to everything which is not directed by Decorum and Formality, or which bears the least resemblance to Ease and Good-breeding. Nay so great was her aversion to her Nephew's behaviour that I have often heard her give such hints of it before his face that had not Henry at such times been engaged in conversation with Eloisa, they must have caught his Attention and have very much distressed him. The alteration in my Sister's behaviour which I have before hinted at, now took place. The Agreement we had entered into of admiring each other's productions she no longer seemed to regard, and tho' I constantly applauded even every Country-dance,[37] She play'd, yet not even a pidgeon-pye of my making could obtain from her a single word of approbation. This was certainly enough to put any one in a Passion; however, I was as cool as a Cream-cheese and having formed my plan and concerted a scheme of Revenge, I was determined to let her have her own way and not even to make her a single reproach. My Scheme was to treat her as she treated me, and tho' she might even draw my own Picture or play Malbrook[38] (which is the only tune I ever really liked) not to say so much as 'Thank you Eloisa'; tho' I had for many years constantly hollowed whenever she played, Bravo, Bravissimo, Encora, Da Capo, allegretto, con espressione, and Poco presto[39] with many other such outlandish words, all of them as Eloisa told me expressive of my Admiration; and so indeed I suppose they are, as I see some of them in every Page of every Music book, being the Sentiments I imagine of the Composer.

I executed my Plan with great Punctuality; I can not say success, for Alas! my silence while she played seemed not in the least to displease her; on the contrary she actually said to me one day 'Well Charlotte, I am very glad to find that you have at last left off that ridiculous custom of applauding my Execution on the Harpsichord[40] till you made my head ake, and yourself hoarse. I feel very much obliged to you for keeping your Admiration to yourself.' I never shall forget the very witty answer I made to this speech.

'Eloisa' (said I) 'I beg you would be quite at your Ease with respect to all such fears in future, for be assured that I shall always keep my Admiration to myself and my own pursuits and never extend it to yours.' This was the only very severe thing I ever said in my Life; not but that I have often felt myself extremely satirical but it was the only time I ever made my feelings public.

I suppose there never were two young people who had a greater affection for each other than Henry and Eloisa; no, the Love of your Brother for Miss Burton could not be so strong tho' it might be more violent. You may imagine therefore how provoked my Sister must have been to have him play her such a trick. Poor Girl! she still laments his Death with undiminushed Constancy, notwithstanding he has been dead more than six weeks; but some people mind such things more than others. The ill state of Health into which his Loss has thrown her makes her so weak, and so unable to support the least exertion, that she has been in tears all this Morning merely from having taken Leave of M[rs] Marlowe who with her Husband, Brother and Child are to leave Bristol this Morning. I am sorry to have them go because they are the only family with whom we have here any acquaintance, but I never thought of crying; to be sure Eloisa and M[rs] Marlowe have always been more together than with me, and have therefore contracted a kind of affection for each other, which does not make Tears so inexcusable in them as they would be in me. The Marlowes are going to Town; Cleveland accompanies them; as neither Eloisa nor I could catch him I hope You or Matilda may have better Luck. I know not when we shall leave Bristol, Eloisa's Spirits are so low that she is very averse to moving, and yet is certainly by no means mended by her residence here. A week or two will I hope determine our Measures—in the mean time beleive me

etc—etc—Charlotte Lutterell

Letter the Eighth

Miss Lutterell to Mrs Marlowe

Bristol April 4th

I feel myself greatly obliged to you my dear Emma for such a mark of your affection as I flatter myself was conveyed in the proposal you made me of our Corresponding; I assure you that it will be a great releif to me to write to you and as long as my Health and Spirits will allow me, you will find me a very constant Correspondent; I will not say an entertaining one, for you know my situation sufficiently not to be ignorant than in me Mirth would be improper and I know my own Heart too well not to be sensible that it would be unnatural. You must not expect News for we see no one with whom we are in the least acquainted, or in whose proceedings we have any Interest. You must not expect Scandal for by the same rule we are equally debarred either from hearing or inventing it.—You must expect from me nothing but the melancholy effusions of a broken Heart which is ever reverting to the Happiness it once enjoyed and which ill supports its present wretchedness. The Possibility of being able to write, to speak to you of my lost Henry will be a Luxury to me, and your Goodness will not I know refuse to read what it will so much releive my Heart to write. I once thought that to have what is in general called a Freind (I mean one of my own Sex to whom I might speak with less reserve than to any other person) independant of my Sister would never be an object of my wishes, but how much was I mistaken! Charlotte is too much engrossed by two confidential Correspondents of that sort, to supply the place of one to me, and I hope you will not think me girlishly romantic, when I say that to have some kind and compassionate Freind who might listen to my Sorrows without endeavouring to console me was what I had for some time wished for, when our acquaintance with you, the intimacy which followed it and the particular affectionate Attention you paid me almost from the first, caused me to entertain the flattering Idea of those attentions being improved on a closer acquaintance into a Freindship which, if you were what my wishes formed you would be the greatest Happiness I could be capable of enjoying. To find that such Hopes are realized is a satisfaction indeed, a satisfaction which is now almost the only one I can ever experience.—I feel myself so languid that I am sure were you with me you would oblige me to leave off writing, and I cannot give you a greater proof of my Affection for you than by acting as I know you would wish me to do, whether Absent or Present. I am my dear Emma's sincere freind

E. L.

Letter the Ninth

Mrs Marlowe to Miss Lutterell

Grosvenor Street,[41] April 10th

Need I say my dear Eloisa how wellcome your Letter was to me? I cannot give a greater proof of the pleasure I received from it, or of the Desire I feel that our Correspondence may be regular and frequent than by setting you so good an example as I now do in answering it before the end of the week—. But do not imagine that I claim any merit in being so punctual; on the contrary I assure you, that it is a far greater Gratification to me to write to you, than to spend the Evening either at a Concert or a Ball. Mr Marlowe is so desirous of my appearing at some of the Public places every evening that I do not like to refuse him, but at the same time so much wish to remain at Home, that independant of the Pleasure I experience in devoting any portion of my Time to my Dear Eloisa, yet the Liberty I claim from having a Letter to write of spending an Evening at home with my little Boy, You know me well enough to be sensible, will of itself be a sufficient Inducement (if one is necessary) to my maintaining with Pleasure a Correspondence with you. As to the Subjects of your Letters to me, whether Grave or Merry, if they concern you they must be equally interesting to me; Not but that I think the Melancholy Indulgence of your own Sorrows by repeating them and dwelling on them to me, will only encourage and increase them, and that it will be more prudent in you to avoid so sad a subject; but yet knowing as I do what a soothing and Melancholy Pleasure it must afford you, I cannot prevail on myself to deny you so great an Indulgence, and will only insist on your not expecting me to encourage you in it, by my own Letters; on the contrary I intend to fill them with such lively Wit and enlivening Humour as shall even provoke a Smile in the sweet but Sorrowfull Countenance of my Eloisa.

In the first place you are to learn that I have met your Sister's three freinds Lady Lesley and her Daughters, twice in Public since I have been here. I know you will be impatient to hear my opinion of the Beauty of three Ladies of whom You have heard so much. Now, as you are too ill and too unhappy to be vain, I think I may venture to inform you that I like none of their faces so well as I do your own. Yet they are all handsome—Lady Lesley indeed I have seen before; her Daughters I beleive would in general be said to have a finer face than her Ladyship, and Yet what with the charms of a Blooming Complexion, a little Affectation and a great deal of Small-talk, (in each of which She is superior to the Young Ladies) she will I dare say gain herself as many Admirers as the more regular features of Matilda, and Margaret. I am sure you will agree with me in saying that they can none of them be of a proper size for real Beauty,[42] when you know that two of them are taller and the other shorter than ourselves. In spite of this Defect (or rather by reason of it) there is something very noble and majestic in the figures of the Miss Lesleys, and something agreably Lively in the Appearance of their pretty little Mother-in-law. But tho' one may be majestic and the other Lively, yet the faces of neither possess that Bewitching Sweetness of my Eloisa's, which her present Languor is so far from diminushing. What would my Husband and Brother say of us, if they knew all the fine things I have been saying to you in this Letter. It is very hard that a pretty Woman is never to be told she is so by any one of her own Sex, without that person's being suspected to be either her determined Enemy, or her professed Toad-eater.[43] How much more amiable are women in that particular! one Man may say forty civil things to another without our supposing that he is ever paid for it, and provided he does his Duty by our Sex, we care not how Polite he is to his own.

Mrs Lutterell will be so good as to accept my Compliments, Charlotte, my Love, and Eloisa the best wishes for the recovery of her Health and Spirits that can be offered by her Affectionate Freind

E. Marlowe

I am afraid this Letter will be but a poor Specimen of my Powers in the Witty Way; and your opinion of them will not be greatly increased when I assure you that I have been as entertaining as I possibly could—.

Letter the Tenth

From Miss Margaret Lesley to Miss Charlotte Lutterell

Portman Square April 13th

My dear Charlotte

We left Lesley-Castle on the 28th of Last Month, and arrived safely in London after a Journey of seven Days; I had the pleasure of finding your Letter here waiting my Arrival, for which you have my grateful Thanks. Ah! my dear Freind I every day more regret the serene and tranquil Pleasures of the Castle we have left, in exchange for the uncertain and unequal Amusements of this vaunted City. Not that I will pretend to assert that these uncertain and unequal Amusements are in the least Degree unpleasing to me; on the contrary I enjoy them extremely and should enjoy them even more, were I not certain that every appearance I make in Public but rivetts the Chains of those unhappy Beings whose Passion it is impossible not to pity, tho' it is out of my power to return. In short my Dear Charlotte it is my sensibility for the sufferings of so many amiable Young Men, my Dislike of the extreme Admiration I meet with, and my Aversion to being so celebrated both in Public, in Private, in Papers, and in Printshops,[44] that are the reasons why I cannot more fully enjoy, the Amusements so various and pleasing of London. How often have I wished that I possessed as little personal Beauty as you do; that my figure were as inelegant; my face as unlovely; and my Appearance as unpleasing as yours! But Ah! what little chance is there of so desirable an Event; I have had the Small-pox,[45] and must therefore submit to my unhappy fate.

I am now going to intrust you my dear Charlotte with a secret which has long disturbed the tranquility of my days, and which is of a kind to require the most inviolable Secrecy from you. Last Monday se'night[46] Matilda and I accompanied Lady Lesley to a Rout[47] at the Honourable Mrs Kickabout's;[48] we were escorted by Mr Fitzgerald who is a very amiable Young Man in the main, tho' perhaps a little singular in his Taste—He is in love with Matilda—. We had scarcely paid our Compliments to the Lady of the House and curtseyed to half a Score different people when my Attention was attracted by the appearance of a Young Man the most lovely of his Sex, who at that moment entered the Room with another Gentleman and Lady. From the first moment I beheld him, I was certain that on him depended the future Happiness of my Life.[49] Imagine my surprise when he was introduced to me by the name of Cleveland—I instantly recognized him as the Brother of Mrs Marlowe, and the acquaintance of my Charlotte at Bristol. M^r^ and Mrs M. were the Gentleman and Lady who accompanied him. (You do not think Mrs Marlowe handsome?) The elegant address of Mr Cleveland, his polished Manners and Delightful Bow, at once confirmed my attachment. He did not speak; but I can imagine every thing he would have said, had he opened his Mouth. I can picture to myself the cultivated Understanding, the Noble Sentiments, and elegant Language which would have shone so conspicuous in the conversation of Mr Cleveland. The approach of Sir James Gower (one of my too numerous Admirers) prevented the Discovery of any such Powers, by putting an end to a Conversation we had never commenced, and by attracting my attention to himself. But Oh! how inferior are the accomplishments of Sir James to those of his so greatly envied Rival! Sir James is one of the most frequent of our Visitors, and is almost always of our Parties. We have since often met M^r and Mrs Marlowe but no Cleveland—he is always engaged some where else. Mrs Marlowe fatigues me to Death every time I see her by her tiresome Conversations about You and Eloisa. She is so Stupid! I live in the hope of seeing her irrisistable Brother to night, as we are going to Lady Flambeau's,[50] who is I know intimate with the Marlowes. Our party will be Lady Lesley, Matilda, Fitzgerald, Sir James Gower, and myself. We see little of Sir George, who is almost always at the Gaming-table. Ah! my poor Fortune, where art thou by this time? We see more of Lady L. who always makes her appearance (highly rouged) at Dinner-time. Alas! what Delightful Jewels will she be decked in this evening at Lady Flambeau's! Yet I wonder how she can herself delight in wearing them; surely she must be sensible of the ridiculous impropriety of loading her little diminutive figure with such superfluous ornaments; is it possible that she can not know how greatly superior an elegant simplicity is to the most studied apparel? Would she but present them to Matilda and me, how greatly should we be obliged to her. How becoming would Diamonds be on our fine majestic figures! And how surprising it is that such an Idea should never have occurred to <u>her</u>: I am sure if I have reflected in this Manner once, I have fifty times. Whenever I see Lady Lesley dressed in them such reflections immediately come across me. My own Mother's Jewels too! But I will say no more on so melancholy a Subject—Let me entertain you with something more pleasing—Matilda had a letter this Morning from Lesley, by which we have the pleasure of finding that he is at Naples has turned Roman-catholic, obtained one of the Pope's Bulls[51] for annulling his 1st Marriage and has since actually married a Neapolitan Lady of great Rank and Fortune. He tells us moreover that much the same sort of affair has befallen his first wife the worthless Louisa who is likewise at Naples has turned Roman-catholic, and is soon to be married to a Neapolitan Nobleman of great and Distinguished Merit. He says, that they are at present very good Freinds, have quite forgiven all past errors and intend in future to be very good Neighbours. He invites Matilda and me to pay him a visit in Italy and to bring him his little Louisa whom both her Mother, Step-Mother, and himself are equally desirous of beholding. As to our accepting his invitation, it is at present very uncertain; Lady Lesley advises us to go without loss of time; Fitzgerald offers to escort us there, but Matilda has some doubts of the Propriety of such a Scheme—She owns it would be very agreable. I am certain she likes the Fellow. My Father desires us not to be in a hurry, as perhaps if we wait a few months both he and Lady Lesley will do themselves the pleasure of attending us. Lady Lesley says no, that nothing will ever tempt her to forego the Amusements of Brighthelmstone for a Journey to Italy merely to see our Brother. 'No' (says the disagreable woman) 'I have once in my life been fool enough to travel I don't know how many hundred Miles to see two of the Family, and I found it did not answer, so Deuce take me, if ever I am so foolish again.' So says her Ladyship, but Sir George still perseveres in saying that perhaps in a Month or two, they may accompany us.

Adeiu my Dear Charlotte—

Y[r] faithful Margaret Lesley

The History of England

from the reign of
Henry the 4th
to the death of
Charles the 1st [1]

By a partial, prejudiced, and ignorant Historian.[2]

To Miss Austen[3] eldest daughter of the Revd George Austen, this Work is inscribed with all due respect by

The Author

N.B. There will be very few Dates in this History.

Henry the 4th [4]

Henry the 4th ascended the throne of England much to his own satisfaction in the year 1399, after having prevailed on his cousin and predecessor Richard the 2d, to resign it to him, and to retire for the rest of his Life[5] to Pomfret Castle,[6] where he happened to be murdered.[7] It is to be supposed that Henry was Married,[8] since he had certainly four sons, but it is not in my power to inform the Reader who was his Wife. Be this as it may, he did not live for ever, but falling ill, his son the Prince of Wales came and took away the crown;[9] whereupon the King made a long speech, for which I must refer the Reader to Shakespear's Plays, and the Prince made a still longer. Things being thus settled between them the King died, and was succeeded by his son Henry who had previously beat Sir William Gascoigne.[10]

Henry the 5th[11]

This Prince after he succeeded to the throne grew quite reformed and Amiable, forsaking all his dissipated Companions,[12] and never thrashing Sir William again. During his reign, Lord Cobham[13] was burnt alive, but I forget what for.[14] His Majesty then turned his thoughts to France,[15] where he went and fought the famous Battle of Agincourt.[16] He afterwards married the King's daughter Catherine, a very agreable Woman by Shakespear's account.[17] Inspite of all this however he died, and was succeeded by his son Henry.

Henry the 6th[18]

I cannot say much for this Monarch's Sense[19]—Nor would I if I could, for he was a Lancastrian. I suppose you know all about the Wars between him and the Duke of York who was of the right side;[20] If you do not, you had better read some other History, for I shall not be very diffuse in this, meaning by it only to vent my Spleen[21] against, and shew my Hatred to all those people whose parties or principles do not suit with mine, and not to give information. This King married Margaret of Anjou,[22] a Woman whose distresses and Misfortunes[23] were so great as almost to make me who hate her, pity her. It was in this reign that Joan of Arc lived and made such a row among the English.[24] They should not have burnt her—but they did. There were several Battles between the Yorkists and Lancastrians, in which the former (as they ought) usually conquered. At length they were entirely over come; The King was murdered—The Queen was sent home—and Edward the 4th Ascended the Throne.

Edward the 4th

This Monarch was famous only for his Beauty and his Courage, of which the Picture we have here given of him,[25] and his undaunted Behaviour in marrying one Woman while he was engaged to another,[26] are sufficient proofs. His wife was Elizabeth Woodville, a Widow who, poor Woman!,[27] was afterwards confined in a Convent by that Monster of Iniquity and Avarice Henry the 7th. One of Edward's Mistresses was Jane Shore, who has had a play written about her,[28] but it is a tragedy and therefore not worth reading. Having performed all these noble actions, his Majesty died, and was succeeded by his Son.

Edward the 5th

This unfortunate Prince lived so little a while that no body had time to draw his picture.[29] He was murdered by his Uncle's Contrivance, whose name was Richard the 3^{d}.

Richard the 3d [30]

The Character of this Prince has been in general very severely treated by Historians, but as he was a York, I am rather inclined to suppose him a very respectable Man.[31] It has indeed been confidently asserted that he killed his two Nephews and his Wife, but it has also been declared that he did not kill his two Nephews,[32] which I am inclined to beleive true;[33] and if this is the case, it may also be affirmed that he did not kill his Wife,[34] for if Perkin Warbeck was really the Duke of York,[35] why might not Lambert Simnel[36] be the Widow of Richard. Whether innocent or guilty, he did not reign long in peace, for Henry Tudor E. of Richmond as great a Villain as ever lived, made a great fuss about getting the Crown and having killed the King at the battle of Bosworth,[37] he suceeded to it.

Henry the 7th

This Monarch soon after his accession married the Princess Elizabeth of York, by which alliance he plainly proved that he thought his own right inferior to hers, tho' he pretended to the contrary.[38] By this Marriage he had two sons and two daughters, the elder of which daughters was married to the King of Scotland and had the happiness of being grandmother[39] to one of the first Characters in the World. But of <u>her</u>, I shall have occasion to speak more at large in future. The Youngest, Mary, married first the King of France and secondly the D. of Suffolk, by whom she had one daughter, afterwards the Mother of Lady Jane Grey, who tho' inferior to her lovely Cousin the Queen of Scots, was yet an amiable young Woman[40] and famous for reading Greek while other people were hunting. It was in the reign of Henry the 7th that Perkin Warbeck and Lambert Simnel before mentioned made their appearance, the former of whom was set in the Stocks, took shelter in Beaulieu Abbey, and was beheaded with the Earl of Warwick, and the latter was taken into the King's kitchen. His Majesty died, and was succceded by his son Henry whose only merit was his not being <u>quite</u> so bad as his daughter Elizabeth.

Henry the 8th[41]

It would be an affront to my Readers were I to suppose that they were not as well acquainted with the particulars of this King's reign as I am myself. It will therefore be saving them the task of reading again what they have read before, and myself the trouble of writing what I do not perfectly recollect, by giving only a slight sketch of the principal Events which marked his reign. Among these may be ranked Cardinal Wolsey's telling the father Abbott of Leicester Abbey that 'he was come to lay his bones among them',[42] the reformation in Religion, and the King's riding through the Streets of London with Anna Bullen.[43] It is however but Justice, and my Duty to declare that this amiable Woman was entirely innocent of the Crimes with which she was accused, of which her Beauty, her Elegance, and her Sprightliness were sufficient proofs, not to mention her solemn protestations of Innocence, the weakness of the Charges against her, and the King's Character; all of which add some confirmation, tho' perhaps but slight ones when in comparison with those before alledged in her favour. Tho' I do not profess giving many dates, yet as I think it proper to give some and shall of course Make choice of those which it is most necessary for the Reader to know, I think it right to inform him that her letter to the King was dated on the 6th of May.[44] The Crimes and Cruelties of this Prince,[45] were too numerous to be mentioned, (as this history I trust has fully shewn;) and nothing can be said in his vindication, but that his abolishing Religious Houses[46] and leaving them to the ruinous depredations of time has been of infinite use to the landscape of England in general,[47] which probably was a principal motive for his doing it,[48] since otherwise why should a Man who was of no Religion himself be at so much trouble to abolish one which had for Ages been established in the Kingdom. His Majesty's 5th wife[49] was the Duke of Norfolk's Neice who, tho' universally acquitted of the crimes for which she was beheaded, has been by many people supposed to have led an abandoned Life before her Marriage— Of this however I have many doubts, since she was a relation of that noble Duke of Norfolk who was so warm in the Queen of Scotland's cause,[50] and who at last fell a victim to it. The king's last wife contrived to survive him, but with difficulty effected it.[51] He was succeeded by his only son Edward.

Edward the 6th[52]

As this prince was only nine years old at the time of his Father's death, he was considered by many people as too young to govern, and the late King happening to be of the same opinion, his mother's Brother the Duke of Somerset[53] was chosen Protector of the realm during his minority. This Man was on the whole of a very amiable Character, and is somewhat of a favourite with me,[54] tho' I would by no means pretend to affirm that he was equal to those first of Men Robert Earl of Essex, Delamere, or Gilpin.[55] He was beheaded, of which he might with reason have been proud, had he known that such was the death of Mary Queen of Scotland;[56] but as it was impossible that he should be conscious of what had never happened, it does not appear that he felt particularly delighted with the manner of it. After his decease the Duke of Northumberland[57] had the care of the King and the Kingdom, and performed his trust of both so well that the King died and the Kingdom was left to his daughter in law the Lady Jane Grey, who has been already mentioned as—reading Greek.[58] Whether she really understood that language or whether such a Study proceeded only from an excess of vanity[59] for which I beleive she was always rather remarkable, is uncertain. Whatever might be the cause, she preserved the same appearance of knowledge, and contempt of what was generally esteemed pleasure, during the whole of her Life, for she declared herself displeased with being appointed Queen, and while conducting to the Scaffold, she wrote a Sentence in Latin and another in Greek on seeing the dead Body of her Husband accidentally passing that way.

Mary[60]

This Woman had the good luck of being advanced to the throne of England, inspite of the superior pretensions, Merit and <u>Beauty</u> of her Cousins Mary Queen of Scotland and Jane Grey. Nor can I pity the Kingdom for the misfortunes they experienced during her Reign, since they fully deserved them, for having allowed her to succeed her Brother—which was a double peice of folly, since they might have foreseen that as she died without Children, she would be succeeded by that disgrace to humanity, that pest of society, Elizabeth. Many were the people who fell Martyrs to the protestant Religion during her reign; I suppose not fewer than a dozen.[61] She married Philip King of Spain who in her Sister's reign was famous for building Armadas. She died without issue, and then the dreadful moment came in which the destroyer of all comfort, the deceitful Betrayer of trust reposed in her, and the Murderess of her Cousin succeeded to the Throne.—

Elizabeth[62]

It was the peculiar Misfortune of this Woman to have bad Ministers[63]—Since wicked as she herself was, she could not have committed such extensive Mischeif, had not these vile and abandoned Men connived at, and encouraged her in her

Crimes. I know that it has by many people been asserted and beleived that Lord Burleigh, Sir Francis Walsingham,[64] and the rest of those who filled the cheif Offices of State were deserving, experienced, and able Ministers. But Oh! how blinded such Writers and such Readers must be to true Merit, to Merit despised, neglected and defamed, if they can persist in such opinions when they reflect that these Men, these boasted Men were such Scandals to their Country and their Sex as to allow and assist their Queen in confining for the space of nineteen years, a *Woman* who if the claims of Relationship and Merit were no avail, yet as a Queen and as one who condescended to place confidence in her, had every reason to expect Assistance and protection; and at length in allowing Elizabeth to bring this amiable Woman to an untimely, unmerited, and scandalous Death. Can any one if he reflects but for a moment on this blot, this everlasting blot upon their Understanding and their Character, allow any praise to Lord Burleigh or Sir Francis Walsingham? Oh! what must this bewitching Princess whose only freind was then the Duke of Norfolk, and whose only ones are now Mr Whitaker, Mrs Lefroy, Mrs Knight[65] and myself, who was abandoned by her Son,[66] confined by her Cousin, Abused, reproached and villified by all, what must not her most noble mind have suffered when informed that Elizabeth had given orders for her Death! Yet she bore it with a most unshaken fortitude; firm in her Mind; Constant in her Religion; and prepared herself to meet the cruel fate to which she was doomed, with a magnanimity that could alone proceed from conscious Innocence. And yet could you Reader have beleived it possible that some hardened and zealous Protestants have even abused her for that Steadfastness in the Catholic Religion which reflected on her so much credit? But this is a striking proof of *their* narrow Souls and prejudiced Judgements who accuse her. She was executed in the Great Hall at Fortheringay Castle (sacred Place!) on Wednesday the 8th of February—1586[67]—to the everlasting Reproach of Elizabeth, her Ministers, and of England in general. It may not be unnecessary before I entirely conclude my account of this ill-fated Queen, to observe that she had been accused of several crimes during the time of her reigning in Scotland, of which I now most seriously do assure my Reader that she was entirely innocent; having never been guilty of anything more than Imprudencies into which she was betrayed by the openness of her Heart, her Youth, and her Educatian. Having I trust by this assurance entirely done away every Suspicion and every doubt which might have arisen in the Reader's mind, from what other Historians have written of her, I shall proceed to mention the remaining Events that marked Elizabeth's reign. It was about this time that Sir Francis Drake the first English Navigator who sailed round the World, lived, to be the ornament of his Country and his profession. Yet great as he was, and justly celebrated as a Sailor, I cannot help foreseeing that he will be equalled in this or the next Century by one who tho' now but young,[68] already promises to answer all the ardent and sanguine expectations of his Relations and Freinds, amongst whom I may class the amiable Lady to whom this work is dedicated, and my no less amiable Self.

Though of a different profession, and shining in a different Sphere of Life, yet equally conspicuous in the Character of an Earl, as Drake was in that of a Sailor, was Robert Devereux Lord Essex. This unfortunate young Man was not unlike in Character to that equally unfortunate one Frederic Delamere. The simile may be carried still farther, and Elizabeth the torment of Essex may be compared to the Emmeline of Delamere.[69] It would be endless to recount the misfortunes of this noble and gallant Earl. It is sufficient to say that he was beheaded on the 25th of Febry,[70] after having been Lord Leuitenant of Ireland, after having clapped his hand on his sword,[71] and after performing many other services to his Country. Elizabeth did not long survive his loss, and died so miserable[72] that were it not an injury to the memory of Mary I should pity her.

James the 1st

Though this King had some faults, among which and as the most principal, was his allowing his Mother's death, yet considered on the whole I cannot help liking him.[73] He married Anne of Denmark, and had several Children; fortunately for him his eldest son Prince Henry died before his father or he might have experienced the evils which befell his unfortunate Brother.[74]

As I am myself partial to the roman catholic religion,[75] it is with infinite regret that I am obliged to blame the Behaviour of any Member of it; yet Truth being I think very excusable in an Historian, I am necessitated to say that in this reign the roman Catholics of England did not behave like Gentlemen to the protestants. Their Behaviour indeed to the Royal Family and both Houses of Parliament might justly be considered by them as very uncivil,[76] and even Sir Henry Percy tho' certainly the best bred Man of the party, had none of that general politeness which is so universally pleasing, as his Attentions were entirely confined to Lord Mounteagle.[77]

Sir Walter Raleigh[78] flourished in this and the preceding reign, and is by many people held in great veneration and respect—But as he was an enemy of the noble Essex, I have nothing to say in praise of him, and must refer all those who may wish to be acquainted with the particulars of his Life, to Mr Sheridan's play of the Critic,[79] where they will find many interesting Anecdotes as well of him as of his freind Sir Christopher Hatton.—His Majesty was of that amiable disposition which inclines to Freindships, and in such points was possessed of a keener penetration in Discovering Merit[80] than many other people. I once heard an excellent Sharade on a Carpet, of which the subject I am now on reminds me, and as I think it may afford my Readers some Amusement to find it out, I shall here take the liberty of presenting it to them.

Sharade[81]

My first is what my second was to King James the 1st,[82] and you tread on my whole. The principal favourites of his Majesty were Car, who was afterwards created Earl of Somerset and whose name may have some share in the above-mentioned Sharade, and George Villiers afterwards Duke of Buckingham.[83] On his Majesty's death he was succeeded by his son Charles.

Charles the 1st

This amiable Monarch seems born to have suffered Misfortunes equal to those of his lovely Grandmother;[84] Misfortunes which he could not deserve since he was her descendant. Never certainly were there before so many detestable Characters at one time in England as in this period of its History; Never were amiable Men so scarce. The number of them throughout the whole Kingdom amounting only to five, besides the inhabitants of Oxford who were always loyal to their King and faithful to his interests. The names of this noble five who never forgot the duty of the Subject, or swerved from their attachment to his Majesty, were as follows—

The King himself, ever stedfast in his own support, Archbishop Laud, Earl of Strafford, Viscount Faulkland and Duke of Ormond,[85] who were scarcely less strenuous or zealous in the cause. While the Villains of the time would make too long a list to be written or read; I shall therefore content myself with mentioning the leaders of the Gang.[86] Cromwell, Fairfax, Hampden, and Pym may be considered as the original Causers of all the disturbances, Distresses, and Civil Wars in which England for many years was embroiled. In this reign as well as in that of Elizabeth, I am obliged in spite of my Attachment to the Scotch, to consider them as equally guilty with the generality of the English, since they dared to think differently from their Sovereign, to forget the Adoration which as Stuarts it was their Duty to pay them, to rebel against, dethrone and imprison the unfortunate Mary; to oppose, to deceive, and to sell the no less unfortunate Charles. The Events of this Monarch's reign are too numerous for my pen, and indeed the recital of any Events (except what I make myself) is uninteresting to me; my principal reason for undertaking the History of England being to prove the innocence of the Queen of Scotland, which I flatter myself with having effectually done, and to abuse Elizabeth, tho' I am rather fearful of having fallen short in the latter part of my Scheme.—. As therefore it is not my intention to give any particular account of the distresses into which this King was involved through the misconduct and Cruelty of his Parliament, I shall satisfy myself with vindicating him from the Reproach of Arbitrary and tyrannical Government with which he has often been Charged. This, I feel, is not difficult to be done, for with one argument I am certain of satisfying every sensible and well disposed person whose opinions have been properly guided by a good Education—and this Argument is that he was a **Stuart**.

Finis

Saturday Nov: 26th 1791

To Miss Cooper[1]

Cousin

Conscious of the Charming Character which in every Country, and every Clime[2] in Christendom is Cried, Concerning you, with Caution and Care I Commend to your Charitable Criticism this Clever Collection of Curious Comments, which have been Carefully Culled, Collected and Classed by your Comical Cousin

The Author.

A Collection of Letters

Letter the first

From a Mother to her freind

My Children begin now to claim all my attention in a different Manner from that in which they have been used to receive it, as they are now arrived at that age when it is necessary for them in some measure to become conversant with the World.[3] My Augusta is 17 and her Sister scarcely a twelvemonth younger. I flatter myself that their education has been such as will not disgrace their appearance in the World, and that they will not disgrace their Education I have every reason to beleive. Indeed they are sweet Girls—. Sensible yet unaffected—Accomplished yet Easy—. Lively yet Gentle—. As their progress in every thing they have learnt has been always the same, I am willing to forget the difference of age, and to introduce them together into Public. This very Evening is fixed on as their first entrée[4] into Life, as we are to drink tea with Mrs Cope and her Daughter. I am glad that we are to meet no one for my Girls' sake, as it would be awkward for them to enter too wide a Circle on the very first day. But we shall proceed by degrees—. Tomorrow Mr Stanly's family will drink tea with us, and perhaps the Miss Phillips's will meet them. On Tuesday we shall pay Morning-Visits[5]—On Wednesday we are to dine at Westbrook. On Thursday we have Company at home. On Friday we are to be at a private Concert at Sir John Wynne's—and on Saturday we expect Miss Dawson to call in the Morning—which will complete my Daughters' Introduction into

Life. How they will bear so much dissipation I cannot imagine; of their Spirits I have no fear, I only dread their health.

This mighty affair is now happily over, and my Girls are out.—As the moment approached for our departure, you can have no idea how the sweet Creatures trembled with fear and expectation. Before the Carriage drove to the door, I called them into my dressing-room, and as soon as they were seated thus addressed them. 'My dear Girls, the moment is now arrived when I am to reap the rewards of all my Anxieties and Labours towards you during your Education. You are this Evening to enter a World in which you will meet with many wonderfull Things; Yet let me warn you against suffering yourselves to be meanly swayed by the Follies and Vices of others, for beleive me, my beloved Children, that if you do—I shall be very sorry for it.' They both assured me that they would ever remember my Advice with Gratitude, and follow it with Attention; That they were prepared to find a World full of things to amaze and shock them: but that they trusted their behaviour would never give me reason to repent the Watchful Care with which I had presided over their infancy[6] and formed their Minds— 'With such expectations and such intentions' (cried I) 'I can have nothing to fear from you—and can chearfully conduct you to Mrs Cope's without a fear of your being seduced by her Example, or contaminated by her Follies. Come, then my Children' (added I) 'the Carriage is driving to the door, and I will not a moment delay the happiness you are so impatient to enjoy.' When we arrived at Warleigh, poor Augusta could scarcely breathe, while Margaret was all Life and Rapture. 'The long-expected Moment is now arrived' (said she) 'and we shall soon be in the World.'—In a few Moments we were in Mrs Cope's parlour—, where with her daughter she sate ready to receive us. I observed with delight the impression my Children made on them—. They were indeed two sweet, elegant-looking Girls, and tho' somewhat abashed from the peculiarity of their Situation, Yet there was an ease in their Manners and Address which could not fail of pleasing—. Imagine my dear Madam how delighted I must have been in beholding as I did, how attentively they observed every object they saw, how disgusted with some Things, how enchanted with others, how astonished at all! On the whole however they returned in raptures with the World, its Inhabitants, and Manners.

Y^rs Ever—A—F—

Letter the second

From a Young Lady crossed in Love to her freind

Why should this last disappointment hang so heavily on my Spirits? Why should I feel it more, why should it wound me deeper than those I have experienced before? Can it be that I have a greater affection for Willoughby[7] than I had for his amiable predecessors—? Or is it that our feelings become more acute from being often wounded? I must suppose my dear Belle that this is the Case, since I am not conscious of being more sincerely attached to Willoughby than I was to Neville, Fitzowen, or either of the Crawfords, for all of whom I once felt the most lasting affection that ever warmed a Woman's heart. Tell me then dear Belle why I still sigh when I think of the faithless Edward, or why I weep when I behold his Bride? for too surely this is the case—. My Freinds are all alarmed for me; They fear my declining health; they lament my want of Spirits; they dread the effects of both. In hopes of releiving my Melancholy,[8] by directing my thoughts to other objects, they have invited several of their freinds to spend the Christmas with us. Lady Bridget Dashwood and her Sister-in-Law Miss Jane are expeded on Friday; and Colonel Seaton's family will be with us next week. This is all most kindly meant by my Uncle and Cousins; but what can the presence of a dozen indifferent people do to me, but weary and distress me—. I will not finish my Letter till some of our Visitors are arrived.

Friday Evening—

Lady Bridget came this Morning, and with her, her sweet Sister Miss Jane—. Although I have been acquainted with this charming Woman above fifteen years, Yet I never before observed how lovely she is. She is now about 35, and in spite of sickness, Sorrow and Time is more blooming than I ever saw a Girl of 17. I was delighted with her, the moment she entered the house, and she appeared equally pleased with me, attaching herself to me during the remainder of the day. There is something so sweet, so mild in her Countenance, that she seems more than Mortal. Her Conversation is as bewitching as her appearance—; I could not help telling her how much she engaged my Admiration—. 'Oh! Miss Jane' (said I)—and stopped from an inability at the moment of expressing myself as I could wish—'Oh! Miss Jane' (I repeated)—I could not think of words to suit my feelings—She seemed waiting for my Speech—. I was confused—distressed—. My thoughts were bewildered—and I could only add—'How do you do?' She saw and felt for my Embarrassment and with admirable presence of mind releived me from it by saying— 'My dear Sophia be not uneasy at having exposed Yourself—I will turn the Conversation without appearing to notice it.' Oh! how I loved her for her kindness! 'Do you ride as much as you used to do?' said she—. 'I am advised to ride by my Physician,[9] We have delightful Rides round us, I have a Charming horse, am uncommonly fond of the Amusement,' replied I quite recovered from my Confusion, 'and in short I ride a great deal.' 'You are in the right my Love,' said She, Then repeating the following Line which was an extempore and equally adapted to recommend both Riding and Candour—

'Ride where you may, Be Candid where You can,'[10] She added, '<u>I</u> rode once, but it is many years ago'—She spoke this in so Low and tremulous a Voice, that I was silent—Struck with her Manner of Speaking I could make no reply. 'I have not ridden,' continued she fixing her Eyes on my face, 'since I was married.'

I was never so surprised— 'Married, Ma'am!' I repeated. 'You may well wear that look of astonishment', said she, 'since what I have said must appear improbable to you—Yet nothing is more true than that I once was married.'

'Then why are you called Miss Jane?'

'I married, my Sophia, without the consent or knowledge of my father—the late Admiral Annesley. It was therefore necessary to keep the secret from him and from every one, till some fortunate opportunity might offer of revealing it—. Such an opportunity alas! was but too soon given in the death of my dear Cap$^{t.}$ Dashwood—Pardon these tears,' continued Miss Jane wiping her Eyes, 'I owe them to my Husband's Memory, He fell my Sophia, while fighting for his Country in America[11] after a most happy Union of seven years—. My Children, two sweet Boys and a Girl, who had constantly resided with my Father and me, passing with him and with every one as the Children of a Brother (tho' I had ever been an only Child) had as yet been the Comforts of my Life. But no sooner had I lossed my Henry, than these sweet Creatures fell sick and died—. Conceive, dear Sophia, what my feelings must have been when as an Aunt I attended my Children to their early Grave—. My Father did not survive them many weeks. He died, poor Good old Man, happily ignorant to his last hour of my Marriage.'

'But did you not own it, and assume his name at your husband's death?'

'No; I could not bring myself to do it; more especially when in my Children, I lost all inducement for doing it. Lady Bridget, and Yourself are the only persons who are in the knowledge of my having ever been either Wife or Mother. As I could not prevail on myself to take the name of Dashwood (a name which after my Henry's death I could never hear without emotion) and as I was conscious of having no right to that of Annesley, I dropt all thoughts of either,[12] and have made it a point of bearing only my Christian one since my Father's death.' She paused— 'Oh! my dear Miss Jane' (said I) 'how infinitely am I obliged to you for so entertaining a Story! You cannot think how it has diverted me! But have you quite done?'

'I have only to add, my dear Sophia, that my Henry's elder Brother dieing about the same time, Lady Bridget became a Widow like myself, and as we had always loved each other in idea from the high Character in which we had ever been spoken of, though we had never met, we determined to live together. We wrote to one another on the same subject by the same post, so exactly did our feelings and our Actions coincide! We both eagerly embraced the proposals we gave and received of becoming one family, and have from that time lived together in the greatest affection.'

'And is this all?' said I, 'I hope you have not done.'

'Indeed I have; and did you ever hear a Story more pathetic?'

'I never did—and it is for that reason it pleases me so much, for when one is unhappy nothing is so delightful to one's Sensations as to hear of equal Misery.'

'Ah! but my Sophia why <u>are you</u> unhappy?'

'Have you not heard, Madam, of Willoughby's Marriage?'

'But my Love why lament <u>his</u> perfidy, when you bore so well that of many young Men before?'

'Ah! Madam, I was used to it then, but when Willoughby broke his Engagements I had not been dissapointed for half a year.'

'Poor Girl!' said Miss Jane.

Letter the third

From A young Lady in distress'd Circumstances to her freind

A few days ago I was at a private Ball given by Mr Ashburnham. As my Mother never goes out she entrusted me to the care of Lady Greville who did me the honour of calling for me in her way and of allowing me to sit forwards,[13] which is a favour about which I am very indifferent especially as I know it is considered as confering a great obligation on me. 'So Miss Maria' (said her Ladyship as she saw me advancing to the door of the Carriage) 'you seem very smart to night—<u>My</u> poor Girls will appear quite to disadvantage by <u>you</u>—I only hope your Mother may not have distressed herself to set <u>you</u> off. Have you got a new Gown on?'

'Yes Ma'am,' replied I with as much indifference as I could assume.

'Aye, and a fine one too I think—' (feeling it, as by her permission I seated myself by her) 'I dare say it is all very smart—But I must own, for you know I always speak my mind, that I think it was quite a needless peice of expence—Why could not you have worn your old striped one?[14] It is not my way to find fault with people because they are poor, for I always think that they are more to be despised and pitied than blamed for it, especially if they cannot help it, but at the same time I must say that in my opinion your old striped Gown would have been quite fine enough for its Wearer—for to tell you the truth (I always speak my mind) I am very much afraid that one half of the people in the room will not know whether you have a Gown on or not—But I suppose you intend to make your fortune tonight—: Well, the sooner the better; and I wish you success.'

'Indeed, Ma'am, I have no such intention—'

'Who ever heard a Young Lady own that she was a Fortune-hunter?' Miss Greville laughed, but I am sure Ellen felt for me.

'Was your Mother gone to bed before you left her?' said her Ladyship—

'Dear Ma'am,' said Ellen, 'it is but nine o'clock.'

'True, Ellen, but Candles cost money, and Mrs Williams is too wise to be extravagant.'

'She was just sitting down to supper, Ma'am—'

'And what had she got for Supper?' 'I did not observe.' 'Bread and Cheese I suppose.' 'I should never wish for a better supper,' said Ellen. 'You have never any reason' replied her Mother, 'as a better is always provided for you.' Miss Greville laughed excessively, as she constantly does at her Mother's wit.

Such is the humiliating Situation in which I am forced to appear while riding in her Ladyship's Coach—I dare not be impertinent, as my Mother is always admonishing me to be humble and patient if I wish to make my way in the world. She insists on my accepting every invitation of Lady Greville, or you may be certain that I would never enter either her House, or her Coach, with the disagreable certainty I always have of being abused for my Poverty while I am in them.—When we arrived at Ashburnham, it was nearly ten o'clock, which was an hour and a half later than we were desired to be there; but Lady Greville is too fashionable (or fancies herself to be so) to be punctual. The Dancing however was not begun as they waited for Miss Greville. I had not been long in the room before I was engaged to dance by Mr Bernard, but just as we were going to stand up, he recollected that his Servant had got his white Gloves,[15] and immediately ran out to fetch them. In the mean time the Dancing began and Lady Greville in passing to another room went exactly before me—She saw me and instantly stopping, said to me though there were several people close to us;

'Hey day, Miss Maria! What cannot you get a partner? Poor Young Lady! I am afraid your new Gown was put on for nothing. But do not despair; perhaps you may get a hop[16] before the Evening is over.' So saying, she passed on without hearing my repeated assurance of being engaged, and leaving me very provoked at being so exposed before every one—Mr Bernard however soon returned and by coming to me the moment he entered the room, and leading me to the Dancers, my Character I hope was cleared from the imputation Lady Greville had thrown on it, in the eyes of all the old Ladies who had heard her speech. I soon forgot all my vexations in the pleasure of dancing and of having the most agreable partner in the room. As he is moreover heir to a very large Estate I could see that Lady Greville did not look very well pleased when she found who had been his Choice—She was determined to mortify me, and accordingly when we were sitting down between the dances, she came to me with more than her usual insulting importance attended by Miss Mason and said loud enough to be heard by half the people in the room, 'Pray, Miss Maria, in what way of business was your Grandfather? for Miss Mason and I cannot agree whether he was a Grocer or a Bookbinder.'[17] I saw that she wanted to mortify me, and was resolved if I possibly could to prevent her seeing that her scheme succeeded. 'Neither Madam; he was a Wine Merchant.' 'Aye, I knew he was in some such low way—He broke[18] did not he?' 'I beleive not Ma'am.' 'Did not he abscond?' 'I never heard that he did.' 'At least he died insolvent?' 'I was never told so before.' 'Why, was not your Father as poor as a Rat?'[19] 'I fancy not.' 'Was not he in the King's Bench[20] once?' 'I never saw him there.' She gave me such a look, and turned away in a great passion; while I was half delighted with myself for my impertinence, and half afraid of being thought too saucy.[21] As Lady Greville was extremely angry with me, she took no further notice of me all the Evening, and indeed had I been in favour I should have been equally neglected, as she was got into a party of great folks and she never speaks to me when she can to any one else. Miss Greville was with her Mother's party at Supper, but Ellen preferred staying with the Bernards and me. We had a very pleasant Dance and as Lady G —— slept all the way home, I had a very comfortable ride.

The next day while we were at dinner Lady Greville's Coach stopped at the door, for that is the time of day she generally contrives it should. She sent in a message by the Servant to say that 'she should not get out but that Miss Maria must come to the Coach-door, as she wanted to speak to her, and that she must make haste and come immediately—' 'What an impertinent Message Mama!' said I—'Go Maria—' replied She—Accordingly I went and was obliged to stand there at her Ladyship's pleasure though the Wind was extremely high and very cold.

'Why I think, Miss Maria, you are not quite so smart as you were last night—But I did not come to examine your dress, but to tell you that you may dine with us the day after tomorrow—Not tomorrow, remember, do not come tomorrow, for we expect Lord and Lady Clermont and Sir Thomas Stanley's family—There will be no occasion for your being very fine for I shan't send the Carriage—If it rains you may take an umbrella—'[22] I could hardly help laughing at hearing her give me leave to keep myself dry—'And pray remember to be in time, for I shan't wait—I hate my Victuals over-done—But you need not come before the time—How does your Mother do? She is at dinner is not she?' 'Yes, Ma'am, we were in the middle of dinner when your Ladyship came.' 'I am afraid you find it very cold, Maria,' said Ellen. 'Yes, it is an horrible East wind'—said her Mother—'I assure you I can hardly bear the window down—But you are used to be blown about the wind, Miss Maria, and that is what has made your Complexion so ruddy and coarse. You young Ladies who cannot often ride in a Carriage never mind what weather you trudge in, or how the wind shews your legs.[23] I would not have my Girls stand out of doors as you do in such a day as this.[24] But some sort of people have no feelings either of cold or Delicacy—Well, remember that we shall expect you on Thursday at 5 o'clock—You must tell your Maid to come for you at night—There will be no Moon—and you will have an horrid walk home—My Compliments to your Mother—I am afraid your dinner will be cold—Drive on—' And away she went, leaving me in a great passion with her as she always does.

Maria Williams

Letter the fourth

From a young Lady rather impertinent to her freind

We dined yesterday with Mr Evelyn where we were introduced to a very agreable looking Girl his Cousin. I was extremely pleased with her appearance, for added to the charms of an engaging face, her manner and voice had something peculiarly interesting in them. So much so, that they inspired me with a great curiosity to know the history of her Life, who were her Parents, where she came from, and what had befallen her, for it was then only known that she was a relation of Mr Evelyn, and that her name was Grenville. In the evening a favourable opportunity offered to me of attempting at least to know what I wished to know, for every one played at Cards but Mrs Evelyn, My Mother, Dr Drayton, Miss Grenville and myself, and as the two former were engaged in a whispering Conversation, and the Doctor fell asleep, we were of necessity obliged to entertain each other. This was what I wished and being determined not to remain in ignorance for want of asking, I began the Conversation in the following Manner.

'Have you been long in Essex, Ma'am?'

'I arrived on Tuesday.'

'You came from Derbyshire?'

'No, Ma'am!' appearing surprised at my question, 'from Suffolk.'[25] You will think this a good dash[26] of mine my dear Mary, but you will know that I am not wanting for Impudence when I have any end in veiw. 'Are you pleased with the Country, Miss Grenville? Do you find it equal to the one you have left?'

'Much superior, Ma'am, in point of Beauty.' She sighed. I longed to know for why.

'But the face of any Country however beautiful' said I, 'can be but a poor consolation for the loss of one's dearest Freinds.' She shook her head, as if she felt the truth of what I said. My Curiosity was so much raised, that I was resolved at any rate to satisfy it.

'You regret having left Suffolk then, Miss Grenville?' 'Indeed I do.' 'You were born there I suppose?' 'Yes, Ma'am, I was and passed many happy years there—'

'That is a great comfort—' said I— 'I hope Ma'am that you never spent any *un*happy one's there.'

'Perfect Felicity is not the property of Mortals, and no one has a right to expect uninterrupted Happiness—*Some* Misfortunes I have certainly met with—'

'*What* Misfortunes, dear Ma'am?' replied I, burning with impatience to know everything. '*None*, Ma'am, I hope that have been the effect of any wilfull fault in me.' 'I dare say not Ma'am, and have no doubt but that any sufferings you may have experienced could arise only from the cruelties of Relations or the Errors of Freinds.' She sighed—'You seem unhappy, my dear Miss Grenville—Is it in my power to soften your Misfortunes.' '*Your* power Ma'am,' replied she extremely surprised; 'it is in *no one's* power to make me happy.' She pronounced these words in so mournfull and solemn an accent, that for some time I had not courage to reply. I was actually silenced. I recovered myself however in a few moments and looking at her with all the affection I could, 'My dear Miss Grenville,' said I, 'you appear extremely young—and may probably stand in need of some one's advice whose regard for you, joined to superior Age, perhaps superior Judgement might authorise her to give it—. I am that person, and I now challenge you to accept the offer I make you of my Confidence and Freindship, in return to which I shall only ask for yours—'

'You are extremely obliging, Ma'am'—said She—'and I am highly flattered by your attention to me—. But I am in no difficulty, no doubt, no uncertainty of situation in which any Advice can be wanted. Whenever I am, however,' continued she, brightening into a complaisant smile, 'I shall know where to apply.'

I bowed, but felt a good deal mortified by such a repulse; Still however I had not given up my point. I found that by the appearance of Sentiment and Freindship nothing was to be gained and determined therefore to renew my Attacks by Questions and Suppositions.

'Do you intend staying long in this part of England, Miss Grenville?'

'Yes, Ma'am, some time I beleive.'

'But how will Mr and Mrs Grenville bear your Absence?'

'They are neither of them alive, Ma'am.'

This was an answer I did not expect—I was quite silenced, and never felt so awkward in my Life—.

Letter the fifth

From a Young Lady very much in love to her Freind

My Uncle gets more stingy, my Aunt more particular, and I more in love every day. What shall we all be at this rate by the end of the year! I had this morning the happiness of receiving the following Letter from my dear Musgrove.[27]

Sackville[28] St: Jan^{ry} 7th

It is a month to day since I beheld my lovely Henrietta, and the sacred anniversary must and shall be kept in a manner becoming the day—by writing to her. Never shall I forget the moment when her Beauties first broke on my sight—No time as you well know can erase it from my Memory. It was at Lady Scudamore's. Happy Lady Scudamore to live within a mile of the divine Henrietta! When the lovely Creature first entered the room, Oh! what were my sensations? The sight of you was like the sight of a wonderful fine Thing. I started—I gazed at her with Admiration—She appeared every moment more Charming, and the unfortunate Musgrove became a Captive to your Charms before I had time to look about me. Yes Madam, I had the happiness of adoring you, an unhappiness for which I cannot be too grateful. 'What,' said he to himself, 'is Musgrove allowed to die for Henrietta? Enviable Mortal! and may he pine for her who is the object of universal Admiration, who is adored by a Colonel, and toasted[29] by a Baronet!—' Adorable Henrietta how beautiful you are! I declare you are quite divine! You are more than Mortal. You are an Angel. You are Venus herself. Inshort, Madam, you are the prettiest Girl I ever saw in my Life—and her Beauty is encreased in her Musgrove's Eyes, by permitting him to love her and allowing me to hope. And Ah! Angelic Miss Henrietta, Heaven is my Witness how ardently I do hope for the death of your villanous Uncle and his Abandoned[30] Wife, Since my fair one will not consent to be mine till their decease has placed her in affluence above what my fortune can procure—. Though it is an improvable Estate—.[31] Cruel Henrietta to persist in such a resolution! I am at present with my Sister where I mean to continue till my own house which tho' an excellent one is at present somewhat out of repair, is ready to receive me. Amiable princess of my Heart farewell—Of that Heart which trembles while it signs itself your most ardent Admirer

and devoted humble Servt

T. Musgrove

There is a pattern for a Love-letter[32] Matilda! Did you ever read such a masterpeice of Writing? Such Sense, Such

Sentiment, Such purity of Thought, Such flow of Language and such unfeigned Love in one Sheet? No, never I can answer for it, since a Musgrove is not to be met with by every Girl. Oh! how I long to be with him! I intend to send him the following in answer to his Letter tomorrow.

My dearest Musgrove—. Words can not express how happy your Letter made me; I thought I should have cried for Joy, for I love you better than any body in the World. I think you the most amiable, and the handsomest Man in England, and so to be sure you are. I never read so sweet a Letter in my Life. Do write me another just like it, and tell me you are in love with me in every other line. I quite die to see you. How shall we manage to see one another? for we are so much in love that we cannot live asunder. Oh! my dear Musgrove you cannot think how impatiently I wait for the death of my Uncle and Aunt—If they will not die soon, I beleive I shall run mad, for I get more in love with you every day of my Life. How happy your Sister is to enjoy the pleasure of your Company in her house, and how happy every body in London must be because you are there. I hope you will be so kind as to write to me again soon, for I never read such sweet Letters as yours. I am, my dearest Musgrove, most truly and faithfully yours for ever and ever

Henrietta Halton

I hope he will like my answer; it is as good a one as I can write, though nothing to his; Indeed I had always heard what a dab[33] he was at a Love-letter. I saw him you know for the first time at Lady Scudamore's—And when I saw her Ladyship afterwards she asked me how I liked her Cousin Musgrove?

'Why upon my word' said I, 'I think he is a very handsome young Man.'

'I am glad you think so,' replied she, 'for he is distractedly in love with you.'

'Law! Lady Scudamore,' said I, 'how can you talk so ridiculously?'

'Nay, 'tis very true,' answered She, 'I assure you, for he was in love with you from the first moment he beheld you.'

'I wish it may be true,' said I, 'for that is the only kind of love I would give a farthing[34] for—There is some Sense in being in love at first sight.'

'Well, I give you Joy of your conquest,' replied Lady Scudamore, 'and I beleive it to have been a very complete one; I am sure it is not a contemptible one, for my Cousin is a charming young fellow, has seen a great deal of the World, and writes the best Love-letters I ever read.'

This made me very happy, and I was excessively pleased with my conquest. However I thought it was proper to give myself a few Airs—So I said to her—

'This is all very pretty, Lady Scudamore, but you know that we young Ladies who are Heiresses must not throw ourselves away upon Men who have no fortune at all.'

'My dear Miss Halton,' said She, 'I am as much convinced of that as you can be, and I do assure you that I should be the last person to encourage your marrying any one who had not some pretensions to expect a fortune with you. Mr Musgrove is so far from being poor that he has an estate of Several hundreds an year[35] which is capable of great Improvement, and an excellent House, though at present it is not quite in repair.'

'If that is the case,' replied I, 'I have nothing more to say against him, and if as you say he is an informed young Man and can write good Love-letters, I am sure I have no reason to find fault with him for admiring me, tho' perhaps I may not marry him for all that, Lady Scudamore.'

'You are certainly under no obligation to marry him,' answered her Ladyship, 'except that which love himself will dictate to you, for if I am not greatly mistaken you are at this very moment unknown to yourself, cherishing a most tender affection for him.'

'Law, Lady Scudamore,' replied I blushing, 'how can you think of such a thing?'

'Because every look, every word betrays it,' answered She; 'Come, my dear Henrietta, consider me as a freind, and be sincere with me—Do not you prefer Mr Musgrove to any man of your acquaintance?'

'Pray do not ask me such questions, Lady Scudamore,' said I turning away my head, 'for it is not fit for me to answer them.'

'Nay my Love,' replied she, 'now you confirm my suspicions. But why, Henrietta, should you be ashamed to own a well-placed Love, or why refuse to confide in me?'

'I am not ashamed to own it;' said I taking Courage. 'I do not refuse to confide in you or blush to say that I do love your cousin Mr Musgrove, that I am sincerely attached to him, for it is no disgrace to love a handsome Man. If he were plain indeed I might have had reason to be ashamed of a passion which must have been mean since the Object would have been unworthy. But with such a figure and face, and such beautiful hair as your Cousin has, why should I blush to own that such Superior Merit has made an impression on me.'

'My sweet Girl' (said Lady Scudamore embracing me with great Affection) 'what a delicate way of thinking you have in these Matters, and what a quick discernment for one of your years! Oh! how I honour you for such Noble Sentiments!'

'Do you, Ma'am?' said I; 'You are vastly obliging. But pray, Lady Scudamore, did your Cousin himself tell you of his Affection for me? I shall like him the better if he did, for what is a Lover without a Confidante?'

'Oh! my Love' replied She, 'you were born for each other. Every word you say more deeply convinces me that your Minds are actuated by the invisible power of simpathy, for your opinions and Sentiments so exactly coincide. Nay, the colour of your Hair is not very different. Yes, my dear Girl, the poor despairing Musgrove did reveal to me the story of his Love—. Nor was I surprised at it—I know not how it was, but I had a kind of presentiment that he <u>would</u> be in love with you.'

'Well, but how did he break it to you?'

'It was not till after supper. We were sitting round the fire together talking on indifferent subjects, though to say the truth the Conversation was cheifly on my side, for he was thoughtful and silent, when on a sudden he interrupted me in the midst of something I was saying, by exclaiming in a most Theatrical tone—

"Yes I'm in love I feel it now
And Henrietta Halton has undone me—"'[36]

'Oh! What a sweet Way' replied I, 'of declaring his Passion! To make such a couple of charming Lines about me! What a pity it is that they are not in rhime!'

'I am very glad you like it,' answered She; 'To be sure there was a great deal of Taste in it. "And are you in love with her, Cousin?" said I. "I am very sorry for it, for unexceptionable as you are in every respect, with a pretty Estate capable of Great improvements, and an excellent House tho' somewhat out of repair, Yet who can hope to aspire with success to the adorable Henrietta who has had an offer from a Colonel and been toasted by a Baronet—"' '<u>That</u> I have—' cried I. Lady Scudamore continued. '"Ah, dear Cousin," replied he, "I am so well convinced of the little Chance I can have of winning her who is adored by thousands, that I need no assurances of yours to make me more thoroughly so. Yet surely neither you or the fair Henrietta herself will deny me the exquisite Gratification of dieing for her, of falling a victim of her Charms. And when I am dead"—continued he—'

'Oh Lady Scudamore,' said I wiping my eyes, 'that such a sweet Creature should talk of dieing!'

'It is an affecting Circumstance indeed,' replied Lady Scudamore. '"When I am dead," said he, "Let me be carried and lain at her feet, and perhaps she may not disdain to drop a pitying tear on my poor remains."'

'Dear Lady Scudamore' interrupted I, 'say no more on this affecting Subject. I cannot bear it.'

'Oh! how I admire the sweet Sensibility of your Soul, and as I would not for Worlds wound it too deeply, I will be silent.'

'Pray go on' said I. She did so.

'"And then," added he, "Ah! Cousin, imagine what my transports will be when I feel the dear precious drops trickle o'er my face! Who would not die to taste such extacy! And when I am interred, may the divine Henrietta bless some happier Youth with her affection, May he be as tenderly attached to her as the hapless Musgrove and while he crumbles to dust, May they live an example of Felicity in the Conjugal state!" '

'Did you ever hear any thing so pathetic? What a charming wish, to be lain at my feet when he was dead! Oh! what an exalted mind he must have to be capable of such a wish! Lady Scudamore went on.'

' "Ah! my dear Cousin," replied I to him, "Such noble behaviour as this, must melt the heart of any Woman however obdurate it may naturally be; and could the divine Henrietta but hear your generous wishes for her happiness, all gentle as is her Mind, I have not a doubt but that she would pity your affection and endeavour to return it." "Oh! Cousin," answered he, "do not endeavour to raise my hopes by such flattering Assurances. No, I cannot hope to please this angel of a Woman, and the only thing which remains for me to do, is to die." "True Love is ever desponding," replied I, "but I, my dear Tom, will give you even greater hopes of conquering this fair one's heart, than I have yet given you, by assuring you that I watched her with the strictest attention during the whole day, and could plainly discover that she cherishes in her bosom though unknown to herself, a most tender affection for you." '

'Dear Lady Scudamore,' cried I, 'This is more than I ever knew!'

'Did not I say that it was unknown to yourself? "I did not," continued I to him, "encourage you by saying this at first, that Surprise might render the pleasure Still Greater." "No, Cousin," replied he in a languid voice, "nothing will convince me that I can have touched the heart of Henrietta Halton, and if you are deceived yourself, do not attempt deceiving me." Inshort my Love it was the work of some hours for me to persuade the poor despairing Youth that you had really a preference for him; but when at last he could no longer deny the force of my arguments, or discredit what I told him, his transports, his Raptures, his Extacies are beyond my power to describe.'

'Oh! the dear Creature,' cried I, 'how passionately he loves me! But, dear Lady Scudamore, did you tell him that I was totally dependant on my Uncle and Aunt?'

'Yes, I told him every thing.'

'And what did he say?'

'He exclaimed with virulence against Uncles and Aunts; Accused the Laws of England for allowing them to possess their Estates when wanted by their Nephews or Neices, and wished he were in the House of Commons, that he might reform the Legislature, and rectify all its abuses.'

'Oh! the sweet Man! What a spirit he has!' said I.

'He could not flatter himself, he added, that the adorable Henrietta would condescend for his Sake to resign those Luxuries and that Splendor to which She had been used, and accept only in exchange the Comforts and Elegancies which his limited Income could afford her, even supposing that his house were in Readiness to receive her. I told him that it could not be expected that she would; it would be doing her an injustice to suppose her capable of giving up the power she now possesses and so nobly uses of doing such extensive Good to the poorer part of her fellow Creatures, merely for the gratification of you and herself.'

'To be sure,' said I, 'I am very Charitable every now and then. And what did Mr Musgrove say to this?'

'He replied that he was under a melancholy Necessity of owning the truth of what I said, and therefore if he should be the happy Creature destined to be the Husband of the Beautiful Henrietta he must bring himself to wait, however impatiently, for the fortunate day, when she might be freed from the power of worthless Relations and able to bestow herself on him.'

What a noble Creature he is! Oh! Matilda what a fortunate one I am, who am to be his Wife! My Aunt is calling to me to come and make the pies.[37] So adeiu my dear freind,

and beleive me yours etc.—H. Halton

Finis

[Scraps]

To Miss Fanny Catherine Austen[1]

My dear Neice

As I am prevented by the great distance between Rowling and Steventon[2] from superintending Your Education Myself, the care of which will probably on that account devolve on your Father and Mother, I think it is my particular Duty to prevent your feeling as much as possible the want of my personal instructions, by addressing to You on paper my Opinions and Admonitions on the conduct of Young Women,[3] which you will find expressed in the following pages. I am my dear Neice

Your affectionate Aunt

The Author

The female philosopher[1]
a Letter

My dear Louisa

Your friend Mr Millar called upon us yesterday in his way to Bath, whither he is going for his health; two of his daughters were with him, but the oldest and the three Boys are with their Mother in Sussex. Though you have often told me that Miss Millar was remarkably handsome, You never mentioned anything of her Sisters' beauty; yet they are certainly extremely pretty. I'll give you their description.—Julia is eighteen; with a countenance in which Modesty, Sense and Dignity are happily blended, she has a form which at once presents you with Grace, Elegance and Symmetry. Charlotte who is just Sixteen is shorter than her Sister, and though her figure cannot boast the easy dignity of Julia's, yet it has a pleasing plumpness which is in a different way as estimable. She is fair and her face is expressive sometimes of softness the most bewitching, and at others of Vivacity the most striking. She appears to have infinite Wit and a good humour unalterable; her conversation during the half hour they set with us, was replete with humorous Sallies, Bonmots and repartées;[2] while the sensible, the amiable Julia uttered Sentiments of Morality[3] worthy of a heart like her own.

Mr Millar appeared to answer the character I had always received of him. My Father met him with that look of Love, that social Shake, and Cordial kiss[4] which marked his gladness at beholding an old and valued friend from whom thro' various circumstances he had been separated nearly twenty Years. Mr Millar observed (and very justly too) that many events had befallen each during that interval of time, which gave occasion to the lovely Julia for making most sensible reflections on the many changes in their situation which so long a period had occasioned, on the advantages of some, and the disadvantages of others. From this subject she made a short digression to the instability of human pleasures and the uncertainty of their duration, which led her to observe that all earthly Joys must be imperfect. She was proceeding to illustrate this doctrine by examples from the Lives of great Men when the Carriage came to the Door and the amiable Moralist with her Father and Sister was obliged to depart, but not without a promise of spending five or six months with us[5] on their return. We of course mentioned You, and I assure you that ample Justice was done to your Merits by all. 'Louisa Clarke' (said I) 'is in general a very pleasant Girl, yet sometimes her good humour is clouded by Peevishness, Envy and Spite. She neither wants Understanding nor is without some pretensions to Beauty, but these are so very trifling, that the value she sets on her personal charms, and the adoration she expects them to be offered are at once a striking example of her vanity, her pride, and her folly.' So said I, and to my opinion every one added weight by the concurrence of their own.

Your affec[te] Arabella[6] Smythe

The first Act of a Comedy

Characters

Popgun	Maria
Charles	Pistoletta
Postilion[1]	Hostess
Chorus of Ploughboys	Cook
and	and
Strephon[2]	Chloe

Scene—an Inn
Enter Hostess, Charles, Maria and Cook

Hostess to Maria: If the gentry in the Lion[3] should want beds, shew them number 9.—
Maria: Yes Mistress.

exit Maria

Hostess to Cook: If their Honours in the Moon ask for the bill of fare,[4] give it them.
Cook: I wull, I wull.[5] exit Cook
Hostess to Charles: If their Ladyships in the Sun ring their Bell—answer it.
Charles: Yes, Ma'am.—

Exeunt Severally

Scene changes to the Moon, and discovers
Popgun and Pistoletta.

Pistoletta: Pray papa, how far is it to London?
Popgun: My Girl, my Darling, my favourite of all my Children, who art the picture of thy poor Mother, who died two months ago, with whom I am going to Town to marry Strephon, and to whom I mean to bequeath my whole Estate, it wants seven Miles.

Scene changes to the Sun—
Enter Chloe and a chorus of ploughboys.[6]

Chloe: Where am I? At Hounslow—.[7] Where go I? To London—. What to do? To be married—. Unto whom?
Unto Strephon: Who is he? A Youth. Then I will sing a Song.

Song

I go to Town
And when I come down,
I shall be married to Stree-phon[8]
And that to me will be fun.

Chorus: Be fun, be fun, be fun,
And that to me will be fun.

Enter Cook

Cook: Here is the bill of fare.
Chloe reads: 2 Ducks, a leg of beef, a stinking partridge,[9] and a tart.—I will have the leg of beef and the partridge.

exit Cook

And now I will sing another song.

Song

I am going to have my dinner,
After which I shan't be thinner,
I wish I had here Strephon
For he would carve the partridge if it should
be a tough one.

Chorus: Tough one, tough one, tough one,
For he would carve the partridge if it
Should be a tough one.

Exit Chloe and Chorus—.

Scene changes to the inside of the Lion.
Enter Strephon and Postilion

Streph: You drove me from Staines to this place, from whence I mean to go to Town to marry Chloe. How much is your due?

Post: Eighteen pence.

Streph: Alas, my friend, I have but a bad guinea[10] with which I mean to support myself in Town. But I will pawn to you an undirected Letter[11] that I received from Chloe.

Post: Sir, I accept your offer.

End of the first Act

A Letter from a Young Lady, whose feelings being too Strong for her Judgement led her into the commission of Errors which her Heart disapproved.

Many have been the cares and vicissitudes of my past life, my beloved Ellinor, and the only consolation I feel for their bitterness is that on a close examination of my conduct, I am convinced that I have strictly deserved them. I murdered my father at a very early period of my Life, I have since murdered my Mother, and I am now going to murder my Sister. I have changed my religion so often that at present I have not an idea of any left. I have been a perjured witness in every public tryal for these last twelve Years, and I have forged my own Will. In short there is scarcely a crime that I have not committed—But I am now going to reform. Colonel Martin of the Horse guards[1] has paid his Addresses to me, and we are to be married in a few days. As there is something singular in our Courtship, I will give you an account of it. Colonel Martin is the second son of the late Sir John Martin who died immensely rich, but bequeathing only one hundred thousand pound apiece to his three younger Children, left the bulk of his fortune, about eight Million to the present Sir Thomas. Upon his small pittance the Colonel lived tolerably contented for nearly four months when he took it into his head to determine on getting the whole of his eldest Brother's Estate. A new will was forged and the Colonel produced it in Court—but nobody would swear to it's being the right Will except himself, and he had sworn so much that Nobody beleived him. At that moment I happened to be passing by the door of the Court, and was beckoned in by the Judge who told the Colonel that I was a Lady ready to witness anything for the cause of Justice, and advised him to apply to me. In short the Affair was soon adjusted. The Colonel and I swore to its' being the right will, and Sir Thomas has been obliged to resign all his illgotten Wealth. The Colonel in gratitude waited on me the next day with an offer of his hand—. I am now going to murder my Sister.

Yours Ever,

Anna Parker

A Tour through Wales[1]
in a Letter from a young Lady

My dear Clara

I have been so long on the ramble[2] that I have not till now had it in my power to thank you for your Letter—. We left our dear home on last Monday Month;[3] and proceeded on our tour through Wales, which is a principality contiguous to England and gives the title to the Prince of Wales. We travelled on horseback by preference. My Mother rode upon our little poney and Fanny and I walked by her side or rather ran, for my Mother is so fond of riding fast that She galloped all the way. You may be sure that we were in a fine perspiration[4] when we came to our place of resting. Fanny has taken a great many Drawings of the Country, which are very beautiful, tho' perhaps not such exact resemblances as might be wished, from their being taken as she ran along. It would astonish you to see all the Shoes we wore out in our Tour. We determined to take a good Stock with us and therefore each took a pair of our own besides those we set off in. However we were obliged to have them both capped and heelpeiced[5] at Carmarthen, and at last when they were quite gone, Mama was so kind as to lend us a pair of blue Sattin Slippers,[6] of which we each took one and hopped home from Hereford[7] delightfully—

I am your ever affectionate

Elizabeth Johnson

A Tale

A Gentleman whose family name I shall conceal, bought a small Cottage in Pembrokeshire[1] about two Years ago. This daring Action was suggested to him by his elder Brother who promised to furnish two rooms and a Closet[2] for him, provided he would take a small house near the borders of an extensive Forest, and about three Miles from the Sea. Wilhelminus[3] gladly accepted the Offer and continued for some time searching after such a retreat when he was one morning agreably releived fiom his Suspence by reading this advertisement in a Newspaper.

To be Lett

> A neat Cottage on the borders of an extensive forest and about three Miles from the Sea. It is ready furnished except two rooms and a Closet.

The delighted Wilhelminus posted away immediately to his brother, and shewed him the advertisement. Robertus congratulated him and sent him in his Carriage to take possession of the Cottage. After travelling for three days and six Nights without Stopping, they arrived at the Forest and following a track which led by it's side down a steep Hill over which ten Rivulets meandered, they reached the Cottage in half an hour. Wilhelminus alighted, and after knocking for some time without receiving any answer or hearing anyone stir within, he opened the door which was fastened only by a wooden latch and entered a small room, which he immediately perceived to be one of the two that were unfurnished—From thence he proceeded into a Closet equally bare. A pair of Stairs[4] that went out of it led him into a room above, no less destitute, and these apartments he found composed the whole of the House. He was by no means displeased with this discovery, as he had the comfort of reflecting that he should not be obliged to lay out any thing on furniture himself—. He returned immediately to his Brother, who took him next day to every Shop in Town, and bought what ever was requisite to furnish the two rooms and the Closet. In a few days everything was completed, and Wilhelminus returned to take possession of his Cottage. Robertus accompanied him, with his Lady the amiable Cecilia and her two lovely Sisters Arabella and Marina to whom Wilhelminus was tenderly attached, and a large number of Attendants.—An ordinary Genius[5] might probably have been embarrassed in endeavouring to accomodate so large a party, but Wilhelminus with admirable presence of Mind gave order for the immediate erection of two noble Tents in an open Spot in the Forest adjoining to the house. Their Construction was both simple and elegant—A Couple of old blankets, each supported by four sticks, gave a striking proof of that Taste for Architecture and that happy ease in overcoming difficulties which were some of Wilhelminus's most striking Virtues.

Finis

End of the Second Volume

Volume the Third

Manuscript page 1 of 'Catharine, or The Bower', in Jane Austen's notebook *Volume the Third*. (By permission of the British Library.)

VOLUME THE THIRD

Jane Austen—May 6th 1792.[1]

Contents[2]

To Miss Mary Lloyd,[1]
The following Novel is by permission
Dedicated,
by her Obed[t] humble Serv[t]
The Author

Evelyn[2]

In a retired part of the County of Sussex there is a village (for what I know to the Contrary) called Evelyn, perhaps one of the most beautiful Spots in the south of England. A Gentleman passing through it on horseback about twenty years ago, was so entirely of my opinion in this respect, that he put up at the little Alehouse in it and enquired with great earnestness whether there were any house to be lett in the Parish.[3] The Landlady, who as well as every one else in Evelyn was remarkably amiable, shook her head at this question, but seemed unwilling to give him any answer. He could not bear this uncertainty—yet knew not how to obtain the information he desired. To repeat a question which had already appear'd to make the good woman uneasy was impossible—. He turned from her in visible agitation. 'What a situation am I in!' said he to himself as he walked to the window and threw up the sash.[4] He found himself revived by the Air, which he felt to a much greater degree when he had opened the window than he had done before. Yet it was but for a moment—. The agonizing pain of Doubt and Suspence again weighed down his Spirits. The good woman who had watched in eager silence every turn of his Countenance with that benevolence which characterizes the inhabitants of Evelyn, intreated him to tell her the cause of his uneasiness. 'Is there anything, Sir, in my power to do that may releive Your Greifs—Tell me in what Manner I can sooth them, and beleive me that the freindly balm of Comfort and Assistance shall not be wanting; for indeed, Sir, I have a simpathetic Soul.'

'Amiable Woman' (said Mr Gower, affected almost to tears by this generous offer) 'This Greatness of mind in one to whom

I am almost a Stranger, serves but to make me the more warmly wish for a house in this sweet village—. What would I not give to be your Neighbour, to be blessed with your Acquaintance, and with the farther knowledge of your virtues! Oh! with what pleasure would I form myself by such an example! Tell me then, best of Women, is there no possibility?—I cannot speak—You know my Meaning—.'

'Alas! Sir,' replied Mrs Willis, 'there is none. Every house in this village, from the sweetness of the Situation, and the purity of the Air, in which neither Misery, Ill health, or Vice are ever wafted, is inhabited. And yet,' (after a short pause) 'there is a Family, who tho' warmly attached to the spot, yet from a peculiar Generosity of Disposition would perhaps be willing to oblige you with their house.' He eagerly caught at this idea, and having gained a direction to the place, he set off immediately on his walk to it. As he approached the House, he was delighted with its situation. It was in the exact centre of a small circular paddock,[5] which was enclosed by a regular paling, and bordered with a plantation of Lombardy poplars, and Spruce firs alternatively placed in three rows. A gravel walk ran through this beautiful Shrubbery,[6] and as the remainder of the paddock was unincumbered with any other Timber, the surface of it perfectly even and smooth, and grazed by four white Cows[7] which were disposed at equal distances from each other, the whole appearance of the place as Mr Gower entered the Paddock was uncommonly striking. A beautifully-rounded, gravel road without any turn or interruption[8] led immediately to the house. Mr Gower rang—the Door was soon opened. 'Are M^r^ and Mrs Webb at home?' 'My Good Sir, they are'—replied the Servant; And leading the way, conducted Mr Gower upstairs into a very elegant Dressing room, where a Lady rising from her seat, welcomed him with all the Generosity which Mrs Willis had attributed to the Family.

'Welcome best of Men[9]—Welcome to this House, and to everything it contains. William, tell your Master of the happiness I enjoy—invite him to partake of it—. Bring up some Chocolate[10] immediately; Spread a Cloth in the dining Parlour, and carry in the venison pasty—.[11] In the mean time let the

Gentleman have some sandwiches, and bring in a Basket of Fruit—Send up some Ices and a bason of Soup, and do not forget some Jellies and Cakes.' Then turning to Mr Gower, and taking out her purse, 'Accept this, my good Sir,—. Beleive me you are welcome to everything that is in my power to bestow.—I wish my purse were weightier, but Mr Webb must make up my deficiences—. I know he has cash in the house to the amount of an hundred pounds, which he shall bring you immediately.' Mr Gower felt overpowered by her generosity as he put the purse in his pocket, and from the excess of his Gratitude, could scarcely express himself intelligibly when he accepted her offer of the hundred pounds. Mr Webb soon entered the room, and repeated every protestation of Freindship and Cordiality which his Lady had already made. The Chocolate, the Sandwiches, the Jellies, the Cakes, the Ice, and the Soup soon made their appearance, and Mr Gower having tasted something of all, and pocketted the rest, was conducted into the dining parlour, where he eat a most excellent Dinner and partook of the most exquisite Wines, while M^{r} and Mrs Webb stood by him still pressing him to eat and drink a little more. 'And now my good Sir,' said Mr Webb, when Mr Gower's repast was concluded, 'what else can we do to contribute to your happiness and express the Affection we bear you. Tell us what you wish more to receive, and depend upon our gratitude for the communication of your wishes.' 'Give me then your house and Grounds; I ask for nothing else.' 'It is yours,' exclaimed both at once; 'from this moment it is yours.' The Agreement concluded on and the present accepted by Mr Gower, Mr Webb rang to have the Carriage ordered, telling William at the same time to call the Young Ladies.

'Best of Men,' said Mrs Webb, 'we will not long intrude upon your Time.'

'Make no Apologies dear Madam,' replied Mr Gower, 'You are welcome to stay this half hour if you like it.'

They both burst forth into raptures of Admiration at his politeness, which they agreed served only to make their Conduct appear more inexcusable in trespassing on his time.

The Young Ladies soon entered the room. The eldest of

them was about seventeen, the other, several years younger. Mr Gower had no sooner fixed his Eyes on Miss Webb than he felt that something more was necessary to his happiness than the house he had just received—Mrs Webb introduced him to her daughter. 'Our dear freind Mr Gower, my Love—He has been so good as to accept of this house, small as it is, and to promise to keep it for ever.' 'Give me leave to assure you, Sir,' said Miss Webb, 'that I am highly sensible of your kindness in this respect, which from the shortness of my Father's and Mother's acquaintance with you, is more than usually flattering.'

Mr Gower bowed—'You are too obliging, Ma'am—I assure you that I like the house extremely—and if they would complete their generosity by giving me their eldest daughter in marriage with a handsome portion,[12] I should have nothing more to wish for.' This compliment brought a blush into the cheeks of the lovely Miss Webb, who seemed however to refer herself to her father and Mother. They looked delighted at each other—At length Mrs Webb breaking silence, said—'We bend under a weight of obligations to you which we can never repay. Take our girl, take our Maria, and on her must the difficult task fall, of endeavouring to make some return to so much Benefiscence.' Mr Webb added, 'Her fortune is but ten thousand pounds,[13] which is almost too small a sum to be offered.' This objection however being instantly removed by the generosity of Mr Gower, who declared himself satisfied with the sum mentioned, Mr and Mrs Webb, with their youngest daughter took their leave, and on the next day, the nuptials of their eldest with Mr Gower were celebrated.[14]—This amiable Man now found himself perfectly happy; united to a very lovely and deserving young woman, with an handsome fortune, an elegant house, settled in the village of Evelyn, and by that means enabled to cultivate his acquaintance with Mrs Willis, could he have a wish ungratified?—For some months he found that he could not, till one day as he was walking in the Shrubbery with Maria leaning on his arm, they observed a rose full-blown lying on the gravel; it had fallen from a rose tree which with three others had been planted by Mr Webb to give a pleasing variety[15] to the walk.

These four Rose trees served also to mark the quarters of the Shrubbery, by which means the Traveller might always know how far in his progress round the Paddock he was got—. Maria stooped to pick up the beautiful flower, and with all her Family Generosity presented it to her Husband. 'My dear Frederic,' said she, 'pray take this charming rose.' 'Rose!' exclaimed Mr Gower—. 'Oh! Maria, of what does not that remind me! Alas, my poor Sister, how have I neglected you!' The truth was that Mr Gower was the only son of a very large Family, of which Miss Rose Gower was the thirteenth daughter. This Young Lady whose merits deserved a better fate than she met with, was the darling of her relations—From the clearness of her skin and the Brilliancy of her Eyes, she was fully entitled to all their partial affection. Another circumstance contributed to the general Love they bore her, and that was one of the finest heads of hair in the world. A few Months before her Brother's Marriage, her heart had been engaged by the attentions and charms of a young Man whose high rank and expectations seemed to foretell objections from his Family to a match which would be highly desirable to theirs. Proposals were made on the young Man's part, and proper objections on his Father's—He was desired to return from Carlisle where he was with his beloved Rose, to the family seat in Sussex.[16] He was obliged to comply, and the angry father then finding from his Conversation how determined he was to marry no other woman, sent him for a fortnight to the Isle of Wight under the care of the Family Chaplain, with the hope of overcoming his Constancy by Time and Absence in a foreign Country.[17] They accordingly prepared to bid a long adieu to England—The young Nobleman was not allowed to see his Rosa. They set sail—A storm arose which baffled the arts of the Seamen. The Vessel was wrecked on the coast of Calshot[18] and every Soul on board perished. This sad Event soon reached Carlisle, and the beautiful Rose was affected by it, beyond the power of Expression. It was to soften her affliction by obtaining a picture of her unfortunate Lover that her brother undertook a Journey into Sussex, where he hoped that his petition would not be rejected, by the severe yet afflicted Father. When he reached Evelyn he was not many miles from —— Castle, but the pleasing events which befell him in that place had for a while made him totally forget the object of his Journey and his unhappy Sister. The little incident of the rose however brought everything concerning her to his recollection again, and he bitterly repented his neglect. He returned to the house immediately and agitated by Greif, Apprehension and Shame wrote the following Letter to Rosa.

July 14th—. Evelyn

My dearest Sister

As it is now four months since I left Carlisle, during which period I have not once written to you, You will perhaps unjustly accuse me of Neglect and Forgetfulness. Alas! I blush when I own the truth of your Accusation.—Yet if you are still alive, do not think too harshly of me, or suppose that I could for a moment forget the situation of my Rose. Beleive me I will forget you no longer, but will hasten as soon as possible to —— Castle if I find by your answer that you are still alive. Maria joins me in every dutiful and affectionate wish, and I am yours sincerely

F. Gower

He waited in the most anxious expectation for an answer to his Letter, which arrived as soon as the great distance from Carlisle would admit of.—But alas, it came not from Rosa.

Carlisle July 17th

Dear Brother

My Mother has taken the liberty of opening your Letter to poor Rose, as she has been dead these six weeks. Your long absence and continued Silence gave us all great uneasiness and hastened her to the Grave. Your Journey to —— Castle therefore may be spared. You do not tell us where you have been since the time of your quitting Carlisle, nor in any way account for your tedious absence, which gives us some surprise. We all unite in Comp^{ts} to Maria, and beg to know who she is—.

Y^{r} affec^{te} Sister

M. Gower

This Letter, by which Mr Gower was obliged to attribute to his own conduct, his Sister's death, was so violent a shock to his feelings, that in spite of his living at Evelyn where Illness was scarcely ever heard of, he was attacked by a fit of the gout,[19] which confining him to his own room afforded an opportunity to Maria of shining in that favourite character of Sir Charles Grandison's, a nurse.[20] No woman could ever appear more amiable than Maria did under such circumstances, and at last by her unremitting attentions had the pleasure of seeing him gradually recover the use of his feet. It was a blessing by no means lost on him, for he was no sooner in a condition to leave the house, that he mounted his horse, and rode to —— Castle, wishing to find whether his Lordship softened by his Son's death, might have been brought to consent to the match, had both <u>he</u> and Rosa been alive. His amiable Maria followed him with her Eyes till she could see him no longer, and then sinking into her chair overwhelmed with Greif, found that in his absence she could enjoy no comfort.

Mr Gower arrived late in the evening at the castle, which was situated on a woody Eminence commanding a beautiful prospect of the Sea. Mr Gower did not dislike the situation, tho' it was certainly greatly inferior to that of his own house. There was an irregularity in the fall of the ground, and a profusion of old Timber which appeared to him illsuited to the stile of the Castle, for it being a building of a very ancient date, he thought it required the Paddock of Evelyn lodge to form a Contrast, and enliven the structure.[21] The gloomy appearance of the old Castle frowning on him as he followed it's winding approach, struck him with terror.[22] Nor did he think himself safe, till he was introduced into the Drawing room where the Family were assembled to tea. Mr Gower was a perfect stranger to every one in the Circle but tho' he was always timid in the Dark and easily terrified when alone, he did not want that more necessary and more noble courage which enabled him without a Blush to enter a large party of superior Rank, whom he had never seen before, and to take his Seat amongst them with perfect Indifference. The name of Gower was not unknown to Lord ——. He felt distressed and astonished; Yet rose and received him with all the politeness of a well-bred Man. Lady —— who felt a deeper Sorrow at the loss of her Son, than his Lordship's harder heart was capable of, could hardly keep her Seat when she found that he was the Brother of her lamented Henry's Rosa. 'My Lord,' said Mr Gower as soon as he was seated, 'You are perhaps surprised at receiving a visit from a Man whom you could not have the least expectation of seeing here. But my Sister, my unfortunate Sister, is the real cause of my thus troubling you: That luckless Girl is now no more—and tho' she can receive no pleasure from the intelligence, yet for the satisfaction of her Family I wish to know whether the Death of this unhappy Pair has made an impression on your heart sufficiently strong to obtain that consent to their Marriage which in happier circumstances you would not be persuaded to give Supposing that they now were both alive.' His Lordship seemed lossed in astonishment. Lady —— could not support the mention of her Son, and left the room in tears; the rest of the Family remained attentively listening, almost persuaded that Mr Gower was distracted. 'Mr Gower,' replied his Lordship 'This is a very odd question—It appears to me that you are supposing an impossibility—No one can more sincerely regret the death of my Son than I have always done, and it gives me great concern to know that Miss Gower's was hastened by his—. Yet to suppose them alive is destroying at once the Motive for a change in my sentiments concerning the affair.' 'My Lord,' replied Mr Gower in anger, 'I see that you are a most inflexible Man, and that not even the death of your Son can make you wish his future Life happy. I will no longer detain your Lordship. I see, I plainly see that you are a very vile Man—And now I have the honour of wishing all your Lordships, and Ladyships a good Night.' He immediately left the room, forgetting in the heat of his Anger the lateness of the hour, which at any other time would have made him tremble, and leaving the whole Company unanimous in their opinion of his being Mad. When however he had mounted his horse and the great Gates of the Castle had shut him out, he felt an universal tremor through out his whole frame. If we consider his Situation indeed, alone, on horseback, as late in the year as August, and in the day, as nine o'clock, with no light to direct him but that of the Moon almost full, and the Stars which alarmed him by their twinkling, who can refrain from pitying him?—No house within a quarter of a mile, and a Gloomy Castle blackened by the deep shade of Walnuts and Pines, behind him.—He felt indeed almost distracted with his fears, and shutting his Eyes till he arrived at the Village to prevent his seeing either Gipsies or Ghosts,[23] he rode on a full gallop all the way.

[JA's manuscript ends here. The following continuation of 'Evelyn' is in the hand of her nephew James Edward Austen-Leigh, written in the notebook *Volume the Third* c.1815–16 on pages Austen had left blank for a later addition and possibly with her blessing and advice.[24]]

On his return home, he rang the housebell, but no one appeared, a second time he rang, but the door was not opened, a third and a fourth with as little success, when observing the dining parlour window open he leapt in, and persued his way through the house till he reached Maria's Dressingroom, where he found all the servants assembled at tea. Surprized at so very unusual a sight, he fainted, on his recovery he found himself on the Sofa, with his wife's maid kneeling by him, chafing his temples with Hungary water—.[25] From her he learned that his beloved Maria had been so much grieved at his departure that she died of a broken heart about 3 hours after his departure.

He then became sufficiently composed to give necessary orders for her funeral which took place the Monday following this being the Saturday—When Mr Gower had settled the order of the procession he set out himself[26] to Carlisle, to give vent to his sorrow in the bosom of his family—He arrived there in high health and spirits, after a delightful journey of 3 days and a ½—What was his surprize on entering the Breakfast parlour to see Rosa, his beloved Rosa, seated on a Sofa; at the sight of him she fainted and would have fallen had not a Gentleman sitting with his back to the door, started up and saved her from sinking to the ground—She very soon came to herself and then introduced this gentleman to her Brother as her Husband a Mr Davenport—

'But my dearest Rosa,' said the astonished Gower, 'I thought you were dead and buried.' 'Why, my dear Frederick,' replied Rosa 'I wished you to think so, hoping that you would spread the report about the country and it would thus by some means reach —— Castle. By this I hoped some how or other to touch the hearts of its inhabitants. It was not till the day before yesterday that I heard of the death of my beloved Henry which I learned from M^{r} D—— who concluded by offering me his hand. I accepted it with transport, and was married yesterday—' Mr Gower, embraced his sister and shook hands with Mr Davenport, he then took a stroll into the town—As he passed by a public house he called for a pot of beer,[27] which was brought him immediately by his old friend Mrs Willis—

Great was his astonishment at seeing Mrs Willis in Carlisle. But not forgetful of the respect he owed her, he dropped on one knee, and received the frothy cup from her, more grateful to *him* than Nectar[28]—He instantly made her an offer of his hand and heart, which she graciously condescended to accept, telling him that she was only on a visit to her cousin, who kept the *Anchor* and should be ready to return to Evelyn, whenever he chose—The next morning they were married and immediately proceeded to Evelyn—When he reached home, he recollected that he had never written to M^{r} and Mrs Webb to inform them of the death of their daughter, which he rightly supposed they knew nothing of, as they never took in any newspapers—He immediately dispatched the following Letter—

Evelyn—Augst 19th 1809

Dearest Madam,

How can words express the poignancy of my feelings! Our Maria, our beloved Maria is no more, she breathed her last, on Saturday the 12th of Augst—I see you now in an agony of grief lamenting not your own, but my loss—Rest satisfied I am happy, possessed of my lovely Sarah what more can I wish for?—

I remain

respectfully Yours

F. Gower

Westgate Builgs[29] Augst 22d

Generous, best of Men

how truly we rejoice to hear of your present welfare and happiness! and how truly grateful are we for your unexampled generosity in writing to condole with us on the late unlucky accident which befel our Maria—I have enclosed a draught[30] on our banker for 30 pounds, which Mr Webb joins with me in entreating you and the aimiable Sarah to accept—

Your most grateful
Anne Augusta Webb

Mr and Mrs Gower resided many years at Evelyn enjoying perfect happiness the just reward of their virtues. The only alteration which took place at Evelyn was that Mr and Mrs Davenport settled there in Mrs Willis's former abode and were for many years the proprietors of the White Horse Inn—

To Miss Austen[1]

Madam

Encouraged by your warm patronage of The beautiful Cassandra, and The History of England, which through your generous support, have obtained a place in every library in the Kingdom, and run through threescore Editions,[2] I take the liberty of begging the same Exertions in favour of the following Novel, which I humbly flatter myself, possesses Merit beyond any already published, or any that will ever in future appear, except such as may proceed from the pen of Your Most Grateful Humble Serv[t]

The Author

Steventon August 1792—

Catharine,
or the Bower[3]

Catharine had the misfortune, as many heroines have had before her,[4] of losing her Parents when she was very young, and of being brought up under the care of a Maiden Aunt, who while she tenderly loved her, watched over her conduct with so scrutinizing a severity, as to make it very doubtful to many people, and to Catharine amongst the rest, whether she loved her or not. She had frequently been deprived of a real pleasure through this jealous Caution, had been sometimes obliged to relinquish a Ball because an Officer was to be there, or to dance with a Partner of her Aunt's introduction in preference to one of her own Choice. But her Spirits were naturally good, and not easily depressed, and she possessed such a fund of vivacity and good humour as could only be damped by some very serious vexation.—Besides these antidotes against every disappointment, and consolations under them, she had another, which afforded her constant releif in all her misfortunes, and that was a fine shady Bower, the work of her own infantine Labours assisted by those of two young Companions who had resided in the same village—. To this Bower, which terminated a very pleasant and retired walk in her Aunt's Garden, she always wandered whenever anything disturbed her, and it possessed such a charm over her senses, as constantly to tranquillize her mind and quiet her spirits—Solitude and reflection might perhaps have had the same effect in her Bed Chamber, yet Habit had so strengthened the idea which Fancy had first suggested, that such a thought never occurred to Kitty who was firmly persuaded that her Bower alone could restore her to herself. Her imagination was warm, and in her Freindships, as well as in the whole tenure[5] of her Mind, she was enthousiastic.[6] This beloved Bower had been the united work of herself and two amiable Girls, for whom since her earliest Years, she had felt the tenderest regard. They were the daughters of the Clergyman of the Parish with whose Family, while it had continued there, her Aunt had been on the most intimate terms, and the little Girls tho' separated for the greatest part of the Year by the different Modes of their Education, were constantly together during the holidays of the Miss Wynnes. In those days of happy Childhood, now so often regretted by Kitty, this arbour had been formed, and separated perhaps for ever from these dear freinds, it encouraged more than any other place the tender and Melancholy recollections of hours rendered pleasant by <u>them</u>, at once so sorrowful, yet so soothing! It was now two years since the death of Mr Wynne, and the consequent dispersion of his Family who had been left by it in great distress. They had been reduced to a state of absolute dependance on some relations, who though very opulent, and very nearly connected with them, had with difficulty been prevailed on to contribute anything towards their Support. Mrs Wynne was fortunately spared the knowledge and participation of their distress, by her release from a painful illness a few months before the death of her husband.—The eldest daughter had been obliged to accept the offer of one of her cousins to equip her for the East Indies,[7] and tho' infinitely against her inclinations had been necessitated to embrace the only possibility that was offered to her, of a Maintenance;[8] Yet it was <u>one</u>, so opposite to all her ideas of Propriety, so contrary to her Wishes, so repugnant to her feelings, that she would almost have preferred Servitude to it, had Choice been allowed her—. Her personal Attractions had gained her a husband as soon as she had arrived at Bengal,[9] and she had now been married nearly a twelvemonth. Splendidly, yet unhappily married. United to a Man of double her own age, whose disposition was not amiable, and whose Manners were unpleasing, though his Character was respectable. Kitty had heard twice from her freind since her marriage, but her Letters were always unsatisfactory, and though she did not openly avow her feelings, yet every line proved her to be Unhappy. She spoke with pleasure of nothing, but of those Amusements which they had shared together and which could return no more, and seemed to have no happiness in veiw but that of returning to England again. Her sister had been taken by another relation the Dowager[10] Lady Halifax as a companion[11] to her Daughters, and had accompanied her family into Scotland about the same time of Cecilia's leaving England. From Mary therefore Kitty had the power of hearing more frequently, but her Letters were scarcely more comfortable—. There was not indeed that hopelessness of sorrow in her situation as in her sister's; she was not married, and could yet look forward to a change in her circumstances; but situated for the present without any immediate hope of it, in a family where, tho' all were her relations she had no freind, she wrote usually in depressed Spirits, which her separation from her Sister and her Sister's Marriage had greatly contributed to make so.—Divided thus from the two she loved best on Earth, while Cecilia and Mary were still more endeared to her by their loss, everything that brought a remembrance of them was doubly cherished, and the Shrubs they had planted, and the keepsakes they had given were rendered sacred—. The living of Chetwynde[12] was now in the possession of a Mr Dudley, whose Family unlike the Wynnes were productive only of vexation and trouble to Mrs Percival[13] and her Neice. Mr Dudley, who was the Younger Son of a very noble Family,[14] of a Family more famed for their Pride than their opulence, tenacious of his Dignity, and jealous of his rights, was forever quarrelling, if not with Mrs Percival herself, with her Steward and Tenants concerning tythes,[15] and with the principal Neighbours themselves concerning the respect and parade, he exacted. His Wife, an ill-educated, untaught Woman of ancient family, was proud of that family almost without knowing why, and like him too was haughty and quarrelsome, without considering for what. Their only daughter, who inherited the ignorance, the insolence, and pride of her parents, was from that Beauty of which she was unreasonably vain, considered by them as an irresistable Creature, and looked up to as the future restorer, by a Splendid Marriage, of the dignity which their reduced Situation and Mr Dudley's being obliged to take orders for a Country Living had so much lessened. They at once despised the Percivals as people of mean family, and envied them as people of fortune. They were jealous of their being more respected than themselves and while they affected to consider them as of no Consequence, were continually seeking to lessen them in the opinion of the Neighbourhood by Scandalous and Malicious reports. Such a family as this, was ill-calculated to console Kitty for the loss of the Wynnes, or to fill up by their Society, those occasionally irksome hours which in so retired a Situation would sometimes occur for want of a Companion. Her aunt was most excessively fond of her, and miserable if she saw her for a moment out of spirits; Yet she lived in such constant apprehension of her marrying imprudently if she were allowed the opportunity of choosing, and was so dissatisfied with her behaviour when she saw her with Young Men, for it was, from her natural disposition remarkably open and unreserved, that though she frequently wished for her Neice's sake, that the Neighbourhood were larger, and that She had used herself to mix more with it, yet the recollection of there being young Men in almost every Family in it, always conquered the Wish. The same fears that prevented Mrs Percival's joining much in the Society of her Neighbours, led her equally to avoid inviting her relations to spend any time in her House—She had therefore constantly regretted the annual attempt of a distant relation to visit her at Chetwynde, as there was a young Man in the Family of whom she had heard many traits that alarmed her. This Son was however now on his travels,[16] and the repeated solicitations of Kitty, joined to a consciousness of having declined with too little Ceremony the frequent overtures of her Freinds to be admitted, and a real wish to see them herself, easily prevailed on her to press with great Earnestness the pleasure of a visit from them during the Summer. M^r and Mrs Stanley were accordingly to come, and Catharine, in having an object to look forward to, a something to expect that must inevitably releive the dullness of a constant tete-a-tete with her Aunt, was so delighted, and her spirits so elevated, that for the three or four days immediately preceding their Arrival, she could scarcely fix herself to any employment. In this point Mrs Percival always thought her defective, and frequently complained of a want of Steadiness and perseverance in her occupations, which were by no means congenial to the eagerness of Kitty's Disposition, and perhaps not often met with in any young person. The tediousness too of her Aunt's conversation and the want of agreable Companions greatly encreased this desire of Change in her Employments, for Kitty found herself much sooner tired of Reading, Working,[17] or Drawing, in Mrs Percival's parlour than in her own Arbour, where Mrs Percival for fear of its being damp never accompanied her.

As her Aunt prided herself on the exact propriety and Neatness with which everything in her Family was conducted, and had no higher Satisfaction than that of knowing her house to be always in complete Order, as her fortune was good, and her Establishment Ample, few were the preparations necessary for the reception of her Visitors. The day of their arrival so long expected, at length came, and the Noise of the Coach and 4 as it drove round the sweep,[18] was to Catharine a more interesting sound, than the Music of an Italian Opera, which to most Heroines is the hight of Enjoyment.[19] M^r and Mrs Stanley[20] were people of Large Fortune and high Fashion. He was a Member of the house of Commons, and they were therefore most agreably necessitated to reside half the Year in Town;[21] where Miss Stanley had been attended by the most capital Masters from the time of her being six years old to the last Spring, which comprehending a period of twelve Years had been dedicated to the acquirement of Accomplishments[22] which were now to be displayed and in a few Years entirely neglected. She was elegant in her appearance, rather handsome, and naturally not deficient in Abilities; but those Years which ought to have been spent in the attainment of useful knowledge and Mental Improvement, had been all bestowed in learning Drawing, Italian and Music, more especially the latter, and she now united to these Accomplishments, an Understanding unimproved by reading and a Mind totally devoid either of Taste or Judgement. Her temper was by Nature good, but unassisted by reflection, she had neither patience under Disappointment, nor could sacrifice her own inclinations to promote the happiness of others. All her Ideas were towards the Elegance of her appearance, the fashion of her dress, and the Admiration she wished them to excite. She professed a love of Books without Reading, was Lively without Wit, and generally Good humoured without Merit. Such was Camilla Stanley; and Catharine, who was prejudiced by her appearance, and who from her solitary Situation was ready to like anyone, tho' her Understanding and Judgement would not otherwise have been easily satisfied, felt almost convinced when she saw her, that Miss Stanley would be the very companion She wanted, and in some degree make amends for the loss of Cecilia and Mary Wynne. She therefore attached herself to Camilla from the first day of her arrival, and from being the only young People in the house, they were by inclination constant Companions. Kitty was herself a great reader, tho' perhaps not a very deep one, and felt therefore highly delighted to find that Miss Stanley was equally fond of it. Eager to know that their sentiments as to Books were similar, she very soon began questioning her new Acquaintance on the subject; but though She was well read in Modern history[23] herself, she chose rather to speak first of Books of a lighter kind, of Books universally read and Admired.

'You have read Mrs Smith's Novels,[24] I suppose?' said she to her Companion—. 'Oh! Yes,' replied the other, 'and I am quite delighted with them—They are the sweetest things in the world—' 'And which do you prefer of them?' 'Oh! dear, I think there is no comparison between them—Emmeline is so much better than any of the others—'

'Many people think so, I know; but there does not appear so great a disproportion in their Merits to me; do you think it is better written?'

'Oh! I do not know anything about that—but it is better in everything—Besides, Ethelinde is so long—' 'That is a very common Objection I beleive,' said Kitty, 'but for my own part, if a book is well written, I always find it too short.'

'So do I, only I get tired of it before it is finished.' 'But did not you find the story of Ethelinde very interesting? And the

Descriptions of Grasmere,[25] are not they Beautiful?' 'Oh! I missed them all, because I was in such a hurry to know the end of it'—. Then from an easy transition she added, 'We are going to the Lakes[26] this Autumn, and I am quite Mad with Joy; Sir Henry Devereux has promised to go with us, and that will make it so pleasant, you know—'

'I dare say it will; but I think it is a pity that Sir Henry's powers of pleasing were not reserved for an occasion where they might be more wanted.—However I quite envy you the pleasure of such a Scheme.'

'Oh! I am quite delighted with the thoughts of it; I can think of nothing else. I assure you I have done nothing for this last Month but plan what Cloathes I should take with me, and I have at last determined to take very few indeed besides my travelling Dress,[27] and so I advise you to do, when ever you go; for I intend in case we should fall in with any races, or stop at Matlock or Scarborough,[28] to have some Things made for the occasion.'

'You intend then to go into Yorkshire?'

'I beleive not—indeed I know nothing of the Route, for I never trouble myself about such things—. I only know that we are to go from Derbyshire to Matlock and Scarborough, but to which of them first, I neither know nor care—I am in hopes of meeting some particular freinds of mine at Scarborough—Augusta told me in her last Letter that Sir Peter talked of going; but then you know that is so uncertain. I cannot bear Sir Peter, he is such a horrid Creature—'

'He is, is he?' said Kitty, not knowing what else to say.

'Oh! he is quite Shocking.' Here the Conversation was interrupted, and Kitty was left in a painful Uncertainty, as to the particulars of Sir Peter's Character; She knew only that he was Horrid and Shocking, but why, and in what, yet remained to be discovered. She could scarcely resolve what to think of her new Acquaintance; She appeared to be shamefully ignorant as to the Geography of England, if she had understood her right, and equally devoid of Taste and Information. Kitty was however unwilling to decide hastily; she was at once desirous of doing Miss Stanley justice, and of having her own Wishes in her answered; she determined therefore to suspend all Judgement for some time. After Supper, the Conversation turning on the State of Affairs in the political World, Mrs Percival, who was firmly of opinion that the whole race of Mankind were degenerating, said that for her part, Everything she beleived was going to rack and ruin, all order was destroyed over the face of the World,[29] The house of Commons she heard did not break up sometimes till five in the Morning, and Depravity never was so general before; concluding with a wish that she might live to see the Manners of the People in Queen Elizabeth's reign, restored again. 'Well, Ma'am,' said her Neice,[30] 'but I hope you do not mean with the times to restore Queen Elizabeth herself.'

'Queen Elizabeth,' said Mrs Stanley, who never hazarded a remark on History that was not well founded, 'lived to a good old Age, and was a very Clever Woman.'

'True Ma'am,' said Kitty; 'but I do not consider either of those Circumstances as meritorious in herself, and they are very far from making me wish her return, for if she were to come again with the same Abilities and the same good Constitution She might do as much Mischeif and last as long as she did before—'[31] Then turning to Camilla who had been sitting very silent for some time, she added, 'What do you think of Elizabeth, Miss Stanley? I hope you will not defend her.'

'Oh! dear,' said Miss Stanley, 'I know nothing of Politics,[32] and cannot bear to hear them mentioned.' Kitty started at this repulse, but made no answer; that Miss Stanley must be ignorant of what she could not distinguish from Politics she felt perfectly convinced.—'She retired to her own room, perplexed in her opinion about her new Acquaintance, and fearful of her being very unlike Cecilia and Mary. She arose the next morning to experience a fuller conviction of this, and every future day encreased it—. She found no variety in her conversation; She received no information from her but in fashions, and no Amusement but in her performance on the Harpsichord; and after repeated endeavours to find her what she wished, she was obliged to give up the attempt and to consider it as fruitless. There had occasionally appeared a something like humour in

Camilla which had inspired her with hopes, that she might at least have a natural genius, tho' not an improved one, but these Sparklings of Wit happened so seldom, and were so ill-supported that she was at last convinced of their being merely accidental. All her stock of knowledge was exhausted in a very few Days, and when Kitty had learnt from her, how large their house in Town was, when the fashionable Amusements began, who were the celebrated Beauties and who the best Millener, Camilla had nothing further to teach, except the Characters of any of her Acquaintance as they occurred in Conversation, which was done with equal Ease and Brevity, by saying that the person was either the sweetest Creature in the world, and one of whom she was doatingly fond, or horrid, shocking and not fit to be seen.

As Catharine was very desirous of gaining every possible information as to the Characters of the Halifax Family,[33] and concluded that Miss Stanley must be acquainted with them, as she seemed to be so with every one of any Consequence, she took an opportunity as Camilla was one day enumerating all the people of rank that her Mother visited, of asking her whether Lady Halifax were among the number.

'Oh! Thank you for reminding me of her; She is the sweetest Woman in the world, and one of our most intimate Acquaintance; I do not suppose there is a day passes during the six Months that we are in Town, but what we see each other in the course of it—. And I correspond with all the Girls.'

'They <u>are</u> then a very pleasant Family?' said Kitty. 'They ought to be so indeed, to allow of such frequent Meetings, or all Conversation must be at end.'

'Oh! dear, not at all,' said Miss Stanley, 'for sometimes we do not speak to each other for a month together. We meet perhaps only in Public,[34] and then you know we are often not able to get near enough; but in that case we always nod and smile.'

'Which does just as well—. But I was going to ask you whether you have ever seen a Miss Wynne with them?'

'I know who you mean perfectly—she wears a blue hat—. I have frequently seen her in Brook Street,[35] when I have been at Lady Halifax's Balls—She gives one every Month during the

Winter—. But only think how good it is in her to take care of Miss Wynne, for she is a very distant relation, and so poor that, as Miss Halifax told me, her Mother was obliged to find her in Cloathes.[36] Is not it shameful?'

'That she should be so poor? it is indeed, with such wealthy connexions as the Family have.'

'Oh! no; I mean, was not it shameful in Mr Wynne to leave his Children so distressed, when he had actually the Living of Chetwynde and two or three Curacies,[37] and only four Children to provide for—. What would he have done if he had had ten, as many people have?'

'He would have given them all a good Education and have left them all equally poor.'

'Well I do think there never was so lucky a Family. Sir George Fitzgibbon you know sent the eldest girl to India entirely at his own Expence, where they say she is most nobly married and the happiest Creature in the World—Lady Halifax you see has taken care of the youngest and treats her as if she were her Daughter; She does not go out into Public with her to be sure; but then she is always present when her Ladyship gives her Balls, and nothing can be kinder to her than Lady Halifax is; she would have taken her to Cheltenham[38] last year, if there had been room enough at the Lodgings, and therefore I do not think that she can have anything to complain of. Then there are the two Sons; one of them the Bishop of M —— has got into the Army as a Leiutenant I suppose; and the other is extremely well off I know, for I have a notion that somebody puts him to School somewhere in Wales.[39] Perhaps you knew them when they lived here?'

'Very well, We met as often as your Family and the Halifaxes do in Town, but as we seldom had any difficulty in getting near enough to speak, we seldom parted with merely a Nod and a Smile. They were indeed a most charming Family, and I beleive have scarcely their Equals in the World; The Neighbours we now have at the Parsonage, appear to more disadvantage in coming after them.'

'Oh! horrid Wretches! I wonder you can endure them.'

'Why, what would you have one do?'

'Oh! Lord, If I were in your place, I should abuse them all day long.'

'So I do, but it does no good.'

'Well, I declare it is quite a pity that they should be suffered to live. I wish my Father would propose knocking all their Brains out, some day or other when he is in the House. So abominably proud of their Family! And I dare say after all, that there is nothing particular in it.'

'Why Yes, I beleive thay <u>have</u> reason to value themselves on it, if any body has; for you know he is Lord Amyatt's Brother.'

'Oh! I know all that very well, but it is no reason for their being so horrid. I remember I met Miss Dudley last Spring with Lady Amyatt at Ranelagh,[40] and she had such a frightful Cap on, that I have never been able to wear any of them since.— And so you used to think the Wynnes very pleasant?'

'You speak as if their being so were doubtful! Pleasant! Oh! they were every thing that could interest and attach. It is not in my power to do Justice to their Merits, tho' not to feel them, I think must be impossible. They have unfitted me for any Society but their own!'

'Well, That is just what I think of the Miss Halifaxes; by the bye, I must write to Caroline tomorrow, and I do not know what to say to her. The Barlows too are just such other sweet Girls; but I wish Augusta's hair was not so dark. I cannot bear Sir Peter—Horrid Wretch! He is <u>always</u> laid up with the Gout, which is exceedingly disagreable to the Family.'

'And perhaps not very pleasant to <u>himself</u>—. But as to the Wynnes; do you really think them very fortunate?'

'Do I? Why, does not every body? Miss Halifax and Caroline and Maria all say that they are the luckiest Creatures in the World. So does Sir George Fitzgibbon and so do Every body.'

'That is, Every body who have themselves conferred an obligation on them. But do you call it lucky, for a Girl of Genius and Feeling to be sent in quest of a Husband to Bengal, to be married there to a Man of whose Disposition she has no opportunity of judging till her Judgement is of no use to her, who may be a Tyrant, or a Fool or both for what she knows to the Contrary. Do you call <u>that</u> fortunate?'

'I know nothing of all that; I only know that it was extremely good in Sir George to fit her out and pay her Passage, and that she would not have found Many who would have done the same.'

'I wish she had not found one,' said Kitty with great Eagerness, 'she might then have remained in England and been happy.'

'Well, I cannot conceive the hardship of going out in a very agreable Manner with two or three sweet Girls for Companions, having a delightful voyage to Bengal or Barbadoes[41] or wherever it is, and being married soon after one's arrival to a very charming Man immensely rich—. I see No hardship in all that.'

'Your representation of the Affair,' said Kitty laughing, 'certainly gives a very different idea of it from Mine. But supposing all this to be true, still, as it was by no means certain that she would be so fortunate either in her voyage, her Companions, or her husband; in being obliged to run the risk of their proving very different, she undoubtedly experienced a great hardship—. Besides, to a Girl of any Delicacy, the voyage in itself, since the object of it is so universally known, is a punishment that needs no other to make it very severe.'

'I do not see that at all. She is not the first Girl who has gone to the East Indies for a Husband, and I declare I should think it very good fun if I were as poor.'

'I beleive you would think very differently then. But at least you will not defend her Sister's situation? Dependant even for her Cloathes on the bounty of others, who of course do not pity her, as by your own account, they consider her as very fortunate.'

'You are extremely nice[42] upon my word; Lady Halifax is a delightful Woman, and one of the sweetest tempered Creatures in the World; I am sure I have every reason to speak well of her, for we are under most amazing Obligations to her. She has frequently chaproned me when my Mother has been indisposed, and last Spring she lent me her own horse three times, which was a prodigious favour, for it is the most beautiful Creature that ever was seen, and I am the only person she ever lent it to.'[43]

'And then,' continued she, 'the Miss Halifaxes are quite delightful—. Maria is one of the cleverest Girls that ever were known—Draws in Oils,[44] and plays anything by sight. She promised me one of her Drawings before I left Town, but I entirely forgot to ask her for it—. I would give anything to have one.'

'But was not it very odd,' said Kitty, 'that the Bishop should send Charles Wynne to sea,[45] when he must have had a much better chance of providing for him in the Church, which was the profession that Charles liked best, and the one for which his Father had intended him? The Bishop I know had often promised M[r] Wynne a living, and as he never gave him one, I think it was incumbant on him to transfer the promise to his Son.'

'I beleive you think he ought to have resigned his Bishopric to him; you seem determined to be dissatisfied with every thing that has been done for them.'

'Well,' said Kitty, 'this is a subject on which we shall never agree, and therefore it will be useless to continue it farther, or to mention it again—' She then left the room, and running out of the House was soon in her dear Bower where she could indulge in peace all her affectionate Anger against the relations of the Wynnes, which was greatly heightened by finding from Camilla that they were in general considered as having acted particularly well by them—. She amused herself for some time in Abusing, and Hating them all, with great spirit, and when this tribute to her regard for the Wynnes, was paid, and the Bower began to have its usual influence over her Spirits, she contributed towards settling them, by taking out a book, for she had always one about her, and reading—. She had been so employed for nearly an hour, when Camilla came running towards her with great Eagerness, and apparently great Pleasure—. 'Oh! my Dear Catharine,' said she, half out of Breath—'I have such delightful News for You—But you shall guess what it is—We are all the happiest Creatures in the World; would you beleive it, the Dudleys have sent us an invitation to a Ball at their own House—. What Charming People they are! I had no idea of there being so much Sense in the whole

Family—I declare I quite doat upon them—. And it happens so fortunately too, for I expect a new Cap from Town tomorrow which will just do for a Ball—Gold Net.[46]—It will be a most angelic thing—Every Body will be longing for the pattern—' The expectation of a Ball was indeed very agreable intelligence to Kitty, who fond of Dancing and seldom able to enjoy it, had reason to feel even greater pleasure in it than her Freind; for to her, it was now no novelty—. Camilla's delight however was by no means inferior to Kitty's, and she rather expressed the most of the two. The Cap came and every other preparation was soon completed; while these were in agitation the Days passed gaily away, but when Directions were no longer necessary, Taste could no longer be displayed, and Difficulties no longer overcome, the short period that intervened before the day of the Ball hung heavily on their hands, and every hour was too long. The very few Times that Kitty had ever enjoyed the Amusement of Dancing was an excuse for her impatience, and an apology for the Idleness it occasioned to a Mind naturally very Active; but her Freind without such a plea was infinitely worse than herself. She could do nothing but wander from the house to the Garden, and from the Garden to the avenue, wondering when Thursday would come, which she might easily have ascertained, and counting the hours as they passed which served only to lengthen them—. They retired to their rooms in high Spirits on Wednesday night, but Kitty awoke the next Morning with a violent Toothake. It was in vain that she endeavoured at first to deceive herself; her feelings were witnesses too acute of it's reality; with as little success did she try to sleep it off, for the pain she suffered prevented her closing her Eyes—. She then summoned her Maid and with the Assistance of the Housekeeper, every remedy that the receipt book[47] or the head of the latter contained, was tried, but ineffectually; for though for a short time releived by them, the pain still returned. She was now obliged to give up the endeavour, and to reconcile herself not only to the pain of a Toothake, but to the loss of a Ball; and though she had with so much eagerness looked forward to the day of its arrival, had received such pleasure in the necessary preparations, and promised herself so much delight in it, Yet she was not so totally void of philosophy as many Girls of her age, might have been in her situation. She considered that there were Misfortunes of a much greater magnitude than the loss of a Ball, experienced every day by some part of Mortality,[48] and that the time might come when She would herself look back with Wonder and perhaps with Envy on her having known no greater vexation. By such reflections as these, she soon reasoned herself into as much Resignation and Patience as the pain she suffered, would allow of, which after all was the greatest Misfortune of the two, and told the sad Story when she entered the Breakfast room, with tolerable Composure. Mrs Percival more greived for her toothake than her Disappointment, as she feared that it would not be possible to prevent her Dancing with a Man if she went, was eager to try everything that had already been applied to alleviate the pain, while at the same time She declared it was impossible for her to leave the House. Miss Stanley who joined to her concern for her Freind, felt a mixture of Dread lest her Mother's proposal that they should all remain at home, might be accepted, was very violent in her sorrow on the occasion, and though her apprehensions on the subject were soon quieted by Kitty's protesting that sooner than allow any one to stay with her, she would herself go, she continued to lament it with such unceasing vehemence as at last drove Kitty to her own room. Her Fears for herself being now entirely dissipated left her more than ever at leisure to pity and persecute her Freind who tho' safe when in her own room, was frequently removing from it to some other in hopes of being more free from pain, and then had no opportunity of escaping her—.

'To be sure, there never was anything so shocking,' said Camilla; 'To come on such a day too! For one would not have minded it you know had it been at any other time. But it always is so. I never was at a Ball in my Life, but what something happened to prevent somebody from going! I wish there were no such things as Teeth in the World; they are nothing but plagues to one, and I dare say that People might easily invent something to eat with instead of them; Poor Thing! what pain you are in! I declare it is quite Shocking to look at you. But you won't have it out, will you? For Heaven's sake don't; for there is nothing I dread so much. I declare I had rather undergo the greatest Tortures in the World than have a tooth drawn.[49] Well! how patiently you do bear it! how can you be so quiet? Lord, if I were in your place I should make such a fuss, there would be no bearing me. I should torment you to Death.'

'So you do, as it is,' thought Kitty.

'For my own part, Catharine' said Mrs Percival 'I have not a doubt but that you caught this toothake by sitting so much in that Arbour, for it is always damp. I know it has ruined your Constitution entirely; and indeed I do not beleive it has been of much service to mine; I sate down in it last May to rest myself, and I have never been quite well since—. I shall order John to pull it all down I assure you.'

'I know you will not do that, Ma'am,' said Kitty, 'as you must be convinced how unhappy it would make me.'

'You talk very ridiculously, Child; it is all whim and Nonsense. Why cannot you fancy this room an Arbour?'

'Had this room been built by Cecilia and Mary, I should have valued it equally, Ma'am, for it is not merely the name of an Arbour, which charms me.'

'Why indeed, Mrs Percival,' said Mrs Stanley, 'I must think that Catharine's affection for her Bower is the effect of a Sensibility that does her Credit. I love to see a Freindship between Young Persons and always consider it as a sure mark of an aimiable affectionate disposition. I have from Camilla's infancy taught her to think the same, and have taken great pains to introduce her to young people of her own age who were likely to be worthy of her regard. Nothing forms the taste more than sensible and Elegant Letters—. Lady Halifax thinks just like me—. Camilla corresponds with her Daughters, and I beleive I may venture to say that they are none of them the worse for it.'

These ideas were too modern to suit Mrs Percival who considered a correspondence between Girls as productive of no good, and as the frequent origin of imprudence and Error by the effect of pernicious advice and bad Example. She could not therefore refrain from saying that for her part, she had lived fifty Years in the world without having ever had a correspondent, and did not find herself at all the less respectable for it—. M[rs] Stanley could say nothing in answer to this, but her Daughter who was less governed by Propriety, said in her thoughtless way, 'But who knows what you might have been, Ma'am, if you had had a Correspondent; perhaps it would have made you quite a different Creature. I declare I would not be without those I have for all the World. It is the greatest delight of my Life, and you cannot think how much their Letters have formed my taste as Mama says, for I hear from them generally every week.'

'You received a Letter from Augusta Barlow to day, did not you, my Love?' said her Mother—. 'She writes remarkably well I know.'

'Oh! Yes Ma'am, the most delightful Letter you ever heard of. She sends me a long account of the new Regency walking dress[50] Lady Susan has given her, and it is so beautiful that I am quite dieing with envy for it.'

'Well, I am prodigiously happy to hear such pleasing news of my young freind; I have a high regard for Augusta, and most sincerely partake in the general Joy on the occasion. But does she say nothing else? it seemed to be a long Letter—Are they to be at Scarborough?'

'Oh! Lord, she never once mentions it, now I recollect it; and I entirely forgot to ask her when I wrote last. She says nothing indeed except about the Regency.' 'She must write well' thought Kitty, 'to make a long Letter upon a Bonnet and Pelisse.'[51] She then left the room tired of listening to a conversation which tho' it might have diverted her had she been well, served only to fatigue and depress her, while in pain. Happy was it for her, when the hour of dressing came, for Camilla satisfied with being surrounded by her Mother and half the Maids in the House did not want her assistance, and was too agreably employed to want her Society. She remained therefore alone in the parlour, till joined by M[r] Stanley and her Aunt, who however after a few enquiries, allowed her to continue undisturbed and began their usual conversation on Politics. This was a subject on which they could never agree, for M[r] Stanley who considered himself as perfectly qualified by his Seat in the

House, to decide on it without hesitation, resolutely maintained that the Kingdom had not for ages been in so flourishing and prosperous a state,[52] and M[rs] Percival with equal warmth, tho' perhaps less argument, as vehemently asserted that the whole Nation would speedily be ruined, and everything as she expressed herself be at sixes and sevens. It was not however unamusing to Kitty to listen to the Dispute, especially as she began then to be more free from pain, and without taking any share in it herself, she found it very entertaining to observe the eagerness with which they both defended their opinions, and could not help thinking that M[r] Stanley would not feel more disappointed if her Aunt's expectations were fulfilled, than her Aunt would be mortified by their failure. After waiting a considerable time M[rs] Stanley and her daughter appeared, and Camilla in high Spirits, and perfect good humour with her own looks, was more violent than ever in her lamentations over her Freind as she practised her Scotch Steps[53] about the room—. At length they departed, and Kitty better able to amuse herself than she had been the whole Day before, wrote a long account of her Misfortunes to Mary Wynne. When her Letter was concluded she had an opportunity of witnessing the truth of that assertion which says that Sorrows are lightened by Communication, for her toothake was then so much releived that she began to entertain an idea of following her Freinds to M[r] Dudley's. They had been gone an hour, and as every thing relative to her Dress was in complete readiness, She considered that in another hour[54] since there was so little a way to go, She might be there—. They were gone in M[r] Stanley's Carriage and therefore She might follow in her Aunt's. As the plan seemed so very easy to be executed, and promising so much pleasure, it was after a few Minutes deliberation finally adopted, and running up stairs, She rang in great haste for her Maid. The Bustle and Hurry which then ensued for nearly an hour was at last happily concluded by her finding herself very well-dressed and in high Beauty. Anne was then dispatched in the same haste to order the Carriage, while her Mistress was putting on her gloves, and arranging the folds of her dress. In a few Minutes she heard the Carriage drive up to the Door, and tho' at first surprised at the expedition with which it had been got ready, she concluded after a little reflection that the Men had received some hint of her intentions beforehand, and was hastening out of the room, when Anne came running into it in the greatest hurry and agitation, exclaiming 'Lord, Ma'am! Here's a Gentleman in a Chaise and four[55] come, and I cannot for my Life conceive who it is! I happened to be crossing the hall when the Carriage drove up, and I knew nobody would be in the way to let him in but Tom, and he looks so awkward you know, Ma'am, now his hair is just done up,[56] that I was not willing the gentleman should see him, and so I went to the door myself. And he is one of the handsomest young Men you would wish to see; I was almost ashamed of being seen in my Apron, Ma'am, but however he is vastly handsome and did not seem to mind it at all.—And he asked me whether the Family were at home; and so I said everybody was gone out but you, Ma'am, for I would not deny you because I was sure you would like to see him. And then he asked me whether Mr and Mrs Stanley were not here, and so I said Yes, and then—'

'Good Heavens!' said Kitty, 'what can all this mean! And who can it possibly be! Did you never see him before? And Did not he tell you his Name?'

'No, Ma'am, he never said anything about it—So then I asked him to walk into the parlour, and he was prodigious agreable, and—'

'Whoever he is,' said her Mistress, 'he has made a great impression upon you, Nanny—But where did he come from? and what does he want here?'

'Oh! Ma'am, I was going to tell you, that I fancy his business is with You; for he asked me whether you were at leisure to see anybody, and desired I would give his Compliments to you, and say he should be very happy to wait on you—However I thought he had better not come up into your Dressing room, especially as everything is in such a litter, so I told him if he would be so obliging as to stay in the parlour, I would run up stairs and tell you he was come, and I dared to say that you would wait upon <u>him</u>. Lord, Ma'am, I'd lay anything that he is come to ask you to dance with him tonight, and has got his Chaise ready to take you to Mr Dudley's.'

Kitty could not help laughing at this idea, and only wished it might be true, as it was very likely that she would be too late for any other partner—'But what, in the name of wonder, can he have to say to me? Perhaps he is come to rob the house—he comes in stile at least; and it will be some consolation for our losses to be robbed by a Gentleman in a Chaise and 4—. What Livery[57] has his Servants?'

'Why that is the most wonderful thing about him, Ma'am, for he has not a single servant with him, and came with hack horses;[58] But he is as handsome as a Prince for all that, and has quite the look of one—. Do, dear Ma'am, go down, for I am sure you will be delighted with him—'

'Well, I beleive I must go; but it is very odd! What can he have to say to me.' Then giving one look at herself in the Glass, she walked with great impatience, tho' trembling all the while from not knowing what to expect, down Stairs, and after pausing a moment at the door to gather Courage for opening it, she resolutely entered the room.

The Stranger, whose appearance did not disgrace the account she had received of it from her Maid, rose up on her entrance, and laying aside the Newspaper he had been reading, advanced towards her with an air of the most perfect Ease and Vivacity, and said to her, 'It is certainly a very awkward circumstance to be thus obliged to introduce myself, but I trust that the necessity of the case will plead my Excuse, and prevent your being prejudiced by it against me—. Your name, I need not ask, Ma'am—. Miss Percival is too well known to me by description to need any information of that.' Kitty, who had been expecting him to tell his own name, instead of hers, and who from having been little in company, and never before in such a situation, felt herself unable to ask it, tho' she had been planning her speech all the way down stairs, was so confused and distressed by this unexpected address that she could only return a slight curtesy to it, and accepted the chair he reached her, without knowing what she did. The gentleman then continued. 'You are, I dare say, surprised to see me returned from France so soon, and nothing indeed but business could have brought me to England; a very Melancholy affair has now occasioned it, and I was unwilling to leave it without paying my respects to the Family in Devonshire[59] whom I have so long wished to be acquainted with—.' Kitty, who felt much more surprised at his supposing her to be so, than at seeing a person in England, whose having ever left it was perfectly unknown to her, still continued silent from Wonder and Perplexity, and her visitor still continued to talk. 'You will suppose, Madam, that I was not the less desirous of waiting on you, from your having M^r and Mrs Stanley with you—. I hope they are well? And Mrs Percival, how does she do?' Then without waiting for an answer he gaily added, 'But my dear Miss Percival, you are going out I am sure; and I am detaining you from your appointment. How can I ever expect to be forgiven for such injustice! Yet how can I, so circumstanced, forbear to offend! You seem dressed for a Ball? But this is the Land of gaiety I know; I have for many years been desirous of visiting it. You have Dances I suppose at least every week—But where are the rest of your party gone, and what kind Angel in compassion to me, has excluded you from it?'

'Perhaps Sir,' said Kitty extremely confused by his manner of speaking to her, and highly displeased with the freedom of his Conversation towards one who had never seen him before and did not now know his name, 'perhaps Sir, you are acquainted with M^r and Mrs Stanley; and your business may be with them?'

'You do me too much honour, Ma'am,' replied he laughing, 'in supposing me to be acquainted with M^r and Mrs Stanley; I merely know them by sight; very distant relations; only my Father and Mother; Nothing more I assure you.'

'Gracious Heaven!' said Kitty, 'are you Mr Stanley then?—I beg a thousand pardons—Though really upon recollection I do not know for what—for you never told me your name—'

'I beg your pardon—I made a very fine speech when you entered the room, all about introducing myself; I assure you it was very great for me.'

'The speech had certainly great Merit,' said Kitty smiling; 'I thought so at the time; but since you never mentioned your name in it, as an introductory one it might have been better.'

There was such an air of good humour and Gaiety in

Stanley, that Kitty, tho' perhaps not authorized to address him with so much familiarity on so short an acquaintance, could not forbear indulging the natural Unreserve and Vivacity of her own Disposition, in speaking to him, as he spoke to her. She was intimately acquainted too with his Family who were her relations, and she chose to consider herself entitled by the connexion to forget how little a while they had known each other. 'Mr and Mrs Stanley and your Sister are extremely well,' said She, 'and will I dare say be very much surprised to see you—But I am sorry to hear that your return to England has been occasioned by an unpleasant circumstance.'

'Oh! Don't talk of it,' said he, 'it is a most confounded shocking affair, and makes me miserable to think of it; But where are my Father and Mother, and your Aunt gone? Oh! Do you know that I met the prettiest little waiting maid in the World, when I came here; she let me into the house; I took her for you at first.'

'You did me a great deal of honour, and give me more credit for good nature than I deserve, for I never go to the door when any one comes.'[60]

'Nay do not be angry; I mean no offence. But tell me, where are you going to so smart?[61] Your carriage is just coming round.'

'I am going to a Dance at a Neighbour's, where your Family and my Aunt are already gone.'

'Gone, without you! what's the meaning of that? But I suppose you are like myself, rather long in dressing.'

'I must have been so indeed, if that were the case for they have been gone nearly these two hours; The reason however was not what you suppose—I was prevented going by a pain—'

'By a pain!' interrupted Stanley, 'Oh! heavens, that is dreadful indeed! No Matter where the pain was. But my dear Miss Percival, what do you say to my accompanying you? And suppose you were to dance with me too? I think it would be very pleasant.'

'I can have no objection to either I am sure,' said Kitty laughing to find how near the truth her Maid's conjecture had been; 'on the contrary I shall be highly honoured by both, and I can answer for Your being extremely welcome to the Family who give the Ball.'[62]

'Oh! hang them; who cares for that; they cannot turn me out of the house. But I am afraid I shall cut a sad figure among all your Devonshire Beaux in this dusty, travelling apparel,[63] and I have not wherewithal to change it. You can procure me some powder perhaps, and I must get a pair of Shoes from one of the Men, for I was in such a devil of a hurry to leave Lyons[64] that I had not time to have anything pack'd up but some linen.'[65] Kitty very readily undertook to procure for him everything he wanted, and telling the footman to shew him into Mr Stanley's dressing room, gave Nanny orders to send in some powder and pomatum,[66] which orders Nanny chose to execute in person. As Stanley's preparations in dressing were confined to such very trifling articles, Kitty of course expected him in about ten minutes; but she found that it had not been merely a boast of vanity in saying that he was dilatory in that respect, as he kept her waiting for him above half an hour, so that the Clock had struck ten before he entered the room and the rest of the party had gone by eight.

'Well,' said he as he came in, 'have not I been very quick? I never hurried so much in my Life before.'

'In that case you certainly have,' replied Kitty, 'for all Merit you know is comparative.'

'Oh! I knew you would be delighted with me for making so much haste—. But come, the Carriage is ready; so, do not keep me waiting.' And so saying he took her by the hand, and led her out of the room.

'Why, my dear Cousin,' said he when they were seated, 'this will be a most agreable surprize to every body to see you enter the room with such a smart Young Fellow as I am—I hope your Aunt won't be alarmed.'

'To tell you the truth,' replied Kitty, 'I think the best way to prevent it, will be to send for her, or your Mother before we go into the room, especially as you are a perfect stranger, and must of course be introduced to M^r^ and Mrs Dudley—'

'Oh! Nonsense,' said he; 'I did not expect <u>you</u> to stand upon such Ceremony; Our acquaintance with each other renders all such Prudery,[67] ridiculous; Besides, if we go in together, we shall be the whole talk of the Country—'

'To me' replied Kitty, 'that would certainly be a most powerful inducement; but I scarcely know whether my Aunt would consider it as such—. Women at her time of life, have odd ideas of propriety you know.'

'Which is the very thing that you ought to break them of; and why should you object to entering a room with me where all our relations are, when you have done me the honour to admit me without any chaprone into your Carriage? Do not you think your Aunt will be as much offended with you for one, as for the other of these mighty crimes?'

'Why really' said Catharine, 'I do not know but that she may; however, it is no reason that I should offend against Decorum a second time, because I have already done it once.'

'On the contrary, that is the very reason which makes it impossible for you to prevent it, since you cannot offend for the first time again.'

'You are very ridiculous,' said she laughing, 'but I am afraid your arguments divert me too much to convince me.'

'At least they will convince you that I am very agreable, which after all, is the happiest conviction for me, and as to the affair of Propriety we will let that rest till we arrive at our Journey's end—. This is a monthly Ball[68] I suppose. Nothing but Dancing here—.'

'I thought I had told you that it was given by a Mr Dudley—'

'Oh! aye so you did; but why should not Mr Dudley give one every month? By the bye who is that Man? Everybody gives Balls now I think; I beleive I must give one myself soon—. Well, but how do you like my Father and Mother? And poor little Camilla too, has not she plagued you to death with the Halifaxes?' Here the Carriage fortunately stopped at Mr Dudley's, and Stanley was too much engaged in handing her out of it, to wait for an answer, or to remember that what he had said required one. They entered the small vestibule which Mr Dudley had raised to the Dignity of a Hall,[69] and Kitty immediately desired the footman who was leading the way upstairs, to inform either Mrs Percival, or Mrs Stanley of her arrival, and beg them to come to her, but Stanley unused to any contradiction and impatient to be amongst them, would neither allow her to wait, or listen to what she said, and forcibly seizing her arm within his, overpowered her voice with the rapidity of his own, and Kitty half angry, and half laughing was obliged to go with him up stairs, and could even with difficulty prevail on him to relinquish her hand before they entered the room. M[rs] Percival was at that very moment engaged in conversation with a Lady at the upper end of the room, to whom she had been giving a long account of her Neice's unlucky disappointment, and the dreadful pain that she had with so much fortitude, endured the whole Day—'I left her however,' said She, 'thank heaven!, a little better, and I hope she has been able to amuse herself with a book, poor thing! for she must otherwise be very dull. She is probably in bed by this time, which while she is so poorly, is the best place for her you know, Ma'am.' The Lady was going to give her assent to this opinion, when the Noise of voices on the stairs, and the footman's opening the door as if for the entrance of Company, attracted the attention of every body in the room; and as it was in one of those Intervals between the Dances when every one seemed glad to sit down, M[rs] Percival had a most unfortunate opportunity of seeing her Neice whom she had supposed in bed, or amusing herself as the height of gaity with a book, enter the room most elegantly dressed, with a smile on her Countenance, and a glow of mingled Chearfulness and Confusion on her Cheeks, attended by a young Man uncommonly handsome, and who without any of her Confusion, appeared to have all her vivacity. M[rs] Percival, colouring with anger and astonishment, rose from her Seat, and Kitty walked eagerly towards her, impatient to account for what she saw appeared wonderful to every body, and extremely offensive to <u>her</u>, while Camilla on seeing her Brother ran instantly towards him, and very soon explained who he was by her words and her actions. M[r] Stanley, who so fondly doated on his Son, that the pleasure of seeing him again after an absence of three Months prevented his feeling for the time any anger against him for returning to England without his knowledge, received him with equal surprise and delight; and soon comprehending the cause of his Journey, forbore any further conversation with him, as he was eager to see his Mother, and it was necessary that he should be introduced to Mr Dudley's family. This introduction to any one but Stanley would have been highly unpleasant, for they considered their dignity injured by his coming uninvited to their house, and received him with more than their usual haughtiness; But Stanley who with a vivacity of temper seldom subdued, and a contempt of censure not to be overcome, possessed an opinion of his own Consequence, and a perseverance in his own schemes which were not to be damped by the conduct of others, appeared not to perceive it. The Civilities therefore which they coldly offered, he received with a gaiety and ease peculiar to himself, and then attended by his Father and Sister walked into another room where his Mother was playing at Cards,[70] to experience another Meeting, and undergo a repetition of pleasure, Surprise and Explanations. While these were passing, Camilla eager to communicate all she felt to some one who would attend to her, returned to Catharine, and seating herself by her, immediately began—'Well, did you ever know anything so delightful as this? But it always is so; I never go to a Ball in my Life but what something or other happens unexpectedly that is quite charming!'

'A Ball' replied Kitty, 'seems to be a most eventful thing to You—'

'Oh! Lord, it is indeed—But only think of my brother's returning so suddenly—And how shocking a thing it is that has brought him over! I never heard anything so dreadful—!'

'What is it pray that has occasioned his leaving France? I am sorry to find that it is a melancholy event.'

'Oh! it is beyond anything you can conceive! His favourite Hunter[71] who was turned out in the park on his going abroad, somehow or other fell ill—No, I beleive it was an accident, but however it was something or other, or else it was something else, and so they sent an Express[72] immediately to Lyons where my Brother was, for they knew that he valued this Mare more than anything else in the World besides; and so my Brother set off directly for England, and without packing up another Coat;

I am quite angry with him about it; it was so shocking you know to come away without a change of Cloathes—'

'Why indeed,' said Kitty, 'it seems to have been a very shocking affair from beginning to end.'

'Oh! it is beyond anything You can conceive! I would rather have had <u>anything</u> happen than that he should have lossed that mare.'

'Except his coming away without another coat.'

'Oh! yes, that has vexed me more than you can imagine—. Well, and so Edward got to Brampton[73] just as the poor Thing was dead; but as he could not bear to remain there <u>then</u>, he came off directly to Chetwynde on purpose to see us—. I hope he may not go abroad again.'

'Do you think he will not?'

'Oh! dear, to be sure he must, but I wish he may not with all my heart—. You cannot think how fond I am of him! By the bye are not you in love with him yourself?'

'To be sure I am,' replied Kitty laughing, 'I am in love with every handsome Man I see.'

'That is just like me—<u>I</u> am always in love with every handsome Man in the World.'

'There you outdo me,' replied Catharine 'for I am only in love with those I <u>do</u> see.' Mrs Percival who was sitting on the other side of her, and who began now to distinguish the words, <u>Love</u> and <u>handsome Man</u>, turned hastily towards them, and said 'What are you talking of, Catharine?' To which Catharine immediately answered with the simple artifice of a Child, 'Nothing, Ma'am.' She had already received a very severe lecture from her Aunt on the imprudence of her behaviour during the whole evening; She blamed her for coming to the Ball, for coming in the same Carriage with Edward Stanley, and still more for entering the room with him.[74] For the last-mentioned offence Catharine knew not what apology to give, and tho' she longed in answer to the second to say that she had not thought it would be civil to make Mr Stanley <u>walk</u>, she dared not so to trifle with her aunt, who would have been but the more offended by it. The first accusation however she considered as very unreasonable, as she thought herself perfectly justified in coming. This conversation continued till Edward Stanley entering the room came instantly towards her, and telling her that every one waited for her to begin the next Dance led her to the top of the room,[75] for Kitty, impatient to escape from so unpleasant a Companion, without the least hesitation, or one civil scruple at being so distinguished, immediately gave him her hand, and joyfully left her Seat. This Conduct however was highly resented by several young Ladies present, and among the rest by Miss Stanley whose regard for her brother tho' excessive, and whose affection for Kitty tho' prodigious, were not proof against such an injury to her importance and her peace. Edward had however only consulted his own inclinations in desiring Miss Percival to begin the Dance, nor had he any reason to know that it was either wished or expected by anyone else in the Party. As an heiress she was certainly of consequence, but her Birth gave her no other claim to it, for her Father had been a Merchant. It was this very circumstance which rendered this unfortunate affair so offensive to Camilla, for tho' she would sometimes boast in the pride of her heart, and her eagerness to be admired that she did not know who her grandfather had been, and was as ignorant of everything relative to Genealogy as to Astronomy, (and she might have added, Geography) yet she was really proud of her family and Connexions, and easily offended if they were treated with Neglect. 'I should not have minded it,' said she to her Mother, 'if she had been anybody else's daughter; but to see her pretend to be above me, when her Father was only a tradesman,[76] is too bad! It is such an affront to our whole Family! I declare I think Papa ought to interfere in it, but he never cares about anything but Politics. If I were Mr Pitt or the Lord Chancellor,[77] he would take care I should not be insulted, but he never thinks about me; And it is so provoking that Edward should let her stand there. I wish with all my heart that he had never come to England! I hope she may fall down and break her neck, or sprain her Ancle.' Mrs Stanley perfectly agreed with her daughter concerning the affair, and tho' with less violence, expressed almost equal resentment at the indignity. Kitty in the meantime remained insensible of having given any one Offence, and therefore unable either to offer an apology, or make a reparation; her whole attention was occupied by the happiness she enjoyed in dancing with the most elegant young Man in the room, and every one else was equally unregarded. The Evening indeed to her, passed off delightfully; he was her partner during the greatest part of it,[78] and the united attractions that he possessed of Person, Address and vivacity, had easily gained that preference from Kitty which they seldom fail of obtaining from every one. She was too happy to care either for her Aunt's illhumour which she could not help remarking, or for the Alteration in Camilla's behaviour which forced itself at last on her observation. Her Spirits were elevated above the influence of Displeasure in any one, and she was equally indifferent as to the cause of Camilla's, or the continuance of her Aunt's. Though Mr Stanley could never be really offended by any imprudence or folly in his Son that had given him the pleasure of seeing him, he was yet perfectly convinced that Edward ought not to remain in England, and was resolved to hasten his leaving it as soon as possible; but when he talked to Edward about it, he found him much less disposed towards returning to France, than to accompany them in their projected tour, which he assured his Father would be infinitely more pleasant to him, and that as to the affair of travelling he considered it of no importance, and what might be pursued at any little odd time, when he had nothing better to do. He advanced these objections in a manner which plainly shewed that he had scarcely a doubt of their being complied with, and appeared to consider his father's arguments in opposition to them, as merely given with a veiw to keep up his authority, and such as he should find little difficulty in combating. He concluded at last by saying, as the chaise in which they returned together from Mr Dudley's reached Mrs Percival's, 'Well Sir, we will settle this point some other time, and fortunately it is of so little consequence, that an immediate discussion of it is unnecessary.' He then got out of the chaise and entered the house without waiting for his Father's reply. It was not till their return that Kitty could account for that coldness in Camilla's behaviour to her, which had been so pointed as to render it impossible to be entirely unnoticed. When however they were seated in the Coach with the two other Ladies, Miss Stanley's indignation was no longer to be suppressed from breaking out into words, and found the following vent.

'Well, I must say this, that I never was at a stupider Ball in my Life! But it always is so; I am always disappointed in them for some reason or other. I wish there were no such things.'

'I am sorry, Miss Stanley,' said Mrs Percival drawing herself up, 'that you have not been amused; every thing was meant for the best I am sure, and it is a poor encouragement for your Mama to take you to another if you are so hard to be satisfied.'

'I do not know what you mean, Ma'am, about Mama's taking me to another. You know I am come out.'[79]

'Oh! dear Mrs Percival,' said Mrs Stanley, 'you must not beleive every thing that my lively Camilla says, for her spirits are prodigiously high sometimes, and she frequently speaks without thinking. I am sure it is impossible for any one to have been at a more elegant or agreable dance, and so she wishes to express herself I am certain.'

'To be sure I do,' said Camilla very sulkily, 'only I must say that it is not very pleasant to have any body behave so rude to one as to be quite shocking! I am sure I am not at all offended, and should not care if all the World were to stand above me, but still it is extremely abominable, and what I cannot put up with. It is not that I mind it in the least, for I had just as soon stand at the bottom as at the top all night long, if it was not so very disagreable—. But to have a person come in the middle of the Evening and take everybody's place is what I am not used to, and tho' I do not care a pin about it myself, I assure you I shall not easily forgive or forget it.'

This speech which perfectly explained the whole affair to Kitty, was shortly followed on her side by a very submissive apology, for she had too much good Sense to be proud of her family, and too much good Nature to live at variance with any one. The Excuses she made, were delivered with so much real concern for the Offence, and such unaffected Sweetness, that it was almost impossible for Camilla to retain that anger which had occasioned them; She felt indeed most highly gratified to find that no insult had been intended and that Catharine was very far from forgetting the difference in their birth for which she could *now* only pity her, and her good humour being restored with the same Ease in which it had been affected, she spoke with the highest delight of the Evening, and declared that she had never before been at so pleasant a Ball. The same endeavours that had procured the forgiveness of Miss Stanley ensured to her the cordiality of her Mother, and nothing was wanting but Mrs Percival's good humour to render the happiness of the others complete; but She, offended with Camilla for her affected Superiority, Still more so with her brother for coming to Chetwynde, and dissatisfied with the whole Evening, continued silent and Gloomy and was a restraint on the vivacity of her Companions. She eagerly seized the very first opportunity which the next Morning offered to her of speaking to Mr Stanley on the subject of his Son's return, and after having expressed her opinion of its being a very silly affair that he came at all, concluded with desiring him to inform Mr Edward Stanley that it was a rule with her never to admit a young Man into her house as a visitor for any length of time.

'I do not speak, Sir,' she continued, 'out of any disrespect to You, but I could not answer it to myself to allow of his stay; there is no knowing what might be the consequence of it, if he were to continue here, for girls nowadays will always give a handsome young Man the preference before any other, tho' for why, I never could discover, for what after all is Youth and Beauty? It is but a poor substitute for real worth and Merit; Beleive me Cousin that, what ever people may say to the contrary, there is certainly nothing like Virtue for making us what we ought to be, and as to a young Man's, being young and handsome and having an agreable person, it is nothing at all to the purpose for he had much better be respectable. I always *did* think so, and I always *shall*, and therefore you will oblige me very much by desiring your Son to leave Chetwynde, or I cannot be answerable for what may happen between him and my Neice. You will be surprised to hear *me* say it,' she continued, lowering her voice, 'but truth will out, and I must own that

Kitty is one of the most impudent Girls that ever existed.[80] I assure you Sir, that I have seen her sit and laugh and whisper with a young Man whom she has not seen above half a dozen times. Her behaviour indeed is scandalous, and therefore I beg you will send your Son away immediately, or everything will be at sixes and sevens.' Mr Stanley, who from one part of her Speech had scarcely known to what length her insinuations of Kitty's impudence were meant to extend, now endeavoured to quiet her fears on the occasion, by assuring her, that on every account he meant to allow only of his son's continuing that day with them, and that she might depend on his being more earnest in the affair from a wish of obliging her. He added also that he knew Edward to be very desirous himself of returning to France, as he wisely considered all time lost that did not forward the plans in which he was at present engaged, tho' he was but too well convinced of the contrary himself. His assurance in some degree quieted Mrs Percival, and left her tolerably releived of her Cares and Alarms, and better disposed to behave with civility towards his Son during the short remainder of his stay at Chetwynde. Mr Stanley went immediately to Edward, to whom he repeated the Conversation that had passed between Mrs Percival and himself, and strongly pointed out the necessity of his leaving Chetwynde the next day, since his word was already engaged for it. His son however appeared struck only by the ridiculous apprehensions of Mrs Percival; and highly delighted at having occasioned them himself, seemed engrossed alone in thinking how he might encrease them, without attending to any other part of his Father's Conversation. Mr Stanley could get no determinate Answer from him, and tho' he still hoped for the best, they parted almost in anger on his side. His Son though by no means disposed to marry, or any otherwise attached to Miss Percival than as a good-natured lively Girl who seemed pleased with him, took infinite pleasure in alarming the jealous fears of her Aunt by his attentions to her, without considering what effect they might have on the Lady herself. He would always sit by her when she was in the room, appear dissatisfied if she left it, and was the first to enquire whether she meant soon to return. He was delighted with her Drawings, and enchanted with her performance on the Harpsichord; Everything that she said, appeared to interest him; his Conversation was addressed to her alone, and she seemed to be the sole object of his attention. That such efforts should succeed with one so tremblingly alive[81] to every alarm of the kind as Mrs Percival, is by no means unnatural, and that they should have equal influence with her Neice whose imagination was lively, and whose Disposition romantic,[82] who was already extremely pleased with him, and of course desirous that he might be so with her, is as little to be wondered at. Every moment as it added to the conviction of his liking her, made him still more pleasing, and strengthened in her Mind a wish of knowing him better. As for Mrs Percival, she was in tortures the whole Day; Nothing that she had ever felt before on a similar occasion was to be compared to the sensations which then distracted her; her fears had never been so strongly, or indeed so reasonably excited.—Her dislike of Stanley, her anger at her Neice, her impatience to have them separated conquered every idea of propriety and Good-breeding, and though he had never mentioned any intention of leaving them the next day, she could not help asking him after Dinner, in her eagerness to have him gone, at what time he meant to set out.

'Oh! Ma'am,' replied he, 'if I am off by twelve at night, you may think yourself lucky; and if I am not, you can only blame yourself for having left so much as the hour of my departure to my own disposal.' Mrs Percival coloured very highly at this speech, and without addressing herself to any one in particular, immediately began a long harangue on the shocking behaviour of modern Young Men, and the wonderful Alteration that had taken place in them, since her time, which she illustrated with many instructive anecdotes of the Decorum and Modesty which had marked the Characters of those whom she had known, when she had been young. This however did not prevent his walking in the Garden with her Neice, without any other companion for nearly an hour in the course of the Evening. They had left the room for that purpose with Camilla at a time when Mrs Percival had been out of it, nor was it for some time after her return to it, that she could discover where they were. Camilla had taken two or three turns with them in the walk which led to the Arbour, but soon growing tired of listening to a Conversation in which she was seldom invited to join, and from its turning occasionally on Books, very little able to do it, she left them together in the arbour, to wander alone to some other part of the Garden, to eat the fruit, and examine Mrs Percival's Greenhouse. Her absence was so far from being regretted, that it was scarcely noticed by them, and they continued conversing together on almost every subject, for Stanley seldom dwellt long on any, and had something to say on all, till they were interrupted by her Aunt.

Kitty was by this time perfectly convinced that both in Natural Abilities, and acquired information, Edward Stanley was infinitely superior to his Sister. Her desire of knowing that he was so, had induced her to take every opportunity of turning the Conversation on History and they were very soon engaged in an historical dispute, for which no one was more calculated[83] than Stanley who was so far from being really of any party, that he had scarcely a fixed opinion on the Subject. He could therefore always take either side, and always argue with temper.[84] In his indifference on all such topics he was very unlike his Companion, whose judgement being guided by her feelings which were eager and warm, was easily decided, and though it was not always infallible, she defended it with a Spirit and Enthouisasm which marked her own reliance on it. They had continued therefore for sometime conversing in this manner on the character of Richard the 3d,[85] which he was warmly defending when he suddenly seized hold of her hand, and exclaiming with great emotion, 'Upon my honour you are entirely mistaken,' pressed it passionately to his lips, and ran out of the arbour. Astonished at this behaviour, for which she was wholly unable to account, she continued for a few Moments motionless on the Seat where he had left her, and was then on the point of following him up the narrow walk through which he had passed, when on looking up the one that lay immediately before the arbour, she saw her Aunt walking towards her with more than her usual quickness. This explained at once the reason of his leaving her, but his leaving her in such Manner was rendered still more inexplicable by it. She felt a considerable degree of confusion at having been seen by her in such a place with Edward, and at having that part of his conduct, for which she could not herself account, witnessed by one to whom all gallantry was odious. She remained therefore confused, distressed and irresolute, and suffered her Aunt to approach her, without leaving the Arbour. Mrs Percival's looks were by no means calculated to animate the spirits of her Neice, who in silence awaited her accusation, and in silence meditated her Defence. After a few Moments suspence, for Mrs Percival was too much fatigued to speak immediately, she began with great Anger and Asperity, the following harangue. 'Well; this is beyond anything I could have supposed. Profligate[86] as I knew you to be, I was not prepared for such a sight. This is beyond any thing you ever did before; beyond any thing I ever heard of in my Life! Such Impudence, I never witnessed before in such a Girl! And this is the reward for all the cares I have taken in your Education; for all my troubles and Anxieties; and Heaven knows how many they have been! All I wished for, was to breed you up virtuously; I never wanted you to play upon the Harpsichord, or draw better than any one else; but I had hoped to see you respectable and good; to see you able and willing to give an example of Modesty and Virtue to the Young people here abouts. I bought you Blair's Sermons,[87] and Cœlebs in Search of a Wife,[88] I gave you the key to my own Library,[89] and borrowed a great many good books of my Neighbours for you, all to this purpose. But I might have spared myself the trouble—Oh! Catharine, you are an abandoned Creature, and I do not know what will become of you. I am glad however,' she continued softening into some degree of Mildness, 'to see that you have some shame for what you have done, and if you are really sorry for it, and your future life is a life of penitence and reformation perhaps you may be forgiven. But I plainly see that every thing is going to sixes and sevens and all order will soon be at an end throughout the Kingdom.'

'Not however, Ma'am, the sooner, I hope, from any conduct of mine,' said Catharine in a tone of great humility, 'for upon my honour I have done nothing this evening that can contribute to overthrow the establishment of the kingdom.'

'You are Mistaken, Child,' replied she; 'the welfare of every Nation depends upon the virtue of it's individuals, and any one who offends in so gross a manner against decorum and propriety is certainly hastening it's ruin.[90] You have been giving a bad example to the World, and the World is but too well disposed to receive such.'

'Pardon me, Madam,' said her Neice; 'but I <u>can</u> have given an Example only to <u>You</u>, for You alone have seen the offence. Upon my word however there is no danger to fear from what I have done; Mr Stanley's behaviour has given me as much surprise, as it has done to You, and I can only suppose that it was the effect of his high spirits, authorized in his opinion by our relationship. But do you consider, Madam, that it is growing very late? Indeed You had better return to the house.' This speech as she well knew, would be unanswerable with her Aunt, who instantly rose, and hurried away under so many apprehensions for her own health, as banished for the time all anxiety about her Neice, who walked quietly by her side, revolving within her own Mind the occurrence that had given her Aunt so much alarm. 'I am astonished at my own imprudence,' said Mrs Percival; 'How could I be so forgetful as to sit down out of doors at such a time of night? I shall certainly have a return of my rheumatism after it—I begin to feel very chill already. I must have caught a dreadful Cold by this time—I am sure of being lain-up all the winter after it—' Then reckoning with her fingers, 'Let me see; This is July; the cold weather will soonbecomingin—August—September—October—November—December—January—February—March—April—Very likely I may not be tolerable again before May. I must and will have that arbour pulled down—it will be the death of me; who knows <u>now</u>, but what I may never recover—Such things <u>have</u> happened—My particular freind Miss Sarah Hutchinson's death was occasioned by nothing more—She staid out late one Evening in April, and got wet through for it rained very hard, and never changed her Cloathes when she came home—It is unknown how many people have died in consequence of catching Cold! I do not beleive there is a disorder in the World except the Smallpox which does not spring from it.' It was in vain that

Kitty endeavoured to convince her that her fears on the occasion were groundless; that it was not yet late enough to catch cold, and that even if it were, she might hope to escape any other complaint, and to recover in less than ten Months. Mrs Percival only replied that she hoped she knew more of Ill health than to be convinced in such a point by a Girl who had always been perfectly well, and hurried up stairs leaving Kitty to make her apologies to Mr and Mrs Stanley for going to bed—. Tho' Mrs Percival seemed perfectly satisfied with the goodness of the Apology herself, yet Kitty felt somewhat embarrassed to find that the only one she could offer to their Visitors was that her Aunt had *perhaps* caught cold, for Mrs Percival charged her to make light of it, for fear of alarming them. Mr and Mrs Stanley however who well knew that their Cousin was easily terrified on that Score, received the account of it with very little surprise, and all proper concern. Edward and his Sister soon came in, and Kitty had no difficulty in gaining an explanation of his Conduct from him, for he was too warm on the subject himself, and too eager to learn its success, to refrain from making immediate Enquiries about it; and She could not help feeling both surprised and offended at the ease and Indifference with which he owned that all his intentions had been to frighten her Aunt by pretending an affection for *her*, a design so very incompatible with that partiality which she had at one time been almost convinced of his feeling for her. It is true that she had not yet seen enough of him to be actually in love with him, yet she felt greatly disappointed that so handsome, so elegant, so lively a young Man should be so perfectly free from any such Sentiment as to make it his principal Sport. There was a Novelty in his character which to *her* was extremely pleasing; his person was uncommonly fine, his Spirits and Vivacity suited to her own, and his Manners at once so animated and insinuating, that she thought it must be impossible for him to be otherwise than amiable, and was ready to give him Credit for being perfectly so. He knew the powers of them himself; to them he had often been endebted for his father's forgiveness of faults which had he been awkward and inelegant would have appeared very serious; to them, even more than to his person or his fortune, he owed the regard which almost every one was disposed to feel for him, and which Young Women in particular were inclined to entertain. Their influence was acknowledged on the present occasion by Kitty, whose Anger they entirely dispelled, and whose Chearfulness they had power not only to restore, but to raise—. The Evening passed off as agreably as the one that had preceded it; they continued talking to each other, during the cheif part of it, and such was the power of his Address, and the Brilliancy of his Eyes, that when they parted for the Night, tho' Catharine had but a few hours before totally given up the idea, yet she felt almost convinced again that he was really in love with her. She reflected on their past Conversation, and tho' it had been on various and indifferent subjects, and she could not exactly recollect any speech on his side expressive of such a partiality, she was still however nearly certain of it's being so; But fearful of being vain enough to suppose such a thing without sufficient reason, she resolved to suspend her final determination on it, till the next day, and more especially till their parting which she thought would infallibly explain his regard if any he had—. The more she had seen of him, the more inclined was she to like him, and the more desirous that he should like *her*. She was convinced of his being naturally very clever and very well disposed, and that his thoughtlessness and negligence, which tho' they appeared to *her* as very becoming in *him*, she was aware would by many people be considered as defects in his Character, merely proceeded from a vivacity always pleasing in Young Men, and were far from testifying a weak or vacant Understanding. Having settled this point within herself, and being perfectly convinced by her own arguments of it's truth, she went to bed in high Spirits, determined to study his Character, and watch his Behaviour still more the next day. She got up with the same good resolutions and would probably have put them in execution, had not Anne informed her as soon as she entered the room that Mr Edward Stanley was already gone. At first she refused to credit the information, but when her Maid assured her that he had ordered a Carriage the evening before to be there at seven o'clock in the Morning and that she herself had actually seen him depart in it a little after eight, she could no longer deny her beleif to it. 'And this,' thought she to herself blushing with anger at her own folly, 'this is the affection for me of which I was so certain. Oh! what a silly Thing is Woman! How vain, how unreasonable![91] To suppose that a young Man would be seriously attached in the course of four and twenty hours, to a Girl who has nothing to recommend her but a good pair of eyes! And he is really gone! Gone perhaps without bestowing a thought on me! Oh! why was not I up by eight o'clock? But it is a proper punishment for my Lazyness and Folly, and I am heartily glad of it. I deserve it all, and ten times more for such insufferable vanity. It will at least be of service to me in that respect; it will teach me in future <u>not</u> to think Every Body is in love with me. Yet I <u>should</u> like to have seen him before he went, for perhaps it may be many Years before we meet again. By his Manner of leaving us however, he seems to have been perfectly indifferent about it. How very odd, that he should go without giving us Notice of it, or taking leave of any one! But it is just like a Young Man, governed by the whim of the moment, or actuated merely by the love of doing anything oddly! Unaccountable Beings indeed! And Young Women are equally ridiculous! I shall soon begin to think like my Aunt that everything is going to Sixes and Sevens, and that the whole race of Mankind are degenerating.' She was just dressed, and on the point of leaving her room to make her personal enquiries after M[rs] Percival, when Miss Stanley knocked at her door, and on her being admitted began in her Usual Strain a long harangue upon her Father's being so shocking as to make Edward go at all, and upon Edward's being so horrid as to leave them at such an hour in the Morning. 'You have no idea,' said she, 'how surprised I was, when he came into my Room to bid me good bye—'

'Have you seen him then, this Morning?' said Kitty.

'Oh Yes! And I was so sleepy that I could not open my eyes. And so he said, "Camilla, goodbye to you for I am going away—. I have not time to take leave of any body else, and I dare not trust myself to see Kitty, for then you know I should never get away—"'

'Nonsense,' said Kitty; 'he did not say that, or he was in joke if he did.'

'Oh! no I assure you he was as much in earnest as he ever was in his life; he was too much out of spirits to joke then. And he desired me when we all met at Breakfast to give his Comp[ts] to your Aunt, and his Love to You, for you was a nice Girl he said, and he only wished it were in his power to be more with You. You were just the Girl to suit him, because you were so lively and good-natured, and he wished with all his heart that you might not be married before he came back, for there was nothing he liked better than being here. Oh! You have no idea what fine things he said about You, till at last I fell asleep and he went away. But he certainly is in love with you—I am sure he is—I have thought so a great while I assure You.'

'How can You be so ridiculous?' said Kitty smiling with pleasure; 'I do not beleive him to be so easily affected. But he did desire his Love to me then? And wished I might not be married before his return? And said I was a Nice Girl, did he?'

'Oh! dear, Yes, and I assure You it is the greatest praise in his opinion, that he can bestow on any body; I can hardly ever persuade him to call me one, tho' I beg him sometimes for an hour together.'

'And do You really think that he was sorry to go?'

'Oh! You can have no idea how wretched it made him. He would not have gone this Month, if my Father had not insisted on it; Edward told me so himself yesterday. He said that he wished with all his heart he had never promised to go abroad, for that he repented it more and more every day; that it interfered with all his other schemes, and that since Papa had spoke to him about it, he was more unwilling to leave Chetwynde than ever.'

'Did he really say all this? And why would your father insist upon his going?' 'His leaving England interfered with all his other plans, and his Conversation with M[r] Stanley had made him still more averse to it.' 'What can this Mean?'

'Why that he is excessively in love with You to be sure; what other plans can he have? And I suppose my father said that if he had not been going abroad, he should have wished him to marry you immediately.—But I must go and see your Aunt's plants—There is one of them that I quite doat on—and two or three more besides—'

'Can Camilla's explanation be true?' said Catharine to herself, when her freind had left the room. 'And after all my doubts and Uncertainties, can Stanley really be averse to leaving England for my sake only? "His plans interrupted." And what indeed can his plans be, but towards Marriage? Yet so soon to be in love with me!—But it is the effect perhaps only of a warmth of heart which to me is the highest recommendation in any one. A Heart disposed to love—And such under the appearance of so much Gaity and Inattention, is Stanley's! Oh! how much does it endear him to me! But he is gone—Gone perhaps for Years—Obliged to tear himself from what he most loves, his happiness is sacrificed to the vanity of his Father! In what anguish he must have left the house! Unable to see me, or to bid me adeiu, while I, senseless wretch, was daring to sleep. This, then explained his leaving us at such a time of day—. He could not trust himself to see me—. Charming Young Man! How much must you have suffered! I knew that it was impossible for one so elegant, and so well bred, to leave any Family in such a Manner, but for a Motive like this unanswerable.' Satisfied, beyond the power of Change, of this, She went in high spirits to her Aunt's apartment, without giving a Moment's recollection on the vanity of Young Women, or the unaccountable conduct of Young Men. —

[JA's manuscript ends here. The following continuation of 'Catharine' in *Volume the Third* is in the hand of her nephew James Edward Austen-Leigh, *c.*1815–16.][92]

Kitty continued in this state of satisfaction during the remainder of the Stanley's visit—Who took their leave with many pressing invitations to visit them in London, when as Camilla said, she might have an opportunity of becoming acquainted with that sweet girl Augusta Halifax—Or Rather (thought Kitty,) of seeing my d^{r} Mary Wynne again—Mrs Percival in answer to Mrs Stanley's invitation replied—That she looked upon London as the hot house of Vice where virtue had long been banished from Society and Wickedness of every description was daily gaining ground—that Kitty was of herself sufficiently inclined to give way to, and indulge in vicious inclinations[93]—and therefore was the last girl in the world to be trusted in London, as she would be totally unable to withstand temptation—

After the departure of the Stanleys Kitty returned to her usual occupations, but Alas! they had lost their power of pleasing. Her bower alone retained its interest in her feelings, and perhaps that was oweing to the particular remembrance it brought to her mind of Ed^{wd} Stanley.

[Second continuation of 'Catharine' in the hand of James Edward Austen-Leigh, post-1845.]

The Summer passed away unmarked by any incident worth narrating, or any pleasure to Catharine save one, which arose from the reciept of a letter from her friend Cecilia now Mrs Lascelles, announcing the speedy return of herself and Husband to England.

A correspondance productive indeed of little pleasure to either party had been established between Camilla and Catharine. The latter had now lost the only Satisfaction she had ever received from the letters of Miss Stanley, as that young Lady having informed her Friend of the departure of her Brother to Lyons now never mentioned his name—Her letters seldom contained any Intelligence except a description of some new Article of Dress, an enumeration of various engagements, a panegyric on Augusta Halifax and perhaps a little abuse of the unfortunate Sir Peter—

The Grove, for so was the Mansion of Mrs Percival at Chetwynde denominated, was situated within five miles from Exeter, but though that Lady possessed a carriage and horses of her own, it was seldom that Catharine could prevail on her to visit that town for the purpose of shopping, on account of the many Officers perpetually Quartered[94] there and who infested the principal Streets—A company of strolling players in their way from some Neighbouring Races having opened a temporary Theatre there, Mrs Percival was prevailed on by her Niece to indulge her by attending the performance once during their stay—Mrs Percival insisted on paying Miss Dudley the compliment of inviting her to join the party, when a new difficulty arose, from the necessity of having Some Gentleman to attend them—

Lady Susan[1]

1

Letter 1.

Lady Susan Vernon to Mr. Vernon.

Langford Decr. —

My dear Brother

I can no longer refuse myself the pleasure of profitting by your kind invitation when we last parted, of spending some weeks with you at Churchill, & therefore if quite convenient to you & Mrs. Vernon to receive me at present, I shall hope within a few days to be introduced to a Sister whom I have so long desired to be ac: quainted with. — My kind friends here are most affectionately urgent with me to prolong my stay, but their hospitable & chearful dispositions lead them

Manuscript page 1 of Jane Austen's fair copy of *Lady Susan*. (By permission of the Pierpont Morgan Library, New York.)

Letter 1

Lady Susan Vernon[2] to Mr Vernon

Langford, Decr

My dear Brother[3]

I can no longer refuse myself the pleasure of profitting by your kind invitation when we last parted, of spending some weeks with you at Churchill,[4] and therefore if quite convenient to you and Mrs Vernon to receive me at present, I shall hope within a few days to be introduced to a Sister, whom I have so long desired to be acquainted with.—My kind friends here are most affectionately urgent with me to prolong my stay, but their hospitable and chearful dispositions lead them too much into society for my present situation and state of mind; and I impatiently look forward to the hour when I shall be admitted into your delightful retirement. I long to be made known to your dear little Children, in whose hearts I shall be very eager to secure an interest.—I shall soon have occasion for all my fortitude, as I am on the point of separation from my own daughter.—The long illness of her dear Father prevented my paying her that attention which Duty and affection equally dictated, and I have but too much reason to fear that the Governess to whose care I consigned her, was unequal to the charge.—I have therefore resolved on placing her at one of the best Private Schools in Town,[5] where I shall have an opportunity of leaving her myself, in my way to you. I am determined you see, not to be denied admittance at Churchill.—It would indeed give me most painful sensations to know that it were not in your power to receive me.—

Yr most obliged and affec: Sister
S. Vernon

Letter 2[d]

Lady Susan to M[rs] Johnson

Langford

You were mistaken my dear Alicia, in supposing me fixed at this place for the rest of the winter. It greives me to say how greatly you were mistaken, for I have seldom spent three months more agreably than those which have just flown away.—At present nothing goes smoothly.—The Females of the Family are united against me.—You foretold how it would be, when I first came to Langford; and Manwaring is so uncommonly pleasing that I was not without apprehensions myself. I remember saying to myself as I drove to the House, 'I like this Man; pray Heaven no harm come of it!'—But I was determined to be discreet, to bear in mind my being only four months a widow, and to be as quiet as possible,—and I have been so;—My dear Creature, I have admitted no one's attentions but Manwaring's, I have avoided all general flirtation whatever, I have distinguished no Creature besides of all the Numbers resorting hither, except Sir James Martin, on whom I bestowed a little notice in order to detach him from Miss Manwaring. But if the World could know my motive there, they would honour me.—I have been called an unkind Mother, but it was the sacred impulse of maternal affection, it was the advantage of my Daughter that led me on; and if that Daughter were not the greatest simpleton on Earth, I might have been rewarded for my Exertions as I ought.—Sir James did make proposals to me for Frederica—but Frederica, who was born to be the torment of my life, chose to set herself so violently against the match, that I thought it better to lay aside the scheme for the present.—I have more than once repented that I did not marry him myself, and were he but one degree less contemptibly weak I certainly should, but I must own myself rather romantic in that respect, and that Riches only, will not satisfy me. The event of all this is very provoking.—Sir James is gone, Maria highly incensed, and Mrs Manwaring insupportably jealous;—so jealous in short, and so enraged against me, that in the fury of her temper I should not be surprised at her appealing to her Guardian if she had the liberty of addressing him—but there your Husband stands my friend, and the kindest, most amiable action of his Life was his throwing her off forever on her Marriage.—Keep up his resentment therefore I charge you.—We are now in a sad state; no house was ever more altered; the whole family are at war, and Manwaring scarcely dares speak to me. It is time for me to be gone; I have therefore determined on leaving them, and shall spend I hope a comfortable day with you in Town within this week.—If I am as little in favour with Mr Johnson as ever, you must come to me at N° 10 Wigmore S^t^[6]—but I hope this may not be the case, for as Mr Johnson with all his faults is a Man to whom that great word 'Respectable' is always given, and I am known to be so intimate with his wife, his slighting me has an awkward Look.—I take Town in my way to that insupportable spot, a Country Village,[7] for I am really going to Churchill.—Forgive me my dear friend, it is my last resource. Were there another place in England open to me, I would prefer it.—Charles Vernon is my aversion, and I am afraid of his wife.—At Churchill however I must remain till I have something better in veiw. My young Lady accompanies me to Town, where I shall deposit her under the care of Miss Summers in Wigmore Street, till she becomes a little more reasonable. She will make good connections there, as the Girls are all of the best Families.—The price is immense, and much beyond what I can ever attempt to pay.—Adeiu. I will send you a line, as soon as I arrive in Town.—

Yours Ever,
S. Vernon

Letter 3

Mrs Vernon to Lady De Courcy

Churchill

My dear Mother

I am very sorry to tell you that it will not be in our power to keep our promise of spending the Christmas with you; and we are prevented that happiness by a circumstance which is not likely to make us any amends.—Lady Susan in a letter to her Brother, has declared her intention of visiting us almost immediately—and as such a visit is in all probability merely an affair of convenience, it is impossible to conjecture its length. I was by no means prepared for such an event, nor can I now account for her Ladyship's conduct.—Langford appeared so exactly the place for her in every respect, as well from the elegant and expensive stile of Living there, as from her particular attachment to Mrs Manwaring, that I was very far from expecting so speedy a distinction, tho' I always imagined from her increasing friendship for us since her Husband's death, that we should at some future period be obliged to receive her.—Mr Vernon I think was a great deal too kind to her, when he was in Staffordshire. Her behaviour to him, independant of her general Character, has been so inexcusably artful and ungenerous since our Marriage was first in agitation,[8] that no one less amiable and mild than himself could have overlooked it at all; and tho' as his Brother's widow[9] and in narrow circumstances it was proper to render her pecuniary assistance, I cannot help thinking his pressing invitation to her to visit us at Churchill perfectly unnecessary.—Disposed however as he always is to think the best of every one, her display of Greif, and professions of regret, and general resolutions of prudence were sufficient to soften his heart, and make him really confide in her sincerity. But as for myself, I am still unconvinced; and plausibly as her Ladyship has now written, I cannot make up my mind, till I better understand her real meaning in coming to us.—You may guess therefore my dear Madam,[10] with what feelings I look forward to her arrival. She will have occasion for all those attractive Powers for which she is celebrated, to gain any share of my regard; and I shall certainly endeavour to guard myself against their influence, if not accompanied by something more substantial.—She expresses a most eager desire of being acquainted with me, and makes very gracious mention of my children, but I am not quite weak enough to suppose a woman who has behaved with inattention if not unkindness to her own child, should be attached to any of mine. Miss Vernon is to be placed at a school in Town before her Mother comes to us, which I am glad of, for her sake and my own. It must be to her advantage to be separated from her Mother; and a girl of sixteen who has received so wretched an education would not be a very desirable companion here.—Reginald has long wished I know to see this captivating Lady Susan, and we shall depend on his joining our party soon.—I am glad to hear that my Father continues so well, and am, with best Love etc.,

Cath Vernon

Letter 4

M[r] De Courcy to M[rs] Vernon

Parklands

My dear Sister

I congratulate you and M[r] Vernon on being about to receive into your family, the most accomplished Coquette in England.—As a very distinguished Flirt, I have been always taught to consider her; but it has lately fallen in my way to hear some particulars of her conduct at Langford, which prove that she does not confine herself to that sort of honest flirtation which satisfies most people, but aspires to the more delicious gratification of making a whole family miserable.—By her behaviour to M[r] Manwaring, she gave jealousy and wretchedness to his wife, and by her attentions to a young man previously attached to M[r] Manwaring's sister, deprived an amiable girl of her Lover.[11]—I learnt all this from a M[r] Smith now in this neighbourhood—(I have dined with him at Hurst and Wilford[12])—who is just come from Langford, where he was a fortnight in the house with her Ladyship, and who is therefore well qualified to make the communication.—

What a Woman she must be!—I long to see her, and shall certainly accept your kind invitation, that I may form some idea of those bewitching powers which can do so much—engaging at the same time and in the same house the affections of two Men who were neither of them at liberty to bestow them—and all this, without the charm of Youth.—I am glad to find that Miss Vernon does not come with her Mother to Churchill, as she has not even Manners to recommend her, and according to M[r] Smith's account, is equally dull and proud. Where Pride and Stupidity unite, there can be no dissimulation worthy notice, and Miss Vernon shall be consigned to unrelenting Contempt; but by all that I can gather, Lady Susan possesses a degree of captivating Deceit which must be pleasing to witness and detect. I shall be with you very soon, and am your affec. Brother

R De Courcy

Letter 5

Lady Susan to M[rs] Johnson

Churchill

I received your note my dear Alicia, just before I left Town, and rejoice to be assured that M[r] Johnson suspected nothing of your engagement the evening before; it is undoubtedly better to deceive him entirely;—since he will be stubborn, he must be tricked.—I arrived here in safety, and have no reason to complain of my reception from M[r] Vernon; but I confess myself not equally satisfied with the behaviour of his Lady.—She is perfectly well bred indeed, and has the air of a woman of fashion, but her Manners are not such as can persuade me of her being prepossessed in my favour.—I wanted her to be delighted at seeing me—I was as amiable as possible on the occasion—but all in vain—she does not like me.—To be sure, when we consider that I did take some pains to prevent my Brother-in-law's marrying her, this want of cordiality is not very surprising—and yet it shews an illiberal and vindictive spirit to resent a project which influenced me six years ago, and which never succeeded at last.—I am sometimes half disposed to repent that I did not let Charles buy Vernon Castle when we were obliged to sell it, but it was a trying circumstance, especially as the sale took place exactly at the time of his marriage—and everybody ought to respect the delicacy of those feelings, which could not endure that my Husband's Dignity should be lessened by his younger brother's having possession of the Family Estate.—Could Matters have been so arranged as to prevent the necessity of our leaving the Castle, could we have lived with Charles and kept him single, I should have been very far from persuading my husband to dispose of it elsewhere;—but Charles was then on the point of marrying Miss De Courcy, and the event has justified me. Here are Children in abundance, and what benefit could have accrued to me from his purchasing Vernon?—My having prevented it, may perhaps have given his wife an unfavourable impression—but where there is a disposition to dislike a motive will never be wanting; and as to money-matters, it has not with-held him from being very useful to me. I really have a regard for him, he is so easily imposed on!

The house is a good one, the Furniture fashionable, everything announces plenty and elegance.—Charles is very rich I am sure; when a Man has once got his name[13] in a Banking House[14] he rolls in money. But they do not know what to do with their fortune, keep very little company, and never go to Town but on business.—We shall be as stupid as possible.—I mean to win my Sister in law's heart through her Children; I know all their names already, and am going to attach myself with the greatest sensibility to one in particular, a young Frederic, whom I take on my lap and sigh over for his dear Uncle's sake.—[15]

Poor Manwaring!—I need not tell you how much I miss him—how perpetually he is in my Thoughts.—I found a dismal letter from him on my arrival here, full of complaints of his wife and sister, and lamentations on the cruelty of his fate. I passed off the letter as his wife's, to the Vernons, and when I write to him, it must be under cover to you.—

Yours Ever,

S.V.

Letter 6

Mrs Vernon to Mr De Courcy

Churchill

Well my dear Reginald, I have seen this dangerous creature, and must give you some description of her, tho' I hope you will soon be able to form your own judgement. She is really excessively pretty.—However you may chuse to question the allurements of a Lady no longer young, I must for my own part declare that I have seldom seen so lovely a Woman as Lady Susan.—She is delicately fair, with fine grey eyes and dark eyelashes; and from her appearance one would not suppose her more than five and twenty, tho' she must in fact be ten years older.—I was certainly not disposed to admire her, tho' always hearing she was beautiful; but I cannot help feeling that she possesses an uncommon union of Symmetry, Brilliancy and Grace.—Her address to me was so gentle, frank and even affectionate, that if I had not known how much she has always disliked me for marrying Mr Vernon, and that we had never met before, I should have imagined her an attached friend.—One is apt I beleive to connect assurance of manner with coquetry, and to expect that an impudent address will necessarily attend an impudent mind;—at least I was myself prepared for an improper degree of confidence in Lady Susan; but her Countenance is absolutely sweet, and her voice and manner winningly mild.—I am sorry it is so, for what is this but Deceit?[16]—Unfortunately one knows her too well.—She is clever and agreable, has all that knowledge of the world which makes conversation easy, and talks very well, with a happy command of Language, which is too often used I beleive to make Black appear White.—She has already almost persuaded me of her being warmly attached to her daughter, tho' I have so long been convinced of the contrary. She speaks of her with so much tenderness and anxiety, lamenting so bitterly the neglect of her education, which she represents however as wholly unavoidable, that I am forced to recollect how many successive Springs her Ladyship spent in Town, while her daughter was left in Staffordshire to the care of servants or a Governess very little better, to prevent my believing whatever she says.

If her manners have so great an influence on my resentful heart, you may guess how much more strongly they operate on Mr Vernon's generous temper.—I wish I could be as well satisfied as he is, that it was really her choice to leave Langford for Churchill; and if she had not staid three months there before she discovered that her friends' manner of Living did not suit her situation or feelings, I might have beleived that concern for the loss of such a Husband as Mr Vernon, to whom her own behaviour was far from unexceptionable,[17] might for a time make her wish for retirement. But I cannot forget the length of her visit to the Manwarings, and when I reflect on the different mode of Life which she led with them, from that to which she must now submit, I can only suppose that the wish of establishing her reputation by following, tho' late, the path of propriety, occasioned her removal from a family where she must in reality have been particularly happy. Your friend Mr Smith's story however cannot be quite true, as she corresponds regularly with Mrs Manwaring; at any rate it must be exaggerated;—it is scarcely possible that two men should be so grossly deceived by her at once.—

Y^rs^ etc.
Cath Vernon

Letter 7

Lady Susan to Mrs Johnson

Churchill

My dear Alicia

You are very good in taking notice of Frederica, and I am grateful for it as a mark of your friendship; but as I cannot have a doubt of the warmth of that friendship, I am far from exacting so heavy a sacrifice. She is a stupid girl, and has nothing to recommend her.—I would not therefore on any account have you encumber one moment of your precious time by sending her to Edward S^t^, especially as every visit is so many hours deducted from the grand affair of Education, which I really wish to be attended to, while she remains with Miss Summers.—I want her to play and sing with some portion of Taste, and a good deal of assurance, as she has my hand and arm, and a tolerable voice. I was so much indulged in my infant years that I was never obliged to attend to anything, and consequently am without those accomplishments which are now necessary to finish a pretty Woman.[18] Not that I am an advocate for the prevailing fashion of acquiring a perfect knowledge in all the Languages Arts and Sciences;—it is throwing time away;—to be Mistress of French, Italian, German, Music, Singing, Drawing etc. will gain a Woman some applause, but will not add one Lover to her list. Grace and Manner after all are of the greatest importance. I do not mean therefore that Frederica's acquirements should be more than superficial, and I flatter myself that she will not remain long enough at school to understand anything thoroughly.—I hope to see her the wife of Sir James within a twelvemonth.—You know on what I ground my hope, and it is certainly a good foundation, for School must be very humiliating to a girl of Frederica's age;[19] and by the bye, you had better not invite her any more on that account, as I wish her to find her situation as unpleasant as possible.—I am sure of Sir James at any time, and could make him renew his application by a Line.—I shall trouble you meanwhile to prevent his forming any other attachment when he comes to Town;—ask him to your House occasionally, and talk to him about Frederica that he may not forget her.—

Upon the whole I commend my own conduct in this affair extremely, and regard it as a very happy mixture of circumspection and tenderness. Some Mothers would have insisted on their daughter's accepting so great an offer on the first overture, but I could not answer it to myself to force Frederica into a marriage from which her heart revolted; and instead of adopting so harsh a measure, merely propose to make it her own choice by rendering her thoroughly uncomfortable till she does accept him. But enough of this tiresome girl.—

You may well wonder how I contrive to pass my time here—and for the first week, it was most insufferably dull.—Now however, we begin to mend;—our party is enlarged by Mrs Vernon's brother, a handsome young Man, who promises me some amusement. There is something about him that rather interests me, a sort of sauciness, of familiarity which I shall teach him to correct. He is lively and seems clever, and when I have inspired him with greater respect for me than his sister's kind offices have implanted, he may be an agreable Flirt.—There is exquisite pleasure in subduing an insolent spirit, in making a person pre-determined to dislike, acknowledge one's superiority.—I have disconcerted him already by my calm reserve; and it shall be my endeavour to humble the Pride of these self-important De Courcies still lower, to convince Mrs Vernon that her sisterly cautions have been bestowed in vain, and to persuade Reginald that she has scandalously belied me. This project will serve at least to amuse me, and prevent my feeling so acutely this dreadful separation from You and all whom I love. Adeiu.

Yours Ever
S. Vernon

Letter 8

Mrs Vernon to Lady De Courcy

Churchill

My dear Mother

You must not expect Reginald back again for some time. He desires me to tell you that the present open weather induces him to accept Mr Vernon's invitation to prolong his stay in Sussex that they may have some hunting together.—He means to send for his Horses immediately,[20] and it is impossible to say when you may see him in Kent. I will not disguise my sentiments on this change from you my dear Madam, tho' I think you had better not communicate them to my Father, whose excessive anxiety about Reginald would subject him to an alarm which might seriously affect his health and spirits. Lady Susan has certainly contrived in the space of a fortnight to make my Brother like her.—In short, I am persuaded that his continuing here beyond the time originally fixed for his return, is occasioned as much by a degree of fascination towards her, as by the wish of hunting with Mr Vernon, and of course I cannot receive that pleasure from the length of his visit which my Brother's company would otherwise give me.—I am indeed provoked at the artifice of this unprincipled Woman. What stronger proof of her dangerous abilities can be given, than this perversion of Reginald's Judgement, which when he entered the house was so decidedly against her?—In his last letter he actually gave me some particulars of her behaviour at Langford, such as he received from a Gentleman who knew her perfectly well, which if true must raise abhorrence against her, and which Reginald himself was entirely disposed to credit.—His opinion of her I am sure, was as low as of any Woman in England, and when he first came it was evident that he considered her as one entitled neither to Delicacy nor respect, and that he felt she would be delighted with the attentions of any Man inclined to flirt with her.

Her behaviour I confess has been calculated to do away such an idea, I have not detected the smallest impropriety in it,—nothing of vanity, of pretension, of Levity—and she is altogether so attractive, that I should not wonder at his being delighted with her, had he known nothing of her previous to this personal acquaintance;—but against reason, against conviction, to be so well pleased with her as I am sure he is, does really astonish me.—His admiration was at first very strong, but no more than was natural; and I did not wonder at his being struck by the gentleness and delicacy of her Manners;—but when he has mentioned her of late, it has been in terms of more extraordinary praise, and yesterday he actually said, that he could not be surprised at any effect produced on the heart of Man by such Loveliness and such Abilities; and when I lamented in reply the badness of her disposition, he observed that whatever might have been her errors, they were to be imputed to her neglected Education and early Marriage, and that she was altogether a wonderful Woman.—

This tendency to excuse her conduct, or to forget it in the warmth of admiration vexes me; and if I did not know that Reginald is too much at home at Churchill to need an invitation for lengthening his visit, I should regret Mr Vernon's giving him any.—

Lady Susan's intentions are of course those of absolute coquetry, or a desire of universal admiration. I cannot for a moment imagine that she has anything more serious in veiw, but it mortifies me to see a young Man of Reginald's sense duped by her at all.—

I am etc.[21]
Cath Vernon

Letter 9

Mrs Johnson to Lady Susan

Edward St

My dearest Friend

I congratulate you on Mr De Courcy's arrival, and advise you by all means to marry him; his Father's Estate is we know considerable, and I beleive certainly entailed.[22]—Sir Reginald is very infirm, and not likely to stand in your way long.—I hear the young Man well spoken of, and tho' no one can really deserve you my dearest Susan, Mr De Courcy may be worth having.—Manwaring will storm of course, but you may easily pacify him. Besides, the most scrupulous point of honour could not require you to wait for his emancipation.[23]—I have seen Sir James,—he came to Town for a few days last week, and called several times in Edward Street. I talked to him about you and your daughter, and he is so far from having forgotten you, that I am sure he would marry either of you with pleasure.—I gave him hopes of Frederica's relenting, and told him a great deal of her improvements.—I scolded him for making Love[24] to Maria Manwaring; he protested that he had been only in joke, and we both laughed heartily at her disappointment, and in short were very agreable.—He is as silly as ever.—.[25]

Yours faithfully
Alicia

Letter 10

Lady Susan to Mrs Johnson

Churchill

I am much obliged to you my dear Friend, for your advice respecting M^r^ De Courcy, which I know was given with the fullest conviction of its expediency, tho' I am not quite determined on following it.—I cannot easily resolve on anything so serious as Marriage, especially as I am not at present in want of money, and might perhaps till the old Gentleman's death, be very little benefited by the match. It is true that I am vain enough to beleive it within my reach.—I have made him sensible of my power, and can now enjoy the pleasure of triumphing over a Mind prepared to dislike me, and prejudiced against all my past actions. His sister too, is I hope convinced how little the ungenerous representations of any one to the disadvantage of another will avail, when opposed to the immediate influence of Intellect and Manner.—I see plainly that she is uneasy at my progress in the good opinion of her Brother, and conclude that nothing will be wanting on her part to counteract me;—but having once made him doubt the justice of her opinion of me, I think I may defy her.—

It has been delightful to me to watch his advances towards intimacy, especially to observe his altered manner in consequence of my repressing by the calm dignity of my deportment, his insolent approach to direct familiarity.—My conduct has been equally guarded from the first, and I never behaved less like a Coquette in the whole course of my Life, tho' perhaps my desire of dominion was never more decided. I have subdued him entirely by sentiment and serious conversation, and made him I may venture to say at least half in Love with me, without the semblance of the most common-place flirtation. Mrs Vernon's consciousness of deserving every sort of revenge that it can be in my power to inflict, for her ill-offices, could alone enable her to perceive that I am actuated by any design in behaviour so gentle and unpretending.—Let her think and act as she chuses however; I have never yet found that the advice of a Sister could prevent a young Man's being in love if he chose it.—We are advancing now towards some kind of confidence, and in short are likely to be engaged in a kind of platonic friendship.—On my side, you may be sure of its never being more, for if I were not already as much attached to another person as I can be to any one, I should make a point of not bestowing my affection on a Man who had dared to think so meanly of me.—

Reginald has a good figure, and is not unworthy the praise you have heard given him, but is still greatly inferior to our friend at Langford.—He is less polished, less insinuating than Manwaring, and is comparatively deficient in the power of saying those delightful things which put one in good humour with oneself and all the world. He is quite agreable enough however, to afford me amusement, and to make many of those hours pass very pleasantly which would be otherwise spent in endeavouring to overcome my sister in law's reserve, and listening to her Husband's insipid talk.—

Your account of Sir James is most satisfactory, and I mean to give Miss Frederica a hint of my intentions very soon.—

Yours etc.

S. Vernon

Letter 11

Mrs Vernon to Lady De Courcy

I really grow quite uneasy my dearest Mother about Reginald, from witnessing the very rapid increase of Lady Susan's influence. They are now on terms of the most particular friendship, frequently engaged in long conversations together, and she has contrived by the most artful coquetry to subdue his Judgement to her own purposes.—It is impossible to see the intimacy between them, so very soon established, without some alarm, tho' I can hardly suppose that Lady Susan's veiws extend to marriage.—I wish you could get Reginald home again, under any plausible pretence. He is not at all disposed to leave us, and I have given him as many hints of my Father's precarious state of health, as common decency will allow me to do in my own house.—Her power over him must now be boundless, as she has entirely effaced all his former ill-opinion, and persuaded him not merely to forget, but to justify her conduct.—Mr Smith's account of her proceedings at Langford, where he accused her of having made Mr Manwaring and a young Man engaged to Miss Manwaring distractedly in love with her, which Reginald firmly beleived when he came to Churchill, is now he is persuaded only a scandalous invention. He has told me so in a warmth of manner which spoke his regret at having ever beleived the contrary himself.—

How sincerely do I greive that she ever entered this house!—I always looked forward to her coming with uneasiness—but very far was it, from originating in anxiety for Reginald.—I expected a most disagreable companion to myself, but could not imagine that my Brother would be in the smallest danger of being captivated by a Woman with whose principles he was so well acquainted, and whose Character he so heartily despised. If you can get him away, it will be a good thing.

Y^rs affec^ly
Cath Vernon

Letter 12

Sir Reginald De Courcy to his Son

Parklands

I know that young Men in general do not admit of any enquiry even from their nearest relations, into affairs of the heart; but I hope my dear Reginald that you will be superior to such as allow nothing for a Father's anxiety, and think themselves privileged to refuse him their confidence and slight his advice.—You must be sensible that as an only son and the representative of an ancient Family, your conduct in Life is most interesting to your connections.—n the very important concern of Marriage especially, there is everything at stake; your own happiness, that of your Parents, and the credit of your name.—I do not suppose that you would deliberately form an absolute engagement of that nature without acquainting your Mother and myself, or at least without being convinced that we should approve your choice; but I cannot help fearing that you may be drawn in by the Lady who has lately attached you, to a Marriage, which the whole of your Family, far and near, must highly reprobate.

Lady Susan's age is itself a material objection, but her want of character is one so much more serious, that the difference of even twelve years[26] becomes in comparison of small account.—Were you not blinded by a sort of fascination, it would be ridiculous in me to repeat the instances of great misconduct on her side, so very generally known.—Her neglect of her husband, her encouragement of other Men, her extravagance and dissipation were so gross and notorious, that no one could be ignorant of them at the time, nor can now have forgotten them.—To our Family, she has always been represented in softened colours by the benevolence of Mr Charles Vernon; and yet in spite of his generous endeavours to excuse her, we know that she did, from the most selfish motives, take all possible pains to prevent his marrying Catherine.—

My Years and increasing Infirmities make me very desirous my dear Reginald, of seeing you settled in the world.—To the Fortune of your wife, the goodness of my own, will make me indifferent; but her family and character must be equally unexceptionable. When your choice is so fixed as that no objection can be made to either, I can promise you a ready and chearful consent; but it is my Duty to oppose a Match, which deep Art only could render probable, and must in the end make wretched.

It is possible that her behaviour may arise only from Vanity, or a wish of gaining the admiration of a Man whom she must imagine to be particularly prejudiced against her; but it is more likely that she should aim at something farther.—She is poor, and may naturally seek an alliance which may be advantageous to herself.—You know your own rights, and that it is out of my power to prevent your inheriting the family Estate. My Ability of distressing you during my Life, would be a species of revenge to which I should hardly stoop under any circumstances.[27]—I honestly tell you my Sentiments and Intentions. I do not wish to work on your Fears, but on your Sense and Affection.—It would destroy every comfort of my Life, to know that you were married to lady Susan Vernon. It would be the death of that honest Pride with which I have hitherto considered my son, I should blush to see him, to hear of him, to think of him.—

I may perhaps do no good, but that of relieving my own mind, by this Letter; but I felt it my Duty to tell you that your partiality for Lady Susan is no secret to your friends, and to warn you against her.—I should be glad to hear your reasons for disbeleiving Mr Smith's intelligence;—you had no doubt of its authenticity a month ago.—

If you can give me your assurance of having no design beyond enjoying the conversation of a clever woman for a short period, and of yeilding admiration only to her Beauty and Abilities without being blinded by them to her faults, you will restore me to happiness; but if you cannot do this, explain to me at least what has occasioned so great an alteration in your opinion of her.

I am etc.
Reg^d^ De Courcy

Letter 13

Lady De Courcy to Mrs Vernon

Parklands

My dear Catherine,

Unluckily I was confined to my room when your last letter came, by a cold which affected my eyes so much as to prevent my reading it myself, so I could not refuse your Father when he offered to read it to me, by which means he became acquainted to my great vexation with all your fears about your Brother. I had intended to write to Reginald myself, as soon as my eyes would let me, to point out as well as I could the danger of an intimate acquaintance with so artful a woman as Lady Susan, to a young Man of his age and high expectations. I meant moreover to have reminded him of our being quite alone now, and very much in need of him to keep up our spirits these long winter evenings. Whether it would have done any good, can never be settled now; but I am excessively vexed that Sir Reginald should know anything of a matter which we foresaw would make him so uneasy.—He caught all your fears the moment he had read your Letter, and I am sure has not had the business out of his head since;—he wrote by the same post to Reginald, a long letter full of it all, and particularly asking [for] an explanation of what he may have heard from Lady Susan to contradict the late shocking reports. His answer came this morning, which I shall enclose to you, as I think you will like to see it; I wish it was more satisfactory, but it seems written with such a determination to think well of Lady Susan, that his assurances as to Marriage etc., do not set my heart at ease.—I say all I can however to satisfy your Father, and he is certainly less uneasy since Reginald's letter. How provoking it is my dear Catherine, that this unwelcome Guest of yours, should not only prevent our meeting this Christmas, but be the occasion of so much vexation and trouble.—Kiss the dear Children for me.—

Your affec: Mother
C. De Courcy

Letter 14

Mr De Courcy to Sir Reginald

Churchill

My dear Sir

I have this moment received your Letter, which has given me more astonishment than I ever felt before. I am to thank my Sister I suppose, for having represented me in such a light as to injure me in your opinion, and give you all this alarm.—I know not why she should chuse to make herself and her family uneasy by apprehending an Event, which no one but herself I can affirm, would ever have thought possible. To impute such a design to Lady Susan would be taking from her every claim to that excellent understanding which her bitterest Enemies have never denied her; and equally low must sink my pretensions to common sense, if I am suspected of matrimonial veiws in my behaviour to her.—Our difference of age must be an insuperable objection, and I entreat you my dear Sir to quiet your mind, and no longer harbour a suspicion which cannot be more injurious to your own peace than to our Understandings.

I can have no veiw in remaining with Lady Susan than to enjoy for a short time (as you have yourself expressed it) the conversation of a Woman of high mental powers. If Mrs Vernon would allow something to my affection for herself and her husband in the length of my visit, she would do more justice to us all;—but my Sister is unhappily prejudiced beyond the hope of conviction against Lady Susan.—From an attachment to her husband which in itself does honour to both, she cannot forgive those endeavours at preventing their union, which have been attributed to selfishness in Lady Susan. But in this case, as well as in many others, the World has most grossly injured that Lady, by supposing the worst, where the motives of her conduct have been doubtful.—

Lady Susan had heard something so materially to the disadvantage of my Sister, as to persuade her that the happiness of Mr Vernon, to whom she was always much attached, would be absolutely destroyed by the Marriage. And this circumstance while it explains the true motive of Lady Susan's conduct, and removes all the blame which has been so lavished on her, may also convince us how little the general report of any one ought to be credited, since no Character however upright, can escape the malevolence of Slander. If my Sister in the security of retirement, with as little opportunity as inclination to do Evil, could not avoid Censure, we must not rashly condemn those who living in the World and surrounded with temptation, should be accused of Errors which they are known to have the power of committing.—

I blame myself severely for having so easily beleived the scandalous tales invented by Charles Smith to the prejudice of Lady Susan, as I am now convinced how greatly they have traduced her. As to Mrs Manwaring's jealousy, it was totally his own invention; and his account of her attaching Miss Manwaring's Lover was scarcely better founded. Sir James Martin had been drawn in by that young Lady to pay her some attention, and as he is a Man of fortune, it was easy to see that <u>her</u> veiws extended to Marriage.—It is well known that Miss Manwaring is absolutely on the catch for a husband, and no one therefore can pity her, for losing by the superior attractions of another woman, the chance of being able to make a worthy Man completely miserable.—Lady Susan was far from intending such a conquest, and on finding how warmly Miss Manwaring resented her Lover's defection, determined, in spite of M^r and Mrs Manwaring's most earnest entreaties, to leave the family.—I have reason to imagine that she did receive serious Proposals from Sir James, but her removing from Langford immediately on the discovery of his attachment, must acquit her on that article, with every Mind of common candour.[28]—You will, I am sure my dear Sir, feel the truth of this reasoning, and will hereby learn to do justice to the character of a very injured Woman.—

I know that Lady Susan in coming to Churchill was governed only by the most honourable and amiable intentions.—Her prudence and economy are exemplary, her regard for Mr Vernon equal even to his deserts, and her wish of obtaining my sister's good opinion merits a better return than it has received.—As a Mother she is unexceptionable. Her solid affection for her Child is shewn by placing her in hands, where her Education will be properly attended to; but because she has not the blind and weak partiality of most Mothers, she is accused of wanting Maternal Tenderness.—Every person of Sense however will know how to value and commend her well directed affection, and will join me in wishing that Frederica Vernon may prove more worthy than she has yet done, of her Mother's tender cares.

I have now my dear Sir, written my real sentiments of Lady Susan; you will know from this Letter, how highly I admire her Abilities, and esteem her Character; but if you are not equally convinced by my full and solemn assurance that your fears have been most idly created, you will deeply mortify and distress me.—

I am etc.

R De Courcy

Letter 15

Mrs Vernon to Lady De Courcy

Churchill

My dear Mother

I return you Reginald's letter, and rejoice with all my heart that my Father is made easy by it. Tell him so, with my congratulations;—but between ourselves, I must own it has only convinced me of my Brother's having no present intention of marrying Lady Susan—not that he is in no danger of doing so three months hence.—He gives a very plausible account of her behaviour at Langford, I wish it may be true, but his intelligence must come from herself, and I am less disposed to beleive it, than to lament the degree of intimacy subsisting between them, implied by the discussion of such a subject.

I am sorry to have incurred his displeasure, but can expect nothing better while he is so very eager in Lady Susan's justification.—He is very severe against me indeed, and yet I hope I have not been hasty in my judgement of her.—Poor Woman! tho' I have reasons enough for my dislike, I can not help pitying her at present as she is in real distress, and with too much cause.—She had this morning a letter from the Lady with whom she has placed her daughter, to request that Miss Vernon might be immediately removed, as she had been detected in an attempt to run away. Why, or whither she intended to go, does not appear; but as her situation seems to have been unexceptionable, it is a sad thing and of course highly afflicting to Lady Susan.—

Frederica must be as much as sixteen, and ought to know better, but from what her Mother insinuates I am afraid she is a perverse girl. She has been sadly neglected however, and her Mother ought to remember it.—

Mr Vernon set off for Town as soon as she had determined what should be done. He is if possible to prevail on Miss

Summers to let Frederica continue with her, and if he cannot succeed, to bring her to Churchill for the present, till some other situation can be found for her.—Her Ladyship is comforting herself meanwhile by strolling along the Shrubbery[29] with Reginald, calling forth all his tender feelings I suppose on this distressing occasion. She has been talking a great deal about it to me, she talks vastly well, I am afraid of being ungenerous or I should say she talks <u>too</u> well to feel so very deeply. But I will not look for Faults. She may be Reginald's Wife—Heaven forbid it!—but why should I be quicker sighted than anybody else?—Mr Vernon declares that he never saw deeper distress than hers, on the receipt of the Letter—and is his Judgement inferior to mine?—

She was very unwilling that Frederica should be allowed to come to Churchill, and justly enough, as it seems a sort of reward to Behaviour deserving very differently. But it was impossible to take her any where else, and she is not to remain here long.—

'It will be absolutely necessary,' said she, 'as you my dear Sister must be sensible, to treat my daughter with some severity while she is here;—a most painful necessity, but I will <u>endeavour</u> to submit to it.—I am afraid I have been often too indulgent, but my poor Frederica's temper could never bear opposition well. You must support and encourage me—You must urge the necessity of reproof, if you see me too lenient.'

All this sounds very reasonably.—Reginald is so incensed against the poor silly Girl!—Surely it is not to Lady Susan's credit that he should be so bitter against her daughter; his idea of her must be drawn from the Mother's description.—

Well, whatever may be his fate, we have the comfort of knowing that we have done our utmost to save him. We must commit the event to an Higher Power.—

Yours Ever etc.
Cath Vernon

Letter 16

Lady Susan to Mrs Johnson

Churchill

Never my dearest Alicia, was I so provoked in my life as by a Letter this morning from Miss Summers. That horrid girl of mine has been trying to run away.—I had not a notion of her being such a little Devil before;—she seemed to have all the Vernon Milkiness; but on receiving the letter in which I declared my intentions about Sir James, she actually attempted to elope; at least, I cannot otherwise account for her doing it.—She meant I suppose to go to the Clarkes in Staffordshire, for she has no other acquaintance. But she shall be punished, she shall have him. I have sent Charles to Town to make matters up if he can, for I do not by any means want her here. If Miss Summers will not keep her, you must find me out another school, unless we can get her married immediately.—Miss S. writes word that she could not get the young Lady to assign any cause for her extraordinary conduct, which confirms me in my own private explanation of it.—

Frederica is too shy I think, and too much in awe of me, to tell tales; but if the mildness of her Uncle should get anything from her, I am not afraid. I trust I shall be able to make my story as good as hers.—If I am vain of anything, it is of my eloquence. Consideration and Esteem as surely follow command of Language, as Admiration waits on Beauty. And here I have opportunity enough for the exercise of my Talent, as the cheif of my time is spent in Conversation. Reginald is never easy unless we are by ourselves, and when the weather is tolerable, we pace the shrubbery for hours together.—I like him on the whole very well, he is clever and has a good deal to say, but he is sometimes impertinent and troublesome.—There is a sort of ridiculous delicacy about him which requires the fullest explanation of whatever he may have heard to my disadvantage, and is never satisfied till he thinks he has ascertained the beginning and end of everything.—

This is one sort of Love—but I confess it does not particularly recommend itself to me.—I infinitely prefer the tender and liberal spirit of Manwaring, which impressed with the deepest conviction of my merit, is satisfied that whatever I do must be right; and look with a degree of contempt on the inquisitive and doubting Fancies of that Heart which seems always debating on the reasonableness of its Emotions. Manwaring is indeed beyond compare superior to Reginald—superior in everything but the power of being with me.—Poor fellow! he is quite distracted by Jealousy, which I am not sorry for, as I know no better support of Love.—He has been teizing me[30] to allow of his coming into this country, and lodging somewhere near me incog[31]—but I forbid anything of the kind.—Those women are inexcusable who forget what is due to themselves and the opinion of the World.—

S. Vernon

Letter 17

Mrs Vernon to Lady De Courcy

Churchill

My dear Mother

Mr Vernon returned on Thursday night, bringing his neice with him. Lady Susan had received a line from him by that day's post informing her that Miss Summers had absolutely refused to allow of Miss Vernon's continuance in her Academy. We were therefore prepared for her arrival, and expected them impatiently the whole evening.—They came while we were at Tea,[32] and I never saw any creature look so frightened in my life as Frederica when she entered the room.—

Lady Susan who had been shedding tears before and shewing great agitation at the idea of the meeting, received her with perfect self-command, and without betraying the least tenderness of spirit.—She hardly spoke to her, and on Frederica's bursting into tears as soon [as] we were seated, took her out of the room and did not return for some time; when she did, her eyes looked very red, and she was as much agitated as before.—We saw no more of her daughter.—

Poor Reginald was beyond measure concerned to see his fair friend in such distress, and watched her with so much tender solicitude that I, who occasionally caught her observing his countenance with exultation, was quite out of patience.—This pathetic representation lasted the whole evening, and so ostentatious and artful a display has entirely convinced me that she did in fact feel nothing.—

I am more angry with her than ever since I have seen her daughter.—The poor girl looks so unhappy that my heart aches for her.—Lady Susan is surely too severe, because Frederica does not seem to have the sort of temper to make severity necessary.—She looks perfectly timid, dejected and penitent.—

She is very pretty, tho' not so handsome as her Mother, nor at all like her. Her complexion is delicate, but neither so fair, nor so blooming as Lady Susan's—and she has quite the Vernon cast of countenance, the oval face and mild dark eyes, and there is peculiar sweetness in her look when she speaks either to her Uncle or me, for as we behave kindly to her, we have of course engaged her gratitude.—Her Mother has insinuated that her temper is untractable, but I never saw a face less indicative of any evil disposition than hers; and from what I now see of the behaviour of each to the other, the invariable severity of Lady Susan, and the silent dejection of Frederica, I am led to beleive as heretofore that the former has no real Love for her daughter and has never done her justice, or treated her affectionately.

I have not yet been able to have any conversation with my neice; she is shy, and I think I can see that some pains are taken to prevent her being much with me.—Nothing satisfactory transpires as to her reason for running away.—Her kindhearted Uncle you may be sure, was too fearful of distressing her, to ask many questions as they travelled.—I wish it had been possible for me to fetch her instead of him;—I think I should have discovered the truth in the course of a Thirty mile Journey.—

The small Pianoforté has been removed within these few days at Lady Susan's request, into her Dressing room, and Frederica spends great part of the day there; <u>practising</u> it is called, but I seldom hear any noise when I pass that way.—What she does with herself there I do not know, there are plenty of books in the room, but it is not every girl who has been running wild the first fifteen years of her life, that can or will read.—Poor Creature! the prospect from her window is not very instructive, for that room overlooks the Lawn you know with the Shrubbery on one side, where she may see her Mother walking for an hour together, in earnest conversation with Reginald.—A girl of Frederica's age must be childish indeed, if such things do not strike her.—Is it not inexcusable to give such an example to a daughter?—Yet Reginald still thinks Lady Susan the best of Mothers—still condemns Frederica as a worthless girl!—He is convinced that her attempt to run away, proceeded from no justifiable cause, and had no provocation. I am sure I cannot say that it <u>had</u>, but while Miss Summers declares that Miss Vernon shewed no sign of Obstinacy or Perverseness during her whole stay in Wigmore S^{t} till she was detected in this scheme, I cannot so readily credit what Lady Susan has made him and wants to make me beleive, that it was merely an impatience of restraint, and a desire of escaping from the tuition of Masters which brought on the plan of an elopement.—Oh! Reginald, how is your Judgement enslaved!—He scarcely dares even allow her to be handsome, and when I speak of her beauty, replies only that her eyes have no Brilliancy.

Sometimes he is sure that she is deficient in Understanding, and at others that her temper only is in fault. In short when a person is always to deceive, it is impossible to be consistent. Lady Susan finds it necessary for her own justification that Frederica should be to blame, and probably has sometimes judged it expedient to accuse her of ill-nature and sometimes to lament her want of sense. Reginald is only repeating after her Ladyship.—

I am etc.
Cath Vernon

Letter 18

From the same to the same

Churchill

My dear Madam

I am very glad to find that my description of Frederica Vernon has interested you, for I do beleive her truly deserving of our regard, and when I have communicated a notion that has recently struck me, your kind impression in her favour will I am sure be heightened. I cannot help fancying that she is growing partial to my brother, I so very often see her eyes fixed on his face with a remarkable expression of pensive admiration!—He is certainly very handsome—and yet more—there is an openness in his manner that must be highly prepossessing, and I am sure she feels it so.—Thoughtful and pensive in general her countenance always brightens with a smile when Reginald says anything amusing; and let the subject be ever so serious that he may be conversing on, I am much mistaken if a syllable of his uttering, escape her.—

I want to make <u>him</u> sensible of all this, for we know the power of gratitude on such a heart as his; and could Frederica's artless affection detach him from her Mother, we might bless the day which brought her to Churchill. I think my dear Madam, you would not disapprove of her as a Daughter. She is extremely young to be sure, has had a wretched Education and a dreadful example of Levity in her Mother; but yet I can pronounce her disposition to be excellent, and her natural abilities very good.—

Tho' totally without accomplishment, she is by no means so ignorant as one might expect to find her, being fond of books and spending the cheif of her time in reading. Her Mother leaves her more to herself now than she <u>did</u>, and I have her with me as much as possible, and have taken great pains to overcome her timidity. We are very good friends, and tho' she never opens her lips before her Mother, she talks enough when alone with me, to make it clear that if properly treated by Lady Susan she would always appear to much greater advantage. There cannot be a more gentle, affectionate heart, or more obliging manners, when acting without restraint. Her little Cousins are all very fond of her.—

Y[rs] affec[ly]
Cath Vernon

Letter 19

Lady Susan to Mrs Johnson

Churchill

You will be eager I know to hear something farther of Frederica, and perhaps may think me negligent for not writing before.—She arrived with her Uncle last Thursday fortnight, when of course I lost no time in demanding the reason of her behaviour, and soon found myself to have been perfectly right in attributing it to my own letter.—The purport of it frightened her so thoroughly that with a mixture of true girlish perverseness and folly, without considering that she could not escape from my authority by running away from Wigmore Street, she resolved on getting out of the house, and proceeding directly by the stage to her friends the Clarkes, and had really got as far as the length of two streets in her journey, when she was fortunately miss'd, pursued, and overtaken.—

Such was the first distinguished exploit of Miss Frederica Susanna Vernon, and if we consider that it was atchieved at the tender age of sixteen we shall have room for the most flattering prognostics of her future renown.—I am excessively provoked however at the parade of propriety which prevented Miss Summers from keeping the girl; and it seems so extraordinary a peice of nicety,[33] considering what are my daughter's family connections, that I can only suppose the Lady to be governed by the fear of never getting her money.—Be that as it may however, Frederica is returned on my hands, and having now nothing else to employ her, is busy in pursueing the plan of Romance begun at Langford.—She is actually falling in love with Reginald De Courcy.—To disobey her Mother by refusing an unexceptionable offer is not enough; her affections must likewise be given without her Mother's approbation.—I never saw a girl of her age, bid fairer to be the sport of Mankind. Her feelings are tolerably lively, and she is so charmingly artless in their display, as to afford the most reasonable hope of her being ridiculed and despised by every Man who sees her.—

Artlessness will never do in Love matters, and that girl is born a simpleton who has it either by nature or affectation.—I am not yet certain that Reginald sees what she is about; nor is it of much consequence;—she is now an object of indifference to him, she would be one of contempt were he to understand her Emotions.—Her beauty is much admired by the Vernons, but it has no effect on <u>him</u>. She is in high favour with her Aunt altogether—because she is so little like myself of course. She is exactly the companion for Mrs Vernon, who dearly loves to be first, and to have all the sense and all the wit of the Conversation to herself;—Frederica will never eclipse her.—When she first came, I was at some pains to prevent her seeing much of her Aunt, but I have since relaxed, as I beleive I may depend on her observing the rules I have laid down for their discourse.—

But do not imagine that with all this Lenity, I have for a moment given up my plan of her marriage;—No, I am unalterably fixed on that point, tho' I have not yet quite resolved on the manner of bringing it about.—I should not chuse to have the business brought forward here, and canvassed by the wise heads of M^r^ and Mrs Vernon; and I cannot just now afford to go to Town.—Miss Frederica therefore must wait a little.—

Yours Ever
S. Vernon

Letter 20

Mrs Vernon to Lady De Courcy

Churchill

We have a very unexpected Guest with us at present, my dear Mother.—He arrived yesterday.—I heard a carriage at the door as I was sitting with my children while they dined, and supposing I should be wanted left the Nursery soon afterwards and was half way down stairs, when Frederica as pale as ashes came running up, and rushed by me into her own room.—I instantly followed, and asked her what was the matter.—'Oh!' cried she, 'he is come, Sir James is come—and what am I to do?' This was no explanation; I begged her to tell me what she meant. At that moment we were interrupted by a knock at the door;—it was Reginald, who came by Lady Susan's direction to call Frederica down.—'It is Mr De Courcy,' said she, 'colouring violently, Mama has sent for me, and I must go.'—

We all three went down together, and I saw my Brother examining the terrified face of Frederica with surprise.—In the breakfast room we found Lady Susan and a young Man of genteel appearance,[34] whom she introduced to me by the name of Sir James Martin, the very person, as you may remember, whom it was said she had been at pains to detach from Miss Manwaring.—But the conquest it seems was not designed for herself, or she has since transferred it to her daughter, for Sir James is now desperately in love with Frederica, and with full encouragement from Mama.—The poor girl however I am sure dislikes him; and tho' his person and address are very well, he appears both to Mr Vernon and me a very weak young Man.—

Frederica looked so shy, so confused, when we entered the room, that I felt for her exceedingly. Lady Susan behaved with great attention to her Visitor, and yet I thought I could perceive that she had no particular pleasure in seeing him.—Sir James talked a good deal, and made many civil excuses to me for the liberty he had taken in coming to Churchill, mixing more frequent laughter with his discourse than the subject required;—said many things over and over again, and told Lady Susan three times that he had seen Mrs Johnson a few Evenings before.—He now and then addressed Frederica, but more frequently her Mother.—The poor girl sat all this time without opening her lips;—her eyes cast down, and her colour varying every instant, while Reginald observed all that passed, in perfect silence.—

At length Lady Susan, weary I beleive of her situation, proposed walking, and we left the two Gentlemen together to put on our Pelisses.—[35]

As we went upstairs Lady Susan begged permission to attend me for a few moments in my Dressing room, as she was anxious to speak with me in private.—I led her thither accordingly, and as soon as the door was closed she said, 'I was never more surprised in my life than by Sir James's arrival, and the suddenness of it requires some apology to You my dear Sister, tho' to me as a Mother, it is highly flattering.—He is so warmly attached to my daughter that he could exist no longer without seeing her.—Sir James is a young Man of an amiable disposition, and excellent character;—a little too much of the Rattle[36] perhaps, but a year or two will rectify that, and he is in other respects so very eligible a Match for Frederica that I have always observed his attachment with the greatest pleasure, and am persuaded that you and my Brother will give the alliance your hearty approbation.—I have never before mentioned the likelihood of its taking place to any one, because I thought that while Frederica continued at school, it had better not be known to exist;—but now, as I am convinced that Frederica is too old ever to submit to school confinement, and have therefore begun to consider her union with Sir James as not very distant, I had intended within a few days to acquaint yourself and Mr Vernon with the whole business.—I am sure my dear Sister, you will excuse my remaining silent on it so long, and agree with me that such circumstances, while they continue from any cause in suspense, cannot be too cautiously concealed.—When you have the happiness of bestowing your sweet little Catherine some years hence on a Man, who in connection and character is alike unexceptionable, you will know what I feel now;—tho' Thank Heaven! you cannot have all my reasons for rejoicing in such an Event.—Catherine will be amply provided for, and not like my Frederica endebted to a fortunate Establishment for the comforts of Life.'—

She concluded by demanding my congratulations.—I gave them somewhat awkwardly I beleive;—for in fact, the sudden disclosure of so important a matter took from me the power of speaking with any clearness.—She thanked me however most affectionately for my kind concern in the welfare of herself and her daughter, and then said,

'I am not apt to deal in professions, my dear M[rs] Vernon, and I never had the convenient talent of affecting sensations foreign to my heart; and therefore I trust you will beleive me when I declare that much as I had heard in your praise before I knew you, I had no idea that I should ever love you as I now do;—and I must farther say that your friendship towards me is more particularly gratifying, because I have reason to beleive that some attempts were made to prejudice you against me.—I only wish that They—whoever they are—to whom I am endebted for such kind intentions, could see the terms on which we now are together, and understand the real affection we feel for each other!—But I will not detain you any longer.—God bless you, for your goodness to me and my girl, and continue to you all your present happiness.'

What can one say of such a Woman, my dear Mother?—such earnestness, such solemnity of expression!—And yet I cannot help suspecting the truth of everything she said.—

As for Reginald, I beleive he does not know what to make of the matter.—When Sir James first came, he appeared all astonishment and perplexity. The folly of the young Man, and the confusion of Frederica entirely engrossed him; and tho' a little private discourse with Lady Susan has since had its effect, he is still hurt I am sure at her allowing of such a Man's attentions to her daughter.—

Sir James invited himself with great composure to remain here a few days;—hoped we would not think it odd, was aware of its being very impertinent, but he took the liberty of a relation, and concluded by wishing with a laugh, that he might be really one soon.—Even Lady Susan seemed a little disconcerted by this forwardness;—in her heart I am persuaded, she sincerely wishes him gone.—

But something must be done for this poor Girl, if her feelings are such as both her Uncle and I beleive them to be. She must not be sacrificed to Policy or Ambition, she must not be even left to suffer from the dread of it.—The Girl, whose heart can distinguish Reginald De Courcy, deserves, however he may slight her, a better fate than to be Sir James Martin's wife.—As soon as I can get her alone, I will discover the real Truth, but she seems to wish to avoid me.—I hope this does not proceed from anything wrong, and that I shall not find out I have thought too well of her.—Her behaviour before Sir James certainly speaks the greatest consciousness and Embarrassment; but I see nothing in it more like Encouragement.—

Adeiu my dear Madam,

Y[rs] etc. Cath Vernon

Letter 21

Miss Vernon to M^r De Courcy

Sir,

I hope you will excuse this liberty, I am forced upon it by the greatest distress, or I should be ashamed to trouble you.—I am very miserable about Sir James Martin, and have no other way in the world of helping myself but by writing to you, for I am forbidden ever speaking to my Uncle or Aunt on the subject; and this being the case, I am afraid my applying to you will appear no better than equivocation, and as if I attended only to the letter and not the spirit of Mama's commands, but if You do not take my part, and persuade her to break it off, I shall be half-distracted, for I can not bear him.—No human Being but You could have any chance of prevailing with her.—If you will therefore have the unspeakable great kindness of taking my part with her, and persuading her to send Sir James away, I shall be more obliged to you than it is possible for me to express.—I always disliked him from the first, it is not a sudden fancy I assure you Sir, I always thought him silly and impertinent and disagreable, and now he is grown worse than ever.—I would rather work for my bread than marry him.—I do not know how to apologise enough for this Letter, I know it is taking so great a liberty, I am aware how dreadfully angry it will make Mama, but I must run the risk.—

I am Sir, Your most Hum^ble Servt
F. S. V.

Letter 22[d]

Lady Susan to M[rs] Johnson

Churchill

This is insufferable!—My dearest friend, I was never so enraged before, and must releive myself by writing to you, who I know will enter into all my feelings.—Who should come on Tuesday but Sir James Martin?—Guess my astonishment and vexation—for as you well know, I never wished him to be seen at Churchill. What a pity that you should not have known his intentions!—Not content with coming, he actually invited himself to remain here a few days. I could have poisoned him;—I made the best of it however, and told my story with great success to Mrs Vernon who, whatever might be her real sentiments, said nothing in opposition to mine. I made a point also of Frederica's behaving civilly to Sir James, and gave her to understand that I was absolutely determined on her marrying him.—She said something of her misery, but that was all.—I have for some time been more particularly resolved on the Match, from seeing the rapid increase of her affection for Reginald, and from not feeling perfectly secure that a knowledge of <u>that</u> affection might not in the end awaken a return.—Contemptible as a regard founded only on compassion, must make them both,[37] in my eyes, I felt by no means assured that such might not be the consequence.—It is true that Reginald had not in any degree grown cool towards me;—but yet he had lately mentioned Frederica spontaneously and unnecessarily, and once had said something in praise of her person.—

<u>He</u> was all astonishment at the appearance of my visitor; and at first observed Sir James with an attention which I was pleased to see not unmixed with jealousy;—but unluckily it was impossible for me really to torment him, as Sir James tho' extremely gallant to me, very soon made the whole party understand that his heart was devoted to my daughter.—

I had no great difficulty in convincing De Courcy when we were alone, that I was perfectly justified, all things considered, in desiring the match; and the whole business seemed most comfortably arranged. They could none of them help perceiving that Sir James was no Solomon,[38] but I had positively forbidden Frederica's complaining to Charles Vernon or his wife, and they had therefore no pretence for Interference, tho' my impertinent Sister I beleive wanted only opportunity for doing so.—

Everything however was going on calmly and quietly; and tho' I counted the hours of Sir James's stay, my mind was entirely satisfied with the posture of affairs.—Guess then what I must feel at the sudden disturbance of all my schemes, and that too from a quarter, whence I had least reason to apprehend it.—Reginald came this morning into my Dressing room, with a very unusual solemnity of countenance, and after some preface informed me in so many words, that he wished to reason with me on the Impropriety and Unkindness of allowing Sir James Martin to address my Daughter, contrary to her inclination.—I was all amazement.—When I found that he was not to be laughed out of his design, I calmly required an explanation, and begged to know by what he was impelled, and by whom commissioned to reprimand me.

He then told me, mixing in his speech a few insolent compliments and illtimed expressions of Tenderness to which I listened with perfect indifference, that my daughter had acquainted him with some circumstances concerning herself, Sir James, and me, which gave him great uneasiness.—

In short, I found that she had in the first place actually written to him, to request his interference, and that on receiving her Letter he had conversed with her on the subject of it, in order to understand the particulars and assure himself of her real wishes!

I have not a doubt but that the girl took this opportunity of making downright Love to him; I am convinced of it, from the manner in which he spoke of her. Much good, may such Love do him!—I shall ever despise the Man who can be gratified by the Passion, which he never wished to inspire, nor solicited the avowal of.—I shall always detest them both.—He can have no true regard for me, or he would not have listened to her;—And she, with her little rebellious heart and indelicate feelings to throw herself into the protection of a young Man[39] with whom she had scarcely ever exchanged two words before. I am equally confounded at her Impudence and his Credulity.—How dared he beleive what she told him in my disfavour!—Ought he not to have felt assured that I must have unanswerable Motives for all that I had done!—Where was his reliance on my Sense or Goodness then; where the resentment which true Love would have dictated against the person defaming me, that person, too, a Chit, a Child, without Talent or Education, whom he had been always taught to despise?—

I was calm for some time, but the greatest degree of Forbearance may be overcome; and I hope I was afterwards sufficiently keen.—He endeavoured, long endeavoured to soften my resentment, but that woman is a fool indeed who while insulted by accusation, can be worked on by compliments.—At length he left me, as deeply provoked as myself, and he shewed his anger more.—I was quite cool, but he gave way to the most violent indignation.—I may therefore expect it will sooner subside; and perhaps his may be vanished for ever, while mine will be found still fresh and implacable.

He is now shut up in his apartment, whither I heard him go, on leaving mine.—How unpleasant, one would think, must his reflections be!—But some people's feelings are incomprehensible.—I have not yet tranquillized myself enough to see Frederica. She shall not soon forget the occurrences of this day.—She shall find that she has poured forth her tender Tale of Love in vain, and exposed herself forever to the contempt of the whole world, and the severest Resentment of her injured Mother.—

Yrs affecly
S. Vernon

Letter 23

Mrs Vernon to Lady De Courcy

Churchill

Let me congratulate you, my dearest Mother. The affair which has given us so much anxiety is drawing to a happy conclusion. Our prospect is most delightful;—and since matters have now taken so favourable a turn, I am quite sorry that I ever imparted my apprehensions to you; for the pleasure of learning that the danger is over, is perhaps dearly purchased by all that you have previously suffered.—

I am so much agitated by Delight that I can scarcely hold a pen, but am determined to send you a few lines by James, that you may have some explanation of what must so greatly astonish you, as that Reginald should be returning to Parklands.—

I was sitting about half an hour ago with Sir James in the Breakfast parlour, when my Brother called me out of the room.—I instantly saw that something was the matter;—his complexion was raised, and he spoke with great emotion.—You know his eager manner, my dear Madam, when his mind is interested.—

'Catherine,' said he, 'I am going home today. I am sorry to leave you, but I must go.—It is a great while since I have seen my Father and Mother.—I am going to send James forward with my Hunters[40] immediately, if you have any Letter therefore he can take it.—I shall not be at home myself till Wednesday or Thursday, as I shall go through London, where I have business.—But before I leave you,' he continued, speaking in a lower voice and with still greater energy, 'I must warn you of one thing.—Do not let Frederica Vernon be made unhappy by that Martin.—He wants to marry her—her Mother promotes the Match—but she cannot endure the idea of it.—Be assured that I speak from the fullest conviction of the Truth of what I say.—I <u>know</u> that Frederica is made wretched by Sir James' continuing here.—She is a sweet girl, and deserves a better fate.—Send him away immediately. <u>He</u> is only a fool—but what her Mother can mean, Heaven only knows!—Good bye,' he added shaking my hand with earnestness—'I do not know when you will see me again. But remember what I tell you of Frederica;—you <u>must</u> make it your business to see justice done her.—She is an amiable girl, and has a very superior Mind to what we have ever given her credit for.'—

He then left me and ran upstairs.—I would not try to stop him, for I knew what his feelings must be; the nature of mine as I listened to him, I need not attempt to describe.—For a minute or two I remained in the same spot, overpowered by wonder—of a most agreable sort indeed; yet it required some consideration to be tranquilly happy.—

In about ten minutes after my return to the parlour, Lady Susan entered the room.—I concluded of course that she and Reginald had been quarreling, and looked with anxious curiosity for a confirmation of my beleif in her face.—Mistress of Deceit however she appeared perfectly unconcerned, and after chatting on indifferent subjects for a short time, said to me,

'I find from Wilson that we are going to lose M^r^ De Courcy.—Is it true that he leaves Churchill this morning?'

I replied that it was.—

'He told us nothing of all this last night,' said she laughing, 'or even this morning at Breakfast. But perhaps he did not know it himself.—Young Men are often hasty in their resolutions—and not more sudden in forming, than unsteady in keeping them.—I should not be surprised if he were to change his mind at last, and not go.'—

She soon afterwards left the room.—I trust however my dear Mother, that we have no reason to fear an alteration of his present plan; things have gone too far.—They must have quarrelled, and about Frederica too.—Her calmness astonishes me.—What delight will be yours in seeing him again, in seeing him still worthy your Esteem, still capable of forming your Happiness!

When I next write, I shall be able I hope to tell you that Sir James is gone, Lady Susan vanquished, and Frederica at peace.—We have much to do, but it shall be done.—I am all impatience to know how this astonishing change was effected.—I finish as I began, with the warmest congratulations.—

Y^{rs} Ever,
Cath Vernon

Letter 24

From the same to the same

Churchill

Little did I imagine my dear Mother, when I sent off my last letter, that the delightful perturbation of spirits I was then in, would undergo so speedy, so melancholy a reverse!—I never can sufficiently regret that I wrote to you at all.—Yet who could have foreseen what has happened? My dear Mother, every hope which but two hours ago made me so happy, is vanished. The quarrel between Lady Susan and Reginald is made up, and we are all as we were before. One point only is gained; Sir James Martin is dismissed.—What are we now to look forward to?—I am indeed disappointed. Reginald was all but gone; his horse was ordered, and almost brought to the door!—Who would not have felt safe?—

For half an hour I was in momentary expectation of his departure.—After I had sent off my Letter to you, I went to Mr Vernon and sat with him in his room, talking over the whole matter.—I then determined to look for Frederica, whom I had not seen since breakfast.—I met her on the stairs and saw that she was crying.

'My dear Aunt,' said she, 'he is going, Mr De Courcy is going, and it is all my fault. I am afraid you will be angry, but indeed I had no idea it would end so.'—

'My Love,' replied I, 'do not think it necessary to apologize to me on that account.—I shall feel myself under an obligation to anyone who is the means of sending my brother home;—because, (recollecting myself) I know my Father wants very much to see him. But what is it that <u>you</u> have done to occasion all this?'—

She blushed deeply as she answered, 'I was so unhappy about Sir James that I could not help—I have done something very wrong I know—but you have not an idea of the misery I have been in, and Mama had ordered me never to speak to you or my Uncle about it,—and,—'

'You therefore spoke to my Brother, to engage *his* interference;' said I, wishing to save her the explanation.

'No—but I wrote to him.—I did indeed.—I got up this morning before it was light—I was two hours about it—and when my Letter was done, I thought I never should have courage to give it.—After breakfast however, as I was going to my own room I met him in the passage, and then as I knew that everything must depend on that moment, I forced myself to give it.—He was so good as to take it immediately;—I dared not look at him—and ran away directly.—I was in such a fright that I could hardly breathe.—My dear Aunt, you do not know how miserable I have been.'

'Frederica,' said I, 'you ought to have told *me* all your distresses.—You would have found in me a friend always ready to assist you.—Do you think that your Uncle and I should not have espoused your cause as warmly as my Brother?'—

'Indeed I did not doubt your goodness,' said she, colouring again, 'but I thought that M^r De Courcy could do anything with my Mother;—but I was mistaken;—they have had a dreadful quarrel about it, and he is going.—Mama will never forgive me, and I shall be worse off than ever.'

'No, you shall not,' replied I.—'In such a point as this, your Mother's prohibition ought not to have prevented your speaking to me on the subject. She has no right to make you unhappy, and she shall *not* do it.—Your applying however to Reginald can be productive only of Good to all parties. I beleive it is best as it is.—Depend upon it that you shall not be made unhappy any longer.'

At that moment, how great was my astonishment at seeing Reginald come out of Lady Susan's Dressing room. My heart misgave me instantly. His confusion on seeing me was very evident.—Frederica immediately disappeared.

'Are you going?'—said I. 'You will find Mr Vernon in his own room.'

'No Catherine,' replied he.—'I am *not* going.—Will you let me speak to you a moment?'

We went into my room. 'I find,' continued he, his confusion increasing as he spoke, 'that I have been acting with my usual foolish Impetuosity.—I have entirely misunderstood Lady Susan, and was on the point of leaving the house under a false impression of her conduct.—There has been some very great mistake—we have been all mistaken I fancy.—Frederica does not know her Mother—Lady Susan means nothing but her Good—but Frederica will not make a friend of her.—Lady Susan therefore does not always know what will make her daughter happy.—Besides I could have no right to interfere—Miss Vernon was mistaken in applying to me.—In short Catherine, everything has gone wrong—but it is now all happily settled.—Lady Susan I beleive wishes to speak to you about it, if you are at leisure.'—

'Certainly;' replied I, deeply sighing at the recital of so lame a story.—I made no remarks however, for words would have been in vain. Reginald was glad to get away, and I went to Lady Susan; curious indeed to hear her account of it.—

'Did not I tell you,' said she with a smile, 'that your Brother would not leave us after all?'

'You did indeed,' replied I very gravely, 'but I flattered myself that you would be mistaken.'

'I should not have hazarded such an opinion,' returned she, 'if it had not at that moment occurred [to] me, that his resolution of going might be occasioned by a Conversation in which we had been this morning engaged, and which had ended very much to his Dissatisfaction from our not rightly understanding each other's meaning.—This idea struck me at the moment, and I instantly determined that an accidental dispute in which I might probably be as much to blame as himself, should not deprive you of your Brother.—If you remember, I left the room almost immediately.—I was resolved to lose no time in clearing up these mistakes as far as I could.—The case was this.—Frederica had set herself violently against marrying Sir James,—'

'And can your Ladyship wonder that she should?' cried I with some warmth.—'Frederica has an excellent Understanding, and Sir James has none.'

'I am at least very far from regretting it, my dear Sister,' said she; 'on the contrary, I am grateful for so favourable a sign of my Daughter's sense. Sir James is certainly under par,—(his boyish manners make him appear the worse),—and had Frederica possessed the penetration, the abilities, which I could have wished in my daughter, or had I even known her to possess so much as she does, I should not have been anxious for the match.'

'It is odd that you alone should be ignorant of your Daughter's sense.'

'Frederica never does justice to herself;—her manners are shy and childish.—She is besides afraid of me; she scarcely loves me.—During her poor Father's life she was a spoilt child; the severity which it has since been necessary for me to shew, has entirely alienated her affection;—neither has she any of that Brilliancy of Intellect, that Genius, or Vigour of Mind which will force itself forward.'

'Say rather that she has been unfortunate in her Education.'

'Heaven knows my dearest Mrs Vernon, how fully I am aware of <u>that</u>; but I would wish to forget every circumstance that might throw blame on the memory of one, whose name is sacred with me.'

Here she pretended to cry.—I was out of patience with her.—'But what,' said I, 'was your Ladyship going to tell me about your disagreement with my Brother?'—

'It originated in an action of my Daughter's, which equally marks her want of Judgement, and the unfortunate Dread of me I have been mentioning.—She wrote to M^r^ De Courcy.'—

'I know she did.—You had forbidden her speaking to Mr Vernon or to me on the cause of her distress: what could she do therefore but apply to my Brother?'

'Good God!—' she exclaimed, 'what an opinion must you have of me!—Can you possibly suppose that I was aware of her unhappiness? that it was my object to make my own child miserable, and that I had forbidden her speaking to you on the subject, from a fear of your interrupting the Diabolical scheme?—Do you think me destitute of every honest, every natural feeling?—Am I capable of consigning her to everlasting Misery, whose welfare it is my first Earthly Duty to promote?'

'The idea is horrible.—What then was your intention when you insisted on her silence?'

'Of what use my dear Sister, could be any application to you, however the affair might stand? Why should I subject you to entreaties, which I refused to attend to myself?—Neither for your sake, for hers, nor for my own, could such a thing be desireable.—Where my own resolution was taken, I could not wish for the interference, however friendly, of another person.—I was mistaken, it is true, but I beleived myself to be right.'

'But what was this mistake, to which your Ladyship so often alludes? From whence arose so astonishing a misapprehension of your Daughter's feelings?—Did not you know that she disliked Sir James?—'

'I knew that he was not absolutely the Man she would have chosen.—But I was persuaded that her objections to him did not arise from any perception of his Deficiency.—You must not question me however my dear Sister, too minutely on this point'—continued she, taking me affectionately by the hand.—'I honestly own that there is something to conceal.—Frederica makes me very unhappy.—Her applying to M^r^ De Courcy hurt me particularly.'

'What is it that you mean to infer,' said I, 'by this appearance of mystery?—If you think your daughter at all attached to Reginald, her objecting to Sir James could not less deserve to be attended to, than if the cause of her objecting had been a consciousness of his folly.—And why should your Ladyship at any rate quarrel with my brother for an interference which you must know, it was not in his nature to refuse, when urged in such a manner?'

'His disposition you know is warm, and he came to expostulate with me, his compassion all alive for this ill-used Girl, this Heroine in distress!—We misunderstood each other. He beleived me more to blame than I really was; I considered his interference as less excusable than I now find it. I have a real regard for him, and was beyond expression mortified to find it as I thought so ill bestowed. We were both warm, and of course both to blame.—His resolution of leaving Churchill is consistent with his general eagerness;—when I understood his intention however, and at the same time began to think that we had perhaps been equally mistaken in each other's meaning, I resolved to have an explanation before it were too late.—For any Member of your Family I must always feel a degree of affection, and I own it would have sensibly hurt me, if my acquaintance with M[r] De Courcy had ended so gloomily. I have now only to say farther, that as I am convinced of Frederica's having a reasonable dislike to Sir James, I shall instantly inform him that he must give up all hope of her.—I reproach myself for having ever, tho' so innocently, made her unhappy on that score.—She shall have all the retribution in my power to make;—if she value her own happiness as much as I do, if she judge wisely and command herself as she ought, she may now be easy.—Excuse me, my dearest Sister, for thus trespassing on your time, but I owed it to my own Character; and after this explanation I trust I am in no danger of sinking in your opinion.'

I could have said 'Not much indeed;'—but I left her almost in silence.—It was the greatest stretch of Forbearance I could practise. I could not have stopped myself, had I begun.—Her assurance, her Deceit—but I will not allow myself to dwell on them;—they will strike you sufficiently. My heart sickens within me.—

As soon as I was tolerably composed, I returned to the Parlour. Sir James's carriage was at the door, and he, merry as usual, soon afterwards took his leave.—How easily does her Ladyship encourage, or dismiss a Lover!—

In spite of this release, Frederica still looks unhappy, still fearful perhaps of her Mother's anger, and tho' dreading my Brother's departure jealous, it may be, of his staying.—I see how closely she observes him and Lady Susan.—Poor Girl, I have now no hope for her. There is not a chance of her affection being returned.—He thinks very differently of her, from what he used to do, he does her some justice, but his reconciliation with her Mother precludes every dearer hope.—

Prepare my dear Madam, for the worst.—The probability of their marrying is surely heightened. He is more securely hers than ever.—When that wretched Event takes place, Frederica must wholly belong to us.—

I am thankful that my last Letter will precede this by so little, as every moment that you can be saved from feeling a Joy which leads only to disappointment is of consequence.—

Y[rs] Ever,
Cath Vernon

Letter 25

Lady Susan to Mrs Johnson

Churchill

I call on you dear Alicia, for congratulations. I am again myself;—gay and triumphant.—When I wrote to you the other day, I was in truth in high irritation, and with ample cause.—Nay, I know not whether I ought to be quite tranquil now, for I have had more trouble in restoring peace than I ever intended to submit to.—This Reginald has a proud spirit of his own!—A spirit too, resulting from a fancied sense of superior Integrity which is peculiarly insolent.—I shall not easily forgive him I assure you. He was actually on the point of leaving Churchill!—I had scarcely concluded my last, when Wilson brought me word of it.—I found therefore that something must be done, for I did not chuse to have my character at the mercy of a Man whose passions were so violent and resentful.—It would have been trifling with my reputation, to allow of his departing with such an impression in my disfavour;—in this light, condescension was necessary.—

I sent Wilson to say that I desired to speak with him before he went.—He came immediately. The angry emotions which had marked every feature when we last parted, were partially subdued. He seemed astonished at the summons, and looked as if half wishing and half fearing to be softened by what I might say.—

If my Countenance expressed what I aimed at, it was composed and dignified—and yet with a degree of pensiveness which might convince him that I was not quite happy.

'I beg your pardon Sir, for the liberty I have taken in sending to you,' said I; 'but as I have just learnt your intention of leaving this place to day, I feel it my duty to entreat that you will not on my account shorten your visit here, even an hour.—I am perfectly aware that after what has passed between us, it would ill suit the feelings of either to remain longer in the same house.

So very great, so total a change from the intimacy of Friendship, must render any future intercourse the severest punishment;—and your resolution of quitting Churchill is undoubtedly in unison with our situation and with those lively feelings which I know you to possess.—But at the same time, it is not for me to suffer such a sacrifice, as it must be, to leave Relations to whom you are so much attached and are so dear. My remaining here cannot give that pleasure to M^r^ and Mrs Vernon which your society must;—and my visit has already perhaps been too long. My removal therefore, which must at any rate take place soon, may with perfect convenience be hastened;—and I make it my particular request that I may not in any way be instrumental in separating a family so affectionately attached to each other.—Where I go is of no consequence to anyone; of very little to myself; but you are of importance to all your connections.'

Here I concluded, and I hope you will be satisfied with my speech.—Its effect on Reginald justifies some portion of vanity, for it was no less favourable than instantaneous.—Oh! how delightful it was, to watch the variations of his Countenance while I spoke, to see the struggle between returning Tenderness and the remains of Displeasure.—There is something agreable in feelings so easily worked on. Not that I would envy him their possession, nor would for the world have such myself, but they are very convenient when one wishes to influence the passions of another. And yet this Reginald, whom a very few words from me softened at once into the utmost submission, and rendered more tractable, more attached, more devoted than ever, would have left me in the first angry swelling of his proud heart, without deigning to seek an explanation!—

Humbled as he now is, I cannot forgive him such an instance of Pride; and am doubtful whether I ought not to punish him, by dismissing him at once after this our reconciliation, or by marrying and teizing him for ever.—But these measures are each too violent to be adopted without some deliberation. At present my Thoughts are fluctuating between various schemes.—I have many things to compass.—I must punish Frederica, and pretty severely too, for her application to Reginald;—I must punish him for receiving it so favourably, and for the rest of his conduct. I must torment my Sister-in-law for the insolent triumph of her Look and Manner since Sir James has been dismissed—for in reconciling Reginald to me, I was not able to save that ill-fated young Man;—and I must make myself amends for the humiliations to which I have stooped within these few days.—To effect all this I have various plans.—I have also an idea of being soon in Town, and whatever may be my determination as to the rest, I shall probably put that project in execution—for London will be always the fairest field of action, however my veiws may be directed, and at any rate, I shall there be rewarded by your society and a little Dissipation for a ten weeks' penance at Churchill.—

I beleive I owe it to my own Character, to complete the match between my daughter and Sir James, after having so long intended it.—Let me know your opinion on this point.—Flexibility of Mind, a Disposition easily biassed by others, is an attribute which you know I am not very desirous of obtaining;—nor has Frederica any claim to the indulgence of her whims, at the expence of her Mother's inclination.—Her idle Love for Reginald too;—it is surely my duty to discourage such romantic nonsense.—All things considered therefore, it seems encumbent on me to take her to Town, and marry her immediately to Sir James.

When my own will is effected, contrary to his, I shall have some credit in being on good terms with Reginald, which at present in fact I have not, for tho' he is still in my power, I have given up the very article by which our quarrel was produced, and at best, the honour of victory is doubtful.—

Send me your opinion on all these matters, my dear Alicia, and let me know whether you can get Lodgings to suit me within a short distance of you.—

Y[r] most attached

S. Vernon

Letter 26

Mrs Johnson to Lady Susan

Edward S^t

I am gratified by your reference, and this is my advice; that you come to Town yourself without loss of time, but that you leave Frederica behind. It would surely be much more to the purpose to get yourself well established by marrying Mr De Courcy, than to irritate him and the rest of his family, by making her marry Sir James.—You should think more of yourself, and less of your Daughter.—She is not of a disposition to do you credit in the World, and seems precisely in her proper place, at Churchill with the Vernons;—but <u>You</u> are fitted for Society, and it is shameful to have you exiled from it.—Leave Frederica therefore to punish herself for the plague she has given you, by indulging that romantic tender-heartedness which will always ensure her misery enough; and come yourself to Town, as soon as you can.—

I have another reason for urging this.—Manwaring came to Town last week, and has contrived, in spite of Mr Johnson, to make opportunities of seeing me.—He is absolutely miserable about you, and jealous to such a degree of De Courcy, that it would be highly unadvisable for them to meet at present; and yet if you do not allow him to see you here, I cannot answer for his not committing some great imprudence—such as going to Churchill for instance, which would be dreadful.—Besides, if you take my advice, and resolve to marry De Courcy, it will be indispensably necessary for you to get Manwaring out of the way, and you only can have influence enough to send him back to his wife.—

I have still another motive for your coming. Mr Johnson leaves London next Tuesday. He is going for his health to Bath,[41] where if the waters are favourable to his constitution and my wishes, he will be laid up with the Gout many weeks.—During his absence we shall be able to chuse our own society, and have true enjoyment.—I would ask you to Edward S[t] but that he once forced from me a kind of promise never to invite you to my house. Nothing but my being in the utmost distress for Money, could have extorted it from me.—I can get you however a very nice Drawing room-apartment in Upper Seymour S[t], and we may be always together, there or here, for I consider my promise to M[r] Johnson as comprehending only (at least in his absence) your not sleeping in the House.—

Poor Manwaring gives me such histories of his wife's jealousy!—Silly Woman, to expect constancy from so charming a Man!—But she was always silly; intolerably so, in marrying him at all. She, the Heiress of a large Fortune, he without a shilling!—One Title I know she might have had, besides Baronets. Her folly in forming the connection was so great, that tho' Mr Johnson was her Guardian and I do not in general share his feelings, I never can forgive her.—

Adeiu, Yours, Alicia

Letter 27

Mrs Vernon to Lady De Courcy

Churchill

This Letter my dear Mother, will be brought you by Reginald. His long visit is about to be concluded at last, but I fear the separation takes place too late to do us any good.—She is going to Town, to see her particular friend, Mrs Johnson. It was at first her intention that Frederica should accompany her for the benefit of Masters, but we over-ruled her there. Frederica was wretched in the idea of going, and I could not bear to have her at the mercy of her Mother. Not all the Masters in London could compensate for the ruin of her comfort. I should have feared too for her health, and for everything in short but her Principles; there I beleive she is not to be injured, even by her Mother, or all her Mother's friends;—but with those friends (a very bad set I doubt not) she must have mixed, or have been left in total solitude, and I can hardly tell which would have been worse for her.—If she is with her Mother moreover, she must alas! in all probability, be with Reginald—and that would be the greatest evil of all.—

Here, we shall in time be at peace.—Our regular employments, our Books and conversation, with Exercise, the Children, and every domestic pleasure in my power to procure her, will, I trust, gradually overcome this youthful attachment. I should not have a doubt of it, were she slighted for any other woman in the world, than her own Mother.—

How long Lady Susan will be in Town, or whether she returns here again, I know not.—I could not be cordial in my invitation; but if she chuses to come, no want of cordiality on my part will keep her away.—

I could not help asking Reginald if he intended being in Town this winter, as soon as I found that her Ladyship's steps would be bent thither; and tho' he professed himself quite undetermined, there was a something in his Look and voice as he spoke, which contradicted his words.—I have done with Lamentation.—I look upon the Event as so far decided, that I resign myself to it in despair. If he leaves you soon for London, everything will be concluded.—

Yours affec[ly]
Cath Vernon

Letter 28

Mrs Johnson to Lady Susan

Edward St

My dearest Friend,

I write in the greatest distress; the most unfortunate event has just taken place. Mr Johnson has hit on the most effectual manner of plaguing us all.—He had heard I imagine by some means or other, that you were soon to be in London, and immediately contrived to have such an attack of the Gout, as must at least delay his journey to Bath, if not wholly prevent it.—I am persuaded the Gout is brought on, or kept off at pleasure;—it was the same, when I wanted to join the Hamiltons to the Lakes;[42] and three years ago when I had a fancy for Bath, nothing could induce him to have a Gouty symptom.

I have received yours, and have engaged the Lodgings in consequence.—I am pleased to find that my Letter had so much effect on you, and that De Courcy is certainly your own.—Let me hear from you as soon as you arrive, and in particular tell me what you mean to do with Manwaring.—It is impossible to say when I shall be able to see you. My confinement must be great. It is such an abominable trick, to be ill here, instead of at Bath, that I can scarcely command myself at all.—At Bath, his old Aunts would have nursed him, but here it all falls upon me—and he bears pain with such patience that I have not the common excuse for losing my temper.

Yrs Ever, Alicia

Letter 29

Lady Susan to Mrs Johnson

Upper Seymour S^{t}

My dear Alicia

There needed not this last fit of the Gout to make me detest Mr Johnson; but now the extent of my aversion is not to be estimated.—To have you confined, a Nurse in his apartment!—My dear Alicia, of what a mistake were you guilty in marrying a Man of his age!—just old enough to be formal, ungovernable and to have the Gout—too old to be agreable, and too young to die.

I arrived last night about five, and had scarcely swallowed my dinner when Manwaring made his appearance.—I will not dissemble what real pleasure his sight afforded me, nor how strongly I felt the contrast between his person and manners, and those of Reginald, to the infinite disadvantage of the latter.—For an hour or two, I was even stagger'd in my resolution of marrying him—and tho' this was too idle and nonsensical an idea to remain long on my mind, I do not feel very eager for the conclusion of my Marriage, or look forward with much impatience to the time when Reginald according to our agreement is to be in Town.—I shall probably put off his arrival, under some pretence or other. He must not come till Manwaring is gone.

I am still doubtful at times, as to Marriage.—If the old Man would die, I might not hesitate; but a state of dependance on the caprice of Sir Reginald, will not suit the freedom of my spirit;—and if I resolve to wait for that event, I shall have excuse enough at present, in having been scarcely ten months a Widow.

I have not given Manwaring any hint of my intention—or allowed him to consider my acquaintance with Reginald as more than the commonest flirtation;—and he is tolerably appeased.—Adeiu till we meet.—I am enchanted with my Lodgings.

Y^rs Ever,
S. Vernon

Letter 30

Lady Susan to M^r De Courcy

Upper Seymour S^t

I have received your Letter; and tho' I do not attempt to conceal that I am gratified by your impatience for the hour of meeting, I yet feel myself under the necessity of delaying that hour beyond the time originally fixed.—Do not think me unkind for such an exercise of my power, or accuse me of Instability, without first hearing my reasons.—In the course of my journey from Churchill, I had ample leisure for reflection on the present state of our affairs, and every reveiw has served to convince me that they require a delicacy and cautiousness of conduct, to which we have hitherto been too little attentive.—We have been hurried on by our feelings to a degree of Precipitance which ill accords with the claims of our Friends, or the opinion of the World.—We have been unguarded in forming this hasty Engagement; but we must not complete the imprudence by ratifying it, while there is so much reason to fear the Connection would be opposed by those Friends on whom you depend.

It is not for us to blame any expectation on your Father's side of your marrying to advantage; where possessions are so extensive as those of your Family, the wish of increasing them, if not strictly reasonable, is too common to excite surprise or resentment.—He has a right to require a woman of fortune in his daughter in law; and I am sometimes quarreling with myself for suffering you to form a connection so imprudent.—But the influence of reason is often acknowledged too late by those who feel like me.—

I have now been but a few months a widow; and however little endebted to my Husband's memory for any happiness derived from him during an Union of some years, I cannot forget that the indelicacy of so early a second marriage, must subject me to the censure of the World, and incur what would be still more insupportable, the displeasure of Mr Vernon.—I might perhaps harden myself in time against the injustice of general reproach; but the loss of his valued Esteem, I am as you well know, ill fitted to endure;—and when to this, may be added the consciousness of having injured you with your Family, how am I to support myself.—With feelings so poignant as mine, the conviction of having divided the son from his Parents, would make me, even with you, the most miserable of Beings.—

It will surely therefore be advisable to delay our Union, to delay it till appearances are more promising, till affairs have taken a more favourable turn.—To assist us in such a resolution, I feel that absence will be necessary. We must not meet. Cruel as this sentence may appear, the necessity of pronouncing it, which can alone reconcile it to myself, will be evident to you when you have considered our situation in the light in which I have found myself imperiously obliged to place it.—You may be, you must be well assured that nothing but the strongest conviction of Duty, could induce me to wound my own feelings by urging a lengthened separation; and of Insensibility to yours, you will hardly suspect me.—Again therefore I say that we ought not, we must not yet meet.—By a removal for some Months from each other, we shall tranquillize the sisterly fears of Mrs Vernon, who, accustomed herself to the enjoyment of riches, considers Fortune as necessary every where, and whose Sensibilities are not of a nature to comprehend ours.—

Let me hear from you soon, very soon. Tell me that you submit to my Arguments, and do not reproach me for using such.—I cannot bear reproaches. My spirits are not so high as to need being repressed.—I must endeavour to seek amusement abroad, and fortunately many of my Friends are in Town—among them, the Manwarings. You know how sincerely I regard both Husband and wife.—

I am ever, Faithfully Yours
S. Vernon

Letter 31

Lady Susan to Mrs Johnson

Upper Seymour St

My dear Friend,

That tormenting creature Reginald is here. My Letter, which was intended to keep him longer in the Country, has hastened him to Town. Much as I wish him away however, I cannot help being pleased with such a proof of attachment. He is devoted to me, heart and soul.—He will carry this note himself, which is to serve as an Introduction to you, with whom he longs to be acquainted. Allow him to spend the Evening with you, that I may be in no danger of his returning here.—I have told him that I am not quite well, and must be alone—and should he call again there might be confusion, for it is impossible to be sure of servants.—Keep him therefore I entreat you in Edward St.—You will not find him a heavy companion, and I allow you to flirt with him as much as you like. At the same time do not forget my real interest;—say all that you can to convince him that I shall be quite wretched if he remain here;—you know my reasons—Propriety and so forth.—I would urge them more myself, but that I am impatient to be rid of him, as Manwaring comes within half an hour. Adeiu.

S.V.

Letter 32

Mrs Johnson to Lady Susan

Edward S^t

My dear Creature,

I am in agonies, and know not what to do, nor what you can do.—M^r De Courcy arrived, just when he should not. Mrs Manwaring had that instant entered the House, and forced herself into her Guardian's presence, tho' I did not know a syllable of it till afterwards, for I was out when both she and Reginald came, or I would have sent him away at all events; but she was shut up with Mr Johnson, while he waited in the Drawing room for me.

She arrived yesterday in pursuit of her Husband;—but perhaps you know this already from himself.—She came to this house to entreat my Husband's interference, and before I could be aware of it, everything that you could wish to be concealed, was known to him; and unluckily she had wormed out of Manwaring's servant that he had visited you every day since your being in Town, and had just watched him to your door herself!—What could I do?—Facts are such horrid things!—All is by this time known to De Courcy, who is now alone with Mr Johnson.—Do not accuse me;—indeed, it was impossible to prevent it.—Mr Johnson has for some time suspected De Courcy of intending to marry you, and would speak with him alone, as soon as he knew him to be in the House.—

That detestable Mrs Manwaring, who for your comfort, has fretted herself thinner and uglier than ever, is still here, and they have been all closeted together. What can be done?—If Manwaring is now with you, he had better be gone.—At any rate I hope he will plague his wife more than ever.—With anxious wishes,

Y^rs faithfully
Alicia

Letter 33

Lady Susan to Mrs Johnson

Upper Seymour S^{t}

This Eclaircissement[43] is rather provoking.—How unlucky that you should have been from home! I thought myself sure of you at 7.—I am undismayed however. Do not torment yourself with fears on my account.—Depend upon it, I can make my own story good with Reginald. Manwaring is just gone; he brought me the news of his wife's arrival. Silly Woman! what does she expect by such Manoeuvres?—Yet, I wish she had staid quietly at Langford.—

Reginald will be a little enraged at first, but by Tomorrow's Dinner, everything will be well again.—

Adeiu.

S.V.

Letter 34

Mr De Courcy to Lady Susan

Hotel

I write only to bid you Farewell.—The spell is removed. I see you as you are.—Since we parted yesterday, I have received from indisputable authority, such an history of you as must bring the most mortifying conviction of the Imposition I have been under, and the absolute necessity of an immediate and eternal separation from you.—You cannot doubt to what I allude;—Langford—Langford—that word will be sufficient.—I received my information in Mr Johnson's house, from Mrs Manwaring herself.—

You know how I have loved you, you can intimately judge of my present feelings; but I am not so weak as to find indulgence in describing them to a woman who will glory in having excited their anguish, but whose affection they have never been able to gain.

R De Courcy

Letter 35

Lady Susan to Mr De Courcy

Upper Seymour St

I will not attempt to describe my astonishment on reading the note, this moment received from you. I am bewilder'd in my endeavours to form some rational conjecture of what Mrs Manwaring can have told you, to occasion so extraordinary a change in your sentiments.—Have I not explained everything to you with respect to myself which could bear a doubtful meaning, and which the illnature of the World had interpreted to my Discredit?—What can you now have heard to stagger your Esteem for me?—Have I ever had a concealment from you?—Reginald, you agitate me beyond expression.—I cannot suppose that the old story of Mrs Manwaring's jealousy can be revived again, or at least, be listened to again.—Come to me immediately, and explain what is at present absolutely incomprehensible.—Beleive me, the single word of Langford is not of such potent intelligence, as to supersede the necessity of more.—If we are to part, it will at least be handsome to take your personal Leave.—But I have little heart to jest; in truth, I am serious enough—for to be sunk, tho' but an hour, in your opinion, is an humiliation to which I know not how to submit. I shall count every moment till your arrival.

S.V.

Letter 36

Mr De Courcy to Lady Susan

Hotel

Why would you write to me?—Why do you require particulars? – But since it must be so, I am obliged to declare that all the accounts of your misconduct during the life and since the death of Mr Vernon which had reached me in common with the World in general, and gained my entire beleif before I saw you, but which you by the exertion of your perverted Abilities had made me resolve to disallow, have been unanswerably proved to me.—Nay, more, I am assured that a Connection, of which I had never before entertained a thought, has for some time existed, and still continues to exist between you and the Man, whose family you robbed of its Peace, in return for the hospitality with which you were received into it!—That you have corresponded with him ever since your leaving Langford—not with his wife—but with him—and that he now visits you every day.—Can you, dare you deny it?—And all this at the time when I was an encouraged, an accepted Lover!—From what have I not escaped!—I have only to be grateful.—Far from me be all Complaint, and every sigh of regret. My own Folly had endangered me, my Preservation I owe to the kindness, the Integrity of another.—But the unfortunate Mrs Manwaring, whose agonies while she related the past, seem'd to threaten her reason—how is she to be consoled?

After such a discovery as this, you will scarcely affect farther wonder at my meaning in bidding you Adeiu.—My Understanding is at length restored, and teaches me no less to abhor the Artifices which had subdued me, than to despise myself for the weakness, on which their strength was founded.—

R De Courcy

Letter 37

Lady Susan to Mr De Courcy

Upper Seymour St

I am satisfied—and will trouble you no more when these few Lines are dismissed.—The Engagement which you were eager to form a fortnight ago, is no longer compatible with your veiws, and I rejoice to find that the prudent advice of your Parents has not been given in vain.—Your restoration to Peace will, I doubt not, speedily follow this act of filial Obedience, and I flatter myself with the hope of surviving *my* share in this disappointment.

S.V.

Letter 38

Mrs Johnson to Lady Susan

Edward St

I am greived, tho' I cannot be astonished at your rupture with Mr De Courcy;—he had just informed Mr Johnson of it by letter. He leaves London he says to day.—Be assured that I partake in all your feelings, and do not be angry if I say that our intercourse even by Letter must soon be given up.—It makes me miserable—but Mr Johnson vows that if I persist in the Connection, he will settle in the Country for the rest of his life—and you know it is impossible to submit to such an extremity while any other alternative remains.—

You have heard of course that the Manwarings are to part;[44] I am afraid Mrs M. will come home to us again. But she is still so fond of her Husband and frets so much about him that perhaps she may not live long.—

Miss Manwaring is just come to Town to be with her Aunt, and they say, that she declares she will have Sir James Martin before she leaves London again.—If I were you, I would certainly get him myself.—I had almost forgot to give you my opinion of De Courcy, I am really delighted with him, he is full as handsome I think as Manwaring, and with such an open, goodhumoured Countenance that one cannot help loving him at first sight.—Mr Johnson and he are the greatest friends in the World. Adeiu, my dearest Susan. I wish matters did not go so perversely. That unlucky visit to Langford!—But I dare say you did all for the best, and there is no defying Destiny.—

Yr sincerely attached

Alicia

Letter 39

Lady Susan to Mrs Johnson

Upper Seymour S^t^

My dear Alicia

I yeild to the necessity which parts us. Under such circumstances you could not act otherwise. Our friendship cannot be impaired by it; and in happier times, when your situation is as independant as mine, it will unite us again in the same Intimacy as ever. For this I shall impatiently wait; and meanwhile can safely assure you that I never was more at ease, or better satisfied with myself and everything about me, than at the present hour.—Your Husband I abhor—Reginald I despise—and I am secure of never seeing either again. Have I not reason to rejoice?—Manwaring is more devoted to me than ever; and were he at liberty, I doubt if I could resist even Matrimony offered by <u>him</u>. This Event, if his wife live with you, it may be in your power to hasten. The violence of her feelings, which must wear her out, may be easily kept in irritation.—I rely on your friendship for this.—I am now satisfied that I never could have brought myself to marry Reginald; and am equally determined that Frederica never <u>shall</u>. To-morrow I shall fetch her from Churchill, and let Maria Manwaring tremble for the consequence. Frederica shall be Sir James's wife before she quits my house. <u>She</u> may whimper, and the Vernons may storm;—I regard them not. I am tired of submitting my will to the Caprices of others—of resigning my own Judgement in deference to those, to whom I owe no Duty, and for whom I feel no respect.—I have given up too much—have been too easily worked on; but Frederica shall now find the difference.—

Adeiu, dearest of Friends. May the next Gouty Attack be more favourable—and may you always regard me as unalterably Yours

S. Vernon

Letter 40

Lady De Courcy to M[rs] Vernon

Parklands

My dear Catherine

I have charming news for you, and if I had not sent off my Letter this morning, you might have been spared the vexation of knowing of Reginald's being gone to Town, for he is returned, Reginald is returned, not to ask our consent to his marrying Lady Susan, but to tell us that they are parted forever!—He has been only an hour in the House, and I have not been able to learn particulars, for he is so very low, that I have not the heart to ask questions; but I hope we shall soon know all.—This is the most joyful hour he has ever given us, since the day of his birth. Nothing is wanting but to have you here, and it is our particular wish and entreaty that you would come to us as soon as you can. You have owed us a visit many long weeks.—I hope nothing will make it inconvenient to Mr Vernon, and pray bring all my Grand Children, and your dear Neice is included of course; I long to see her. It has been a sad heavy winter hitherto, without Reginald, and seeing nobody from Churchill; I never found the season so dreary before, but this happy meeting will make us young again.—Frederica runs much in my thoughts, and when Reginald has recovered his usual good spirits, (as I trust he soon will) we will try to rob him of his heart once more, and I am full of hopes of seeing their hands joined at no great distance.

Y[r] affec: Mother
C. De Courcy

Letter 41

Mrs Vernon to Lady De Courcy

Churchill

My dear Madam

Your Letter has surprised me beyond measure. Can it be true that they are really separated—and for ever?—I should be overjoyed if I dared depend on it, but after all that I have seen, how can one be secure?—And Reginald really with you!—My surprise is the greater, because on Wednesday, the very day of his coming to Parklands, we had a most unexpected and unwelcome visit from Lady Susan, looking all chearfulness and good humour, and seeming more as if she were to marry him when she got back to Town, than as if parted from him for ever.—She staid nearly two hours, was as affectionate and agreable as ever, and not a syllable, not a hint was dropped of any Disagreement or coolness between them. I asked her whether she had seen my Brother since his arrival in Town—not as you may suppose with any doubt of the fact—but merely to see how she looked.—She immediately answered without any embarrassment that he had been kind enough to call on her on Monday, but she beleived he had already returned home—which I was very far from crediting.—

Your kind invitation is accepted by us with pleasure, and on Thursday next, we and our little ones will be with you.—Pray Heaven! Reginald may not be in Town again by that time!—

I wish we could bring dear Frederica too, but I am sorry to add that her Mother's errand hither was to fetch her away; and miserable as it made the poor Girl, it was impossible to detain her. I was thoroughly unwilling to let her go, and so was her Uncle; and all that could be urged, we did urge. But Lady Susan declared that as she was now about to fix herself in Town for several Months, she could not be easy if her Daughter were not with her, for Masters, etc. Her Manner, to be sure, was very kind and proper—and Mr Vernon beleives that Frederica will now be treated with affection. I wish I could think so too!—

The poor girl's heart was almost broke at taking leave of us. I charged her to write to me very often, and to remember that if she were in any distress, we should be always her friends.—I took care to see her alone, that I might say all this, and I hope made her a little more comfortable.—But I shall not be easy till I can go to Town and judge of her situation myself.—

I wish there were a better prospect than now appears, of the Match, which the conclusion of your Letter declares your expectation of.—At present it is not very likely.—

Y^{rs} etc.

Cath Vernon

Conclusion

This Correspondence, by a meeting between some of the Parties and a separation between the others, could not, to the great detriment of the Post office Revenue, be continued longer.—Very little assistance to the State could be derived from the Epistolary Intercourse of Mrs Vernon and her Neice, for the former soon perceived by the stile of Frederica's Letters, that they were written under her Mother's inspection, and therefore deferring all particular enquiry till she could make it personally in Town, ceased writing minutely or often.—

Having learnt enough in the meanwhile from her openhearted Brother, of what had passed between him and Lady Susan to sink the latter lower than ever in her opinion, she was proportionably more anxious to get Frederica removed from such a Mother, and placed under her own care; and tho' with little hope of success, was resolved to leave nothing unattempted that might offer a chance of obtaining her Sister in law's consent to it.—Her anxiety on the subject made her press for an early visit to London; and Mr Vernon who, as it must have already appeared, lived only to do whatever he was desired, soon found some accomodating Business to call him thither.—With a heart full of the Matter, Mrs Vernon waited on Lady Susan, shortly after her arrival in Town; and she was met with such an easy and chearful affection as made her almost turn from her with horror.—No remembrance of Reginald, no consciousness of Guilt, gave one look of embarrassment.—She was in excellent spirits, and seemed eager to shew at once, by every possible attention to her Brother and Sister, her sense of their kindness, and her pleasure in their society.

Frederica was no more altered than Lady Susan;—the same restrained Manners, the same timid Look in the presence of her Mother as heretofore, assured her Aunt of her situation's being uncomfortable, and confirmed her in the plan of altering it.— No unkindness however on the part of Lady Susan appeared. Persecution on the subject of Sir James was entirely at an end— his name merely mentioned to say that he was not in London; and in all her conversation she was solicitous only for the welfare and improvement of her Daughter, acknowledging in terms of grateful delight that Frederica was now growing every day more and more what a Parent could desire.—

M[rs] Vernon surprised and incredulous, knew not what to suspect, and without any change in her own veiws, only feared greater difficulty in accomplishing them. The first hope of anything better was derived from Lady Susan's asking her whether she thought Frederica looked quite as well as she had done at Churchill, as she must confess herself to have sometimes an anxious doubt of London's perfectly agreeing with her.— M[rs] Vernon encouraging the doubt, directly proposed her Neice's returning with them into the country. Lady Susan was unable to express her sense of such kindness; yet knew not from a variety of reasons how to part with her Daughter; and as, tho' her own plans were not yet wholly fixed, she trusted it would ere long be in her power to take Frederica into the country herself, concluded by declining entirely to profit by such unexampled attention.—M[rs] Vernon however persevered in the offer of it; and tho' Lady Susan continued to resist, her resistance in the course of a few days seemed somewhat less formidable.

The lucky alarm of an Influenza, decided what might not have been decided quite so soon.—Lady Susan's maternal fears were then too much awakened for her to think of anything but Frederica's removal from the risk of infection. Above all Disorders in the World, she most dreaded the Influenza for her daughter's constitution. Frederica returned to Churchill with her Uncle and Aunt, and three weeks afterwards Lady Susan announced her being married to Sir James Martin.—

M[rs] Vernon was then convinced of what she had only

suspected before, that she might have spared herself all the trouble of urging a removal, which Lady Susan had doubtless resolved on from the first.—Frederica's visit was nominally for six weeks;—but her Mother, tho' inviting her to return in one or two affectionate Letters, was very ready to oblige the whole Party by consenting to a prolongation of her stay, and in the course of two months ceased to write of her absence, and in the course of two more, to write to her at all.

Frederica was therefore fixed in the family of her Uncle and Aunt, till such time as Reginald De Courcy could be talked, flattered and finessed[45] into an affection for her—which, allowing leisure for the conquest of his attachment to her Mother, for his abjuring all future attachments and detesting the Sex, might be reasonably looked for in the course of a Twelvemonth. Three Months might have done it in general, but Reginald's feelings were no less lasting than lively.—

Whether Lady Susan was, or was not happy in her second Choice—I do not see how it can ever be ascertained—for who would take her assurance of it, on either side of the question?—The World must judge from Probability.—She had nothing against her, but her Husband, and her Conscience.

Sir James may seem to have drawn an harder Lot than mere Folly merited.—I leave him therefore to all the Pity that anybody can give him. For myself, I confess that I can pity only Miss Manwaring, who coming to Town and putting herself to an expence in Cloathes, which impoverished her for two years, on purpose to secure him, was defrauded of her due by a Woman ten years older than herself.

Finis

Appendix A

Early poem by Jane Austen*

'This little bag'

This little bag I hope will prove
    To be not vainly made—
For, if you thread and needle want
    It will afford you aid.

And as we are about to part
    T'will serve another end,
For when you look upon the Bag
    You'll recollect your friend.

Jan[ry] 1792

* Verses written to accompany a 'huswife' or small sewing bag made by JA and presented to her friend Mary Lloyd (who later married James Edward Austen) when she left nearby Deane parsonage in 1792. They were written on a slip of paper, folded tightly and inserted into a tiny pocket in the huswife; now in the hands of Austen descendant Mrs Freydis Welland.

Appendix B

Letter by Sophia Sentiment in *The Loiterer*, 28 March 1789*

To the AUTHOR *of the* LOITERER.

Sir,

I write this to inform you that you are very much out of my good graces, and that, if you do not mend your manners, I shall soon drop your acquaintance. You must know, Sir, I am a great reader, and not to mention some hundred volumes of Novels and Plays, have, in the last two summers, actually got through all the entertaining papers of our most celebrated periodical writers, from the Tatler and Spectator to the Microcosm and the Olla Podrida. Indeed I love a periodical work beyond any thing, especially those in which one meets with a great many stories, and where the papers are not too long. I assure you my heart beat with joy when I first heard of your publication, which I immediately sent for, and have taken in ever since.

I am sorry, however, to say it, but really, Sir, I think it the stupidest work of the kind I ever saw: not but that some of the papers are well written; but then your subjects are so badly chosen, that they never interest one.—Only conceive, in eight papers, not one sentimental story about love and honour, and all that.—Not one Eastern Tale full

* *The Loiterer* (31 January 1789–20 March 1790) is a weekly periodical written almost entirely by James and Henry Austen at Oxford (see Introduction). Critics have attributed this letter to JA on stylistic grounds, although the issue is still open to question. It is introduced by James as a letter 'brought us the last week . . . and as it is the first favour of the kind we have ever received from the fair sex (I mean in our capacity of authors) we take the earliest opportunity of laying it before our readers' (*The Loiterer*, ed. Robert L. Mack [Lewiston, NY: Edwin Mellen Press, 2006], p. 51). Not only does the pseudonym recall Sophia in 'Love and Freindship' and the reference to 'the pastry-cook's shop' recall 'The beautifull Cassandra', but JA would also have known *The Mausoleum* (1785), a comedy by William Hayley (whose works she acquired in April 1791) that features a character called Lady Sophia Sentiment (*FR*, 68).

of Bashas and Hermits, Pyramids and Mosques—no, not even an allegory or dream have yet made their appearance in the Loiterer. Why, my dear Sir—what do you think we care about the way in which Oxford men spend their time and money—we, who have enough to do to spend our own. For my part, I never, but once, was at Oxford in my life, and I am sure I never wish to go there again—They dragged me through so many dismal chapels, dusty libraries, and greasy halls, that it gave me the vapours for two days afterwards. As for your last paper, indeed, the story was good enough, but there was no love, and no lady in it, at least no young lady; and I wonder how you could be guilty of such an omission, especially when it could have been so easily avoided. Instead of retiring to Yorkshire, he might have fled into France, and there, you know, you might have made him fall in love with a French *Paysanne*, who might have turned out to be some great person. Or you might have let him set fire to a convent, and carry off a nun, whom he might afterwards have converted, or any thing of that kind, just to have created a little bustle, and made the story more interesting.

In short, you have never yet dedicated any one number to the amusement of our sex, and have taken no more notice of us, than if you thought, like the Turks, we had no souls. From all which I do conclude, that you are neither more nor less than some old Fellow of a College, who never saw any thing of the world beyond the limits of the University, and never conversed with a female, except your bed-maker and laundress. I therefore give you this advice, which you will follow as you value our favour, or your own reputation.—Let us hear no more of your Oxford Journals, your Homelys and Cockney: but send them about their business, and get a new set of correspondents, from among the young of both sexes, but particularly ours; and let us see some nice affecting stories, relating the misfortunes of two lovers, who died suddenly, just as they were going to church. Let the lover be killed in a duel, or lost at sea, or you may make him shoot himself, just as you please; and as for his mistress, she will of course go mad; or if you will, you may kill the lady, and let the lover run mad; only remember, whatever you do, that your hero and heroine must possess a great deal of feeling, and have very pretty names. If you think fit to comply with this my injunction, you may expect to hear from me again, and perhaps I may even give you a little assistance;—but, if not—may your work be condemned to the pastry-cook's shop, and may you always continue a bachelor, and be plagued with a maiden sister to keep house for you.

Your's, as you behave,

SOPHIA SENTIMENT.

Textual Notes

The following list includes significant manuscript emendations and variants (see Note on the Text).

Key:

↑word↓	= insertion above the line
~~word~~	= deletion
[ ]	= used for editorial comments

VOLUME THE FIRST

Page	line	
6	4	my↑muslin↓Cloak
7	4	the ~~Mother~~ ↑Father↓ of
7	10–11	attachment,↑either to the object beloved, or↓ to
8	31	imagined↑them↓ to
10	10	by ~~Rouge~~↑Patches↓, Powder
10	29	she ~~would~~ ↑should↓ return
11	6	accordingly ↑did↓ and
12	21	Roger ~~must~~ ↑first↓ addressed
15	9	once ↑up↓on a
15	20–21	Characters ↑of the party↓ introduced
15	22	were ↑both↓ rather
16	5	be ~~agreable~~ ↑pleasing↓
16	10–11	Entertaining. ~~Such was~~ The Johnsons
16	22	the ~~inconvenience,~~ ↑feirceness↓ of
16	23	concourse ~~of masks~~ by
17	2	bottle ~~by his side~~ ↑in their hand↓) deeply
18	1	her ~~inferior~~ ↑Junior↓ and
18	21–2	soon ~~per~~ ↑dis↓covered the ↑unreturned↓ affection
19	15	and ~~had not~~ might

19	21	following ~~Xmas~~ ↑year↓ by
19	31–2	too ~~much colour.~~ ↑red a look↓ 'But
20	12–13	my idea~~s~~ of the case ~~are~~ ↑is↓ this ['this' written over 'these']
20	24	hot ~~that~~. on
20	25	Words ~~they~~ ↑she↓ almost
20	26	forced ↑her↓ away ~~his Daughter~~ from
21	3	reconciliation ~~her ladyship~~ ↑Lady Williams↓ called
21	10	from ~~a~~ ↑the↓ reflection
21	24–5	do.' [?~~a woman~~] ~~in such a situation is particularly off her guard because her head is not strong enough to support intoxication~~ 'Madam
21	28	time, ↑because↓ as
22	16	who ~~was~~ ↑is↓ a
22	19	I ↑have↓ lived
22	20	time ~~some~~ she
23	29	any ~~other reason~~ ↑thing else,↓ I
23	32–3	should ~~soon~~ ↑shortly↓ do
24	6	you; ~~or~~ ↑since↓ we might ↑otherwise↓ perhaps
24	9	you ↑may↓ easily
25	4–5	Lucy ~~on~~ ↑her↓ thoughts on the subject and ~~when~~ ↑as soon as↓ Miss
25	13	fancy ~~that~~ not
25	16–17	her ~~yesterday~~ ↑the other↓ Evening
25	21	tho' ~~I may be partial; indeed~~ ↑~~I am very~~ partial to her, and↓
25	21–2	~~I beleive I am; yes I am very partial to her.~~ ↑perhaps am blinded by my affection, to her↓. real defects.
26	5	I'~~ll~~ hope
26	37	pleased ↑at↓ and
26	38	made ↑me:↓ but
27	11–12	and ↑of↓ her
27	23	to ~~him~~ ↑Mr Adams↓ for
28	2–3	determined; ↑to, do;↓ and
28	6	her ↑having↓ accomplished
28	17	esteem. ↑That↓ One
28	19	my ↑mind↓ by
29	9	admire ~~the~~ ↑your↓ noble

29	10–11	obligations, ~~less deeply felt for Want of sufficient time, preventing you from~~ ↑yet, let me beg that they may not prevent your↓ [After 'prevent' 'charming dear Lucy' was originally inserted then deleted.]
29	15	arguments, ~~and~~ ↑or↓ refuse
29	26	no ~~plot, but~~ ↑blemish but↓ her
29	30	last ~~having~~ ↑of whom had↓ a ['last' written over 'first']
30	16	is↑at present↓ the
30	20–21	Adams. The Lady's ['The Lady's' written over 'Mrs Adams']
31	11	all ~~is~~ ↑indeed, has been↓ to
32	19	Mr Willmot was ~~a younger~~ the
32	23	were ↑too↓ numerous
32	29	beholding ↑ a↓ family
33	2	to ~~fear—.~~ ↑tremble—. ↓ Robert
33	15	which ~~must~~ ↑much ↓ against
33	24–5	so ~~faultering a manner~~ ↑faltering a voice↓ that
36	6	herself ~~with~~ some
36	13	Mrs ~~Jones~~ ↑Willson↓, who ['Willson' substituted for 'Jones'; elsewhere spelt with one 'l'; in all following cases 'Wilson' was 'Jones']
36	13–14	earth, ~~had~~ ↑was↓ no
36	25–6	and ~~of expressing the Love she bore her.~~ ↑accordingly sate out immediately on the↓ receipt
37	12	pleased ~~by~~ with
37	15	being often ['often' written over 'engaged']
37	18	effected, ↑as↓ the
37	19	being ~~likewise~~ very
37	29	Grace ~~after having read it,~~ ↑as soon as she had read↓ the
37	33–4	return with↑out↓ their
38	9	12,000£ a year ['2' written over first '0' in '10,000']
38	10	to [?~~secure~~] ↑save↓ but
38	31	it ↑be↓ possible
38	37	Her ↑little↓ boys
39	21	steps ~~of~~ ↑at↓ the
40	18–19	you ~~do~~ ↑had↓, and

40	21	which ~~never before struck me with~~ ↑now strikes me as↓ being
40	30	which ↑she↓ entirely
42	23	enamoured ~~with~~ ↑of↓ a
42	25	Husband, ↑whom↓ she
48	8–9	but ~~I would~~ ↑as he knew, that he should↓ have
43	9	greived ~~at~~ ↑by↓ the
43	12	at ~~a~~ ↑the↓ Village
43	28	Percival, ~~with~~ ↑at↓ which
44	2–3	Sir, ~~Permit~~ Your
45	24	a ~~violent~~ ↑dangerous↓ fever
48	8–9	Manners, ↑are↓ polished
49	11	Mother's ↑shop↓ to
50	15	grew ~~arrogant.~~ ↑~~peremptory.~~↓ She
54	2	Miss Hervey ['Hervey' written over ?'Webster']
54	26	of, ↑besides;↓ but
56	10	when ~~they~~ ↑it↓ was
56	13	Sir Arthur Hampton ['Authur' changed to 'Arthur' whenever it occurs in this story.]
58	7–8	went ↑any↓ farther
58	11	has ~~ever~~ ↑always↓ been
58	12–13	Truth. ~~He never told a Lie but once, and that was merely to oblige me. Indeed I may truly say there never was such a Brother!~~ (Exeunt Severally)
59	1	Sophy,↑~~take~~↓ my
59	31	but ~~however~~ Sophy
59	35	with ~~a~~ ↑a toast and↓ nutmeg.
60	7–8	for [?~~Sir Arthur~~] ↑him↓ you
60	13	eats ↑auet↓ pudding
60	16	the ↑~~suet~~↓ Pudding_
60	6	Patronage ~~of~~ ↑to↓ the
64	8	go ~~and dress.~~ ↑away.↓
68	10	and ~~has a great idea of Women's~~↑~~never~~↓ ~~going from home~~ what
68	11	he ~~has a great idea~~ ↑talks a great deal↓ of
68	28	like ~~him.~~ ↑it↓
68	29	am ↑not↓ going
70	10	from herself, he told her ~~that he would~~ ↑he should do,↓ for ['herself' written over 'refusal']
70	19	have ↑him↓ Sophy

70 22 generally mo~~st~~↑re↓ strictly

72 2–3 year;' ~~who keeps a post-chaise and pair, with silver Harness, a boot before and a window to look out at behind?~~ 'Very

72 15 to ~~have made us really so.~~ ↑ensure it in reality.↓ Yet

73 13 be ~~so angry and~~ so

73 37 seen! ~~Pearls as large as those of the Princess Badroulbadour in the 4th Volume of the Arabian Nights, and Rubies, Emeralds, Toppazes, Sapphires, Amythists, Turkey stones, Agate, Beads, Bugles and Garnets~~ ↑and Pearls, Rubies, Emeralds, and Beads↓ out

76 7 have ↑with↓ Mary

76 12–13 Leicestershire. ~~Not related to the Family and even but distantly connected with it. His Sister is married to John Dutton's Wife's Brother. When you have puzzled over this account a little you will understand it.~~ M^{r}

76 35 of ~~general~~ ↑every one's↓ attention

78 6 encouraged her ~~in doing so~~ by

80 17 [Entire fragment crossed out]

A fragment—written to inculcate the practise of Virtue.

We all know that many are unfortunate in their progess through the world, but we do not know all that are so. To seek them out to study their wants, and to leave them unsupplied is the duty, and ought to be the Business of Man. But few have time, fewer still have inclination, and no one has either the one or the other for such employments. Who amidst those that perspire away their Evenings in crouded assemblies can have leisure to bestow a thought on such as sweat under the fatigue of their daily Labour.

81 35 think ~~of~~ ↑to↓ have

82 4 of Warwick~~shire,~~ a

82 20 every Month ['Month' written over 'Year']

VOLUME THE SECOND

Page	line	
89	1	Love and Friendship ['ei' written over 'ie']
89	11	experiencing such ~~cruel~~ ↑dreadful↓ ones
89	14	the ~~reiterated~~ ↑cruel↓ Persecutions
90	7–8	Afflictions of ~~that~~ my past Life
90, 28 to 91	1	Acquirements ~~were~~ ↑had been↓ wonderfull
91	1	I ↑had↓ shortly
91	3	could ↑adorn↓ it
91	4	good Quality and ~~the place of appointment~~ of
91	28	had ~~slept~~ ↑supped↓ one night
92	14	astonished, ~~considerably amazed and somewhat surprized~~ by hearing
92	23–5	replied he) ~~I cannot pretend to assert that any one knocks, tho' for my own part, I own I rather imagine it is a knock at the Door that somebody does. Yet as we have no ocular Demonstration . . .~~ ↑We must not pretend to determine on what motive the person may Knock—tho' that someone <u>does</u> rap at the Door, I am partly convinced↓
92	31	Oh! let ~~us go immediately~~ ↑no time be lost↓
93	20	I felt ~~myself instantaneously in Love with him.~~ ↑that on him the happiness or Misery of my↓ future Life
94	8	marry her ~~if you wish I should.~~ ↑in compliance with your Wishes↓ No
94	12	had ↑perhaps↓ little
94	12–13	expected to ~~have met~~ ↑meet↓ with
94	28	befallen ↑me↓ had
95	14–15	but had ~~not even the~~ ↑never even had the↓ slightest
96	12–13	of ↑ever↓ having willingly
96	17–18	myself ↑(said Edward)↓ Support
96	27	efficacious ~~replied~~ ↑returned↓ Augusta
96	29	~~Did~~ ↑Does↓ it appear

96	30	vile and ~~Vulgar~~ ↑corrupted↓ Palate
96	35	I was ~~interrupted~~ ↑prevented↓ from
97	25	dared ↑to↓ unite
98	12	particular ↑freind,↓ which
98	13	arrived in ~~less than an hour~~ ↑a few hours↓
99	3	~~When we were somewhat recovered from the overpowering effusions of our~~ Towards the close [note by Doody that clause erased here begins Letter the 10th]
99	7	Society ~~yet~~ I cannot
99	22	fortune ↑which↓ Philippa
99	25	endless misery ['endless' written over 'need-less']
100	5	I ↑then↓ enjoyed
100	9	never ~~was~~ ↑~~were~~↓ ↑were↓ a happier
100	9–10	imagine ↑inform↓ you
100	12–13	Marriage with those ↑whom↓ they
100	15	submit to ~~their~~ ↑such↓ despotic ~~will~~ Power
100	18	the ↑good↓ opinion
100	19	World ~~by~~ ↑in↓ so doing
100	36–7	Sensibility of ~~Augus~~ Edward
101	12	promised that ~~he~~ ↑we↓ would
101	28	within ~~six~~ ↑twelve↓ miles
101	30	entered ~~Picadilly~~ ↑Holbourn↓
102	13	and ↑un↓ provided
103	19	follow ~~her~~ ↑it↓ in person
105	31	natural ↑noble↓ Sensibility
106	23	other young ['young' written over 'person']
106	28	assured her ↑that↓ she
106	32	to imagine ↑that↓ he
107	7–8	behave like ~~other People~~ ↑any other Person↓
107	33–4	other place ~~as it was a most agreable Drive~~ ↑~~from its wonderful Celebrity~~↓ ↑although it was at ↑a↓ considerable distance↓ from
108	5–6	suspected it ~~had it not~~ but for
108	9	and ~~with~~ ↑amongst↓ them
109	12	must desire ↑that↓ you
111	3	reflections ~~of Augustus~~ which
112	12	on my ↑Edward's↓ Death
112	13–14	in the least fatigued ['fatigued' written over 'tired']

113	29	allotted ~~her~~ us by
114	2–3	her ~~fair~~ ↑sweet↓ face
114	17	last ↑words↓ she
114	21–2	Village ~~where~~ ↑in which↓
114	32	A ~~mutual~~ ↑general↓ Silence prevailed ~~amongst us all~~
115	12	when ↑on↓ looking
115	33	Edward ↑and↓ the
116	2	singular ↑Service↓ we
116	15	reflected ↑Honour↓ on
116	18–19	with ~~unmanly~~ ↑unjustifiable↓ Reproaches
116	26	~~Beautifull~~ ↑delightful↓ scenes
116	31–2	had ~~many~~ ↑made↓ daily Excursions
117	5	~~always~~ ↑generally↓ accompanied
117	29–30	fears ~~for~~ ↑of↓ the
118	8	befallen ~~them~~ ↑me↓
118	19	my own ↑Mother↓ always
118–19	38, 1	we ~~were determined~~ ↑expected↓
119	7	both ~~dead~~ ↑starved to Death↓
119	21	England ~~Ireland~~ and Wales
119	22–3	We happened to ~~quit~~ be
119	29–30	left the ~~room~~ ↑Town,↓ leaving
120	9	I took up my ~~Lodging~~ ↑Residence↓
120	15	suited to her; ~~Graham~~ she became
120	22	they still ~~continue to~~ Exhibit
120	30	~~Sunday~~ June 13th
122	5–6	will ↑always↓ remain
122	6	as it ↑is↓ carried
122	11–15	Messrs Demand and Co . . . £105.0.0 [Lines added by Henry Austen]
124	4	appear ~~for~~ ever
124	13	the Macduff's ['Macduff' written over 'Macbeth']
124	38	that ~~too~~ ↑two↓ such
125	6	any where ↑else↓ indeed
125	7	~~I~~ ↑We↓ have only ↑to↓ hope.
125	32	~~to find that~~ ↑I had the↓ mortification
126	17–18	going ↑instantly↓ to
126	18	so wildly bent ['wildly' written over 'very']
126	21	room; ~~where~~ we laid her
126	22	in ↑the↓ most
126	26	Waste ↑in our provisions↓ which

126 27 some plan for ['plan' written over 'Scheme']
126 28 the best thing ['best' written over 'only']
126 36 but ↑to↓ no purpose
127 3–4 suffer most ~~for~~ ↑from↓ it
127 16–17 no more, ~~I left~~ ↑but leaving↓ her with my Mother ~~and~~ I ~~taking~~ ↑took↓ down
127 20 Melancholy ~~Account~~ ↑Event↓ to Eloisa
127 23–4 Physicians ~~is~~ are greatly ['s' added to 'Physician' and 'are' written over 'is']
127 24 her going into a Decline ['going into' written over 'being in']
129 9 distressed ~~us~~ ↑her↓ most
129 15–16 most ~~lively~~ ↑chearfull↓ Manner
129 34 removed from a miserable Cottage ['from a miserable' written over 'to an elegant']
131 18–19 actually ~~felled,~~ ↑fell↓ and
131 16 to Miss M. Lesley ['Lesley' written over 'Lutterell']
132 12 remarkably good-tempered when ['tempered' written over 'humoured'
132 21 Caprice on ~~herself~~ ↑her side↓
132 26 violent ~~freindship~~ ↑partiality↓
132 26 soon settled in a downright ['settled in' written over 'turned into']
132 31 when it ~~was~~ first
132 32 London and ~~the Amusements~~ of Brighthelmstone
132 34 satisfy the ~~certainty~~ ↑curiosity↓
133 9 Sir George from the manner ['from' written over 'but']
133 37 my ~~freinds~~ ↑acquaintance↓ to marry
134 6 Lesley ~~and~~ ↑to↓ Miss Charlotte
134 13 imagine ~~that~~ there was little
134 15 must be so gay ['gay' written over 'giddy']
134 21 We ~~therefore~~ contented
134 29 comparison ~~to~~ ↑with↓
134 31 great to ~~have brought us~~ ↑bring her↓
135 17 dungeon-like ~~appearance~~ ↑form↓
135 17–18 Rock ↑to appearance↓ so totally
135 25 Girls ↑such↓ as

136 38 conquer ~~her~~ ↑this↓ passion
136 5 as I expected ['ex' written over 'sus' in 'suspected']
137 19 resemblance ~~with~~ ↑between↓
137 34 you said ~~that~~ you
138 1 you think ~~that~~
138 26 Charlotte ~~that~~ I was
139 4 should ever happen ['ha' written over 'be']
139 18 to be ↑so↓ suspected
140 10–11 suppose ~~that~~ this
140 17 into ~~her~~ ↑its↓ Public-places
140 22–3 Education ~~I always took~~ ↑that I took by far the↓ most
140 29 it ↑has↓ always
141 5 equal ~~of~~ ↑and↓ settled
141 20–21 word of ~~Praise~~ ↑approbation↓
141 27 which ~~was~~ ↑is↓
141 to 142 38 to 1 have at last ['last' written over 'least']
142 9–10 severe ~~speech~~ thing
142 29–30 contracted ~~an~~ ↑a kind of↓ affection
142 33 hope ~~that~~ You
143 11–12 Heart ~~well enough~~ ↑too well not↓ to be
143 20 to write ↑to speak↓ to you
144 23 write ↑to↓ you
145 2 to ~~you~~ me
145 26 sure ~~that~~ you
145 38 by any ↑one↓ of
146 3 Paricular! ↑one↓ Man
146 7 my ~~best~~ Compliments
146 9 her Health ['her' written over 'his']
146 12 afraid ~~that~~ this
146 14 have ~~as~~ been as
146 20–21 arrived safely in ['ly' inserted after 'safe']
147 5 reasons ↑why↓
147 16 ~~On~~ Last Monday ['L' written over 'l' in 'Last']
147 16 Monday ~~sennet~~ ↑se'night↓
148 2–3 had ↑never↓ commenced
148 5–6 most ↑frequent↓ of our ~~most~~ Visitors
148 24 to Matilda and me ['Matilda' written over 'Margaret']

148 35 his ↑1st↓ Marriage

148 38 to 1 has ~~obtained another of the Pope's Bulls for annulling~~ ↑turned Roman-catholic, and is soon to be married↓ to

149 11 owns ~~me to~~ it would

153 13 not ↑have↓ burnt

154 3 have ↑here↓ given

155 6–7 his ↑two↓ Nephews

155 11 reign long in peace ['long in' written over 'for ever']

156 16 former of ~~which~~ ↑whom↓

156 20–21 his ~~Gran~~ daughter

157 7 giving ↑only↓ a slight sketch

157 13–14 Crimes ↑with which↓ she was accused

157 19 those ↑before↓ alledged

158 9 ['5' written over '4']th wife

159 9 manner of ~~his death~~ ↑it,↓

159 15 excess of ~~Cockylorum~~ ↑vanity↓

161 33 She was executed ['She' written over 'I k': JA started to write 'I know']

162 13 or ↑the↓ next

162 14 ↑now↓ but young

165 18 be ~~all~~ considered

165 29–30 is ~~tedious~~ ↑uninteresting↓ to me

168 2 Cousin ['Cousin' written over 'Madam']

168 6 Clever Collection ['Clever' written over 'Collect']

169 5 Manner ~~to~~ ↑from↓

169 21 drink ↑tea↓ with us

170 5–6 fear and expectation ['expectation' written over 'Apprehension']

170 23–4 being ~~contaminated~~ ↑seduced↓ by her Example, or ↑contaminated by↓ her Follies

173 10 wiping ~~my~~ ↑her↓ Eyes

173 31 and ↑have↓ made

174 26–7 favour ~~for~~ ↑about↓ which

175 6 could not ↑you↓

175 8 poor ~~because~~ ↑for↓ I always

175 19 Ellen felt ['Ellen' written over 'Fanny' here and throughout the story]

176	25	of ↑having↓ the most
177	3	I fancy not ~~but your Ladyship knows best~~
177	4–5	Bench once? ~~Just as your Ladyship pleases—it is the same to me~~ ↑I never saw him there↓
177	7	afraid of ~~having~~ being
177	7	saucy ['saucy' written over 'much so']
178	6	your legs ['legs' written over 'Ancles']
178	7	But ~~you~~ ↑~~low~~↓ ↑[~~?odd~~]↓ ~~sort~~ ↑some sort↓ of people
178	12	I am afraid your dinner ['I am afraid' written over 'Drive on']
179	24	uninterrupted ~~Felicity~~ ↑Happiness↓
179	30	could arise only ['arise' written over 'occur']
179	36	silenced. ~~Could you have beleived it Mary?~~
180	22	Absence ~~during a long stay in Essex?~~
181	9	what ↑were↓ my Sensations
181	25–6	fair ↑one↓ will
181	30	excellent ~~House~~ ↑one↓
181	35	T. Musgrove ~~May I hope to receive an answer to this e'er many days have tortured me with Suspence! Any Letter (post paid) will be most welcome~~ [Post-script to letter crossed out]
182	17	Life. ~~How fond we shall be of one another when we are married! Oh, do not you long for the spring?~~
183	12	was proper ['proper' written over 'best']
185	8	~~Indeed~~ ↑To be sure↓
185	11	are ↑in↓ every respect
186	3	example of Felicity ['Felicity' written over 'conjugal']
186	6	he was dead ['was' written over 'were']
186	18	dear Tom ['Tom' written over 'Cousin']
187	4	allowing them ['them' written over 'him']
187	20–21	now and then. ~~I gave away two pence this Morning.~~
187	22	He ~~said~~ ↑replied↓
187	24	destined ~~as~~ ↑to be↓

189	16	way as ~~pleasing~~ ↑estimable↓
189	26	valued friend ['ie' written over 'ei']
190	9–10	Understanding ↑is↓ without
191	27	to Town to marry Strephon ['to' written over 'you']
193	7	have but ['but' written over 'not']
194	1	Young Lady ['y' written over 'ie']
194	3–4	commission of ~~several faults~~ ↑Errors↓ which
194	13	twelve Years ['Years' written over 'months']
194	15	I am ↑now↓ going
197	25	fastened only ↑by↓
198	4	amiable Cecilia ['Cecilia' written over 'Sister']

VOLUME THE THIRD

Page	line	
203	19	agonizing ~~idea~~ ↑pain↓
203	26	↑the↓ freindly balm
204	14	with ~~the remainder of their Lease~~ ↑their house↓
204	15	the ~~House~~ ↑place↓
204	20	in three rows ['three' written over ?'two']
204	22	unincumbered ~~by~~ with
205	10	from the ~~effusions~~ ↑excess↓
205	14	Lady had ~~before expressed~~ ↑already made↓
205	23	we bear ~~for~~ you
206	6–7	to ↑promise to↓ keep
208	6	agitated ~~with~~ ↑by↓ Greif
208	15	I ↑will↓ forget
208	16	will hasten ['hasten' written over 'as soon']
208	23	came not ~~for~~ ↑from↓ Rosa
209	3	his living ['living' written over 'staying']
209	22	greatly ~~superior~~ ↑inferior↓ to
209	25	very ~~old~~ ↑ancient↓ date
210	4–5	lamented ~~Sister~~ ↑Henry's↓ Rosa
211	27	seated on a ~~chaise long~~ Sofa
212	15	the respect~~ful~~ he owed her
212	27	19 ['9' written over 'o']

215	1–2	~~Kitty~~ ↑Catharine↓, or the Bower ['Kitty' inconsistently changed to 'Catharine' or 'Catherine' throughout; standardized in this edition to 'Catharine']
215	21	To this ~~Garden~~ ↑Bower↓ which
216	9	Miss Wynnes; ~~they were companions in their walks, their Schemes and Amusements, and while the sweetness of their dispositions ↑had↓ prevented any serious Quarrels, the trifling disputes which it was impossible wholly to avoid, had been far from lessening their affection.~~
216	31	had gained her ↑a↓ husband
217	24	Mrs ~~Peterson~~ ↑Percival↓ ['Peterson' changed to 'Percival' inconsistently throughout]
217	35	of ↑her↓ parents
218	3	despised the ~~Petersons~~ ↑Percivals↓ as people of ~~no~~ ↑mean↓ family
218	15–16	and ↑was↓ so dissatisfied
218	30–31	the frequent ~~endeavours~~ ↑overtures↓ of
219	19	at length ~~arrived~~ ↑came↓
219	21–2	most Heroines ↑is↓ the hight
219	24	of the house ~~and~~ of Commons
219	30	She was ~~about Kitty's age~~ ↑~~not in~~↓elegant
220	11–12	convinced ↑when she saw her↓ that Miss Stanley
220	19–20	as ↑to↓ Books ['to' written in pencil in a different hand]
220	23	Admired ~~and that have given rise perhaps to more frequent Arguments than any other of the same sort~~
220	33–4	better in everything ['in everything' written over 'all together']
221	9	wanted ↑However↓ I quite
221	12	I have ↑done↓ nothing
221	20–21	I never trouble ['never' written over 'scarce']
222	11	Neice, ~~I beleive you have as good a chance of it as any one else,~~ but
222	28	from ~~History~~ ↑Politics↓ she
223	7	Amusements began ['began' written over 'again']
223	32	we are ~~not always~~ ↑often not↓
223	35	you have ↑ever↓ seen

224	19	out into Public ['into' written over 'with']
224	25–6	has ~~sent to Sea~~ ↑got into the Army↓ as a Leiutenant
224	27	I have ↑a↓ notion
224	30	~~Slightly~~ ↑Very well,↓ We met
225	23	~~Barkers~~ ↑Barlows↓ too
226	6	she might ↑then↓ have
226 to 227	38 to 1	lent it to ~~'If so, Mary Wynne can receive very little advantage from her having it.'~~ And then,↑continued she↓ the Miss Halifaxes
227	5–7	to have one.' ~~Why indeed, if Maria will give my Freind a drawing, she can have nothing to complain of but as she does not write in Spirits, I suppose she has not yet been fortunate enough to be so distinguished.~~ 'But was not it very odd ↑said Kitty↓ that
227	27	tribute to ~~the~~ ↑her↓ regard
227	32	towards ↑her↓ with
228	3	Ball ↑Gold Net!↓—
229	5	Mortality, and ↑that↓ the time
229	36	dare say ↑that↓ People
230	24–5	between young ~~Ladies~~ ↑Persons↓
230	25–6	mark ~~of their being disposed to like one another~~ ↑of an aimiable affectionate disposition↓
230	29	regard. ~~There is something mighty pretty I think in young Ladies corresponding with each other and~~ nothing
231	11	from Augusta ↑Barlow↓ to day
231	15–16	new ~~Bonnet~~ ↑Regency walking dress↓
231	25	about the ~~Bonnet~~ ↑Regency↓
231	26	upon a ~~Jacket and petticoat~~ ↑Bonnet and Pelisse↓
231	27	left ↑the↓ room
231	29	depress ↑her↓ while
231	35	to ~~remain~~ ↑continue↓ undisturbed
232	25	gone ~~but half~~ an hour, and as every ↑thing↓
232	26–7	in ~~an hour and a half~~ ↑another hour↓
232	30	pleasure ~~in itself~~ it was
232	33	for ~~about~~ ↑nearly↓ an hour
232	34–5	Beauty. ~~Nanny~~ ↑Anne↓ was then dispatched
232	36	gloves, ↑and↓ arranging

232	37	dress, ~~and providing herself with Lavender water.~~ In
233	3	when ~~Nanny~~ ↑Anne↓
233	7–8	and ~~as~~ I knew nobody
233	12–13	seen ~~because you know Ma'am I am all over powder~~ ↑in my Apron Ma'am↓
235	36	but ~~as~~ ↑since↓ you
236	22–3	just coming round ['round' written over 'to fetch']
236	24	Neighbour's, ~~of ours~~, where
237	6	You can ~~lend~~ ↑procure↓ me
237	9	time to ~~pack up anything~~ ↑have anything pack'd up↓ but
237	20	gone by ['by' written over 'before']
237	27–8	and led ↑her↓ out
240	7–8	But Stanley who ~~joined to~~ ↑with↓ a vivacity
241, 243	8, 5	Except ~~your Brother's~~ ↑his↓ coming away indeed to her ['to' written over 'with']
243	6–7	united attractions ↑that↓ he possessed
243	10	could not help ~~observing~~ ↑remarking↓
243	16–17	folly ↑in his Son↓ that had given him the pleasure of seeing him ~~son~~ [second 'him' originally 'his']
243	19–20	about it, ↑he found him↓ much less disposed
245	16	opportunity which ~~offered~~ the next Morning ↑offered to her↓ of speaking
245	27–8	Youth and Beauty? ~~Why in fact, it is nothing more than being Young and Handsome—and that~~ ↑It↓ is
245	31	and as to a ~~handsome~~ young Man's
246	1–2	existed. ~~Her intimacies with Young Men are abominable; and it is all the same to her, who it is, no one comes amiss to her—~~. I assure you Sir,
246	29	Answer ↑from him,↓ and
247	17	excited. ~~before—~~. Her dislike
248	5	she left them ↑together in the arbour↓ to wander
248	18	Stanley who ↑was↓ so far
249	23–4	Blair's Sermons, and ~~Seccar's explanation of the Catechism~~ ↑Cœleb's in Search of a Wife↓
251	17–18	difficulty ~~of~~ ↑in↓ gaining ↑an explanation↓ of his Conduct

251	32	animated and insinuating ['insinuating' written over 'gentle']
251	33–4	otherwise ↑than↓ amiable
251	34–5	for being ~~completely~~ ↑perfectly↓ so
252	1–2	were ~~disposed to feel~~ ↑inclined to entertain↓
252	33	had not ~~Nanny~~ ↑Anne↓
254	3	he desired me when ['me' written over 'us']
254	8	might not ↑be↓ married
254	18	bestow on any body ['body' written over 'one']
255	26	Kitty continued in this state of satisfaction [From here the text is written by James Edward Austen-Leigh; emendations are not recorded here]

LADY SUSAN

Page	line	
266	29	is equally ~~heavy~~ ↑dull↓
271	13–14	her own behaviour was ~~not~~ ↑far from↓ unexceptionable
272	15	she has my [?~~illegible word~~] hand and arm
274	18	occasioned as much by ~~the~~ ↑a↓ degree of fascination
275	5–6	she is altogether so ~~pleasing~~ ↑attractive↓
307	8–9	has a very superior ↑Mind↓ to what we have ever given her credit for.
310	28	productive only ~~to~~ ↑of↓ Good to all parties.
310, 37 to 311	1	Will you let me speak to you a moment↑?"↓ ~~in your room?"~~ We went ~~thither directly.~~ ↑into my room.↓
314	16	she may now be ~~at peace~~ ↑easy↓.
316	16–17	resentful.—~~To~~ ↑It would↓ have been trifling with my reputation
316 to 317	33 to 1	it would ill suit the feelings ↑of either↓ to remain longer
318	19	~~Weakness~~ ↑Flexibility↓ of Mind, a Disposition easily biassed by others
323	24	he bears ↑pain↓ with such patience
326	10–11	the present ~~posture~~ ↑state↓ of our affairs
327	25–6	whose ~~feelings~~ ↑Sensibilities↓ are not of a nature to comprehend ours.

Notes

These Notes contain information about many aspects of Jane Austen's world that may be unfamiliar to today's readers, as well as references for literary quotations and works cited. Citations from Jane Austen's novels refer to the relevant volume and chapter number.

The following abbreviations are used in the Notes:

FR	Deirdre Le Faye, *Jane Austen: A Family Record*, 2nd edition (Cambridge, Cambridge University Press, 2004).
JA	Jane Austen
Johnson	Samuel Johnson, *A Dictionary of the English Language*, 2 vols (London, 1775)
Juvenilia	Jane Austen, *Juvenilia*, ed. Peter Sabor, The Cambridge Edition of the Works of Jane Austen (Cambridge: Cambridge University Press, 2006)
Letters	Jane Austen, *Jane Austen's Letters*, ed. Deirdre Le Faye, 3rd edition (Oxford: Oxford University Press, 1995)
OED	*The Oxford English Dictionary Online*
E	*Emma*
MP	*Mansfield Park*
NA	*Northanger Abbey*
P	*Persuasion*
P&P	*Pride and Prejudice*
S&S	*Sense and Sensibility*

VOLUME THE FIRST

1. ***Detached pieces***: The titles of the following individual items appear in the text but are not listed on the title page of the manuscript.

Frederic and Elfrida

1. *To Miss Lloyd*: Martha Lloyd (1765–1843) was a neighbour and lifelong friend of Jane Austen (JA). In Spring 1789, the widowed Mrs Lloyd with her daughters Martha and Mary rented nearby Deane parsonage from Mr Austen until January 1792. Mary married JA's widowed brother James in 1797, but JA always preferred Martha. After the deaths of both Mr Austen and Mrs Lloyd in 1805, Martha came to live with Mrs Austen, Jane and Cassandra. In 1828, Martha, then sixty-three, became the second wife of another widowed Austen brother, Francis. She and her sister Mary died within a few months of each other in 1843.

   The story is among the earliest juvenilia written in 1787 (*Juvenilia*, p. xxviii). The dedication was inserted sometime after the story was transcribed into 'Volume the First'; Southam notes that the dedication 'is remarkable for being in a later hand than that in which the rest of the piece is written' (B. C. Southam, *Jane Austen's Literary Manuscripts: A Study of the Novelist's Development through the Surviving Papers* [Oxford: Oxford University Press, 1964], p. 232, n. 4).
2. *muslin Cloak*: Muslin, a finely woven cotton, was fashionable for women's clothing in the 1790s; here it is used for an item of finery to be worn indoors.
3. *Freind*: For JA's idiosyncratic spelling in her juvenilia, see Note on the Text.
4. *the Father of Frederic*: JA had originally written 'Mother' but corrected herself to ensure that the cousins, in addition to their other similarities, shared the same surname.
5. *at one school*: An improbable claim. Upper- and middle-class education was strictly gendered, and schools for girls offered a more limited curriculum with a focus on the acquisition of feminine accomplishments, such as music, French, screen-painting and elaborate needlework, and skills involved in managing a household and domestic servants.
6. *rules of Propriety*: It was considered to be both indelicate and imprudent for a young lady to be in love before the gentleman had declared his intentions. In *NA* (I, iii) JA challenges this 'rule' through her heroine Catherine Morland and quotes from Samuel Richardson's essay in Johnson's *Rambler* 97 (19 Feb. 1751): 'That a young lady should be in love, and the love of the young gentleman undeclared, is an heterodoxy which prudence, and

even policy, must not allow' (*Works of Samuel Johnson* [New Haven: Yale University Press, 1969], IV, p. 156).

7. ***so much alike . . . knew them apart***: JA is mocking the fictional convention that lovers should resemble each other; here she also satirizes the romance convention of near-identical siblings, such as Viola and Sebastian in Shakespeare's *Twelfth Night*.

8. ***Crankhumdunberry***: A mock-Irish name that also suggests the slang term 'crinkum-crankum', used by writers like Frances Burney (1752–1840) in her novel *Evelina, or The History of a Young Lady's Entrance into the World* (1778) (I, xxi), to suggest something 'full of twists and turns; a winding way; something intricately or fancifully elaborated' (*OED*), a feature of this fantasy in which, for example, two young ladies appear and disappear.

9. ***Grove of Poplars . . . verdant Lawn enamelled . . . variegated flowers***: A mock reference to the artificial symbolic landscape gardening of the time. The setting suggests an idealized pastoral landscape painted or enamelled on an artwork such as a vase.

10. ***purling Stream . . . Valley of Tempé***: This purling (rippling) stream has an impossible source in the beautiful Valley of Tempé, which runs between the mountains of Olympus and Ossa and was celebrated in Ancient Greece as the favourite haunt of Apollo and the Muses. JA mocks both the hackneyed language and artificial pastoral scenes of eighteenth-century poetry, and the inappropriate naming of features in the fashionable English landscape garden. In the popular romance novel *The Female Quixote* (1752) by Charlotte Lennox (1730–1804) the heroine Arabella compares the valley setting of Bath to that of Tempé (VII, iii).

11. ***Damon***: The name of a shepherd singer in Virgil's *Eclogues*; used by English poets for a rustic lover or swain. Here JA again mocks the artificiality of pastoral poetry that was popular in the eighteenth century.

12. ***that very evening***: Social etiquette dictated a formal morning visit (made between 12 noon and 3p.m.) to welcome newcomers, but it would be considered highly improper to make such a visit in the evening.

13. ***elegant dressing room . . . artificial flowers***: The eighteenth-century dressing room, adjoining a lady's bedroom and furnished as a kind of sitting room for private use and to receive select visitors, was a sign of status and most typically a feature of wealthy households. The dressing room would not display artificial flowers (popular for adorning hats and gowns), and new

acquaintances would not be received in the dressing room but more formally in the drawing room or parlour.

14. ***Lovely and too charming Fair one***: Cf. the extravagantly formal address of Arabella in *The Female Quixote*: 'too lovely and unfortunate Fair-one' (VI, iii).

15. ***your forbidding Squint, your greazy tresses and your swelling Back . . . Qualities of your Mind***: Rebecca is depicted as a short-sighted hunchback with unwashed hair covered in oily pomatum, a hair ointment. Such comic descriptions of ugly or physically deformed characters, common in JA's juvenilia, suggest her familiarity with eighteenth-century caricature: see Introduction.

16. ***Indian and English Muslins, and the judicious preference***: JA mocks both the triviality of the subject and the fact there is no preference to be debated. Indian muslin was of such fine quality and so superior to the English product, it was subject to an import tax in 1774 to offer some relief to the manufacturers of English muslin. Henry Tilney in *NA* has the dubious attribute of being 'an excellent judge' of muslin and purchases a gown of 'true Indian muslin' for his sister (I, iii).

17. ***profound Curtesy***: A very low curtsy, as made to a person of the highest rank such as a member of the royal family and signifying the deepest respect.

18. ***ran off with the Coachman***: The most disgraceful conduct in a woman of her social class and a matter of lasting shame for her family, as shown in *Tristram Shandy* (1760–67) by Lawrence Sterne (1713–68), where the eponymous hero's aunt makes a similar indiscretion so mortifying to her nephew that 'The least hint of it was enough to make the blood fly into his face' (I, xxi).

19. ***parents of Frederic proposed to those of Elfrida***: The marriage arrangements approved by parents in romance novels typically thwart or disregard the wishes of the hero and heroine. In this case the situation is reversed, with parents implementing the wishes of a couple who are too delicate ever to express them.

20. ***Patches, Powder, Pomatum and Paint***: JA changed 'Rouge' to 'Patches' in her manuscript not only to achieve the alliteration but to echo a line from *The Rape of the Lock* (1712) by Alexander Pope (1688–1744), 'Puffs, Powder, Patches, Bibles, Billet-doux' (I, 138) and imply a comparison between the bewitching Belinda in Pope's poem and the old-fashioned, ugly Rebecca. The use of black velvet patches in the shape of beauty spots, oily pomatum for holding hair in place, and white and red (rouge) face paint was

no longer stylish in the 1790s. Powder for colouring hair was still used for formal occasions.

21. *lovely vehicle*: A post-chaise (as JA notes); this would be lovely indeed since it was a prestigious and expensive hired carriage, the most rapid form of transport, with horses changed at posting stations during the journey.

22. *postilion*: A person who rides the leading nearside (left-hand side) horse drawing a coach or carriage, especially when one pair only is used and there is no coachman (*OED*).

23. *Portland Place*: A magnificent street with spacious Georgian terraced houses, in the Marylebone district of central London; then newly laid out and one of the most fashionable addresses in London.

24. *old pink Coat*: Probably a reference to 'hunting pink', i.e. red. An old hunting jacket would be a most disreputable garment to wear on a formal visit.

25. *new blue coat*: The most fashionable colour for young men, made popular by the sentimental hero in *The Sorrows of Young Werther* (1774) by Johann Wolfgang von Goethe (1749–1832). The handsome Charles Bingley in *P&P* wears a blue coat, whilst Lydia Bennet wonders if the equally handsome Wickham will 'be married in his blue coat'.

26. *something in the appearance . . . she could not account for it*: JA is aware of the debate regarding the influence of physical beauty or plainness on one's choice of a spouse; she satirizes contemporary courtship where ugliness is overlooked in a rich man or woman. In 'The Three Sisters' Georgiana admits that Mr Watts 'is rather plain to be sure, but then what is Beauty in a Man'.

27. *brace of Partridges, a leash of Pheasants*: Two partridges, three pheasants; together with twelve pigeons and a hare (Leveret), this is a totally implausible supper for the young lady and her aunt.

28. *deep stream . . . pleasure Grounds in Portland Place*: Houses in Portland Place were built in rows of narrow but elegantly designed Georgian terraces with no space for 'pleasure grounds' or a stream.

29. *Reader, your mind must be unworthy to peruse them*: JA's direct address to the reader imitates a common narrative mode in the sentimental fiction she is satirizing here.

30. *smelling Bottle*: A small, ornamental bottle or phial containing smelling-salts (carbonate of ammonia) or hartshorn (an aqueous solution of ammonia) which a lady carried with her for use in case of faintness (*OED*).

31. ***dagger***: JA is parodying the alternative methods of suicide—a bowl of poison or dagger to the heart—offered by Queen Eleanor, the wife of Henry II, to the king's mistress, 'the Fair *Rosamund*'.
32. ***Corydon . . . Bess . . . fess***: Corydon is another traditional name for a rural lover (like that of Damon) used in pastoral poetry. JA parodies the current imitative pastoral poems by introducing the distinctive English name of 'Bess', as well as 'fess' (meaning lively, active and smart), a southern English dialect word (Joseph Wright, ed., *English Dialect Dictionary* [London, 1888–1905], ii, 338).
33. ***Stage Waggon***: A large, heavy wagon with rough benches for the passengers, drawn by up to ten horses that moved at walking pace. The cheapest form of public transport, such wagons were used by the poor and would have been totally unsuitable for this newly married couple.
34. ***seat in Buckinghamshire***: A seat was a family estate or large land-holding, indicating that the Captain is a gentleman of wealth and status. The county of Buckinghamshire was known for its fine estates.
35. ***the dangerous way Elfrida was in***: Reference to another convention of the sentimental novel in which the betrayed heroine generally died of grief. Betrayal in love was also considered medically dangerous, particularly if the news came as a sudden shock.

Jack and Alice

1. ***Francis William Austen Esq[r] . . . the Perseverance***: Frank (1774–1865), JA's older brother by one year, entered the Royal Naval Academy at Portsmouth in April 1786, at the age of twelve; he was eventually promoted to Admiral of the Fleet in 1863. On 23 December 1788, Francis Austen sailed as a Volunteer on HMS *Perseverance* to the East Indies, where he remained for four years, serving on the *Perseverance* as Midshipman from 22 December 1789 until 5 November 1791, then on the *Crown* and the *Minerva* (William R. O'Byrne, *A Naval Biographical Dictionary* [London: John Murray, 1849], p. 27; John H. and Edith C. Hubback, *Jane Austen's Sailor Brothers* [1906; repr. Folcroft Library Editions, 1976], pp. 15–16). He received promotion to Lieutenant on 22 December 1792. Thus the earliest date for this dedication, and possibly the story, is December 1789, when JA had just turned fifteen; Southam (*Literary MSS*, p. 16) and

Sabor (*Juvenilia*, p. xxviii) both date the story 1790. 'The adventures of Mr Harley' was also dedicated to Francis Austen while he served on the *Perseverance*.

'Esqr', the abbreviated form of 'Esquire', originally denoted a landed proprietor (hence a comic elevation of the fifteen-year-old Francis by his sister).

2. ***Mr Johnson***: Possibly referring to the Revd Augustus Johnson, who in 1791 became rector of a living in the gift of the Leigh family that their Austen relatives had hoped to obtain (Brigid Brophy, 'Jane Austen and the Stuarts', *Critical Essays on Jane Austen*, ed. B. C. Southam [London: Routledge, 1968], p. 23).
3. ***Masquerade***: A masked ball, in which the assumption of a disguise and the opportunity for loose behaviour led to frequent criticism. Novelists like Frances Burney (in *Evelina*, 1778 and *Cecilia*, 1782) and Samuel Richardson (1689–1761) (in *The History of Sir Charles Grandison*, 1753), JA's early mentors, depict masquerades as being unsuitable and dangerous for young women; hence Mr Johnson's masquerade for his children suggests his irresponsibility as a parent.
4. ***tickets***: Printed tickets were used for public balls and assemblies. This is an unnecessarily grandiose and formal notice for a small, private ball.
5. ***Pammydiddle***: A nonsense name suggesting 'Pam', a card game in which 'Pam'—the knave of clubs—is the highest trump, and 'to diddle' or cheat.
6. ***Charles Adams***: His name is both an exaggerated compliment in its association with the biblical Adam, the first man created by God, and a parody of Richardson's perfect hero Sir Charles Grandison. For a detailed examination of Austen's references in the juvenilia to *Sir Charles Grandison*, see Jocelyn Harris, *Jane Austen's Art of Memory* (Cambridge: Cambridge University Press, 1989), pp. 228–38.
7. ***none but Eagles . . . Face***: In mythology the eagle is commonly associated with the sun, sacred to Jupiter and associated with pride (James Hall, *Dictionary of Subjects and Symbols in Art* [London: John Murray, 1974]); thus proverbially, 'Only the eagle can gaze at the sun'.
8. ***Sukey***: Diminutive for Susan and Susanna; also slang for a kettle, an appropriate association for Sukey who boils over in this story.
9. ***Jointure***: 'Estate settled on a wife to be enjoyed after her husband's death' (Johnson). This consisted of property or money, and was usually part of the marriage settlement.

10 ***Tho' Benevolent and Candid . . . Polished and Entertaining***: The sentence parodies Johnson's symmetry and antithesis. 'Candid' equated with sincere: cf. 'Free from malice; not desirous to find faults' (Johnson).

11. ***family of Love***: A phrase describing the Grandison family in Richardson's *Sir Charles Grandison* (Part 1, Vol. I, Letter XXVI).

12. ***Drawing Room***: A more private room reserved for the reception of company; generally used for ladies to withdraw to from the dining room after dinner.

13. ***Sultana . . . Masks***: A popular oriental costume with masqueraders (here referred to as 'Masks') was that of a Turkish sultana, the wife, concubine or other woman in a sultan's family.

14. ***Mask representing the Sun***: Mythological characters were also popular with masqueraders. Here Charles Adams represents Apollo, the sun God, patron of music, poetry, archery, prophecy and healing art, and generally associated with the perfection of youthful manhood.

15. ***Dominos***: The most popular of masquerade costumes, a loose cloak of Venetian origin worn with a half-mask covering the upper part of the face and not representing any particular character.

16. ***Flora***: Roman goddess of Flowers and associated with Spring, another popular mythological mask with young women.

17. ***Entertainment***: A formal meal, especially a banquet.

18. ***<u>tout ensemble</u>***: General effect of a person's appearance (French).

19. ***so much her Junior***: 'inferior' deleted in manuscript and 'Junior' inserted, indicating JA's change of mind for a less conventional distinction. This also prepares the way for a more extraordinary union between the two.

20. ***Sir Charles Grandison . . . when at Home***: Richardson's hero is praised by Harriet Byron in the novel for refusing to follow 'fashions established by custom' and for 'never pervert[ing] the meaning of words'. Thus he 'never, for instance, suffers his servants to deny him, when he is at home. If he is busy, he just finds time to say he is, to unexpected visiters' (*Sir Charles Grandison*, Part 2, Vol. IV, Letter XXVI).

21. ***In spite of the wine . . . uncommonly out of spirits***: JA's pun on the double meaning of 'spirits' (as alcohol and cheerfulness) also plays on the conventional medicinal properties of wine in the eighteenth century.

22. ***second attachment***: In the sentimental discourse of the time, there was a general romantic prejudice against second loves, strongly

voiced by Marianne Dashwood in *S&S* (I, xi). Lady Grandison, like Lady Williams, however, sees nothing particularly special about first loves: 'For how few of us are there, who have their first Loves? And indeed how few first Loves are fit to be encouraged?' (*Sir Charles Grandison*, Part 3, Vol. VII, Letter XLIII).

23. ***Life and Adventures***: A parody of romance titles and the fictional convention of characters telling their life stories.

24. ***spend the Winter with her in town***: Members of fashionable society, including the wealthy gentry and aristocracy, left their country estates to take houses in London during the 'Season', which began in Winter after the New Year and continued with a full round of social and sporting events and festivities into June. 'Town' was the fashionable 'West End' in the area of Parliament and Westminster, unlike the vulgar 'City' or mercantile area with its preponderance of merchants and others associated with trade. The Bingley sisters in *P&P* sneer at the Bennets' Gardiner relatives, who are in trade and live in the 'City' area of Cheapside.

25. ***red in her Cheeks, she must have too much colour***: Alice Johnson is red from anger and the effects of wine; but JA is probably referring to a family joke on her own rosy appearance. William Fowle, who saw JA frequently in her youth, described her as 'pretty—certainly pretty—bright and a good deal of color in her face—like a doll' (quoted in *FR*, p. 165).

26. ***'From Words she almost came to Blows'***: An adaptation of the line 'From words they almost came to blows', in a poem by James Merrick (1720–69), 'The Cameleon: A Fable, after Monsieur De La Motte', in which two men argue futilely over the colour of a chameleon. It appears in a popular anthology owned by JA: *A Collection of Poems* (1758), edited by Robert Dodsley (1704–64).

27. ***her Claret***: This red wine, imported from Bordeaux, was considered a gentleman's drink and therefore unconventional, even improper, for Lady Williams to offer this wine to her young guest.

28. ***Citron Grove***: Groves were popular settings in sentimental novels and pastoral poetry, but a grove of citrus trees such as lemon or orange would not be found in an English landscape. This is probably another allusion to *Sir Charles Grandison* and the romantic Italian orange grove in which the hero meets with the lovely Clementina (Part 1, Vol. 2, Letter XXXII).

29 ***Horsepond***: Used for watering and washing horses. The unpicturesque country features of pigsty and horsepond parody the pastoral walks of young ladies in sentimental novels.

30. *fair Nymph*: The term alludes to another heroine who suffers from the hero's use of steel, namely Belinda in Pope's *Rape of the Lock*, whose hair is cut with the Baron's steel scissors: 'What wonder then, fair Nymph! Thy hairs should feel / The conquering force of unresisted Steel?' (III, 177–8).
31. *misfortune . . . your Life and adventures*: It was conventional in sentimental fiction for a secondary character, typically a young and beautiful woman encountered by chance, to relate the cause of her misfortune and distress. Doody and Murray find the word 'adventures' in this context may have a sexual connotation, and suggest that JA's fictional source here is *Emmeline, or The Orphan of the Castle* (1788), by Charlotte Smith (1749–1806), where the heroine Emmeline and a female friend on a similar shaded walk encounter a young, beautiful and distressed woman, Adeline, who immediately on their request embarks on a detailed account of her sufferings including pregnancy and abandonment by her lover (Jane Austen, *Catharine and Other Writings*, ed. Margaret Anne Doody and Douglas Murray [Oxford: Oxford University Press, 1993], pp. 293–4).
32. *North Wales*: North Wales was popular for its sublime mountains and lakes and its picturesque beauty; but it was sparsely populated and remote, a place not normally associated with skilled tailors.
33. *breed me up at her own expence*: The first of several examples in JA's writing of the customary practice of wealthier relatives adopting a child from a large family. Fanny Price and later her sister are adopted by Sir Thomas and Lady Bertram in *MP*. JA's own brother Edward was adopted by wealthy, childless relations, Thomas and Catherine Knight II.
34. *accomplishments requisite for one of my sex and rank . . . Dancing, Music, Drawing and various Languages*: The only accomplishment requisite for a girl brought up by an alehouse keeper was the art of brewing beer. Young ladies of the middle class, gentry and aristocracy, however, were expected to acquire the elegant accomplishments listed here and recommended by conduct writers like John Gregory (1724–73) in his chapter on 'Amusements' in *A Father's Legacy to his Daughters* (1774).
35. *to receive the rents of the Estate*: Charles Adams would receive the rents from his steward, who managed all the affairs of this estate on his behalf, including the collection of rents from the tenant farmers. In *P&P*, Mr Wickham's father had been steward to Mr Darcy.

36. ***Mrs Susan***: A cook, as an upper servant, would be addressed by her surname and, even if unmarried, would have the courtesy title of 'Mrs'. A lower servant such as a kitchen maid would be referred to only by her first name. JA is providing a hint that there is something irregular about this employment, and perhaps an untrained lower servant has been promoted to the position of cook for additional reasons. The fact that Mrs Susan is so intimate with the alehouse keeper suggests that she is a frequent visitor to that establishment, and provides another query on her character.
37. ***her Place***: Her position as cook, referring to a position in domestic service.
38. ***Youth, Beauty, Birth, Wit, Merit, and Money***: JA satirizes the inflated and unrealistic attributes that a gentleman may seek in a wife, a subject she returns to more obliquely in *P&P* with Mr Darcy's exacting requirements on female accomplishments, and Elizabeth Bennet's mocking response: 'I am no longer surprised at your knowing *only* six accomplished women. I rather wonder now at your knowing any' (I, viii). Charles Adams's requirement of 'wit' does not refer to 'learning', which was widely accepted as suspect in a female, but rather to a 'lively wit' or teasing banter and charm that was particularly alluring or sexually attractive when combined with youth and beauty. JA was scathing of marriages based on such criteria. In *P&P*, Mr Bennet, 'captivated by youth and beauty, and that appearance of good humour, that youth and beauty generally give, had married a woman whose weak understanding and illiberal mind, had very early in their marriage put an end to all real affection for her' (II, xix).
39. ***endeavoured to reason him out of his resolution***: A gentleman would never enter into such a conversation with his cook, unless there was some sexual relationship between them, when the matter of whether or not he intended to marry might well come up for discussion. Mrs Susan may also have her own marital designs on her master.
40. ***letter, offering . . . my hand and heart***: It was most improper for a young lady to even write to an unrelated gentleman, let alone propose marriage. In *S&S*, when Elinor Dashwood sees her sister Marianne writing a letter to Mr Willoughby she instantly concludes 'they must be engaged' (II, iv).
41 ***modesty . . . pressed him again on the subject***: The confident and overpowering female again assumes the masculine role,

assuming, like Mr Collins's view of Elizabeth Bennet's refusal of his marriage proposal in *P&P*, that it is due to modesty (I, xix).

42. ***steel traps***: These cruel and legally sanctioned man-traps were set on a gentleman's private grounds in woodland to catch trespassers, especially poachers. Such devices were part of the increasingly harsh Game laws in eighteenth-century England, designed to protect the sporting rights of the rural gentry and used by the nearby St John family, known to the Austens. Their use was finally banned in 1827. (Deirdre Le Faye, *Jane Austen's Country Life* [London: Frances Lincoln, 2014], 142.)

43. ***cruel Charles to wound the hearts and legs***: An example of zeugma, a favourite rhetorical device of JA in which a verb takes two different and incongruous objects. The humour of the sentence itself masks the literal truth that Charles Adams is a very cruel man.

44. ***real defects***: This sentence was revised by JA to highlight the malice that underlies Lady Williams's professed regard for Alice (see Textual Notes).

45. ***Bath***: Initially established as a spa by the ancient Romans, the city of Bath in south-west England was at the height of its reputation as a fashionable resort in the 1780s and 1790s. In JA's work it is often the site at which matches are made, though often of an ill-advised or hasty nature. She visited Bath in November 1797, and lived there with her family from 1801 to 1806. Like Anne Elliot in *P*, she 'disliked Bath, and did not think it agreed with her' (I, ii).

46. ***my self unparalelled***: This long speech of self-praise by the supremely vain Charles Adams is strikingly similar in content and tone to the adulation of Harriet Byron in her description of Sir Charles Grandison, and to a similar eulogy by his sister Charlotte. This novel was reportedly a favourite and admired by the youthful JA (James Edward Austen-Leigh, *A Memoir of Jane Austen* [1871], in *A Memoir of Jane Austen and Other Family Recollections*, ed. Kathryn Sutherland [Oxford: Oxford University Press, 2002], p. 71), but she cannot resist mocking such overblown passages while still distinguishing between the conceited Charles Adams and Grandison as 'a *good man*' (Part 1, Vol. I, Letter XXXVI).

47. ***One freind I have and glory in having but one***: The identity of the 'freind' as Mrs Susan, the cook from Wales, clarifies their irregular relationship. Charles Adams would always retain one or more cooks at his principal estate, and the fact that he has

chosen to bring this servant with him from Wales is another indication that she is his mistress. The word 'freind' in this context is 'mistress', which adds a new insult to Charles's rejection of marriage with Mr Johnson's daughter.

48. ***procure me a home . . . what I most desire***: The common motivation for marriage for dependent single women with little income. In *P&P*, Charlotte Lucas offers the same reason for her acceptance of the marriage proposal of the odious Mr Collins: 'I ask only a comfortable home' (I, xxii). See also Miss Wynne's predicament in 'Catharine'.

49. ***the age of seventeen***: This was the accepted age that a girl 'came out' or made her introduction to polite society and could attend balls and other social functions, and, most importantly, could meet eligible gentlemen.

50. ***raised to the Gallows***: Hanged, usually in a public place. The execution of Sukey, as a young lady of quality, would rate as a huge spectacle. Hanging was specified by English statute law in the case of more than two hundred criminal offences, including minor offences of property such as stealing sheep (Daniel Pool, *What Jane Austen Ate and Charles Dickens Knew* [New York: Simon & Schuster, 1993], p. 134). The sentence, however, was generally commuted to transportation, but not in the case of murder.

51. ***those of her native Country were cheifly engaged***: Reference to the notorious behaviour of the three eldest sons of King George III (r. 1760–1820), who were engaged in illicit liaisons, with no royal bride as yet in sight. The eldest son, George, Prince of Wales (1762–1830), later George IV, was scandalously involved with the Roman Catholic widow Mrs Fitzherbert, to whom he was secretly married, although he made a formal denial before Parliament in December 1787.

52. ***great Mogul***: The Muslim Mogul dynasty had ruled almost all of India in the seventeenth century, but its power declined and a century later the Great Mogul controlled only Delhi and the surrounding area with effective power in the hands of the British. He was treated by the British government as the formal ruler and known as the emperor of Delhi.

Edgar and Emma

1. ***a tale***: 'A slight or petty account of some trifling or fabulous incident' (Johnson). JA uses this term for several of the shortest items in 'Volume the First' to distinguish them from her longer

'novels'; but she is inconsistent and plays with this division, as in the case of 'The Beautifull Cassandra', an inordinately short story designated a 'novel' in twelve chapters. 'Edgar and Emma' is unique in the three volumes of JA's juvenilia in not having a dedicatee. Composed in 1787 (*Juvenilia*, p. xxviii), it may also represent some of JA's earliest writing; Le Faye considers it one of the 'first efforts thought worthy of preservation' (*FR*, p. 66).

2. *three pair of stairs high*: Servants or poor lodgers were usually accommodated in the upper storeys of a house, up a flight (or pair) of stairs.
3. *ninepence among the Ringers*: While a ringing of a peal of church bells marked local events such as marriages and funerals, and national celebrations such as news of a victory, the mere return of the owners of an estate was not generally celebrated in this way. Bell-ringers were paid, but as six to nine ringers were required Sir Godfrey is extremely parsimonious with his distribution of ninepence among them, and has not even supplied the traditional beer or cider usually provided for this strenuous work. Cf. the Revd James Woodforde's payment to bell-ringers in 1786 of two shillings and sixpence 'and a pail of Cyder' (Kirstin Olsen, *All Things Austen: An Encyclopedia of Austen's World*, 2 vols [Westport, CT: Greenwood Press, 2005], p. 75).
4. *Villa*: A small country mansion, usually built in the fashionable Italianate style inspired by the designs of Andrea Palladio and sited on a relatively small landholding. This term also became associated with a pretentious and far less elegant style of architecture, especially favoured by the *nouveau riche*. In this case, the house is totally unsuitable for this large family.
5. *Mr Willmot*: This name has an immediate association with the aristocracy in the name of the libertine English poet John Wilmot, Earl of Rochester (1647–80). With his large brood of children, JA's Mr Willmot appears to have had an equally voracious sexual appetite.
6. *Lead mine*: The predominant share of Mr Willmot's income is evidently derived from the profits of lead mining, a decidedly non-genteel source and an industry associated with harsh and dangerous conditions for its workers.
7. *a ticket in the Lottery*: The device of a state lottery was used in the period 1709–1824 to raise funds for public works, with the attraction of very high dividends.
8. *Coach . . . Carriage*: JA uses both terms to describe the Willmots' vehicle. Carriages were privately owned and expensive to

maintain and even a larger carriage accommodated only four passengers. Mr Austen's carriage, for example, a 'chariot', had a single row of seats for two to three passengers and was drawn by two horses. The term 'coach' was usually applied to the much larger and heavier vehicle for public transport, drawn by a team of at least six horses, with some passengers seated outside. An impossible number of passengers descend from the Willmots' single carriage.

9. ***tremble***: JA originally wrote 'fear', then deleted it; her substitution of 'tremble' more explicitly satirizes the physical effects of sensibility which culminate in Emma sinking 'breathless on a Sopha'.

10. ***Sopha***: Sofa; a long, stuffed seat, introduced to England in the early eighteenth century and inspired by the Eastern 'sopha' with its soft cushions for sitting or reclining in comfort. JA was quick to exploit for comedy its infinite use to the fainting heroines of sentimental fiction, and Lady Bertram in *MP* is seldom absent from the sofa.

11. ***confidante***: The heroine's 'confidante', to whom she could pour out her heart, was a stock convention in romantic fiction. The footman, however, as both a servant and the wrong gender, is an outrageous choice for this role. JA is also continuing her play with furniture with a pun on 'confidente', a fashionable type of settee named by the famous designer George Hepplewhite (*OED*).

12. ***Thomas . . . she unbosomed herself without restraint***: When John Gregory in his conduct book advises his daughters to 'beware of making confidants of your servants', which would 'spoil them and debase yourselves' (*A Father's Legacy to his Daughters*, p. 29), he is referring to female servants such as personal maids. A footman who dared to speak on such a matter to a young lady of the family would be instantly dismissed in disgrace. The luckless Thomas is clearly intent on escape.

13 ***Parlour . . . seated in a social Manner***: Both the term 'parlour' (or sitting room) and the formal circular grouping of guests around the fire were becoming outdated by the 1780s (Mark Girouard, *Life in the English Country House: A Social and Architectural History* [New Haven: Yale University Press, 1979], p. 238). The Austen rectory had its small parlour as well as the 'common parlour' where the family gathered.

14. ***Eton . . . Winchester . . . Queen's Square . . . Convent at Brussells . . . college***: Eton College near Windsor and Winchester College in Hampshire are prestigious boys' schools. Queen's

Square was a prestigious London boarding school for girls from the mid-eighteenth until mid-nineteenth centuries, referred to as the 'Ladies' Eton'. There were no convent schools in England during JA's time, so English Roman Catholic families were obliged to send their daughters abroad to be educated on the Continent. 'College' refers to one of the colleges at the Universities of Oxford or Cambridge.

15. *at Nurse*: The child is with a wet-nurse or foster-mother, of a lower or servant class and reared with her own children for a period of up to two years. All of the Austen children were sent out to nurse, but this practice was increasingly criticized in the second half of the eighteenth century as detrimental to the child and fell out of favour.

Henry and Eliza

1. ***Henry and Eliza***: Composed in late December 1788 or early January 1789 (*Juvenilia*, p. xxviii); the title of the story is a joking allusion to JA's brother Henry Austen (1771–1850) and her cousin Eliza, the Comtesse de Feuillide, née Hancock (1761–1813), and to their leading roles in the private theatricals performed at Steventon rectory on 26 and 28 December 1787. The chosen play was a popular comedy, *The Wonder: A Woman Keeps A Secret!* (1714), by Susanna Centlivre (*c.*1669–1723) and performed throughout the eighteenth century (*FR*, p. 62). The setting is Portugal, with Henry in the role of the dashing hero Don Felix, while Eliza played the beautiful and resourceful heroine Violante. The two are in love and plan to wed, but have to contend with various misunderstandings and misadventures, including the opposing plans of their respective fathers, before they can be finally united. 'Henry and Eliza' is surprisingly percipient: Eliza de Feuillide's husband was guillotined in Paris in 1794 and, like the fictional Eliza, the widow married Henry Austen in 1797.

2. *Miss Cooper*: Jane Cooper (1771–98) was cousin to JA and from early childhood was an intimate companion to the Austen sisters. She was a leading member of the cast of *The Wonder*, and is likely to have played the role of Isabella, the secondary heroine, who is determined to escape the marriage being forced upon her by her father to a rich and elderly suitor. In the following Christmas and New Year holidays there was a new Austen production, a farce, *The Sultan, or A Peep into the Seraglio*

(1775) by Isaac Bickerstaff (*c.*1735–*c.*1812) with Henry Austen in the name role. Eliza de Feuillide had returned to France in the autumn of 1788 and the seventeen-year-old Jane Cooper played opposite him as the heroine Roxalana, the daring and outspoken English harem slave who refuses to accept her servitude. Deirdre Le Faye considers that 'Henry and Eliza' may have been both written and dedicated to Jane Cooper 'during this Christmas period' of December 1788 to January 1789 (*FR*, p. 67).

3. ***smiles of approbation***: An inadequate recompense. It was an accepted right of haymakers to be rewarded in the field with food and beer, a custom that continued for over a century (John Abbey, *Intemperance: Its Bearing Upon Agriculture* [London, 1881]).
4. ***cudgel***: a club. This is extreme behaviour, although there were low wages, poverty and harsh working conditions for agricultural labourers in Hampshire at this time (Barry Stapleton, 'Inherited Poverty and Life-cycle Poverty: Odiham, Hampshire, 1650–1850', *Social History* 18 [1993], p. 250).
5. ***Haycock***: A heap of hay, usually stacked in the shape of a cone.
6. ***Girl not more than 3 months old***: A second comedy performed at Steventon, in January 1788, was a Jacobean comedy, *The Chances* (*c.*1617) by John Fletcher (1579–1625), in which a key early scene features a mysteriously abandoned baby.
7. ***stealing a banknote of 50£ . . . inhuman Benefactors***: Although the theft of even a small amount of money was then a capital offence, in the overwhelming majority of cases the sentence of execution was reprieved. Sir George and Lady Harcourt, however, in turning their young adopted daughter out of doors without money, protection or any place to live, placed her life in grave danger.
8. ***M***: A pretence of mystification; a common novelistic convention at the time, applied also to people as in the following reference to the 'Dutchess of F'. The latter is also a parody of Richardson's use of initials for members of the aristocracy in *Sir Charles Grandison*, as Brian Southam notes: 'This was a convention of epistolary fiction: the letters were supposedly real and so the identity of these lords and ladies was to be respectfully concealed' (*Jane Austen's 'Sir Charles Grandison'* [Oxford: Clarendon Press, 1980], p. 118).
9. ***red Lion***: A tavern or a public house where wine was sold, rather than an inn that also provided accommodation for travellers. The popular emblem of a red lion would have been painted on its sign.

10. ***Humble Companion***: A poor gentlewoman, in a need of a home and income, might be employed at a very small annual wage as a paid companion and subservient confidante to a wealthy older woman.
11. ***Bar***: A very small room close to the entrance, 'where the landlord could greet customers as they entered and keep an eye on things' (Pool, *What Jane Austen Ate*, p. 212).
12. ***going to Service***: Domestic service, as in the case of Richardson's eponymous heroine in his epistolary novel *Pamela*: *Or, Virtue Rewarded* (1740–1) was only acceptable to women of lower class and would require evidence of personal history and past experience.
13. ***reached the same Evening***: A duchess, the highest rank of the aristocracy, would never correspond with or visit a lowly tavern keeper. This blatantly extravagant fantasy mocks the use in sentimental fiction of fortuitous coincidences and highly unlikely events that come to the aid of the distressed heroine.
14. ***seat in Surry***: The estate of the Duchess in Surrey, a county south-west of London and adjoining Hampshire. JA's novel *E* is set in Surrey.
15. ***a private union***: A private union like this without a special licence was illegal. Lord Hardwicke's Marriage Act (1753) formalized the requirements of the marriage ceremony in England and Wales, including the publication of banns (a public notice of the intention to marry, read in the parish church of both bride and groom for the previous three successive Sundays). The publication of banns could only be avoided if the marriage was by a common licence provided by the bishop of the diocese in which the marriage took place, while an expensive special licence granted by the Archbishop of Canterbury was required if the ceremony was in a house or private chapel as in this case. A marriage by special licence was usually favoured by the aristocracy and associated with wealth and high status, as Mrs Bennet proclaims on hearing the news of Elizabeth's engagement to Mr Darcy in *P&P* (III, xvii).
16. ***chaplain***: This clergyman is acting illegally and thus the marriage is invalid.
17. ***assembly***: A public ball, usually funded by subscription and held in Assembly Rooms or other available premises in the nearby town. The local aristocracy was expected to attend to support the assembly.

18. ***300 armed Men . . . some torturelike manner***: A comic medieval fantasy: private armies were curtailed by statutory reform under the first Tudor king, Henry VII (1457–1509).
19. ***12,000£ a year***: A vast amount, and beyond even the annual income of Mr Darcy in *P&P*, whose £10,000 a year from his landed estate places him among the 'Great Landlords' of England (G. E. Mingay, *English Landed Society in the Eighteenth Century* [London: Routledge and Kegan Paul, 1976], pp. 9, 26).
20. ***man of War of 55 Guns, which they had built***: The inclusion of this farcical detail was probably a joking reference to JA's brother Francis Austen, who had graduated from the Naval Academy at Portsmouth at the age of fourteen and been immediately assigned to service in December 1788 on the frigate *Perseverance*. The joke has several comically ludicrous elements: a commissioned warship could never be privately built or owned; and as Brian Southam notes, 'an uneven gun number was an impossibility' (*Jane Austen and the Navy* [London: Hambledon and London, 2000], pp. 47, 26).
21. ***Dover***: The port of Dover, on the south-east English coast at the narrowest section of the English Channel, had long been established as the major port for travel between England and France.
22. ***Newgate***: The principal prison in London since the early thirteenth century, famously featuring in popular eighteenth-century novels such as *Moll Flanders* (1722) by Daniel Defoe (1660–1731). JA uses this word in its alternative meaning of 'Any prison' or 'situation likened to Newgate prison' (*OED*). The Duchess's private keep suggests the mock-medieval dungeons of Gothic fiction.
23. ***a gold Watch for herself***: A ludicrously expensive, luxury item.
24. ***cold collation at one of the Inns***: A light meal of cold meats and salads. In JA's time there was no main meal between breakfast and dinner, which was typically served in the late afternoon. In *P&P*, Lydia and Kitty prepare a refreshment of 'sallad and cucumber' and 'a table set out with such cold meat as an inn larder usually affords' (II, xvi).
25 ***Junketings***: Slang for feasting, partying, merry-making (*OED*).
26. ***to receive some Charitable Gratuity***: Eliza adopts the formal language of polite society to express her very unladylike intention of begging outside the inn.
27. ***Postilion . . . beauty of the prospect***: The postilion, who rides the leading horse drawing a coach or carriage, would hardly have leisure to admire any picturesque scene.

28. *our real Child*: This sudden announcement parodies a convention in sentimental fiction of a mystery surrounding the birth of the heroine and her possible illegitimacy, as in Burney's *Evelina* and Smith's *Emmeline*. This issue is always resolved at the end of the novel when the heroine is revealed to be the legitimate child of titled parents.
29. *the wellfare of my Child*: A parodic reference to Fletcher's *The Chances*, performed at Steventon in January 1788, in which the noble and supposedly unmarried heroine Constantia is in fear of her brother's outrage at the birth of her baby and also secretly abandons the child, but encloses gold and a jewel to provide for its care before mysteriously thrusting it into the arms of a passing gentleman. JA parodies this unlikely scenario with a ludicrous account of Lady Harcourt's dread of her husband's resentment at the birth of a girl, and her secret abandonment of the baby beneath the haycock.

The adventures of Mr Harley

1. *The adventures of Mr Harley*: The title parodies the sentimental novel *The Man of Feeling* (1771) by Henry Mackenzie (1745–1831) and the miscellaneous adventures of its deeply sensitive hero Mr Harley.
2. *Francis Willi^am Austen Midshipman*: As in the case of 'Jack and Alice', the dedication to JA's brother Francis as midshipman on board the HMS *Perseverance* helps to date this story between December 1789 and November 1791.
3. *father for the Church . . . Mother for the Sea*: The choice of an acceptable profession for younger sons who had to work for their living was between the army, the navy, the Church and the law. Southam suggests that a similar debate may well have taken place in the Austen household, with George Austen having serious reservations about sending his young son away to sea but Mrs Austen overcoming her husband's reluctance (*Jane Austen and the Navy*, p. 47).
4. *prevailed on Sir John*: Patronage, in this case probably from a baronet, was commonplace in the eighteenth century. Mr Harley, in *The Man of Feeling*, also requests the patronage of a baronet.
5. *sat-off*: JA uses 'sat' and 'sate' as variants of 'set' as in this case, as well as the alternative meaning of 'sit'. The word is also used in its alternative meanings in the previous 'Henry and Eliza'. The

OED notes that the use of 'sat off' meaning 'to set off' indicated an inferior writer in the late eighteenth century.

6. ***Hogsworth Green, the seat of Emma***: No woman would own a 'seat' or country estate; compare also the farmyard joke in 'Jack and Alice'. Mr Harley in *The Man of Feeling* returns by stage coach to the place where the heiress Miss Walton, the lady he loves, resides with her father on a nearby estate.
7. ***fellow travellers ... Hat, Another with two***: JA continues her parody of Mr Harley's stage-coach journey in *The Man of Feeling*, playing with the boringly pointless details in such passages as the following: 'The company in the stage-coach consisted of a grocer and his wife . . . a young officer, a middle-aged gentlewoman hired as a housekeeper . . . and an elderly well-looking man, with a remarkable old-fashioned periwig.' Harley 'set himself therefore to examine, as usual, the countenances of his companions . . . there was something in that periwig we mentioned peculiarly attractive of Harley's regard' (ch. xxxiii).
8. ***fine dark Eyes***: A favourite feature for JA. The first drafts of *P&P* and *S&S* were written in the 1790s and both heroines, Marianne Dashwood and Elizabeth Bennet, are described as having dark eyes. Mr Darcy in an early chapter of *P&P* is drawn to Elizabeth Bennet by 'the beautiful expression of her dark eyes' and later comments admiringly on her 'fine eyes' (I, vi).
9. ***recollected he had married her***: Mr Harley in *The Man of Feeling* is far too sensitive to propose marriage to Miss Walton and to learn that she intends to accept him. JA mocks this inept hero with her even more inept Mr Harley, who actually forgets that he is married.

Sir William Mountague

1 ***Mountague***: A family name associated with Samuel Richardson's epistolary novel *Clarissa, or The History of a Young Lady* (1747–8), in which the anti-hero Lovelace is heir to his uncle Lord Mountague.

2. ***Charles John Austen Esq[re]***: 'Sir William Mountague' and 'Memoirs of Mr Clifford' were composed in 1788 (*Juvenilia*, p. xxviii), and dedicated to JA's younger brother Charles (1779–1852). In July 1791, shortly after his twelfth birthday, he joined the Naval Academy at Portsmouth, like his brother Francis before him, served in the navy throughout his life and reached the rank of Admiral. Here she flatters her nine-year-old brother with the term 'Esqre' (an

abbreviation of 'Esquire'), addressing him as a gentleman rather than using 'Master', the appropriate title for his age.

3. ***inherited ... from Sir Frederic Mountague***: All are baronets (rather than knights), as this title is inherited. These mocking genealogical details parody the ponderous style of John Debrett's *A New Baronetage of England* (1769). JA's final novel *P* begins with a similar genealogical reference and mocks the vanity of the baronet Sir Walter Elliot (I, i).

4. ***Park well stocked with Deer***: A symbol of status, valued in the late eighteenth century as a source of deer and game birds for the sport of hunting, and 'as a necessary component of picturesque landscape' (Doody and Murray, *Catharine*, p. 300).

5. ***Kilhoobery Park***: A nonsensical mock-Irish name.

6. ***Monday ... first of September***: The beginning of the partridge-shooting season that ran from 1 September until 1 February. Le Faye notes that the day is correct for the year 1788 and suggests that JA 'may have chosen this deliberately in order to lend a spurious air of veracity to the story' (*FR*, p. 66).

7. ***a Shot***: 'One who shoots; an expert in shooting'; the *OED* cites 1780 as the first instance of this meaning. The gentlemanly sport of shooting developed rapidly in the late eighteenth century as guns became easier to handle and more accurate.

8. ***even for such a Cause***: Peter Sabor considers that JA's satiric target here is the landed gentry and their obsession with shooting and hunting (*Juvenilia*, p. 404), a theme she continues in her novels with the equally self-motivated Wickham in *P&P* and Willoughby in *S&S*.

9. ***Surry***: Surrey, one of the 'Home Counties' south of London, known for the beauty of its countryside, as Mrs Elton exclaims in *E*: 'Surrey is the garden of England' (II, xiv).

10. ***Brudenell ... Stanhope***: JA appears to have consulted Debrett's *New Baronetage* for these surnames associated with noble families. Brudenell was the family name of the baronetcy and earldom of Cardigan with the 4th earl, George Brudenell (1712–90), who, in a further link of surnames, changed his name to Montagu in 1749 and was created Duke of Montagu in 1766. Philip Dormer Stanhope (1694–1773), Lord Chesterfield, was succeeded by a distant cousin, Philip Stanhope (1755–1815), as 5th Earl of Chesterfield. JA uses the surnames of Brudenell and Stanhope again in 'The Three Sisters'.

11. ***cruel Murder of her Brother ... 14s***: The word 'Murder' implies a more sinister context than a duel, which, although illegal, was still

widely condoned, as in *S&S* when Colonel Brandon challenges Willoughby for seducing his ward Eliza (II, i). The amount of recompense sought by Miss Stanhope at fourteen shillings is nonsensical; fourteen shillings would purchase two cheap 'plain gowns' for a woman, or a man's 'everyday coat' at five shillings (Vic Gatrell, *City of Laughter: Sex and Satire in Eighteenth-Century London* [London: Atlantic Books, 2006], pp. 244–5).

12. ***privately married***: This is a hasty, illegal marriage: Sir William is only seventeen (not twenty-one) and he has not had time to purchase a marriage licence (see note 15 to 'Henry and Eliza').

13. ***Chariot***: In the eighteenth century, the word was used for a light four-wheeled carriage with seats for up to three passengers. In 1784, the Revd George Austen purchased a chariot drawn by two horses 'for the benefit of his wife and daughters' (*FR*, p. 50). JA would later attend Assembly Balls at Basingstoke in this carriage in company with Cassandra and her mother.

14. ***Brook Street***: A fashionable London street that extends west from Hanover Square to Grosvenor Square, named from Tyburn Brook that flows beneath it.

15. ***free access to Miss Wentworth***: Sir William's conduct deteriorates as the story continues, rapidly becoming that of a hardened libertine in the style of Richardson's Lovelace, and so confirming JA's reference to this character in the family name of Mountague. The story consciously ends in mid-sentence: his predatory nature in relation to women will continue with 'access to Miss Wentworth' like the other prey he hunts.

Memoirs of Mr Clifford

1 ***Charles John Austen . . . generous patronage***: A joking reference to JA's youngest brother Charles (see note 2 to 'Sir William Mountague'), who has been elevated to the role of literary patron, a person of taste and authority whose 'patronage' advanced the interests of a person through the use of money or influence.

2. ***Memoirs***: 'Records of events or history written from the personal knowledge or experience of the writer' (*OED*). Another popular literary form parodied by JA in the journey of a man who does nothing of interest.

3. ***Coach and Four . . . a Chariot, a Chaise, a Landeau, a Landeaulet, a Phaeton, a Gig, a Whisky, an italian Chair, a Buggy, a Curricle <u>and</u> a wheelbarrow***: The catalogue of vehicles and horses is part of JA's joke in providing her young brother with a

story encompassing his interests. Like their modern equivalents, vehicles of Austen's era differed in construction, size, speed and use. A coach, usually used for long-distance travel, was a large, enclosed four-wheeled carriage, built for four to six passengers and drawn by four horses. A chariot was also fairly substantial: see note 13 for 'Sir William Mountague'. A chaise was a light, open carriage for several people, drawn by two or four horses, the leading horse on the left-hand side being ridden by the postilion (driver). The landeau (or landau), an expensive four-wheeled carriage with a retractable hood, was chiefly used for country drives; it was drawn by up to six horses and carried four passengers, with back- and front-facing seats, as in a coach. A landeaulet was small landau; in the final chapter of *P*, Anne—now married to Captain Wentworth—is 'the mistress of a very pretty landaulette', much to the envy of her sister Mary Musgrove (II, xii). The phaeton, a light four-wheeled open carriage, usually drawn by a pair of horses, was a fast and expensive pleasure vehicle driven by the owner and favoured by fashionable young sporting gentleman. The gig and whisky (because it moves smartly or 'whisks' along) were both basic two-wheel, one-horse, all-purpose vehicles; whereas the humbler Italian chair was similar but had no top or springs and was used chiefly for short distances around a park, and the buggy carried only a single passenger. The curricle was a fast, expensive, well-sprung, two-wheeled and two-horse carriage, light and open with a folding hood, favoured by young gentlemen of fashion, with a seat for the owner-driver and one passenger. Mr Darcy in *P&P*, Henry Tilney in *NA* and Willoughby in *S&S* all drive curricles, while John Thorpe in *NA* can only aspire to one and tries to represent his one-horse gig to Catherine Morland as a 'Curricle—hung' (I, vii). The wheelbarrow was a very basic and inexpensive light carriage, drawn by one horse; however, since the modern sense of the term was also current in the eighteenth century (*OED*), a comic double meaning is probably intended here as bathos at the end of the sentence.

4. ***fine stud of Horses . . . six Greys, 4 Bays, eight Blacks and a poney***: The six Greys would be appropriate for the stately landau, while a curricle for example required a handsome, fast and perfectly matched pair. Bay horses are reddish brown in colour with black mane, tail and lower legs, probably Cleveland Bays bred in Yorkshire and very fashionable at this time (Bonnie L. Hendricks, *International Encyclopedia of Horse Breeds* [Nor-

man: Oklahoma University Press, 1995], p. 132). The sole pony ('poney') might be used in the small, one-person buggy, the least expensive of this 'fine stud' (Johnson).

5. ***Devizes***: This small market town in Wiltshire was an important staging place on one of the major coach roads between Bath and London, a distance of approximately 107 miles and easily reached in a coach and four in two days. But Mr Clifford takes six hours just to travel the first stage of nineteen miles to Devizes. The fact that Cleveland Bay horses were known for their qualities of speed and stamina enhances the joke of their incredibly slow progress.
6. ***Overton***: A small town three miles from Steventon in Hampshire and a staging point on the main coach route connecting London with Exeter in Devon. Mr Clifford leaves the major road between Bath and London at Devizes and travels a longer distance instead by way of Andover and Overton, the same route taken by the Austens on their journeys from Steventon to Bath. Devizes is less than forty miles from Overton, with an excellent road for the period, improved and maintained by private turnpike trusts with users paying a toll at each turnpike gate.
7. ***Five months ... celebrated City ... celebrated Physician***: JA mocks both the place and the person. A physician, with his university degree, enjoyed a separate rank and status to the less gentlemanly surgeon or the apothecary, who dispensed medicines. The treatment of Mr Clifford's fever over a period of five months would have been seen at that time as incredibly inept.
8. ***Dean Gate***: Mr Clifford has travelled a short distance to the next coach stop at the Deane Gate Inn which stands at the junction of a then rough and often muddy lane leading to Steventon, just over a mile and a quarter away. It was the stagecoach stop used by JA's brothers and other male relatives and friends travelling to and from Steventon rectory.
9 ***Basingstoke***: A market town and municipal borough, the largest and most important town in the area of Steventon and the place where JA and her sister Cassandra would later attend Assembly Balls. Mr Clifford takes four days to travel this short journey of six miles.
10. ***Clarkengreen ... Worting***: Clarkengreen is a village about two miles east of Deane Gate, and Worting is two miles further towards Basingstoke.
11. ***Mr Robins's***: Mr Robins can be identified as the proprietor of the 'Crown Inn' at Basingstoke, one of the principal coaching inns and known also as the 'Crown Inn and Post House'.

The beautifull Cassandra

1. ***Miss Austen***: Composed in 1788 (*Juvenilia*, p. xxviii), and dedicated to Cassandra Elizabeth (1773–1845), JA's elder sister and therefore addressed as 'Miss Austen' without an initial for her Christian name.
2. ***Phoenix***: In classical mythology, a beautiful bird associated with the sun, known for burning itself to ashes and then rising again with renewed youth; applied to a person of 'matchless beauty; a paragon' (*OED*).
3. ***Millener in Bond Street***: A milliner designs, makes or sells women's hats chiefly to wealthy clients; hence the fashionable shopping location in Bond Street, between Piccadilly and Oxford Street, London.
4. ***fall in love with an elegant Bonnet***: JA's letters show that she was particularly fond of bonnets and their trimmings (see for example *Letters*, p. 16); falling in love with bonnets appears to have been a standing joke between herself and Cassandra, hence the subject of this 'novel'.
5. ***Pastry-cooks where she devoured six ices***: In the days before refrigeration, water ices and ice-cream were luxury items sold by pastry cooks, as in *NA* (I, xv).
6. ***Hackney Coach***: A four-wheeled coach with two horses, kept for hire. A 'hack' means a horse for general use, ordinary riding (*OED*).
7. ***Hampstead***: A village about four miles north from Bond Street, famous for its walks and views of London.
8. ***Bloomsbury Square***: A fashionable address; one of the earliest squares in London.

Amelia Webster

1. ***Mrs Austen***: Written in 1787 and dedicated to JA's mother, Cassandra Leigh Austen (1739–1827), a keen novel reader and witty versifier who would presumably have appreciated this 'romance by telegram', as Juliet McMaster aptly describes it. McMaster makes a strong case for Frances Brooke's *The History of Emily Montague* (1769) as a source (Juliet McMaster, 'Young Jane Austen and the First Canadian Novel: From Emily Montague to "Amelia Webster" and "Love and Freindship"', in *Global Jane Austen: Pleasure, Passion, and Possessiveness in the Jane Austen*

Community, ed. Laurence Raw and Robert G. Dryden [London: Palgrave Macmillan, 2013]).

2. ***from abroad***: In the eighteenth century, the trip 'abroad', or 'tour of the continent', was considered an essential crowning event in the education and finishing of genteel youths.
3. ***Matilda***: A popular name for a Gothic heroine, used by Horace Walpole (1717–97) in *The Castle of Otranto* (1764), by M. G. Lewis (1775–1818) in *The Monk* (1796), and by JA for the imaginary heroine of Henry Tilney's Gothic narrative in *NA* (I, xx).
4. ***Beverley***: A name with romantic and pastoral associations; it appears in *The Rivals* (1775) by Richard Brinsley Sheridan (1751–1816), where it is assumed by Captain Absolute, and also as the surname of the heroine in Burney's *Cecilia*.
5. ***Maud***: A variation of the name Matilda.
6. ***two thousand Pounds***: A fairly modest dowry yielding a yearly income of about £100 per annum. In *P&P*, Mr Collins comments on Elizabeth Bennet's expectations of 'one thousand pounds in the four per cents' (I, xix).
7. ***my paper will only permit me to add***: Given the unlikelihood that Amelia's very short letter could have covered an entire page, this very formulaic ending acts as an ironic indication of the heroine's vacuity.
8. ***Sally***: An affectionate variation on the name Sarah; in the newspaper report at the end of this 'novel', Sally is referred to as 'Sarah'. In *NA*, Catherine Morland's sister prefers to be known as Sarah rather than Sally.
9. ***old hollow oak***: This gestures towards the eighteenth-century epistolary convention of engaging in a correspondence through the use of a hiding place. The eponymous heroine of Richardson's *Clarissa* employs a woodhouse for her correspondence with Lovelace, and that of *Pamela* employs such locations as the interspace between two tiles (Letter 32) in order to conceal her correspondence from Mr B.
10. ***private Correspondence***: This indicates that they are very likely engaged. Compare Elinor's distress in *S&S* when she discovers Marianne's 'impropriety' in writing to Willoughby when they are not engaged (II, vii).
11. ***my Paper reminds me of concluding***: Another ironic framing of both the heroine's trite mode of address and the extreme brevity of her letters. Compare the inelegant phrasing of the ignorant Lucy Steele in *S&S*: 'My paper reminds me to conclude' (III, ii).

12. *telescope*: The popularity of telescopes at this time was linked with the sentimental convention of admiring and contemplating picturesque landscapes. Hervey's misappropriation of this visual and aesthetic aid for the purposes of courtship is framed comically.
13. *Jack . . . Tom*: The gratuitous introduction of two new characters at the end of the 'novel', their abbreviated names and their familiarity with each other emphasizes the author's mock contempt for her readers.

The Visit

1. *Rev[d] James Austen*: Written in 1789 and dedicated to JA's eldest brother James Austen (1765–1819), who was ordained deacon in December 1787 and became a priest in June 1789 (*FR*, pp. 53, 71). It is apt that JA should dedicate this miniature comedic drama to her brother as he directed a series of dramatic performances by the Austen family at Steventon, providing comical prologues and epilogues for them.
2. *'The school for Jealousy' and 'The travelled Man'*: Although there are no eighteenth-century plays with these titles, the format echoes popular titles like Arthur Murphy's *The School for Guardians* (1767), Oliver Goldsmith's *The Good Natur'd Man* (1768), Richard Cumberland's *The Choleric Man* (1774), Richard Brinsley Sheridan's *The School for Scandal* (1777) and Hannah Cowley's *School for Eloquence* (1780). Critics suggest these titles are either fictitious or genuine burlesques written by either James Austen or Jane herself (see Southam in R. W. Chapman, ed., *Minor Works*, Volume 6 of *The Works of Jane Austen*, rev. by B. C. Southam [London: Oxford University Press, 1975], p. 458; see also Paula Byrne, *Jane Austen and the Theatre* [London: Hambledon and London, 2002], p. 21).
3. *Curate*: The curate was entrusted with the care (cure) of the soul and acted as an assistant to the parish priest; he had no living of his own and was 'a source of cheap labour' (Pool, *What Jane Austen Ate*, p. 118). James Austen became curate at Stoke Charity, near Winchester, in July 1788 (*FR*, p. 63).
4. *first composed*: This suggests that the dedication was added some time after the play's earlier composition, possibly in early 1789 (*FR*, pp. 67–8).
5. *Cloe*: Chloe was a traditional name for rustic female characters, derived from the Greek pastoral romance *Daphnis and Chloe* by Longus.

6. ***I am afraid you found your Bed too short***: This allusion to the Procrustean bed comically indicates the grandmother's unsociable refusal to adapt to the behaviour of others. In the original Greek legend, Procrustes offered his bed to strangers and then either truncated or stretched their bodies if they did not extend the same length as his bed.
7. ***The more free, the more Wellcome***: In *High Life Below Stairs* (1759) a two-act farce by James Townley (1714–1778), Kitty declares: 'Lady Charlotte, pray be free; the more free, the more welcome, as they say in my country' (II.i). The allusion is shortly followed through when the aristocratic characters declare their enthusiasm for coarse food traditionally consumed by the servant and labouring classes. This is a reversal of the premise of Townley's play, in which the servants live like aristocrats.
8. ***discovered***: In stage directions this indicates that the characters are already in place when the curtain is raised.
9. ***Exeunt Severally***: In stage directions, this indicates that the characters leave the stage via differing routes.
10. ***Chairs set round in a row***: This, as opposed to the chairs being arranged in clusters, is a formal arrangement typical of more old-fashioned houses.
11. ***hands***: Escorts, or, leads by the hand.
12. ***Miss Fitzgerald at top. Lord Fitzgerald at bottom. Company ranged on each side***: This description, in which the host and hostess are positioned at either end of the table, emphasizes the traditional formality and propriety of the Fitzgeralds' domestic arrangements, thus setting up the incongruity of the type of food that is about to be consumed.
13. ***fried Cowheel and Onion***: The heel of the cow (or 'trotters') was traditionally only used to make jellied broth rather than consumed in its own right. Like many of the dishes that follow, this is the coarse fare traditionally consumed by labourers.
14. ***Sophy will toss off a bumper***: A boisterous expression that indicates downing a glass filled to the brim ('a bumper') quickly rather than sipping in a slow and ladylike fashion.
15. ***Elder wine or Mead***: Cheap, home-made products (made from elderberries and honey respectively) at odds with the expensive wine that would more appropriately deck the aristocratic table of the likes of the Fitzgeralds.
16. ***warm ale with a toast and nutmeg***: This was traditionally a drink for invalids and, as such, is comically at odds with both the formal setting and Sophy's youth and attractiveness.

17. ***red herrings***: Fish preserved in salt was considered an inferior alternative to fresh fish.
18. ***Tripe . . . Liver and Crow***: Like tripe (the stomach lining of oxen or sheep), 'Liver and Crow' refers to a seasoned dish of entrails and giblets usually only consumed by the poor.
19. ***suet pudding***: A traditional boiled pudding made primarily of animal fat and flour which, again, is not associated with the formal, aristocratic table.
20. ***destroyed the Hothouse in order to build a receptacle for the Turkies with its materials***: The possession of a hothouse for the growing of fruits and flowers out of season was an indication of wealth and refinement. This is comically undercut by its being dismantled for the less genteel purpose of housing poultry.
21. ***Come Girls, let us circulate the Bottle***: The wine, typically claret, was customarily passed around the table after the ladies retired to the drawing room, so this suggestion indicates a comical breach of propriety that is sharpened into a gender reversal given the relative reluctance of the male characters to imbibe.
22. ***Goose-berry Wine***: Another instance of a simple, domestically produced beverage that would have been considered inappropriate for a formal gathering of this nature.

The Mystery

1. ***The Mystery***: Written in 1788, the central device of this piece, the use of inaudible whispers, aligns it with George Villiers, the Duke of Buckingham's *The Rehearsal* (1672) and Richard Brinsley Sheridan's *The Critic* (1779), both of which contain famous 'whispering scenes'. JA gently parodies the device by refusing to offer any solid information, only a series of tantalizing fragments.
2. ***the Rev[d] George Austen***: JA's father (1731–1805), rector of Steventon.
3. ***Fanny***: An affectionate variation of Frances, this name is given to several of JA's mature characters: Fanny Dashwood (*S&S*), Fanny Price (*MP*) and Fanny Harville (*P*), and also Fanny in 'The Three Sisters'.
4. ***Spangle***: A bright, metallic fragment usually attached to clothing to create a glittering effect; popular with wealthy men of fashion. It carries associations both of the stage and of clowning.
5. ***Humbug***: This slang term became popular in the mid-eighteenth century and designates trickery and deception, an impostor or fraud.

6. ***Daphne . . . Corydon***: Generic names for rustic characters in the pastoral tradition. Daphne is also the name of a flowering shrub associated with virgin modesty, from the Greek legend of Daphne and Apollo.
7. ***M[rs] Humbug and Fanny, discovered at work***: They would implicitly have been engaged in an occupation like needlework, which was considered a genteel pastime for ladies.
8. ***reclined in an elegant Attitude***: An attitude of studied carelessness and ennui was a fashionable pose for young gentlemen in the late eighteenth century. JA offers a gentle parody of this popular affectation by making the gracefully prone and unconscious aristocrat the final recipient of the secret.

The Three Sisters

1. ***Edward Austen Esq[re]***: JA's third brother (1767–1852), who was adopted and raised by a wealthy, distant cousin, Thomas Knight, and his wife Catherine. He married Elizabeth Bridges in December 1791 and moved to Rowling, near Goodnestone, Kent. Elizabeth's two sisters, Fanny and Sophia, were engaged in the same year, so the topic of the story seems to offer a humorous yet moralizing contrast to the marital prospects of JA's new sisters-in-law. JA probably wrote this piece in late 1791 or early 1792 (*Juvenilia*, p. xxviii; *Literary MSS*, p. 16).
2 ***Settlements***: Refers to property of the husband that, through a pre-nuptial agreement, is determined to be 'settled' on the wife in the event of his death.
3. ***married before me***: Marriage conferred status and it was customary for the eldest daughter to marry first. Lydia Bennet in *P&P* parades her triumph over her elder sisters (III, ix).
4. ***blue spotted with silver . . . plain Chocolate***: Blue and silver is a humorously eccentric and vulgar colour scheme. Mr Watts's preferred chocolate brown is more traditional and tasteful.
5. ***as low as his old one***: Various carriages 'all embodied a certain social dignity' (Pool, *What Jane Austen Ate*, p. 145). It was fashionable and more costly to have a high carriage from which a better view could be enjoyed, and in which young ladies could display themselves to greater advantage. The lower carriage was more economical and also more structurally stable.
6. ***chaprone***: Traditionally, older married women would accompany young unmarried women for the sake of propriety. Here, there is some irony in Mary's enthusiasm for the role, given her

evident immaturity and lack of principles. The situation here is similar to that in *P&P* where the flighty Lydia tactlessly offers to chaperone her older unmarried sisters (III, ix).

7. ***Winter Balls***: During the summer, fashionable society moved from the city to country estates. The winter months were subsequently regarded as the height of the season and the best time to hold larger functions. Winter balls could either be privately hosted or take place in public assembly halls.
8. ***Law***: This euphemism for 'Lord' would have been considered a rather vulgar expression for a lady.
9. ***drinks Tea***: This is not a meal in itself but, rather, refers to the custom of drinking tea after midday dinner, a custom which gradually moved to late afternoon during the eighteenth century.
10. ***then they should fight him***: Duels were becoming quite uncommon at this time, so Mary's comment suggests both callous romanticism and naiveté.
11. ***Miss*** x x x: A playful allusion to the eighteenth-century convention of abbreviating or withholding the names of characters as if they were real people.
12. ***Three thousand a year***: As Georgiana points out, although a good fortune, this sum is by no means a vast one. It is, to be sure, not nearly enough to fulfil Mary's ludicrously extravagant lifestyle expectations; £5,000 a year would be needed for the expenses of the winter London season alone (*Juvenilia*, p. 418).
13. ***Quiet our Minds my dear Anne***: The sudden and slightly incongruous lapse in the facetious tone of the text for this playful sketching-out of a hint of character complexity and moral conundrum seems to signal the emergence of a more serious novelistic style of writing.
14. ***Phaeton***: See note 3 to 'Memoirs of Mr Clifford'.
15. ***Chaise***: See note 3 to 'Memoirs of Mr Clifford'.
16. ***pin money***: Like a 'jointure' (see note 9 to 'Jack and Alice'), pin money was part of the marriage settlement, involving a small personal allowance for the wife's expenses such as those related to dress.
17. ***saddle horse***: A horse broken and reserved for the purposes of riding as opposed to the drawing of carriages.
18. ***valuable Jewels . . . out of number***: At this point, Mary's requests are far in excess of Mr Watts's income. A deleted passage here in the manuscript alludes to the fabulous jewels of the Princess

Badroulbadour from 'The Story of Aladdin' in *The Arabian Nights* (translated into English *c.*1706–21), further emphasizing Mary's fantasy of wealth (see Textual Notes).

19. ***Greenhouse***: The possession of a greenhouse for the growing of fruits and flowers out of season was an indication of wealth and refinement.
20. ***Winter in Bath . . . Autumn at a Watering Place***: Such seasonal enjoyments would be far in excess of Mr Watts's income; even for very wealthy families, an extended stay in Bath and London ('Town') in the same year would have been considered an extravagance. A 'Watering Place' is a spa or seaside resort; 'some Tour' refers to a trip made for the purposes of admiring scenery and could be made either to the Continent or to a scenic part of England.
21. ***Which is the Man***: A comedy (1782) by Hannah Cowley (1743–1809) that was considered for performance at the Steventon theatricals of Christmas 1787–8 but rejected (Penny Gay, *Jane Austen and the Theatre* [Cambridge: Cambridge University Press, 2002], p. 74).
22. ***Writings***: Another reference to the Settlement.
23. ***Special Licence . . . common Licence***: A common licence, granted by a bishop in a church within his diocese, does away with the reading of the banns. Here it represents a compromise between the cheapest matrimonial procedure (the reading of the banns in church over the course of three Sundays, regarded as vulgar by the upper classes) and a special licence.
24. ***Leicestershire***: A Midlands county famous for foxhunting. Following this are four lines deleted in the manuscript (see Textual Notes); Sabor suggests that the conundrum they present may have been too laboured and the reference to JA's brother Edward Knight too personal (*Juvenilia*, p. 421).
25. ***appearance***: Her first public appearance as a married woman.
26. ***I should advise . . . make your Entrée very respectable***: An 'Entrée' is a formal public entrance into a room. Kitty is spitefully undermining Mary's self-representation as an elegant matron by framing her more along the lines of an overworked governess escorting large numbers of girls for money.
27. ***Vixen***: a Shrew (literally, a she-fox).
28. ***Blackguard***: 'A shabby, mean fellow' (Grose, *Dictionary of the Vulgar Tongue* [1785]).
29. ***dressed***: Changed into appropriate evening wear.

Detached Pieces

To Miss Jane Anna Elizabeth Austen

1. ***Miss Jane Anna Elizabeth Austen***: JA's niece (1793–1872) and the daughter of James Austen. Not yet seven weeks old when this piece was composed, she later became Mrs Benjamin Lefroy.
2. ***Treatises for your Benefit***: JA alludes to the extremely popular genre of the advice manual for young ladies. In *P&P*, for example, Mr Collins eagerly reads *Sermons to Young Women* (1766) by James Fordyce (1720–96) to the Bennet girls. See also Mrs Percival's recommendations in JA's 'Catharine'.
3. ***1793***: JA dates these pieces 2 June 1793, except for 'Ode to Pity' dated 3 June 1793. Following this date in the notebook manuscript is a deleted short paragraph titled: 'A fragment—written to inculcate the practise of Virtue' (see Textual Notes).

A beautiful description of the different effects of Sensibility on different Minds

4. ***Sensibility***: In eighteenth-century philosophy and aesthetics, sensibility referred to a receptive capacity to beauty and pathos that was at once physical, emotional and moral.
5. ***book muslin bedgown . . . french net nightcap***: Melissa is finely arrayed. A bedgown is actually a housedress, not necessarily worn for sleeping, and it is made of a very delicate kind of muslin that takes its name from its book-like appearance when folded. A shift is a plain undergarment usually made of ordinary linen or cotton but here made of Chambray gauze, a semi-transparent, very fine cloth made from cambric, a fine linen from Chambray in France. A 'French Nightcap' or 'dormeuse' was fashionable as a day cap 1750–90; it was a crown with a ribbon trimming that fitted over the head with flaps or 'wings' (C. Willet Cunnington and Phillis Cunnington, *Handbook of English Costume in the Eighteenth Century* [London: Faber and Faber, 1972], p. 347).
6. ***hashing up***: To shred, reheat and serve with a binding agent like egg or sauce.
7. ***toasting some cheese***: Like a hash, toasted cheese was a cheap meal not considered appropriate for polite society.
8. ***Curry***: Curry was introduced to England from India and became popular in the eighteenth century. This spicy dish would have been considered inappropriate for an invalid.

9. *cordials*: 'A medicine that increases the force of the heart, or quickens the circulation' (Johnson).

The Generous Curate—a moral Tale, setting forth the Advantages of being Generous and a Curate

10. *Curate*: See note 3 to 'The Visit'.
11. *a moral Tale*: A popular genre of didactic fiction for children, such as *Moral Tales for Young People* (1801) by Maria Edgeworth (1768–1849).
12. *Clergyman*: Unlike the curate of the title, this would be a rector with his own parish, responsible for all official duties including those of his assistant curate.
13. *living*: The clergyman's income derived from tithes and lands that were owned by the parish and rented out. £200 would not have been considered a large sum. JA's father's two livings of Steventon and Deane brought in £100 and £110 per annum respectively, and had to be supplemented by tutoring and by income from one of his cousin Mr Knight's farms amounting to £300 (Irene Collins, *Jane Austen and the Clergy* [London: Hambledon and London, 1994], p. 56).
14. *Royal Academy for Seamen at Portsmouth*: The Royal Naval Academy, later known as the Royal Naval College, accepted boys of eleven to seventeen for training as officers. JA's two youngest brothers, Francis and Charles, both attended this Academy.
15. *small fleet destined for Newfoundland*: The island of Newfoundland was Britain's oldest colony. A naval presence was necessary during frequent wars with France, Spain and Holland, to defend its valuable fisheries.
16. *Newfoundland Dog*: A very large breed of hunting dog, imported to Britain in the seventeenth century and increasingly popular in the late eighteenth and early nineteenth centuries. The poet Lord Byron had several such dogs, and Henry Tilney in *NA* keeps 'a large Newfoundland puppy' (II, xi).
17. *a Curacy of fifty pound a year*: A very small income, only a quarter of that of the clergyman.
18. *twopenny Dame's School*: Women, usually elderly or widowed, would often keep an elementary private school for the poor who wanted to learn basic reading, writing and arithmetic.
19. *genius*: Refers to 'nature, disposition' (Johnson), rather than intellectual brilliance.
20. *brickbats*: Fragments of brick.

Ode to Pity

1. ***Miss Austen***: JA's sister Cassandra; as the eldest daughter she is addressed simply as 'Miss Austen' without the initial of her Christian name.
2. ***Ode to Pity***: The title alludes to William Collins's well-known 'Ode to Pity' (1746), which she would have read in her copy of Dodsley's *Collection of Poems*.
3. ***Myrtle***: Myrtle's association with love stems from the tale of Phaedra piercing its leaves while desperately in love with her stepson, Hippolytus.
4. ***Philomel***: Nightingale, from classical mythology.
5. ***turnpike road***: Road paid for by tolls on vehicles. Introduced in the seventeenth century, they proliferated in the eighteenth.
6. ***The hut, the Cot, the Grot, and Chapel queer***: Cot and Grot are truncations of Cottage and Grotto. These images were popularized by the Graveyard poets and later taken up by Gothic novelists.
7. ***Abbey too a mouldering heap***: Another popular Gothic motif, foreshadowing enthusiasm for abbeys in *NA* (II, ii).

VOLUME THE SECOND

1. ***Ex dono mei Patris***: 'A gift from my father'. The notebook containing the manuscript of 'Volume the Second' was a gift from the Revd George Austen in about 1790, the date of her first item in the notebook.
2. ***Contents***: JA has inserted page numbers beside each of the following contents. The titles under 'Scraps' appear in the text but are not listed on the title page of the manuscript.
3. ***Freindship***: JA has overwritten the letters 'ie' here to produce her usual 'ei' spelling, indicating her indecision over the spelling of this word, although she consistently uses the 'ei' spelling elsewhere in the story: see Note on the Text.

Love and Freindship

1. ***Comtesse De Feuillide***: JA's cousin, Eliza de Feuillide, who was probably staying at Steventon in June 1790 (*FR*, p. 70). JA dates this story 13 June 1790; it is the only story in the juvenilia dedicated to Eliza, although she is referred to in 'Henry and Eliza' and is a possible model for 'Lady Susan'.

2. *in a series of Letters*: This stock phrase signals the epistolary form of the novel, used by Eliza Nugent Bromley (d. 1807) in *Laura and Augustus: An Authentic Story, in a Series of Letters, by a Young Lady* (1784), a major source for 'Love and Freindship'. Besides the same names, Bromley's novel has other plot conventions parodied by JA: female friends, tyrannical fathers, the constant telling of adventures and life histories, extravagant emotions, and even the hero dying and the heroine going mad. For a full exploration of this source, see Juliet McMaster, 'From *Laura and Augustus* to *Love and Freindship*,' in *Thalia: Studies in Literary Humor*, 16: 1–2 (1996), pp. 16–26. For a further possible source in Frances Brooke's *The History of Emily Montague* (1769), see notes to 'Amelia Webster'.
3. *Deceived in Freindship and Betrayed in Love*: From an anonymous song for three voices published in *A Selection of Favorite Catches, Glees, etc. Sung at the Bath Harmonic Society* (1798): 'Welcome, the covert of these aged oaks; / Welcome, each cavern of the horrid rocks; / Far from the world's illusion let me rove, / Deciev'd in Freindship, and betray'd in Love.'
4. *Isabel to Laura*: 'Isabel', a fashionable name, is later used for Isabella Thorpe in *NA* and Isabella Knightley in *E*; 'Laura', an older name, became popular with novelists in the 1780s and 1790s.
5. *Marianne*: The name is given to Marianne Dashwood in *S&S*, a heroine representative of excessive sensibility.
6. *natural*: 'Natural' is here opposed to lawful, meaning that Laura is illegitimate.
7. *italian Opera-girl*: This refers to a woman who dances in the ballet section of the opera rather than a singer. Opera girls often wore revealing costumes and were understood to be sexually available to the wealthy patrons of the opera.
8. *romantic*: Here, romantic refers to the sublime qualities of the landscape, 'full of wild scenery' (Johnson).
9. *Vale of Uske*: Vale of Usk, a picturesque river valley north of Newport in south Wales.
10. *Rendez-vous*: This is a gently malapropos use of the word, which can refer to either a meeting or a favourite meeting place. In the manuscript, JA initially gave the definition of this newly fashionable French term as 'place of appointment' but then deleted it, perhaps to preserve Laura's inappropriate usage.
11. *tremblingly alive*: From Pope's *Essay on Man*: 'Or touch, if tremblingly alive all o'er / To smart, and agonize at ev'ry pore' (I, 189–90).

12. *Minuet Dela Cour*: This translates from the French as 'Minuet of the Court', a highly stylized dance for couples associated with the French court and popular in England and France from *c.* 1650 to 1750.
13. ***one of the first Boarding-schools in London***: For example, the 'ladies' Eton' on Queen's Square, referred to in 'Edgar and Emma' (ch. 3). Boarding schools were an increasingly popular choice for genteel young ladies.
14. ***Southampton***: Southampton is a port city in Hampshire, in the south of England, where JA was at a small boarding school for a short time in 1783. Margaret Anne Doody suggests that the dangerous 'putrid fever' she and Cassandra caught there lends a more sober tone to the following comical reference to Southampton's 'stinking fish' (Doody and Murray, eds, *Catharine*, p. xiii). Certainly the town was known for its dirt and bad air. It was not at all fashionable, so claiming having 'supped one night' there as evidence of worldliness indicates Laura's ludicrous provinciality. JA originally wrote 'slept', then amended this to 'supped' to heighten the joke.
15. ***rustic Cot***: Country cottage; poetic diction of the eighteenth-century pastoral, picturesque tradition.
16. ***We must not pretend . . . I am partly convinced***: JA's major revision here in the manuscript (see deletion in Textual Notes) condenses this speech, probably because she felt it detracted from the main comic effect of the conversation about rapping on the door, as Doody suggests (Doody and Murray, eds, *Catharine*, p. xvii).
17. ***the happiness or Misery of my future Life must depend***: Another stock phrase in the sentimental novel. See, for example, Richardson's *Sir Charles Grandison*: 'On this crisis of time . . . depends an eternity of happiness or misery' (Part 1, Vol. V, Letter XXVIII).
18. ***Lindsay . . . Talbot***: Lindsay is a noble, Scottish name and Talbot a quintessentially English one. Here JA makes a humorous reference to the eighteenth-century novelistic practice of concealing the names of characters as if they were real people.
19. ***Baronet***: The lowest hereditary rank.
20. ***Polydore***: The name of the youngest son of King Priam, this is a highly unusual name for the eighteenth century, though typical for a character in early romance, such as Shakespeare's *Cymbeline*. It is also highly inappropriate to address strangers by their first names.
21. ***obliged my Father***: A humorous reference to the generic plot convention, especially prevalent in eighteenth-century drama, of disagreement between a romantic and strong-willed youth and their father or guardian.

22. ***You have been studying Novels I suspect***: It was typical in the eighteenth century to blame novels for corrupting youth, in particular young women. JA's defence of the novel in *NA* is a famous exception (I, v): see Introduction.
23. ***Bedfordshire, my Aunt's in Middlesex***: Edward is clearly not proficient in geography as Bedfordshire is north-west of London and only about thirty miles north of Middlesex. Instead of travelling this distance he has travelled some hundred miles west to the Vale of Usk.
24. ***who tho' he had never taken orders . . . Church***: As he is not an ordained clergyman, Laura and Edward are not legally married.
25. ***Sophia***: A common name for a sentimental heroine; it means 'wisdom' but is used ironically by JA for rather vacant and fickle young women, as in 'A Collection of Letters'.
26. ***My Life . . . Adorable Angel***: In the eighteenth century, it was acceptable for men to behave affectionately towards one another, but the terms of endearment here employed are humorously excessive and more appropriate for lovers.
27. ***pathetic***: Expressive of pathos; arousing sadness, compassion, or sympathy (*OED*).
28. ***We fainted Alternately on a Sofa***: Compare the similar response in a stage direction in Sheridan's *The Critic*: 'They faint alternately in each other's arms' (III.i).
29. ***Clandestine Marriage***: The secret marriage of minors was prohibited by Hardwicke's Marriage Act of 1753. The phrase derives from the play *The Clandestine Marriage* (1766) by George Colman and David Garrick.
30. ***purloined . . . Escritoire***: Stolen (purloined) from his father's writing desk (escritoire).
31. ***would have blushed at the idea of paying their Debts***: It was considered de rigueur amongst many of the fashionable and wealthy to display a cavalier disregard for debts contracted to tradesmen.
32. ***Execution in the House***: This is the seizure of a debtor's goods through the agency of a writ carried out by a sheriff's officer.
33. ***Officers of Justice***: Sheriff's officers.
34. ***Holbourn***: A district in central London. JA originally wrote 'Picadilly' in her manuscript, a more respectable area of London in the West End.
35. ***Postilion***: See note 22 to 'Frederic and Elfrida'.
36. ***Newgate***: A notorious prison that appears in a number of eighteenth-century novels.

37. *Annuity*: An annual payment, derived from a return on capital, and ceases with the death of the recipient.
38. *travel Post*: A speedy and expensive mode of transportation where the traveller would change horses at various stages, thereby allowing them to travel day and night.
39. *coroneted Coach*: A coach that bears the crest of a family that is part of the peerage, hence the emblem of a coronet or crown.
40. *Matilda*: See note 3 to 'Amelia Webster'.
41. *Philander*: A play on the word 'philanderer', a male flirt.
42. *tell me, have I any other Grand-Children in the House*: A parody of the discovery scene in Frances Burney's *Evelina* (1778), in which the heroine is finally acknowledged by her father Sir John Belmont, who already has a daughter and has just discovered a son (III, xix).
43. *Sorrows of Werter*: Goethe's romantic, sentimental novel, *The Sorrows of Young Werther*, was incredibly popular and fashionable in the eighteenth century.
44. *Auburn*: Red hair briefly became fashionable in the 1780s (see Cunnington and Cunnington, *Handbook of English Costume*, p. 258).
45. *Gretna-Green*: A town in Scotland just north of the English border that was popular with eloping couples because marriages in Scotland between individuals under the age of twenty-one could be performed with expediency and without the permission of parents or guardians. Janetta and M'Kenzie already live in Scotland so their elopement is, in fact, unnecessary.
46. *turn-pike road*: See note 5 to 'Ode to Pity'.
47. *Eastern Zephyr*: A humorous malapropism given that 'Zephyr' is a poetic name for the west wind.
48. *blue sattin Waistcoat*: This type of waistcoat was made popular because of its being worn by the hero of Goethe's *The Sorrows of Young Werther*, whose clothes, behaviour and suicide began a copycat craze throughout Europe.
49. *apropos*: From the French *à propos*, meaning apt or opportune.
50. *Phaeton*: This fashionable open carriage was easily overthrown because of its high centre of gravity. See also note 3 to 'Memoirs of Mr Clifford'.
51. *Life of Cardinal Wolsey*: Thomas Wolsey (1475–1530), cardinal and statesman under Henry VIII, whose fall from wealth and favour was often used as an example of the dangers of pride. Knox-Shaw suggests that not only is JA alluding to Shakespeare's Wolsey in *King Henry VIII* who compares his downfall to a

falling star (III.ii), but she is also drawing on Hugh Blair's comments on this Shakespearean soliloquy that is 'at once instructive and affecting', in his *Lectures on Rhetoric and Belles Lettres* (1783) that JA read (Peter Knox-Shaw, *Jane Austen and the Enlightenment* [Cambridge: Cambridge University Press, 2004], pp. 53–4).

52. ***sensible***: Conscious.
53. ***Cupid's Thunderbolts, avoid the piercing Shafts of Jupiter***: This is reversed, as shafts or arrows are the missiles of Cupid, and thunderbolts of Jupiter.
54. ***Talk not to me of Phaetons . . . Cucumber***: This strongly recalls the mad speech of Tilburina in Sheridan's *The Critic* (III.i), in which a similar effect of staccato delivery and absurd images is achieved.
55. ***Bridget***: In *The Tender Husband* (1705) by Richard Steele (1672–1729), the heroine, Bridget, objects to her own name on the grounds that it is not a name ever given to heroines.
56. ***galloping Consumption***: Rapidly developing tuberculosis. Also used to refer to other wasting diseases.
57. ***Basket***: A compartment hanging off the back of the coach, chiefly intended for luggage; the cheapest and most uncomfortable seat.
58. ***Gilpin's Tour to the Highlands***: *Observations, Relative Chiefly to Picturesque Beauty . . . On Several Parts of Great Britain; Particularly the High-Lands of Scotland* (1788) by William Gilpin (1724–1804). JA's brother Henry noted that: 'She was a warm and judicious admirer of landscape, both in nature and on canvass. At a very early age, she was enamored of Gilpin on the Picturesque.' (Austen-Leigh, *Memoir*, ed. Sutherland, p. 140). JA also refers to Gilpin's picturesque theories elsewhere in the juvenilia and in her novels.
59. ***Stage Coach***: A coach that runs in stages and takes on paying passengers. This would not have been considered an appropriate mode of conveyance for the genteel classes.
60. ***converted it into a Stage***: This represents a humorously dramatic transformation from gentility into the working class.
61. ***Edinburgh from whence he went to Sterling***: Known as the 'Gateway to the Highlands', the ancient city of Stirling in central Scotland is located on the River Forth; the distance from Stirling to the capital of Edinburgh is about forty miles.
62. ***Postchaise***: A small, fast carriage, usually with a closed body and four wheels; see also note 3 to 'Memoirs of Mr Clifford'.

63. ***step into the Basket***: This humorously resembles a formal invitation to a drawing room, and emphasizes that they probably cannot afford to purchase nourishment at the inn.
64. ***Sentimental***: A key term in the eighteenth century referring to a feeling response, engaging the emotions rather than rational thought: see Introduction.
65. ***Staymaker***: A corset maker; a 'stay', or corset, is a laced undergarment stiffened with whalebone to shape and support the figure (*OED*).
66. ***their united fortunes . . . nine Hundred***: This is very imprudent and quite contrary to the usual eighteenth-century practice of living on the interest of a sum of money. The interest on £9,000 would have been sufficient to sustain a very comfortable standard of living.
67. ***the 9th to Silver Buckles***: Although these fashionable items were quite expensive, this is a humorously excessive amount of money to set aside for them as it would enable the purchase of around thirty pairs. Cunnington cites the typical 1788 price for buckles as £3.8s. (*Handbook of English Costume*, p. 424).
68. ***strolling Company of Players***: Travelling actors who would perform plays, generally understood to be of a poor quality, in various locations.
69. ***eclat***: French, meaning brilliance of effect, flamboyance.
70. ***preferment***: Advancement, employment.
71. ***Covent Garden . . . Lewis and Quick***: William Thomas Lewis (*c.*1746–1811) and John Quick (1748–1831), comic actors and managers at Covent Garden, one of the two main London theatres.
72. ***paid the Debt of Nature***: Died; 'To pay the debt of Nature' is a hackneyed euphemism for 'death'.

Lesley Castle

1. ***To Henry Thomas Austen Esqre***: JA's fourth brother (1771–1850). Henry received his BA at Oxford in 1792, which may have supplied the occasion for this dedication since the final letter of 'Lesley Castle' is dated 13 April 1792. Henry has jokingly assumed the role of patron by writing the cash order that follows the dedication.
2. ***Messrs Demand and Co***: A humorous invented name for a bank.
3. ***Matilda***: See note 3 to 'Amelia Webster'.
4. ***Aberdeen***: A university city located on the north-east coast of Scotland; until 1860 it had two universities.

5. *dishonour*: Dishonour's Christian name Rakehelly means 'wild; dissolute' (Johnson); hence 'Rake' or 'Rakehell', 'a lewd, debauched fellow' (Grose, *Dictionary of the Vulgar Tongue*).
6. *Perth*: A city in Perthshire, Scotland, located between the capital Edinburgh and Aberdeen.
7. *the M'Leods ... the Macduffs*: A humorous collection of Scottish names, from literary sources like Shakespeare's *Macbeth*, Burney's *Evelina* and (as Sabor notes, *Juvenilia*, p. 446) Samuel Johnson's *Journey to the Western Islands of Scotland* (1775).
8. *bon-mot ... repartée*: A 'clever remark' and 'lively banter' (French).
9. *I live in Perthshire, You in Sussex*: They live in more or less opposite ends of Great Britain, Sussex being on the south coast of England.
10. *Tunbridge*: Tunbridge Wells was a spa town in Kent, less popular than Bath.
11. *Peggy*: A pet form of Margaret.
12. *Stewed Soup*: Made stock for soup by boiling meat bones.
13. *Whipt syllabub*: Syllabub is a popular English dessert in which cream, sherry, lemon or orange and sugar are whisked vigorously to create a light, frothy consistency.
14. *Eloisa*: A name with melancholy and romantic connotations due to its primary association with the medieval story of Eloise and Abelard, popularized in Alexander Pope's *Eloisa and Abelard* (1717). JA would also have known the sentimental novel *Julie, ou La Nouvelle Héloïse* (1761) by Jean-Jacques Rousseau (1712–88).
15. *dressed*: Prepared for serving.
16. *Decline*: A wasting disease like tuberculosis.
17. *Bristol*: The port city of Bristol in the west of England was near a spa, Bristol Hotwells, which was less expensive than the fashionable one at nearby Bath.
18. *Mistress of those Jewels which once adorned our Mother*: Traditionally a mother's jewels were given to her daughters, but Sir George has instead given them to his second wife.
19. *Dunbeath*: Probably refers to the name of the estate that Margaret Lesley's brother inherited, said to be 'near Aberdeen'.
20. *the healthy air of the Bristol downs*: The air on the Bristol downs (or hills) was touted for its restorative powers, in part to attract punters to the nearby spa.
21. *Chairwomen*: A chairwoman or charwoman is hired to do odd domestic jobs.

22. *Jellies*: This does not refer to sweet jellies, but to clear, jellied stock or aspic in which meat is preserved.
23. *rouges a good deal*: Rouge, or red colour for the cheeks and lips, was becoming unfashionable in the 1780s, suggesting Susan Lesley's lack of taste. In novels, rouge often marks the wearer as frivolous or immoral, hence Susan's protest later in the story when her brother accuses her of an artificial complexion.
24. *Brighthelmstone*: Now called Brighton, this town has been an extremely popular seaside resort since the mid-eighteenth century. The Prince of Wales (later Prince Regent and George IV) moved there in 1784 and built several famous pavilions.
25. *four thousand pounds*: This refers to a capital sum upon whose interest the owner would usually subsist. A sum of this nature would probably bring an annual income of £200 (invested at the typical 5% interest at the time). Here, though, Charlotte believes her friend will simply spend the money all at once.
26. *Curry*: See note 8 to '[Detached peices]'.
27. *set her cap at him*: In *S&S*, Marianne Dashwood objects strongly to the use of this term for attracting a man, stating: 'I abhor every common-place phrase by which wit is intended; and, "setting one's cap at a man," or "making a conquest," are the most odious of all' (I, ix).
28. *Portman-Square*: A fashionable location in London.
29. *Scotch Airs . . . everything Scotch*: The eighteenth century saw a craze for Scottish melodies and songs ('Airs') prompted by the popularity of writers like Allan Ramsay, James Thomson, Robert Fergusson, James Macpherson and, especially, Robert Burns.
30. *toilett*: Usually 'toilette'. It refers both to the dressing table and to the activities of grooming.
31. *Galleries and Antichambers*: Galleries are long passages often found in large medieval and Elizabethan houses; a favourite setting in Gothic novels. They would often be used to display paintings and for women to take exercise in bad weather. JA uses the 'corrupt' spelling of antechamber; 'the chamber that leads to the chief apartment' (Johnson).
32. *Public-places*: This includes concert halls, theatres, dances, museums, exhibitions and pleasure gardens.
33. *Vaux-hall*: Located on the south bank of the river Thames, Vauxhall was a fashionable pleasure garden in London and one of the most popular venues for public entertainment from the seventeenth to the nineteenth centuries. It consisted of several

acres of park, including walkways, shrubberies, cascades, statues and various entertainments.

34. ***cold Beef . . . cut so thin***: Vauxhall was famous for the paper-thin slices of cold beef and ham that could be obtained there.

35. ***Receipts***: Recipes.

36. ***drawing Pullets***: Gutting young chickens in preparation for cooking.

37. ***Country-dance***: Country-dances of rural origin were considered inferior to more formal, courtly dances like the minuet.

38. ***Malbrook***: A French folk-song, 'Malbroucke *s'en va-t-en guerre*' (Marlborough is going to battle), celebrating the military achievements of the Duke of Marlborough and sung to the tune of 'For he's a jolly good fellow' (Doody and Murray, eds, *Catharine*, p. 326).

39. ***Bravo, Bravissimo, Encora, Da Capo, allegretto, con expressione***, and ***Poco presto***: A random and incongruous collection of Italian musical terms, some of which (*Da Capo*, *allegretto*, *con expressione*, *Poco presto*) are technical and descriptive, rather than expressive of admiration as Eloisa believes. *Poco presto* ('a little' and 'very fast') is a particularly nonsensical combination.

40. ***my Execution on the Harpsichord***: Her performance on the harpsichord, the keyboard instrument that most fashionable young women were expected to play. By the 1790s the new pianoforte, mentioned by JA in *Lady Susan*, was replacing this as the family instrument (Patrick Piggott, *The Innocent Diversion: Music in the Life and Writings of Jane Austen* [London: Clover Hill, 1979], pp. 32–7).

41. ***Grosvenor Street***: Fashionable street in London running from Hyde Park to New Bond Street.

42. ***proper size for real Beauty***: A recurring joke in JA's fiction, from 'Love and Freindship' to *P&P* and *E*. Apparently JA herself was fairly tall (*FR*, p. 80), and in all her literary instances the ideal height for a woman seems to veer towards the tall but not too tall, as in the case of Jane Fairfax in *E* (II, ii).

43. ***Toad-eater***: Like the contemporary term 'toady', this term for an insincere sycophant is derived from the practice of the mountebank's assistant who would pretend to swallow a toad so that the mountebank could appear to expel the toxins thus ingested.

44. ***celebrated both in Public, in Private, in Papers, and in Printshops***: Pictures of actresses, society ladies, renowned beauties

and even female criminals were offered for sale in print-sellers' shops.

45. ***Small-pox***: The small pox would often disfigure a woman's face with pock-marks but, having already had it, Margaret is immune to contracting it again.

46. ***Monday se'night***: Monday, seven nights ago, or a week last Monday.

47. ***Rout***: A large gathering or reception as opposed to a dinner party.

48. ***M[rs] Kickabout's***: Like the type names of the eighteenth-century drama, this implies a fashionable woman about town, possibly one who enjoys dancing.

49. ***on him depended the future Happiness of my Life***: This echoes the precipitate sentiments of Laura, the heroine of 'Love and Freindship' upon her first introduction to her future husband Lindsay, aka Talbot.

50. ***Lady Flambeau's***: Another type name reminiscent of the eighteenth-century drama. A 'flambeau' was a flaming torch used to light the way of guests as they went to and from their carriages.

51. ***Pope's Bulls***: A document whose power lies in the affixed papal seal representing a papal edict. In this case the bull is to invalidate Sir Lesley's marriage on the grounds of his spouse being Protestant rather than Roman Catholic.

The History of England

1. ***to the death of Charles the 1st***: JA dates her history 26 November 1791. She sets up her history as a pro-Stuart dramatic tragedy climaxing in the execution of Charles I, boldly inverting the prevailing Whig view of history (see Christopher Kent, 'Learning History with, and from, Jane Austen', in *Jane Austen's Beginnings: The Juvenilia and Lady Susan*, ed. J. David Grey [Ann Arbor, Michigan, and London: UMI Research Press, 1989] p. 64). Her attitude to reading 'real solemn history' is voiced by Catherine Morland in *NA*, 'it tells me nothing that does not either vex or weary me. The quarrels of popes and kings, with wars or pestilences, in every page; the men all so good for nothing, and hardly any women at all—it is very tiresome: and yet I often think it odd that it should be so dull, for a great deal of it must be invention' (I, xiv). Thus a major source for her history,

as she acknowledges, is Shakespeare's history plays from *Richard II* to *Henry VIII*.

The wording of her title indicates that she is parodying the four-volume *The History of England from the Earliest Times to the Death of George II* (1771) by Oliver Goldsmith (1728–74) (all future quotations from Goldsmith refer to this edition, by volume and page number). JA's copy of this work (passed down to her by her brother James, whose signature is in all four volumes) contains over a hundred marginal comments by her, all reflecting her vehement pro-Stuart stance (*Juvenilia*, pp. 316–55). The book is essentially a biased and trivialized abridgement of *The History of England from the Invasion of Julius Caesar to the Revolution in 1688* (6 vols, 1754–62) by the great historian David Hume (1711–76). JA's 'The History of England' is dated November 1791 and was written soon after Goldsmith's publication.

2. ***partial, prejudiced, and ignorant Historian***: JA cannot resist the challenge of Goldsmith's smug concluding remark in his 'Preface' to that, 'as I have endeavoured to get an honest reputation by liberal pursuits, it is hoped the reader will admit my impartiality' (1.viii). JA mocks Goldsmith's claim of impartiality by parodying his Whig Protestant bias with her own declaration of partiality and a fervently Tory pro-Catholic stance, including abuse of those readers who dared to disagree. JA also parodies Goldsmith's scant regard for dates and includes only four dates in her history, as indicated at the foot of her title page.

3. ***To Miss Austen***: Cassandra Austen (1773–1845), whose illustrations to 'The History of England' extend her sister's parody both in terms of the historical monarchs and in relation to the Austen family: see Introduction. All but one of her thirteen medallion portraits are signed 'C E Austen pinx' ('painted it') indicating not only a joking reference to her pretense at professionalism but also her own desire to be taken seriously as a talented artist.

4. ***Henry the 4***th: Henry Bolingbroke (1366–1413), eldest son of John of Gaunt, Duke of Lancaster, and grandson of King Edward III; King of England from 1399 to 1413. During his career he had earned the enmity of his cousin, Richard II, who banished him from England in 1398 and, on the death of John of Gaunt in the following year, confiscated all the Lancastrian estates to the crown. The outraged Bolingbroke invaded England and rallied the nobles in his support. Richard, who had been briefly absent in Ireland, surrendered on his return, and abdicated in favour of

Bolingbroke, who ascended the throne as Henry IV. He was the first of the Lancastrian monarchs.

5. *for the rest of his Life*: An example of JA's black humour, as Richard was murdered four months later at the age of thirty-three.

6. *Pomfret Castle*: Richard II, after being forced to abdicate in September 1399, was imprisoned in the remote Lancastrian fortress of Pontefract Castle in Yorkshire. Both Shakespeare and Goldsmith refer to this castle as 'Pomfret'.

7. *happened to be murdered*: Goldsmith and Shakespeare provide accounts of the murder. Richard died at Pontefract in February 1400, after a short period of imprisonment, but there is no reliable evidence for his murder.

8. *to be supposed that Henry was Married*: The list of characters in Shakespeare's *Henry IV* includes the king and his four sons, but there is no queen. Austen relies on Shakespeare as her source rather than Goldsmith, who notes that 'by his first wife, Mary de Bohun, he had four sons . . . and two daughters' (2.174).

9. *took away the crown*: Goldsmith records that the dying Henry IV, 'was subject to fits, which bereaved him for the time, of his senses', and was so fearful of being usurped as king, that he 'could not be persuaded to sleep, unless the royal diadem were laid upon his pillow' (2.172).

10. *Sir William Gascoigne*: William Gascoigne (*c.*1350–1419), a talented Yorkshire lawyer and advocate, who had loyally served the House of Lancaster and Henry Bolingbroke, was appointed as chief justice of the court of King's Bench when the latter succeeded to the throne in 1399. Goldsmith records that the Prince of Wales struck the judge in court and the 'venerable magistrate' committed the prince to prison (2.171–2); and Shakespeare makes much of Prince Hal's offence and his later praise of the judge, an incident now historically suspect.

11. *Henry the 5th*: King of England from 1413 to 1422. Cassandra's image of this monarch as a young military officer is inspired by H. W. Bunbury's caricature print *The Relief* (1781); but she has made changes to represent JA's brother Henry Austen, then aged twenty-one and in the Royal Regiment of Artillery, the uniform depicted by Cassandra (see Introduction).

12. *forsaking all his dissipated Companions*: Goldsmith records that Henry V, as Prince of Wales, 'ever chose to be surrounded by a set of wretches, who took pride in committing the most illegal acts, with the prince at their head' (2.171), but in one of his 'first steps' as king, 'He had called together his former com-

panions, acquainted them with his intended reformation; exhorted them to follow his example; and thus dismissed them from his presence' (2.176). Shakespeare also dramatizes the king's repudiation of his former friends, especially Falstaff, in *Henry IV*, *Part 2*.

13. ***Lord Cobham***: Sir John Oldcastle (*c.*1378–1417), a distinguished soldier, inherited the title of Lord Cobham in 1409. His friendship with the Prince of Wales had dated from their service together in the Welsh wars. King Henry V, however, was unable to persuade his former friend to recant his support of the Lollards, an English sect associated with the teachings of John Wycliffe. After several escapes from prison, and involvement in a Lollard plot to kidnap the king, Cobham was executed for heresy and treason in 1417. Shakespeare had included the character Sir John Oldcastle in an early version of *Henry IV*, but later changed this name to Falstaff.
14. ***burnt alive, but I forget what for***: It is clear that JA, from the events recorded in her own 'History', is aware that the sentence of being 'burnt alive' was imposed for heresy. Sir John Oldcastle, Lord Cobham, would later be considered as a martyr for English Protestantism. JA, who presents herself as biased towards Catholicism, glosses over such events. This offhand reference is in keeping with her later remark on the executions for heresy in the reign of Queen Mary.
15. ***turned his thoughts to France***: The phrasing suggests that JA is using Shakespeare's *Henry V* rather than Goldsmith as her source: compare Shakespeare's 'For we have now no thought in us but France' (I.ii.302).
16. ***Battle of Agincourt***: JA's reference to this momentous English victory over the French in 1415 identifies this king as a great military leader, and is a compliment to the military ambitions of her brother, Henry Austen, whose image appears as 'Henry the 5th'.
17. ***agreable Woman by Shakespear's account***: In *Henry V* the king successfully woos the French princess, who is not only pleasant and kisses him, but also agrees to marry him (V.ii.231). Austen's joke on the meaning of 'agreable' is an example of her early fascination with wordplay and hidden meanings.
18. ***Henry the 6th***: King of England from 1422 to 1461 and October 1470 to April 1471. Henry VI (1421–71) succeeded to the throne as an infant, and ruled in person from the age of sixteen. He was totally unsuited to government, and was unable to control the

increasingly bitter power struggles between his leading nobles of Lancaster and York and their rival claims to the throne that led to the Wars of the Roses from 1455. Cassandra's portrayal of this monarch in clerical vestments suggests his lack of interest in worldly affairs; the image may also represent the young clergyman Tom Fowle, then aged twenty-seven, a close friend and former pupil at Steventon, and soon to be engaged to Cassandra (1795): see Introduction.

19. ***for this Monarch's Sense***: Henry may have inherited his chronic mental illness from his maternal grandfather, the French king, Charles VI, who also suffered periods of insanity.

20. ***Duke of York . . . the right side***: JA is correct in terms of strict primogeniture as Richard, 3rd Duke of York, was a descendant of Lionel, Duke of Clarence, third son of Edward III. Henry VI was descended from Lionel's younger brother, John of Gaunt, Duke of Lancaster, and his claim to the throne was weaker. Austen's support for the Yorkist cause is based rather on her hatred of the Tudors, and Elizabeth in particular. Henry VII, the first Tudor monarch, would also justify his claim to the throne on his descent from the Duke of Lancaster, John of Gaunt.

21. ***vent my Spleen***: The organ traditionally associated with anger, 'Spleen' in this context means 'violent ill-nature or ill-humour' (*OED*). JA's passionate outpouring against the Lancastrians (red rose) enacts her 'partial' championing of claims of the Yorkists (white rose) in the Wars of the Roses.

22. ***Margaret of Anjou***: (1430–82). The young French queen consort of Henry VI, according to Goldsmith, was 'considered the most accomplished [princess] of the age, both in mind and person' (2.213).

23. ***distresses and Misfortunes***: These began with her marriage in 1445 at the age of fifteen to the mentally unstable king; and her only son, Prince Edward, was killed by Yorkist forces at the Battle of Tewkesbury in 1471. Shakespeare presents her unsympathetically, but Goldsmith comments that 'this extraordinary woman, after having sustained the cause of her husband in twelve battles, after having survived her friends, fortunes, and children, died, a few years after, in privacy in France, very miserable indeed; but with few other claims to our pity, except her courage and her distresses' (2.246).

24. ***Joan of Arc . . . made such a <u>row</u> among the English***: Joan of Arc (*c*.1412–31), a peasant girl, who believed that she was under divine guidance to save France from the English, led the French

forces to a great victory in 1429, before her capture by the English. She was tried before a church court for heresy and sentenced to burn at the stake in 1431. JA's idiomatic usage 'to make a row', referring to making a disturbance or commotion, was considered 'a very low expression' (Johnson).

25. ***Edward the 4th . . . Picture we have here given of him***: Edward IV (1442–83), eldest son of Richard, Duke of York, was King of England from March 1461 to October 1470 and April 1471 to April 1483. According to Goldsmith, 'His best qualities were courage and beauty; his bad, a combination of all the vices' (2.250). Cassandra's doltish image reinforces JA's mockery of his alleged 'beauty'. It was inspired by H. W. Bunbury's caricature print *Recruits* (1780), but Cassandra has made changes to the face and costume to represent their pompous young clergyman cousin Edward Cooper, then aged twenty-two: see Introduction.

26. ***marrying one Woman while he was engaged to another***: In 1464, while Edward IV's council was completing the negotiations for his marriage to Bona of Savoy, the young king secretly married a beautiful lady of the court, Elizabeth Woodville (1437–92), widow of Sir John Grey.

27. ***poor Woman!***: JA's interest in historical women is especially evident here in her record of Edward IV's otherwise uneventful reign. Elizabeth Woodville was confined to Bermondsey Abbey for the final years of her life until her death in 1492; presumably ordered by her son-in-law, Henry VII, so that he could gain access to her lands and wealth.

28. ***Jane Shore . . . a play written about her***: *The Tragedy of Jane Shore: Written in Imitation of Shakespeare's Style* (1714) by Nicholas Rowe (1674–1718) dramatizes the 'tragedy' of this beautiful and seemingly virtuous wife of a rich goldsmith who was seduced by Edward IV. This play was still popular in the early 1790s.

29. ***no body had time to draw his picture***: In fact Goldsmith did include a medallion portrait of this monarch. JA's humorous explanation for the lack of a 'picture' draws attention to the importance of Cassandra's portraits in the meaning of the text, where even absence is significant. Edward V (1470–83) was twelve when he succeeded to the throne in April 1483 and died in June the same year.

30. ***Richard the 3d***: Richard III (1452–85), King of England from 1483 to 1485. Cassandra's image of Richard III may resemble

Richard Buller, who shares the same name and was a pupil at Steventon rectory during this period. Without an image of Buller for comparison, however, this cannot be verified: see Introduction.

31. ***a very respectable Man***: There seems to have been an Austen family joke about the name 'Richard'. In a letter to Cassandra dated 15 September 1796, Austen remarks that 'Mr Richard Harvey's match is put off, till he has got a Better Christian name, of which he has great Hopes' (*Letters*, p. 10). In *NA*, Catherine Morland's clergyman father is described as a 'very respectable man, though his name was Richard' (I, i). It is possible that Richard Buller also came in for some affectionate teasing about his name and may even have shared in the joke against him.

32. ***declared that he did <u>not</u> kill his two Nephews***: Richard served his brother Edward IV loyally but on his death deprived his two sons of their rights to the succession, and had himself proclaimed king. The question of Richard III's guilt of the subsequent murder of his two nephews had become open to debate in the eighteenth century, particularly with the publication in 1768 of the novelist Horace Walpole's *Historic Doubts on the Life and Reign of King Richard the Third*. In JA's 'Catharine', the heroine engages in an 'historical dispute' with Stanley, who is happy to take the opposite view to her by 'warmly defending' the character of Richard III.

33. ***which I am inclined to beleive true***: JA now blithely disregards her statement in the previous chapter, that Edward V was 'murdered by his Uncle's Contrivance'.

34. ***he did not kill his Wife***: Both Shakespeare (*Richard III*, IV.ii. 49–58) and Goldsmith (2.270) represent the king as involved in the murder of his wife, Anne Neville, in 1485, although Richard III made a public denial and assurance of his own grief.

35. ***if Perkin Warbeck was really the Duke of York***: An imposter, who in the reign of Henry VII claimed to be Richard, Duke of York, one of the Princes in the Tower, and was accepted by various European monarchs as well as York family members, until his confession in 1497.

36. ***Lambert Simnel***: Another imposter, who in 1487, two years after the accession of Henry VII, claimed to be Edward, Earl of Warwick, the nephew of the late king, Richard III.

37. ***made a great fuss . . . battle of Bosworth***: By her use of colloquialism, JA is reducing historical events to everyday occurrences. Bosworth was the final battle of the Wars of the Roses, fought in August 1485, with the Yorkist King Richard III defeated and

slain, while the victorious Lancastrian claimant, Henry Tudor, Earl of Richmond, took the throne as Henry VII, reigning from 1485 to 1509. Thus he founded JA's hated Tudor dynasty that culminated in the reign of the 'wicked' Elizabeth I.

38. ***This Monarch . . . pretended to the contrary***: King of England from 1485 to 1509. Henry VII's marriage to Princess Elizabeth, daughter of Edward IV, in January 1486 secured his own position by uniting the two opposing Houses of Lancaster and York.
39. ***had the happiness of being grandmother***: An example of JA's parodic humour. In 1503, Henry VII's elder daughter Margaret Tudor married James IV of Scotland, but since their granddaughter Mary Stuart, Queen of Scots, was born in 1542, a year after Margaret's death, she would hardly have enjoyed such happiness. JA highlights here the absurdity that can result in the Whig historian's 'preoccupation with anticipations and forerunners' (Kent, 'Learning History', p. 65).
40. ***amiable young Woman***: Lady Jane Grey (1537–54) is also described as 'amiable' in Hume's *History of Great Britain* (1754), a possible indication that JA had also read this text (see Kent, 'Learning History', p. 67). Goldsmith describes her as 'the wonder of her age' and includes an account of her 'reading Plato's works in Greek, while all the rest of the family were hunting in the Park' (3.36).
41. ***Henry the 8th***: Henry VIII (1491–1547) was King of England from 1509 to 1547. Cassandra ridicules him in an image suggesting the popular caricatures by James Gillray of the Whig politician Charles James Fox, the arch-enemy of the Austens' friend Warren Hastings at his impeachment trial (a suggestion made to the editor by Annette Upfal). In particular, the red cap of liberty that Gillray uses to mock Fox's enthusiastic support for the revolutionary wars in America and the French Revolution (seen especially the scurrilous caricature *Westminster School*, 1785) is used by Cassandra to reinforce JA's hostility to Henry VIII.
42. ***come to lay his bones among them***: A paraphrase of Goldsmith's description of the last days of Cardinal Wolsey (1475–1530), Henry VIII's powerful Lord Chancellor who was accused of treason (2.361).
43. ***Anna Bullen***: JA follows the spelling used by Shakespeare and Goldsmith for Anne Boleyn (*c.*1507–36), the second wife of Henry VIII and mother of Elizabeth I. When Henry's affections waned, she was accused of adultery, committed to the Tower of London and beheaded.

44. ***dated on the 6th of May***: Anne's letter to the king pleading her own innocence, and that of the men accused with her, is dated 'From my doleful prison in the Tower, this sixth of May'. The letter is reproduced in full by Goldsmith and carries one of only two dates in his book (2.384). Austen's formal elaborate reference to this date mocks Goldsmith's failure, when he does supply a date, to provide the year it was written.
45. ***Crimes and Cruelties of this Prince***: Goldsmith provides a detailed account of the 'crimes and cruelties' (2.418) of Henry VIII, who remains infamous for his six wives and the removal of two by execution.
46. ***abolishing Religious Houses***: In 1534, Parliament passed the Act of Supremacy, which made the monarch 'Supreme Head of the Church in England', enabling Henry VIII to disband and confiscate the wealth of all Roman Catholic monasteries.
47. ***infinite use to the landscape of England in general***: The vogue for visiting medieval monastic ruins in the late eighteenth century was cultivated by the writers of Gothic novels and influenced by the travel writings of Gilpin and his analysis of the picturesque in landscape.
48. ***a principal motive for his doing it***: JA embellishes her previous mockery of Whig historians and their preoccupation with tracing forerunners to historical change. In this example, Henry not only envisions the consequences of his actions more than two hundred years in the future, but arranges his own affairs accordingly.
49. ***His Majesty's 5th wife***: Catherine Howard (*c.*1521–42), niece of Thomas Howard, 3rd Duke of Norfolk, met the same fate as her cousin, Anne Boleyn.
50. ***noble Duke of Norfolk . . . cause***: Thomas Howard, 4th Duke of Norfolk (1538–72), was grandson of the 3rd Duke, and a favoured nobleman in the reign of Elizabeth I. Norfolk, however, was secretly in favour of restoring Catholicism to England; and he was a supporter and would-be suitor of Mary, Queen of Scots—hence JA's *double entendre* implying a 'warm' sexual passion by Norfolk for the young queen. Southam also notes a possible 'sly allusion' to the historical novel *The Recess; or, A Tale of Other Times* (1785) by Sophia Lee (1750–1824), which features a secret marriage between Norfolk and Mary (Jane Austen, *Volume the Second*, ed. Brian Southam [Oxford: Clarendon Press, 1963], p. 215). He was executed for treason in 1572 for his role in a Spanish plot to invade England and place Mary Stuart on the throne.

51. ***The king's last wife . . . with difficulty effected it***: Catherine Parr (1512–48). Henry died in January 1547, and his widow Catherine was secretly married in April to her former suitor, Thomas, Lord Seymour, a brother of Henry VIII's third wife Jane Seymour, but died after the birth of a daughter, in September 1548.
52. ***Edward the 6***[th]: King of England from 1547 to 1553. He succeeded to the throne as an orphaned child of nine and died at the age of fifteen. Cassandra disregards the reality that this king reigned as a child and portrays him as a finely dressed young gentleman, probably JA's wealthy elder brother Edward Austen, then aged twenty-five: see Introduction.
53. ***Duke of Somerset***: Edward Seymour (*c.*1506–52), eldest brother of Henry VIII's third wife Jane Seymour, mother of the young King Edward.
54. ***somewhat of a favourite with me***: Somerset had been an outstanding military commander and had proved his courage and daring in a brilliant victory over the French at Boulogne in 1545. His handsome looks and personal qualities of charm and generosity all added to a romantic image that may have appealed to the young JA.
55. ***those first of Men Robert Earl of Essex, Delamere, or Gilpin***: Robert Devereux, 2nd Earl of Essex (1567–1601) was a dashing young soldier and courtier who became a favourite of the ageing Queen Elizabeth, but fell from favour. Similarly, Frederic Delamere, the ardent suitor of the heroine in Smith's *Emmeline*, is rejected. For William Gilpin, see note 58 to 'Love and Freindship'.
56. ***that such was the death of Mary Queen of Scotland***: Austen uses this episode both to eulogize Mary and to emphasize her central role as heroine in this fictional history. The absurdity of Somerset being proud of his beheading because a future monarch would suffer a similar death continues JA's parody of Goldsmith's penchant for anticipations in his historical commentary.
57. ***Duke of Northumberland***: Goldsmith recounts the rivalry between John Dudley, Duke of Northumberland (1502–53) and Somerset, whose downfall and execution Northumberland had orchestrated. He engineered the marriage of his son to Lady Jane Grey, whom he proclaimed queen against her consent on the death of the young Edward. Despite the considerable sympathy for Lady Jane Grey as the innocent pawn of Northumberland, she and her husband were found guilty of treason and beheaded in 1554.
58. ***mentioned as—reading Greek***: The dash is significant as JA mocks the basis for Lady Jane Grey's reputation for great

learning. Sabor suggests that JA's 'comic treatment' of Lady Jane appeals to contemporary prejudice against learned ladies (*Juvenilia*, p. 464). Her harsh comments in the following passage, however, suggest JA may be employing a defence mechanism, countering her own sensitivity about gaining a similar reputation as another learned 'Jane'.

59. ***vanity***: JA originally wrote the much coarser word 'Cockylorum' ('cockalorum'), meaning 'a self-important little man', and underlined it for emphasis (see Textual Notes). JA's apparent misspelling of this term may have been deliberate to indicate a female gender. The term 'cocky', dating to 1768, is defined as 'Arrogantly pert' and could be applied to a woman (*OED*).

60. ***Mary***: Mary Tudor (1516–58), the daughter of Henry VIII and his first wife, Catherine of Aragon, was Queen of England from 1553 to 1558. A devout Catholic, she married Philip, heir to the throne of Spain, and they attempted to restore Catholicism to England. It was Philip's enormous Spanish Armada of over a hundred ships that famously attempted to invade England in 1588. Cassandra's rather frumpish image may represent Austen's friend and former neighbour Mary Lloyd, then aged twenty-one, who, six years later, would become the second wife of James Austen: see Introduction.

61. ***Martyrs to the protestant Religion . . . dozen***: JA's comic dismissal of 'Bloody Mary's' rigorous enforcement of the heresy laws is part of her pro-Catholic, pro-Stuart stance in her history. Goldsmith records that 'two hundred and seventy-seven suffered by fire, besides those punished by imprisonment, fines, and confiscations' (3.62).

62. ***Elizabeth***: Elizabeth I (1533–1603), daughter of Henry VIII and his second wife, Anne Boleyn; Queen of England from 1558 to 1603, a reign of forty-five peaceful years that have been termed a 'golden age'. Cassandra departs from Goldsmith's format of a single image to portray the two queens who face each other as opposites. The witch-like image of Elizabeth in her garish finery can be identified as that of Austen's mother, Cassandra Leigh Austen, then aged fifty-three, who is formally dressed as if to attend a ball. The image of the young and beautiful Mary, Queen of Scots, also in formal attire, can be positively identified as that of Jane Austen, who would be seventeen on 16 December 1792: see Introduction.

63. ***Misfortune of this Woman to have bad Ministers***: JA parodies and inverts Goldsmith's assertion that it was Elizabeth's 'good fortune, that her ministers were excellent' (3.152). JA continues

her hostility to Elizabeth in 'Catharine', when the heroine says to Camilla Stanley: 'I hope you will not defend her'.

64. ***Lord Burleigh, Sir Francis Walsingham***: JA names the two ministers who were most closely implicated in Mary Stuart's fate. William Cecil (1520–98), created Lord Burleigh in 1571, was Elizabeth's principal and most trusted advisor for the greater part of her reign; and Sir Francis Walsingham (1532–90) was appointed secretary of state in 1573.

65. ***Mr Whitaker, Mrs Lefroy, Mrs Knight***: John Whitaker (1735–1808), author of *Mary, Queen of Scots, Vindicated* (1787); Anne Bridges Lefroy (1749–1804), wife of the rector of Ashe, near Steventon, a mentor and friend of the younger JA; and Catherine Knatchbull Knight (1753–1812), Edward Austen's wealthy adoptive mother. JA may have been alerted to Whitaker's work by a reference in Gilpin's *Observations, Relative Chiefly to Picturesque Beauty* (see note 58 to 'Love and Freindship').

66. ***abandoned by her Son***: James Stuart (1566–1625), James VI of Scotland, was the only son of Mary and her second husband, Lord Darnley. In 1567 Mary was forced to renounce the Scottish throne in favour of her infant son, and she never saw him again. James, who was reared as a Protestant, made only a token effort to save his mother from execution, merely sending a formal protest that would not jeopardize his own position as successor to the childless Elizabeth.

67. ***Fortheringay Castle . . . 1586***: Fotheringay Castle was a heavily fortified castle in Northamptonshire, where Mary was imprisoned for nineteen years until her execution on 8 February 1587. Austen names the year incorrectly as 1586.

68. ***Sir Francis Drake . . . one who tho' now but young***: Francis Drake (*c.*1540–96), considered the greatest seaman of his age, circumnavigated the globe in 1580 with his ship *The Golden Hind*, and played a leading role defeating the Spanish Armada in 1588. JA's comparison is a complimentary reference to her brother Francis, now seventeen, who had been on naval service in the East Indies for nearly two years. Francis became Rear Admiral in 1830, was knighted in 1837, and became Admiral of the Fleet in 1863 at the age of eighty-nine.

69. ***Emmeline of Delamere***: Charlotte Smith's heroine Emmeline was 'tormented' by Delamere's unwanted attentions, his rash conduct including her abduction to Scotland, and his impassioned demands that she marry him. JA has reversed the situation, as in

the case of Essex, whose reckless conduct and treasonable conduct finally led to his execution.

70. ***25th of Febry***: JA omits the year—1601.

71. ***clapped his hand on his sword***: Goldsmith records that Essex had 'turned his back on the queen in a contemptuous manner . . . [and] she gave him a box on the ear'. Essex, in response, 'clapped his hand to his sword; and swore he would not bear such usage even from her father. This offence, though very great, was overlooked by the queen' (3.139). JA implies that this thrreat to Elizabeth was one of his 'services to his Country'.

72. ***died so miserable***: Elizabeth survived Essex by only two years. Goldsmith says that following the execution of her favourite, she 'was never seen to enjoy one happy day more' (3.150).

73. ***James the 1st . . . I cannot help liking him***: Cassandra's image of a fashionably dressed young gentleman may represent James Austen, then aged twenty-seven, thus suggesting here a playful hidden reference by JA to her eldest brother. James I (1566–1625), King of England from 1603 to 1625 and also King of Scotland as James VI (1567–1625), was the first Stuart king of England.

74. ***his unfortunate Brother***: Charles, as king, would suffer the 'evils' of the revolt of his subjects and a long civil war, imprisonment, trial and finally, in 1649, his public execution.

75. ***partial to the roman catholic religion***: A daring remark for the daughter of an Anglican clergyman, but her siblings would have appreciated the joke, as JA affects a pro-Catholic stance in her history in opposition to the openly Protestant bias of Goldsmith and most other eighteenth-century English historians.

76. ***Their Behaviour . . . as very uncivil***: JA is alluding to the Gunpowder Plot of 1605, in which a number of Catholic conspirators, including Guy Fawkes, plotted to kill the king and royal family and blow up the Houses of Parliament. The plot was discovered when one of the conspirators sent an anonymous letter to the Catholic nobleman Lord Monteagle (JA uses Goldsmith's spelling), warning him not to attend at Parliament, and he immediately passed on the letter to Lord Salisbury, the secretary of state. JA follows Goldsmith in identifying (inaccurately) the author of the letter as Sir Henry Percy.

77. ***his Attentions were entirely Confined to Lord Mounteagle***: JA seizes on Goldsmith's phrase, 'his intimate friend and companion' (3.167), to make her own risqué joke implying a homosexual relationship.

78. ***Sir Walter Raleigh***: Walter Raleigh (*c*.1554–1618), a famous courtier, scholar, explorer and sometime favourite of Elizabeth, knighted in 1585. Raleigh testified against his former close associate, the Earl of Essex, at the trial that led to his execution; Raleigh endured a long imprisonment in the Tower of London and was executed by James I.
79. ***with the particulars of his Life . . . the Critic***: Austen, as partial historian, registers her contempt for any such enquiry by directing readers to Sheridan's *The Critic*. The comedy centres on the rehearsal of the playwright Mr Puff's tragedy, *The Spanish Armada*. Whilst Sir Walter Raleigh and Sir Christopher Hatton appear as characters in this ludicrous play-within-a-play, *The Critic* is devoid of further information on Raleigh's life.
80. ***keener penetration in Discovering Merit***: A *double entendre* aimed at the king's sexual preferences, and his appointment of handsome but untalented young men to high office.
81. ***Sharade***: Charade: A riddle in which individual syllables are described or acted out, to discover the meaning of the whole word. The Austens were very fond of charades and, apart from the novels, one of the first Austen items to be published was a collection of charades and conundrums in 1895, written by members of her immediate family, including three by JA herself (Doody and Murray, eds, *Catharine*, p. 369). Emma plays charades with Harriet and Mr Elton (*Emma*, I, ix).
82. ***was to King James the 1st***: Another allusion to the homosexuality of the king, who installed 'Carr', a handsome youth of seventeen, as his favourite or 'pet' in the office of 'gentleman of the bedchamber'. The son of an impoverished Scottish nobleman, Robert Carr (1590–1645) caught the eye of the king when he arrived at the English court in 1607; he was made Viscount Rochester in 1611, a privy councillor in 1612 and Earl of Somerset and Treasurer of Scotland in 1613.
83. ***Duke of Buckingham***: George Villiers (1592–1628), the handsome son of a Leicestershire knight, who replaced Somerset as the king's favourite. Buckingham was appointed Lord High Admiral in 1619, and was virtual ruler of England in the king's final years. He was arrogant and inept, managing to alienate both the upper classes and Parliament from the monarchy. Unfortunately for the Stuart monarchy, Buckingham's policies continued in the first three years of the reign of King Charles I, further isolating the monarch, who had to dissolve Parliament in 1626 to prevent his favourite from being impeached. The

news of his murder in 1628 was met with almost universal rejoicing.

84. ***Charles the 1st . . . his lovely Grandmother***: Austen's marginalia in the family copy of Goldsmith's *History of England* (1771) begins with the reign of Charles I and the Civil War, denouncing Cromwell and again indicating her partiality for the Stuarts. Charles I (1600–49), grandson of Mary, Queen of Scots, was King of England from 1625 to 1649, when he was beheaded for 'high treason' following the defeat in 1645 of Royalist forces by the parliamentary 'New Model Army' commanded by Sir Thomas Fairfax and Oliver Cromwell.

85. ***Archbishop Laud . . . Ormond***: William Laud (1573–1645), Archbishop of Canterbury, executed in 1645; Sir Thomas Wentworth (1593–1641), Earl of Strafford, executed in 1641; Lucius Cary (1610–43), Viscount Falkland, a moderating influence in Parliament; and James Butler (1610–88), Duke of Ormonde, leader of the Royalist forces in Ireland. Strafford was distantly related to JA, through her mother's family the Leighs, and she would later use the surname of Wentworth for her hero in *P*.

86. ***leaders of the Gang***: JA also makes brief and hostile references to Oliver Cromwell ('detestible monster!') and John Hampden in the marginalia of the family copy of Goldsmith's *History of England*. Oliver Cromwell (1599–1658), fervent supporter of Parliament and the execution of the king, was made Lord Protector of the republican commonwealth of England, Scotland and Ireland, until his death five years later. Thomas Fairfax (1612–71) was commander of the parliamentary forces; and John Hampden (1594–1643), a cousin of Cromwell, also served in the parliamentary forces and was killed in the Battle of Chalgrove in June 1643. Goldsmith writes glowingly of Hampden as gaining 'by his inflexible integrity, the esteem even of his enemies. To these he added affability in conversation, temper, art, eloquence in debate, and penetration in counsel' (3.268). JA comments in the marginalia, 'What a pity that such virtues shd be clouded by Republicanism!' (320). John Pym (1583–1643) was a key supporter of Cromwell in Parliament.

A Collection of Letters

1. ***Miss Cooper***: Jane Cooper was JA's cousin. Since she was married to Captain Williams in December 1792 and the dedication cites her maiden name, the letters must pre-date her marriage.

Southam suggests late 1791 or early 1792, 'certainly before "Lesley Castle"' (*Literary MSS*, p. 31).

2. ***Clime***: Contraction of 'climate'; used poetically to indicate a particular region.
3. ***that age . . . become conversant with the World***: Referring to the act of 'coming out'. This was a rite of passage for genteel young women, who, upon reaching a certain age, were understood as taking their place in society.
4. ***entrée***: Here the word is being used to designate the formal entrance into polite society.
5. ***Morning-Visits***: Short, pre-dinner visits made from around midday (after breakfast, which was late) to about 3 p.m. People would often make several such visits in the same day.
6. ***infancy***: Johnson cites 'infancy' as extending in English law from childhood to the age of twenty-one (Johnson).
7. ***Willoughby . . . Crawfords . . . Dashwood***: Surnames later used in JA's novels: Willoughby and the Dashwoods in *S&S*, and the Crawfords in *MP*.
8. ***Melancholy***: Formerly seen as a disease of the nervous system associated with men, melancholy became increasingly understood in the eighteenth century as a feminine complaint, largely due to the impact of the cult of sensibility. (See Janet Todd, ed., *Jane Austen in Context* [Cambridge: Cambridge University Press, 2005], pp. 311–12).
9. ***I am advised to ride by my Physician***: Riding was thought to be beneficial to health. In *MP*, Fanny Price's health deteriorates when she is deprived of the mare Edmund purchases for her use (I, vii).
10. ***Ride where you may, Be Candid where You can***: A humorous appropriation of an aphorism from Pope's *Essay on Man*: 'Laugh where we *must*, be candid where we *can*' (I, 15).
11. ***fighting for his Country in America***: A reference to the American War of Independence (1775–83) between the British and their rebel colonies.
12. ***I dropt all thoughts of either***: This suggests that, on top of the rather suspect legality of her marriage, Miss Jane may also be illegitimate.
13. ***honour of calling for me in her way . . . sit forwards***: The honour is easily bestowed as Lady Greville is on her way to the ball; but sitting forwards, in the direction the carriage is moving, is the preferred position.

14. *old striped one*: By suggesting that Maria should wear an everyday gown to the ball, Lady Greville behaves like Lady Catherine de Bourgh in *P&P*, who, as Mr Collins says, 'will not think the worst of you for being simply dressed' because 'She likes to have the distinction of rank preserved' (II, vi).
15. *white Gloves*: Gentlemen were expected to wear white gloves during a formal dance.
16. *hop*: A colloquialism for a dance, usually one associated with simple country dances.
17. *Grocer or a Bookbinder*: As trades, neither occupation was permissible for a member of polite society. A wine merchant would be socially superior since he dealt in bulk as a wholesaler rather than a retailer, although Lady Greville pays no attention to the distinction.
18. *broke*: As in 'became broke', or bankrupt.
19. *as poor as a Rat*: A more offensive version of the expression 'poor as church mice'.
20. *King's Bench*: King's Bench was primarily a debtors' prison.
21. *too saucy*: JA made a number of revisions to this conversation, perhaps in an effort to preserve realism but still allow Maria some freedom to be impertinent (see Textual Notes).
22. *you may take an umbrella*: Unlike parasols, designed for blocking out the sun while strolling, umbrellas were associated with poverty because they suggested that the bearer was unable to afford a carriage.
23. *shews your legs*: JA originally wrote 'shews your Ancles', a less offensive comment (see Textual Notes).
24. *stand out of doors as you do in such a day as this*: Compare JA's later use of the same situation in *P&P* when Charlotte Collins is kept outdoors in the wind while speaking to Miss de Bourgh (II, v).
25. *Essex ... Derbyshire ... Suffolk*: Her surprise is due to the distance of Derbyshire from Essex, relative to Suffolk, which is much closer.
26. *dash*: A 'sudden stroke; blow' (Johnson).
27. *Musgrove*: The name reappears in *P*, where the heroine's sister Mary has married into the Musgrove family.
28. *Sackville*: A fashionable street in London that runs off Piccadilly.
29. *toasted*: Made the object of a romantic toast among men, a gesture that implied immodesty in the woman toasted.
30. *Abandoned*: This implies dissolute rather than forsaken.
31. *improvable Estate*: Referring here to an estate that would yield more revenue if it were improved or managed better, rather than

to 'improvement' of an estate with reference to the fashionable landscape gardening of the eighteenth century discussed in *MP* by James Rushworth (I, vi) and Henry Crawford (II, vii).

32. ***a pattern for a Love-letter***: Compilations of letters such as those penned by Samuel Richardson in *Letters written to and For Particular Friends on the Most Important Occasions* (1741) were used as models by letter writers.
33. ***dab***: Colloquialism for 'expert'.
34. ***give a farthing***: Echoing the proverbial expression 'not worth a farthing', the smallest English coin, worth only a quarter of a penny.
35. ***Several hundreds an year***: A very small income. Compare the income of Mrs Dashwood and her two daughters of £500 a year, which JA considers as living in much reduced circumstances (*S&S*, I, ii).
36. ***Yes I'm in love . . . has undone me***: Allusion to 'The Je Ne Sais Quoi' by William Whitehead (1715–85): 'Yes, I'm in love, I feel it now, / And Caelia has undone me'; a poem found in JA's copy of Dodsley's *Collection of Poems* (see note 26 to 'Jack and Alice').
37. ***make the pies***: An unladylike occupation. In *P&P*, Mrs Bennet boasts of the genteel upbringing of her daughters compared to Charlotte Lucas, who assists with 'the mince-pies' (I, ix).

[Scraps]

1. ***To Miss Fanny Catherine Austen***: Frances Knight (1793–1882), JA's first niece and the eldest daughter of her brother Edward. Fanny was born on 23 January 1793, so she was only an infant when JA jokes here about superintending her education. This dedication introduces the five following items titled 'Scraps' in the contents list but not here in the text.
2. ***Rowling and Steventon***: Rowling was the estate in east Kent given by the Knights to JA's brother Edward on his marriage. JA's home in Steventon was 100 miles west, in Hampshire.
3. ***Admonitions on the conduct of Young Women***: Conduct books or works of advice to young women were extremely popular in the eighteenth century: see Introduction.

The female philosopher

1. ***female philosopher***: This phrase evokes the conflict between Jacobins and anti-Jacobins, which tended to intensify around

questions of the intellectual capacity of women. JA uses the phrase to mock female aspirations to intellectualism.

2. ***Sallies, Bonmots and repartées***: The meaning of 'sally' derives from military terminology where to 'sally forth' is to make a sudden advance. It denotes a bold witticism or clever retort, as do the following two French words (see note 8 to 'Lesley Castle').
3. ***Sentiments of Morality***: Julia's 'sensible reflections' are derived from conduct books, as in the case of Mary Bennet in *P&P*.
4. ***Cordial kiss***: This would be considered inappropriate as English gentlemen were not encouraged to indulge in physical demonstrations of affection.
5. ***five or six months with us***: To expect to stay for a period of this excessive length is abominably rude.
6. ***Arabella***: A fashionable name, used by JA again in the following 'A Tale'.

The first Act of a Comedy

1. ***Postilion***: See note 22 to 'Frederic and Elfrida'.
2. ***Strephon***: A generic name for a pastoral lover, whose beloved is traditionally called Chloe.
3. ***the Lion***: The public rooms in inns have names such as Lion, Moon and Sun; the bedrooms have numbers.
4. ***bill of fare***: Menu
5. ***I wull, I wull***: This is most likely the phonetic rendering of dialect for 'I will'.
6. ***chorus of ploughboys***: The presence of a chorus aligns this piece with comic opera, which was becoming popular in the late eighteenth century.
7. ***Hounslow***: Like the later Staines, this is a village west of London; Hounslow Heath was notorious for highwaymen.
8. ***Stree-phon***: This is hyphenated to draw attention to the poem's humorously trite rhyming scheme.
9. ***stinking partridge***: Refers to the practice of 'hanging' partridge for a long period of time before consuming it, in order to add flavour.
10. ***bad guinea***: A counterfeit gold coin, worth twenty-one shillings. Forgery was a capital offence.
11. ***undirected Letter***: A letter without an address, probably delivered by hand and of no value.

A letter from a Young Lady

1. ***Horse guards***: The cavalry brigade that protected the royal household, especially the elite regiment known as the Royal Horse Guards.

A Tour through Wales

1. ***A Tour through Wales***: Wales, a fashionable destination for tourists seeking picturesque scenery, was popularized by William Gilpin's *Observations on the River Wye and Several Parts of South Wales* (1782)—a work JA probably knew: see note 58 to 'Love and Freindship'.
2. ***on the ramble***: Engaged in rambling, walking or wandering on a journey for pleasure (*OED*).
3. ***last Monday Month***: A month ago last Monday.
4. ***galloped ... fine perspiration***: This would have been an extremely inappropriate thing for a young lady to mention. Their comic method of travel—unaccompanied, with one pony between three women—is ridiculously implausible.
5. ***capped and heelpeiced***: Repaired by patching the toe and replacing the heel.
6. ***blue Sattin Slippers***: This is evening wear and as such wholly inappropriate for a walking tour.
7. ***hopped home from Hereford***: The alliteration reinforces the burlesque travel narrative. A journey from Hereford, a cathedral town on the Welsh border, to the Johnsons' home in the south of England would be approximately a two-day journey by coach.

A Tale

1. ***Pembrokeshire***: A county in south-west Wales, bordering the coast.
2. ***Closet***: A small, private room, usually adjoining a bedroom.
3. ***Wilhelminus***: A risible, Latinized version of the German name for 'William', as 'Robertus' below is a humorous Latinization of 'Robert'.
4. ***pair of Stairs***: A flight of stairs, from the meaning of 'pair' as 'a set'.
5. ***Genius***: Here the word does not imply unusual intellectual or creative powers, but rather a specific type of 'nature; disposition' (Johnson).

VOLUME THE THIRD

1. *Jane Austen—May 6th 1792*: The volume is titled by JA on the front cover and dated by her at the top of the contents page. A pencil note on the inside front cover in the hand of the Revd George Austen reads: 'Effusions of Fancy by a very Young Lady Consisting of Tales in a Style entirely new'. A note in Cassandra Austen's hand above this reads: 'for James Edward Austen Leigh'. JA appears to have dated this volume at the same time as she wrote the contents page, and transcribed 'Evelyn', then changed the title and the name of the heroine, 'Kitty', when she transcribed 'Catharine' three months later and signed its dedication 'August 1792'. Tentative dating for the composition of 'Evelyn' is December 1791, following 'The History of England' (*FR*, p. 74).
2. ***Contents***: JA has inserted page numbers beside each of the following contents to indicate the appropriate page in her manuscript notebook.
3. ***Kitty***: The heroine's name was originally Kitty, a diminutive of Catherine (generally but not always spelt 'Catharine' by JA in the manuscript). Although JA changed the name on most occasions in the text, she did not revise it here on the contents page.

Evelyn

1. ***Miss Mary Lloyd***: Mary Lloyd (1771–1843), who with her sister Martha was a friend of the Austen sisters, had to move in 1792 with their widowed mother from Deane parsonage, which they had rented from the Austens, to make way for the new curate, James Austen, and his bride. Peter Sabor points out the obvious connections between James's situation and that of the hero of 'Evelyn' (*Jane Austen's Evelyn*, ed. Peter Sabor [Edmonton: Juvenilia Press, 1999], pp. vii and 24). JA also presented Mary with a sewing bag containing a poem, 'This little bag', dated January 1792: see Appendix A.
2. ***Evelyn***: An imaginary village.
3. ***Parish***: A subdivision of an English county, referring to a separate administrative unit with its own church and clergyman.
4. ***sash***: Refers to the wooden part of a sash window, allowing it to be raised and lowered. Sash windows became popular in the late eighteenth century, letting in more light and air than the earlier lead-light windows.

5. *circular paddock*: A ridiculous and uneconomical shape for an enclosed pasture for sheep and cows, especially in its use of palings or pales (pointed lengths of wood arranged closely in a vertical line) and Lombardy poplars—an elegantly tall, narrow species of poplar brought to England from Lombardy in the late eighteenth century for use in ornamental landscapes. Here such planting of huge poplars and firs would obstruct the view. This sentence introduces JA's extended satire on the extravagantly artificial designs of popular landscape gardeners like 'Capability' Lancelot Brown (1715–83), who swept away formal gardens of estates in order to create uninterrupted views of the countryside.
6. *A gravel walk . . . Shrubbery*: A straight gravel walk running through lines of greenery is more perfunctory than picturesque; JA parodies the fashionable winding shrubbery walk that was often designed around the perimeter of an estate in the eighteenth-century emblematic landscape for walks and extensive views, such as William Shenstone's ornamented farm. The shrubbery in *Lady Susan* and that praised by Fanny Price in *MP* are of the more intimate kind recommended later by Humphrey Repton (see Christine Alexander, '"Prospect" and "Perception": Jane Austen and Landscape', *Sensibilities* 11 [Dec. 1995], pp. 17–36).
7. *four white Cows*: This is at humorous variance with the advice of Sir William Gilpin on the picturesque grouping of cattle. In *Observations . . . the High-Lands of Scotland* (1788), he asserts that the ideal group is three and that they must not 'stand in the same attitude and at equal distances' (see Volume II, 'Explanation of the Prints', p. xiii). Elizabeth Bennet alludes to Gilpin's ideal grouping when she refuses to join Miss Bingley, Mr Darcy and Mrs Hurst in a walk in *P&P*: 'The picturesque would be spoilt by admitting a fourth' (I, x).
8. *without any turn or interruption*: The ideal approach to a country house would be winding rather than straight, designed to impress viewers with a variety of pleasing prospects of the house and estate, as in the case of the approach to Pemberley House in *P&P* (III, i).
9. *best of Men*: An ironic reference in the case of the opportunistic and egotistical Mr Gower, since this is a phrase repeatedly used in relation to the noble and superlatively generous eponymous hero of *Sir Charles Grandison* (Doody and Murray, eds, *Catharine*, p. 343).

10. *Chocolate*: Popular since the late seventeenth century, this beverage was considered a luxury.
11. *venison pasty*: Another luxury food item: a pie filled with deer meat.
12. *handsome portion*: A large dowry.
13. *ten thousand pounds*: A substantial dowry; similar to that of Mrs Elton's 'so many thousands' in *E* (I, iv).
14. *on the next day ... celebrated*: As there would have been no time for either banns, a special licence, or a clergyman officiate, this marriage is invalid.
15. *rose tree ... variety*: Like the regular grouping of the cows, the symmetry of four rosebushes contravenes Gilpin's recommendations for picturesque irregularity and 'pleasing variety'.
16. *Carlisle ... Sussex*: Carlisle is a city in Cumberland in the north-west of England, close to the Scottish border, and thus at a great distance from Sussex, on the south coast of England.
17. *Isle of Wight ... in a foreign Country*: A small island off the coast of Hampshire and a popular English resort in the eighteenth century, clearly not a foreign country.
18. *wrecked on the coast of Calshot*: The narrow channel between the mainland and the Isle of Wight, not understood to be dangerous.
19. *fit of the gout*: An inflammatory disease resulting from the overconsumption of rich foods and alcohol, an appropriate malady for the gluttonous Mr Gower.
20. *that favourite character of Sir Charles Grandison's, a nurse*: An allusion to Sir Charles Grandison's advice to marry, since 'Womens sphere is the house, and their shining-place the sick chamber' (Vol. III, Letter XI).
21. *required the Paddock ... enliven the structure*: The castle provides a textbook example of the picturesque with its view of the sea and its rugged irregularity, so Mr Gower's preference for the symmetry of Evelyn Lodge is another ludicrous breach of the rules regarding the picturesque.
22. *winding approach, struck him with terror*: Another nod to the approved mode of the picturesque, and to the motifs of gloomy castles and terrified heroines (not heroes) in the Gothic novels of writers like Ann Radcliffe (1764–1823), whose works JA knew.
23. *Gipsies or Ghosts*: A comic juxtaposition, with the alliteration emphasizing Mr Gower's irrational 'Gothic' fears. Gypsies were, however, feared in the eighteenth century and considered pariahs: compare Harriet Smith's fear of gypsies in *E* (III, iii).

24. ***with her blessing and advice***: James Edward Austen frequently visited his aunt and her family at Chawton in 1815–16, when he was seventeen and eighteen and was also writing a novel that Austen refers to in her letters, so she may have suggested that he complete her earlier works written at the same age (*FR*, p. 240). His older half-sister Anna Lefroy also wrote a continuation of 'Evelyn' on four loose pages that are inserted into the manuscript volume, probably in early December 1814 as Kathryn Sutherland suggests (*Jane Austen's Textual Lives: From Aeschylus to Bollywood* [Oxford: Oxford University Press, 2005], p. 248, n. 96). This is not included in the present edition but interested readers can consult it in Appendix E of *Juvenilia*.
25. ***Hungary water***: An alcohol-based perfume made from rosemary flowers that was also valued as a general remedy when applied to the skin, bathed in or consumed. Named after the Queen of Hungary for whom it was first prepared, it was understood as especially restorative in cases of fainting and hysteria.
26. ***order of the procession he set out himself***: A funeral had a hierarchy of mourners who would follow the hearse, with immediate family heading the procession. Mr Gower's absence from his wife's funeral is highly inappropriate.
27. ***a pot of beer***: It is inappropriate for a man of Mr Gower's station to order beer from a public house. Furthermore, beer, along with gin, brandy and rum, were considered the drinks of the poor and the lower middle class. Wine was a more correct drink for a gentleman.
28. ***Nectar***: The favoured drink of the Gods on Mount Olympus.
29. ***Westgate Buil^{gs}***: A new block in Bath, in which the Austens considered renting lodgings, but in *P* Sir Walter Elliot is annoyed that his daughter Anne visits Mrs Smith in the undesirable Westgate Buildings (II, v).
30. ***draught***: The predecessor of a modern cheque. The draught was issued to the named individual by the bank, which would convert it into cash.

Catharine, or The Bower

1. ***Miss Austen***: Cassandra Austen: See note 1 to 'The beautifull Cassandra'.
2. ***threescore Editions***: Sixty editions, an impossible success for even a very popular work of fiction. Only devotional works went into so many editions in the eighteenth century (J. Paul Hunter,

Before Novels: The Cultural Contexts of Eighteenth-Century English Fiction [New York: W. W. Norton, 1990], p. 235).

3. ***Bower***: A place of solitude, generally associated with medieval gardens; described as 'an arbour; a sheltered place covered with green trees, twined and bent' in Johnson's *Dictionary*. Clara Tuite demonstrates JA's parodic use in 'Catharine' of the Bower of Bliss in *The Faerie Queene*, Book II (1590), by Edmund Spenser (*c.*1552–99): noting that JA comically links Sir Guyon, the Knight of Temperance, with Catharine's Aunt Percival; and Catharine herself with Acrasia, who is captured by the knight and her Bower of Bliss destroyed (*Romantic Austen: Sexual Politics and the Literary Canon* [Cambridge: Cambridge University Press, 2002], pp. 40–49).
4. ***as many heroines have had before her***: Reference to the stereotype of the orphaned heroine in Gothic and sentimental fiction. In *NA*, JA again debunks this expectation when she writes of Catherine Morland's mother that 'instead of dying in bringing the latter into the world, as any body might expect', she continued to live (I, i).
5. ***tenure***: Tenor; an alternative eighteenth-century spelling.
6. ***enthousiastic***: Enthusiastic. In the late seventeenth and early eighteenth centuries, the word referred primarily to excessive religious enthusiasm; but with the rise of the cult of sensibility and the sublime in the late eighteenth century, it came to be associated with an ideal susceptibility to emotional and aesthetic stimuli, an 'elevation of fancy' (Johnson).
7. ***to equip her for the East Indies***: It was much easier to find a husband in the East Indies because of the numerous single young men employed by the East India Company. To equip oneself for such a trip would involve a stock of light clothes and medicines. JA probably had in mind the similar fate of her aunt Philadelphia Hancock: see Introduction.
8. ***Maintenance***: JA here represents marriage as a means of attaining the necessities of life.
9. ***Bengal***: The British name for a region in India, where the East India Company was based; today it is mainly divided between Bangladesh and West Bengal, India.
10. ***Dowager***: A widow who has inherited a substantial property or title from her husband.
11. ***companion***: See note 10 to 'Henry and Eliza'.
12. ***Chetwynde***: A village in Gloucestershire, but the Chetwynde of this story is located in Devonshire.

13. ***M[rs] Percival***: JA substituted the name 'Mrs Percival' throughout the manuscript for 'Mrs Peterson' as the result of 'a new Physician, a D[r] Percival', who came to practise in the Chawton district in 1808, so heightening the relevance of her work for a new audience. The change indicates that she returned to her juvenilia between 1809 and 1811, after settling at Chawton Cottage, Hampshire (see Introduction). JA's letter to Cassandra dated 7 October 1808 notes that Dr Percival was 'the son of the famous D[r] Percival of Manchester, who wrote Moral Tales for Edward to give to me' (*Letters*, p. 145), suggesting that JA may have owned a copy of Thomas Percival's *A Father's Instructions to His Children: Consisting of Tales, Fables, and Reflections* (1775–1800).
14. ***M[r] Dudley . . . the Younger Son of a very noble Family***: Probably a reference to the family of Robert Dudley, Earl of Leicester, favourite of Queen Elizabeth I, whom JA clearly disliked: see 'The History of England'.
15. ***tythes***: Meaning a tenth part; referring to the tradition of giving a tenth of the proceeds from a property to the parish. This meant that a priest's income could vary a great deal depending on whether or not he lived in a wealthy parish.
16. ***on his travels***: Referring to the traditional Grand Tour of Europe, a requisite rite of passage for wealthy young gentlemen like JA's adopted brother Edward, who spent four years in Europe as part of his education.
17. ***Working***: The genteel occupation of needlework, such as embroidery.
18. ***sweep***: A curved carriage drive leading up to the house. This pre-dates the earliest example in the *OED*, which is from the last chapter of *S&S* (1811).
19. ***Music of an Italian Opera, which to most Heroines is the hight of Enjoyment***: The eponymous heroines of Burney's novels *Evelina* and *Cecilia* are both rapturous about the opera.
20. ***Stanley***: Like Dudley, the family name has Elizabethan associations. Henry Stanley, 4th Earl of Derby, participated in the trial of Mary, Queen of Scots—an event condemned by JA in 'The History of England'.
21. ***half the Year in Town***: During the London 'Winter' season, from New Year until 4 June, the King's official birthday.
22. ***acquirement of Accomplishments***: Towards the end of the eighteenth century, a number of female writers, like Catherine Macaulay (1731–91) and Mary Wollstonecraft (1759–97),

became critical of the shallowness of female accomplishments: see Introduction.

23. ***Modern history***: This can mean any work of history dealing with the period beyond antiquity. For JA's attitude to history, see note 1 to 'The History of England'.

24. ***Mrs Smith's Novels***: At the time this story was written, Charlotte Smith had produced *Emmeline* (1788), *Ethelinde* (1789), *Celestina* (1791) and *Desmond* (1792). The four-volume *Emmeline* was one of JA's favourite novels, and she alludes to its hero in her 'History of England'. *Ethelinde* was published in five volumes and is famous for containing passages describing the idyllic beauty of nature.

25. ***Grasmere***: A small lake in the Lake District in Lancashire (now in Cumbria), a popular destination for tourists of the picturesque and sublime landscape.

26. ***the Lakes***: The Lake District in north-west England (including Grasmere), made popular by writers like Gilpin and subsequently famous as the home of Wordsworth and the Lake poets.

27. ***travelling Dress***: For a female, this would most likely have been a riding habit, comprising jacket, waistcoat and skirt, designed not just for riding but 'as an ordinary day- or travelling-dress' (Cunnington and Cunnington, *Handbook of English Costume*, p. 305).

28. ***Matlock or Scarborough***: Matlock is a picturesque town in the Peak District of Derbyshire; Scarborough is a coastal town in east Yorkshire, England's first seaside resort. As it is on the opposite side of England from the Lakes, this indicates Camilla's ignorance of geography.

29. ***all order was destroyed over the face of the World***: This is an only slightly hyperbolized rehearsal of the anti-Jacobin response to the French Revolution in 1790s. Mrs Percival's conservative sentiments parody the warnings of danger to English society articulated in *Reflections on the Revolution in France* (1790) by Edmund Burke (1729–97).

30. ***said her Neice***: In her manuscript, JA has deleted part of Catharine's reply, thus softening it: 'I beleive you have as good a chance of it as any one else'.

31. ***if she were to come again . . . as she did before***: Elizabeth I lived to the age of sixty-nine. For JA's tirade against her, see 'The History of England'.

32. ***Politics***: Whereas it was acceptable for women to speak about history, politics was considered only to be a fit subject for men. Hence Catherine Morland's 'silence' when Henry Tilney launches forth on the subject in *NA* (I, xiv).
33. ***Halifax Family***: The name Halifax indicates the Whig politics of the family, deriving from George Savile, Marquis of Halifax's support of William of Orange.
34. ***in Public***: Places of public assembly such as ballrooms, churches and theatres.
35. ***Brook Street***: See note 14 to 'Sir William Mountague'.
36. ***find her in Cloathes***: To supply her with clothes, a phrase usually used in relation to the upkeep of a servant.
37. ***Curacies***: A clergyman could have more than one 'living' or position, and hire 'curates' on low wages to perform his clerical duties.
38. ***Cheltenham***: A Gloucestershire spa, popular in the late eighteenth century.
39. ***School somewhere in Wales***: Welsh boarding schools were cheaper and less respected than those in England.
40. ***Ranelagh***: London pleasure gardens located in Chelsea; a more expensive version of the older Vauxhall Gardens.
41. ***Barbadoes***: An island in the West Indies known for its sugar-cane production; Barbados, like Bengal in the East Indies, was a British colony.
42. ***nice***: As in finicky or squeamish.
43. ***lent it to***: JA has deleted a sharp reply by Catharine here in the manuscript. She does the same again after Camilla's next comment, making her heroine appear less aggressive (see Textual Notes).
44. ***Draws in Oils***: A sketch or drawing made in oil paint rather than watercolour or crayon. This was understood as a greater achievement.
45. ***to sea***: JA apparently forgot she had changed his career to the army (see above).
46. ***Gold Net***: A fashionable item in the 1790s: a cap with a hairnet woven from golden thread.
47. ***receipt book***: Recipe book, often containing recipes for home remedies.
48. ***Mortality***: Meaning the human race as a whole.
49. ***tooth drawn***: Extracted, without the aid of anaesthetic.
50. ***Regency walking dress***: A later insertion made by JA probably after February 1811, when the Prince of Wales (later George IV)

became regent for his mentally unstable father George III. A Regency walking dress has a shorter hem than an evening dress and is designed for street wear. The substitutions of 'Regency walking dress' and 'Regency' for the word 'Bonnet' here and subsequently are further indications of JA updating her work: see Textual Notes.

51. ***Pelisse***: An elegant long cloak, made of satin or velvet, with arm-holes or sleeves (*OED*).
52. ***Kingdom . . . prosperous a state***: Mr Stanley is a member of the Whig government of William Pitt the Younger (1759–1806), prime minister since 1783 and more popular than his predecessor, Lord North, because he restored confidence in the government after the heavy cost to Britain of the American War of Independence.
53. ***Scotch Steps***: Scottish reels and quicksteps were popular at local assemblies and public dances, but usually considered in bad taste and too lively for elegant young women, as Elizabeth Bennet implies when Mr Darcy asks her to dance a reel at Bingley's private house in *P&P* (I, x).
54. ***gone an hour . . . another hour***: JA changed the timing here in the manuscript to allow Catharine more time to write her letter (see Textual Notes).
55. ***Chaise and four***: A light carriage drawn by four horses, implying Stanley is an elegant and dashing young man.
56. ***now his hair is just done up***: Curled and powdered to look like a wig, as part of his uniform.
57. ***Livery***: The uniform of a servant would be specific to their master and indicate their wealth and status.
58. ***hack horses***: Horses hired from a stable. The necessity of doing so suggests a lower socio-economic status.
59. ***Devonshire***: A county in south-west England, a considerable distance from east England where Mr Stanley has come from.
60. ***go to the door when any one comes***: Usually the responsibility of a servant.
61. ***smart***: Smartly dressed, fashionable, elegant.
62. ***Your being extremely welcome to the Family who give the Ball***: Her assumption entails a serious breach of etiquette.
63. ***travelling apparel***: This would include an overcoat and boots as opposed to the indoor shoes appropriate for a ball.
64 ***Lyons***: This French city was popular on the Grand Tour.
65. ***linen***: Shirts and other small items of clothing made of linen.

66. ***powder and pomatum***: For dressing his hair: see note 56 above and note 20 to 'Frederic and Elfrida'.
67. ***Prudery***: Excessive propriety, primness.
68. ***monthly Ball***: A public ball, funded by subscription.
69. ***the small vestibule which Mr Dudley had raised to the Dignity of a Hall***: This treatment of a small antechamber as if it were the hall of a grand house suggests pretension.
70. ***Cards***: Card playing tended to be the occupation of older people at balls, who were not expected to dance.
71. ***Hunter***: A horse reserved for hunting; often an expensive thoroughbred.
72. ***sent an Express***: A messenger, who could ride rapidly on horseback.
73. ***Brampton***: A village in Cambridgeshire.
74. ***coming in the same Carriage . . . entering the room with him***: Both are serious breaches of decorum. A young lady like Catharine should be chaperoned in such circumstances.
75. ***led her to the top of the room***: To take the head of the line in the dance was a great honour usually reserved for those of a higher rank; neither have the right to this honour, making Edward's presumption an extreme breach of decorum.
76. ***only a tradesman***: Catharine's father was, in fact, a merchant like Camilla's; an important class distinction.
77. ***Mr Pitt or the Lord Chancellor***: William Pitt the Younger was prime minister at the time: see note 52. The Lord Chancellor ranks well above the prime minister, just below the Monarch, although Camilla is clearly ignorant of the distinction.
78. ***her partner during the greatest part of it***: Another breach of etiquette, to dance with the same partner for more than two consecutive dances.
79. ***I am come out***: A lady could only attend evening balls once she was officially 'out' in society, a circumstance that indicated her availability for marriage. See the first letter in 'A Collection of Letters'.
80. ***impudent Girls that ever existed***: Immodest and lacking in propriety. JA softens the serious charges against Catharine by deleting the following sentence in her manuscript here: 'Her intimacies with Young Men are abominable; and it is all the same to her, who it is, no one comes amiss to her—.' (see Textual Notes).

81. ***tremblingly alive***: This quotation from Pope's *Essay on Man* is also used to parody the excessive sentimentality of Laura in 'Love and Freindship'; here it mocks Mrs Percival's unnecessary apprehensions about Catharine.
82. ***Disposition romantic***: Influenced by the imagination (*OED*).
83. ***calculated***: Suited.
84. ***argue with temper***: 'Calmness of mind; moderation' (Johnson).
85. ***Richard the 3^d^***: In 'The History of England', JA suggests that Richard's character 'has been in general very severely treated by Historians' and claims that she herself is inclined by his being a Yorkist to suppose him 'a very respectable Man'.
86. ***Profligate***: Wanton, disposed to vice and dissolution. Edward Stanley's kissing of Catharine's hand 'passionately' goes beyond the accepted gallantry of such an act.
87. ***Blair's Sermons***: The sermons of Hugh Blair (1718–1800), a Scottish divine and Professor of Rhetoric at Edinburgh University, were published between 1777 and 1801. They argue among other things for the importance of modesty and duty for the young.
88. ***Cœlebs in Search of a Wife***: A didactic novel by Hannah More (1745–1833), published in 1809: see Introduction. JA substituted this title for her original, older reference: 'Seccar's explanation of the Catechism', referring to *Lectures on the Catechism of the Church of England* (1769) by Archbishop Thomas Secker (see Textual Notes), thus updating her work. See note 13 above.
89. ***Library***: This could refer to a bookcase or to a room containing books; the text suggests that Mrs Percival is wealthy and has a substantial house with private apartments for guests and possibly a private library.
90. ***the welfare of every Nation . . . hastening its ruin***: This was a common conservative anxiety during the upheavals of the French Revolution and the Napoleonic Wars. Female chastity and propriety were seen as ballasts of national stability against the onrush of social transformation (see Claudia Johnson, 'The Novel of Crisis', in *Jane Austen: Women, Politics and the Novel* [Chicago: University of Chicago Press, 1988], pp. 1–28).
91. ***Oh! what a silly Thing is Woman! How vain, how unreasonable***: A comic inversion of Hamlet's famous speech: 'What a piece of work is a man! / How noble in reason, how infinite in faculties' (Shakespeare, *Hamlet*, II.ii.303–4).

92. ***The following continuation . . . c.1815–16***: See note 24 to 'Evelyn'. The second, further continuation of 'Catharine' by Austen-Leigh that appears below was probably made after 1845 when he inherited *Volume the Third*, as Peter Sabor suggests (*Juvenilia*, p. 364).
93. ***vicious inclinations***: This rather shockingly suggests that Kitty is inclined towards vice, implicitly sexual.
94. ***Quartered***: Provided with quarters, or lodgings.

LADY SUSAN

1. ***Lady Susan***: The fair-copy manuscript is untitled. It received its present title when it was first published by James Edward Austen-Leigh in the appendix to his second edition of *A Memoir of Jane Austen* (1871): see Introduction for further details and for the dedication to Lady Knatchbull, JA's niece.
2. ***Lady Susan Vernon***: Susan Vernon's title (Lady/First name/Surname) derives from her being the child of an Earl or higher nobleman, the daughters of whom are given such an honorific.
3. ***Brother***: In fact, brother-in-law. Although the use is not consistent (see Letter 5), it was not uncommon in familiar contexts to use such near relational terms for in-laws, as in the following use of 'sister'.
4. ***Langford . . . Churchill***: Although common English village names, they refer here to estates.
5. ***Town***: Here and throughout, 'Town' refers to London, especially the West End or Westminster where the upper classes flocked for 'the Season', a series of social events over the winter months (usually New Year until June). London was seen as the centre of sophistication and culture, but was also associated with vice and the commercial interests of the 'City'. The contrast between Town and Country is a feature of eighteenth-century fiction.
6. ***Wigmore S*[t]**: A fashionable West End address in London.
7. ***that insupportable spot, a Country Village***: Compare JA's famous dictum about writing a novel: '3 or 4 Families in a Country Village is the very thing to work on' (*Letters*, p. 275).
8. ***agitation***: Under discussion, being planned.
9. ***widow***: The status of widowhood, which often accorded women both financial and marital independence, was not infrequently viewed with suspicion in JA's time, since such women were seen as

a threat to other wives. Lady Susan refers to this independence in Letter 39. See also Bridget Hill, ed., *Eighteenth-Century Women: An Anthology* (London: George Allen & Unwin, 1984).

10. ***dear Madam***: Mrs Vernon's respectful form for addressing her own mother in writing is not necessarily indicative of over formality. See Reginald's 'My dear Sir', addressing his father (Letter 14).

11. ***Lover***: A word whose meaning has now gained a far stronger complexion. Here, it indicates a fiancé or suitor, but could also mean 'a friend or well-wisher' (*OED*).

12. ***Hurst and Wilford***: Probably country estates, like Parklands and Churchill, that Reginald has visited during the sporting season. September is the hunting and shooting season in the Country, as important to young men of the aristocracy and gentry as the winter London social season. JA's own brothers participated in such activities (*Letters*, p. 10).

13. ***when a Man has once got his name***: 'To get one's name' meant to establish one's validity or worth.

14. ***a Banking House***: Merchant bank, a financial institution in the City of London.

15. ***for his dear Uncle's sake***: Probably because they have the same first name (this is not specified, but Frederica's name is another pointer to this probability).

16. ***her Countenance . . . what is this but Deceit***: JA was no follower of physiognomy, which judged the character of a person by his or her facial features. In this she was probably influenced by her brothers James and Henry Austen, who published an essay in their journal *The Loiterer* (II, no. 51) entitled 'The Science of Physiognomy not to be depended on', written in response to the new vogue for physiognomy initiated in the 1770s by the publication of Lavater's *Essays on Physiognomy*.

17. ***unexceptionable***: The *OED* has 'To whom . . . no exception can be taken; perfectly satisfactory or adequate'. It cites this usage from 1796 in Burney's *Camilla* (Vol. II, Book III, ix): 'She affectionately embraced the unexceptionable Lavinia'.

18. ***those accomplishments which are now necessary to finish a pretty Woman***: About the time JA made her fair copy of *Lady Susan*, she was reading Hannah More's new novel *Coelebs in Search of a Wife* (1809), which refers to the current 'frenzy for accomplishments', seen as essential for the middle-class girl to acquire a husband, especially if, like Frederica, she has no dowry. See 'Catharine' for JA's disapproval of the empty accomplishments women were encouraged to cultivate.

19. *Frederica's age*: Sixteen, an age at which most girls would be part of adult society.
20. *to send for his Horses immediately*: A signal that he means to hunt foxes; Reginald's horses are Hunters (expensive horses used for fox hunting).
21. *I am etc.*: Abbreviated form of formulaic epistolary closure.
22. *entailed*: The estate's succession is legally established and thus non-modifiable, the implicit meaning here being that Sir Reginald De Courcy cannot disinherit his son, who is therefore a 'safe catch'. By contrast, in *P&P*, the entailment of the Bennets' estate on a male heir is of primary concern to the future security of a family of young women.
23. *emancipation*: This could only be attained on the death of Manwaring's wife, an event that Lady Susan later suggests Alicia might help bring about (Letter 39).
24. *making Love*: That is, wooing.
25. *as silly as ever*: The term 'silly' (used six times in *Lady Susan*) had a more markedly derogative sense in JA's time than the somewhat innocuous meaning it carries today: 'silly' implied one was deficient in intellect and feeble-minded (*OED*).
26. *the difference of even twelve years*: If not actually scandalous, the difference in age between Lady Susan and Reginald was less than fully respectable in such social circles, as Sir Reginald's discomfort reveals.
27. *My Ability of distressing you during my Life . . . circumstances*: If he so wished, Sir Reginald could, up to the time of his own death, cut off his son's funding, in all likelihood the younger Reginald's exclusive source of income.
28. *common candour*: Ordinary unbiased assessment. The young JA was well aware of Sheridan's ironic use of 'candour' in his popular plays (in *School for Scandal*, for example, Mrs Candour helps to 'murder characters' with her free-ranging gossip); but Reginald De Courcy's use of the word here carries no irony, an indication of his good nature and perhaps his naivety.
29. *Shrubbery*: A private area of the garden close to the house, laid out with gravel paths and beds of ornamental trees and shrubs. Compare Fanny Price's love of the secluded shrubbery in *MP*; and see also note 6 to 'Evelyn'.
30. *He has been teizing me*: The word here and in Letter 25 clearly had a stronger meaning than that of its current form, suggesting the constant irritation of someone by persistent action that vexes or annoys.

31. <u>*incog*</u>: Incognito, or the disguising of one's real name, title, or character.
32. ***while we were at Tea***: That is, after dinner, possibly as late as 5 p.m. The English habit of 'afternoon tea' did not begin until about the 1840s; before this date, tea was usually served after dinner when the ladies and gentlemen were gathered together in the drawing room (Pool, *What Jane Austen Ate*, p. 209).
33. ***a peice of nicety***: Scrupulousness, being difficult to please or satisfy (*OED*).
34. ***a young Man of genteel appearance***: That is, whose appearance confirms his superior social status as a gentleman, of a similar standing with his hosts. Gentility had strong class connotations but very little moral implication, as Mrs Vernon's comment later in the same paragraph confirms.
35. ***Pelisses***: See note 51 to 'Catharine'.
36. <u>*Rattle*</u>: An eighteenth-century stock character, an indolent bragger. JA uses the term with reference to John Thorpe in *NA*.
37. ***Contemptible as a regard founded only on compassion, must make them both***: Compare the narrator of *NA* on the similar love of Henry Tilney for Catherine: 'I must confess that . . . a persuasion of her partiality for him had been the only cause of giving her a serious thought. It is a new circumstance in romance, I acknowledge, and dreadfully derogatory of an heroine's dignity' (II, xv).
38. ***Solomon***: The Old Testament King Solomon, proverbial for his wisdom.
39. ***to throw herself into the protection of a young Man***: In Richardson's famous epistolary novel, Clarissa similarly seeks the protection of Lovelace to escape being pushed into marriage to a suitor whom she loathes (*Clarissa*).
40. ***Hunters***: See note 20.
41. ***Bath***: See note 45 to 'Jack and Alice'.
42. ***the Lakes***: See note 26 to 'Catharine'.
43. ***Eclaircissement***: A revelation or explanation.
44. ***the Manwarings are to part***: A separation but not an annulment of their relatively recent marriage. Manwaring is not now free to marry Lady Susan.
45. ***finessed***: Something adroitly contrived, suggesting subtle strategy. JA's choice of word here may also reflect her knowledge of card games: the aim in a game of whist is 'To attempt to take a trick by finesse'(1746, *OED*).

Acknowledgements

This book has been a long time in the making. During this time many wonderful Austen scholars and friends have inspired, encouraged and assisted me in so many ways and I thank them all. I owe a special debt of gratitude to my publishers, more recently Simon Winder and Jessica Harrison, who have patiently stuck with me in the expectation that this volume would eventually materialize and, I trust, be of use to all readers of Jane Austen's work. It has also been a pleasure to work with Penguin editors Anna Hervé and Sarah Hulbert.

I am indebted to B. C. Barker-Benfield at the Bodleian Library, Oxford, for enabling me to study the manuscript of Jane Austen's 'Volume the First'; to Sally Brown at the British Library for assisting me in my work on the manuscripts of 'Volume the Second' and 'Volume the Third'; and to Christine Nelson at the Pierpont Morgan Library, New York, for facilitating my research on the manuscript of *Lady Susan* and for helping to identify the handwriting of an associated note. I am grateful to the staff at Jane Austen's House, Chawton, and at Chawton House Library for assistance with my research; and to Freydis Jane Welland for permission to reproduce her manuscript. My thanks are also due to the staff of the University of New South Wales Library, especially Julie Nolan, for their speed in accessing books and information needed to write the explanatory notes.

In preparing these notes, I have drawn on the valuable work of previous editors, especially Brian Southam's edition of *Volume the Third*, Margaret Anne Doody and Douglas Murray's *Catharine and Other Writings*; Peter Sabor's *Juvenilia*; and the Juvenilia Press editions of individual Austen juvenilia. I have benefited from working with Annette Upfal on a Juvenilia Press edition of *Jane Austen's 'The History of England' and Cassandra's Portraits* and with David Owen on *Lady Susan*. I have had the benefit of conversation and advice from William Baker, Margaret Anne Doody, Gillian Dow, Jan Fergus, Susan Allen Ford, Penny Gay, Jocelyn Harris, Clare Lamont, Juliet

McMaster, Lesley Peterson, Gillian Russell, Peter Sabor, Brian Southam, Mary Spongberg, Kathryn Sutherland, Clara Tuite, Joseph Wiesenfarth and John Wiltshire. In the early stages of manuscript transcription I was assisted by Fiona Baird, more recently by Annette Upfal, Roland Alexander and Grace Hellyer on the notes, and throughout by the expertise of my loyal research assistant Donna Couto. My special thanks go to my husband Peter Alexander, whose own literary expertise has been a constant source of help and encouragement.

The work for this edition has been supported by the funding and hospitality I received from several institutions: a Visiting Fellowship at Duke University, Durham, USA; a Visiting Fellowship at Clare Hall, Cambridge, UK; an Australian Research Council Grant; and the continuing support of my own School of the Arts and Media, and of the Faculty of Arts and Social Sciences, University of New South Wales. I am most grateful for their generous support.

I would like to dedicate this volume to Juliet McMaster, FRSC, Distinguished University Professor Emeritus—my friend, research collaborator, mentor and inspiration in all things Austen.

THE STORY OF PENGUIN CLASSICS

Before 1946 . . . 'Classics' are mainly the domain of academics and students; readable editions for everyone else are almost unheard of. This all changes when a little-known classicist, E. V. Rieu, presents Penguin founder Allen Lane with the translation of Homer's *Odyssey* that he has been working on in his spare time.

1946 Penguin Classics debuts with *The Odyssey*, which promptly sells three million copies. Suddenly, classics are no longer for the privileged few.

1950s Rieu, now series editor, turns to professional writers for the best modern, readable translations, including Dorothy L. Sayers's *Inferno* and Robert Graves's unexpurgated *Twelve Caesars*.

1960s The Classics are given the distinctive black covers that have remained a constant throughout the life of the series. Rieu retires in 1964, hailing the Penguin Classics list as 'the greatest educative force of the twentieth century.'

1970s A new generation of translators swells the Penguin Classics ranks, introducing readers of English to classics of world literature from more than twenty languages. The list grows to encompass more history, philosophy, science, religion and politics.

1980s The Penguin American Library launches with titles such as *Uncle Tom's Cabin*, and joins forces with Penguin Classics to provide the most comprehensive library of world literature available from any paperback publisher.

1990s The launch of Penguin Audiobooks brings the classics to a listening audience for the first time, and in 1999 the worldwide launch of the Penguin Classics website extends their reach to the global online community.

The 21st Century Penguin Classics are completely redesigned for the first time in nearly twenty years. This world-famous series now consists of more than 1300 titles, making the widest range of the best books ever written available to millions – and constantly redefining what makes a 'classic'.

The Odyssey continues . . .

The best books ever written

PENGUIN CLASSICS

THE STORY OF PENGUIN CLASSICS

Before 1946 . . . 'Classics' are mainly the domain of academics and students; readable editions for everyone else are almost unheard of. This all changes when a little-known classicist, E. V. Rieu, presents Penguin founder Allen Lane with the translation of Homer's *Odyssey* that he has been working on in his spare time.

1946 Penguin Classics debuts with *The Odyssey*, which promptly sells three million copies. Suddenly, classics are no longer for the privileged few.

1950s Rieu, now series editor, turns to professional writers for the best modern, readable translations, including Dorothy L. Sayers's *Inferno* and Robert Graves's unexpurgated *Twelve Caesars*.

1960s The Classics are given the distinctive black covers that have remained a constant throughout the life of the series. Rieu retires in 1964, hailing the Penguin Classics list as 'the greatest educative force of the twentieth century.'

1970s A new generation of translators swells the Penguin Classics ranks, introducing readers of English to classics of world literature from more than twenty languages. The list grows to encompass more history, philosophy, science, religion and politics.

1980s The Penguin American Library launches with titles such as *Uncle Tom's Cabin*, and joins forces with Penguin Classics to provide the most comprehensive library of world literature available from any paperback publisher.

1990s The launch of Penguin Audiobooks brings the classics to a listening audience for the first time, and in 1999 the worldwide launch of the Penguin Classics website extends their reach to the global online community.

The 21st Century Penguin Classics are completely redesigned for the first time in nearly twenty years. This world-famous series now consists of more than 1300 titles, making the widest range of the best books ever written available to millions – and constantly redefining what makes a 'classic'.

The Odyssey continues . . .